THE DYING LIGHT

THE DYING LIGHT

a Bloodwitch novel

Emily Rooke

For the survivors

CHAPTER 1

harlie was in complete darkness, but he told himself that he
was not afraid.

He had not put up much of a fight when he was jumped
by two men from the Pen gang on his way back from the Pit. He
had long since learnt what to expect when Faulkner wanted
something from him. Even if somebody heard him, he knew better
than to expect anyone's help in Penumbra. It was better not to
resist. That lesson had been drilled into him early on. His only
thought was that, if it had to happen, it was better they took him
from off the streets. At least he was putting no one he cared about
in danger.

They had finally come to a halt. By now, Charlie was too
exhausted to be frightened. There was a searing pain in his head.
He did not know how far from the Karbher Quarter they had taken
him. Judging by the way his legs shook beneath him, however, he
was sure they must have brought him to an entirely different part
of the city. After spending the whole day underground, all he
wanted to do was go home and lose himself to sleep. But that was
not likely to happen anytime soon.

Pinioned between the two men who had attacked him, hooded
as though he were a witch in the custody of Hunters being
prepared for interrogation, Charlie strained to hear something
beyond the pounding of his own heart. He needed to listen for
anything that could provide him with a clue about the place where
they had brought him. Everything was still. The only sound he
could hear was that of the wind as it rustled through the grass. He

shivered, goosepimples prickling along the bare skin of his arms. Then, out of the silence, there came a bored, drawling voice. It was one he recognised instantly.

'Boys, our guest of honour has arrived. Let's give him a proper welcome, shall we?'

Charlie flinched as a long-fingered hand touched the rough material covering his face, settling against his jaw. Faulkner's movements were gentle and leisurely, betraying none of the violence for which Charlie remembered him best. Charlie attempted to shake off his captors, but they were prepared for him. He was kept firmly in place between them as the hood was removed from his head.

'Long time, no see, Charlie,' Faulkner said, his breath tickling Charlie's ear.

Already accustomed to the darkness, Charlie's eyes adjusted quickly to the gloom. His chest tightened as he realised where he was, and who was gathered around him. They had brought him to the Skoto Gate section of the Witchtrap Wall. They were on the outskirts of Penumbra, at the foot of the Elysian mountains. The perfect place to cover up anything they wanted kept hidden.

He was surrounded by Pen boys. The younger ones circled him like dogs, while the senior members flanked their leader, Jay Faulkner. Most of them were eyeing Charlie like he was a fox they had finally managed to get cornered. They looked as though they would like nothing better than to tear him to shreds right there and then. It was only their leader holding them back, and Charlie knew it.

'Why am I here, Faulkner?' he asked, steeling himself. 'I told you before. I'm out.'

Faulkner let out a soft laugh, looking mildly impressed. 'Come on now, Charlie, what sort of reunion is this? It's been a long time. By now you must be, what, sixteen?'

To someone who did not know him, Faulkner might have almost sounded friendly. But Charlie recognised the ghoulish smile curling his lips. He knew what it meant.

'You've forgotten your manners in the time you've been away from us, I see. Perhaps I should refresh your memory. *This* is how you greet an old friend ...'

Charlie had a split second to brace himself against the wave of disgust that rose up from the pit of his stomach. His eyes never leaving Charlie's face, Faulkner stepped forward and wrapped his arms tightly around Charlie's body, enveloping him in a crushing embrace. Charlie closed his eyes and forced himself to keep breathing.

When Faulkner released him, Charlie staggered backwards, his ribs aching. It was only the support of his captors, who were still standing on either side of him, that kept him on his feet.

'You don't look so good, Carroway.' Marko, a boy around his own age who Charlie recognised from the Pit, smirked at him from behind Faulkner. 'It's cold out there on your own, I'd guess.'

'You got what we need, Carroway?' Mikhail, Marko's older cousin, asked. 'You know how this works. You do the job, you get to walk out of here in one piece.'

'He brought these out with him.' One of the men holding Charlie tossed Mikhail a pair of bolt cutters. Charlie recognised them as the ones he had lifted from the storage shed before they took him from the mine earlier that evening. 'They'll do the job.'

'Can I go, then?' Charlie snapped, as Mikhail withdrew into the shadows by the Wall.

Faulkner directed a curt nod to the men guarding Charlie. They released him but did not move away. Charlie rubbed his arms where their fingers had dug into his skin, trying to get some feeling back into them. Faulkner had already closed the distance between them.

'Aren't you curious as to why we brought you out here tonight, Charlie?'

Charlie felt Faulkner's eyes roving over his face before he crouched down, making to tie the lace of his sneakers. His fingers edged towards the flick knife he kept hidden in his sock.

'Don't insult me,' Faulkner said, and Charlie froze. He looked up to see a lazy smile playing around Faulkner's face, and a pistol aimed between his eyes. 'You know I don't trust you with blades anymore, Charlie. Get back on your feet – slowly.'

Charlie stiffened as Faulkner trailed the handgun along the side of his face, his fingers brushing Charlie's skin. A ringing in his ears, Charlie forced himself to concentrate on counting the railings in the Skoto Gate. 'What d'you want from me?' he asked, his teeth gritted.

'I don't suppose you hear much news from the underground these days,' Faulkner drawled, a glint in his cool eyes, 'what with all those paternal responsibilities of yours keeping you busy.'

Charlie heard the blood pounding furiously in his head, even above the laughter of the gang. With deliberate defiance, he raised his eyes to the scarred side of Faulkner's otherwise handsome face, and let his gaze linger there.

Faulkner did not fail to notice. With a click of his fingers, Charlie was forced to his knees on the grass. Out of nowhere, the thought crossed his mind that the kids would probably still be awake, waiting for him to get home.

The force of the blow across his face from Faulkner's gun sent his head snapping to the side. His fingers found the metal collar at his neck, and he drew his nails over the skin beneath it. He was so used to the feel of the cold band at his throat that he barely noticed the press of it there anymore. But sometimes his skin would itch. As though, somewhere inside of him, something was burning. At those times, scratching at himself was his only way of seeking relief.

'Get moving, Carroway.' Marko hauled Charlie to his feet and shoved him forward.

'You've got what you needed from me.' Charlie shook Marko off, glaring at Faulkner. 'I did what you told me to do. I'm on first shift at the Pit again tomorrow, so unless there's something else you want from me, stop wasting my time and let me go home.'

'Not happy being so close to the Witchtrap, Charlie?' Faulkner said, making no attempt to hide the mocking laughter in his words. 'You're not in any danger here. You're among friends, remember? No one's going to hurt you.'

Charlie shivered as laughter rippled through the gang again. 'What're you doing here?'

'All you really need to know is that the rules have changed. We've got some new, powerful friends. There's a special product on the market, and it's in high demand up *there.*'

Frowning, Charlie followed the direction in which Faulkner had jerked his thumb. His eyes came to rest on the dark castle nestled high in the Elysian mountains. From his seat on the High Throne, this was where Nikolai Ignatiev, the Great Protector of Matya, ruled with an iron fist. It was thanks to him that the witch covens were kept at bay, and the people of Penumbra kept safe.

As his gaze returned to Faulkner's face, Charlie noticed something that made him freeze. Something was moving down below them in the shadows near to the Skoto Gate. Charlie recoiled, drawing closer to Faulkner despite himself, as a wave of fear washed over him. Faulkner patted him between the shoulder blades before Charlie shrugged him off.

'Still not a fan of the dark, I see, Charlie,' Faulkner said softly, and Charlie shuddered.

'Keep them quiet,' Mikhail warned, approaching the things moving in the shadows.

At the sound of muffled whimpering and crying, Charlie forced himself to move forward, even as his legs screamed at him to stay away. He peered into the darkness, his eyes narrowed, trying to make out what was going on. He watched as a group of Pen boys led a procession of figures up to the Skoto Gate.

He counted at least thirty people shuffling through the shadows. Dotted amongst the prisoners, adult women supported the elderly, and groups of small girls clustered around older ones. They were dressed in ragged clothes and carried nothing with them at all. Some of them looked frightened, others numb. But it was clear that they were all exhausted. Their clothes, hair and faces were caked with dirt and dried mud. Charlie noticed that there were no men amongst the group, and only a couple of young boys.

He rounded on Faulkner. 'Who are they? What are you doing with them?'

'This is where you come in, Charlie,' Faulkner said, throwing one arm around Charlie's neck and gripping his right shoulder tightly. Charlie winced, as pain lanced through the mass of scar tissue beneath Faulkner's fingers. 'I couldn't leave you out. Honestly, I expected you to be grateful. I thought you might at least want a piece of the action.'

'I don't want anything to do with this,' Charlie said, staring ahead, his jaw clenched.

Most of the prisoners kept their eyes downcast, but one little girl stared back at him, her eyes wide. Her cheeks were stained with tears. Slowly, Charlie reached out a hand to comfort her, but she drew away from him at once. He backed off with a murmured apology.

'Reminding you of those brats of yours, Carroway?' Marko sneered.

Charlie kept his eyes fixed on the little girl long after she had looked away. 'What are you planning to do with them?' He turned to face Faulkner, his fists clenched. 'Where are you taking them?'

'You need to consider your options carefully, Charlie,' Faulkner said. He threw a glance over towards Mikhail and the other gang members positioned along the Wall. 'Hurry up and get them through. We've got another shipment coming in soon. We can't afford any hold-ups.'

Charlie smirked and crossed his arms. 'There's nothing for me to think about.'

Faulkner was smiling again. 'Now, Charlie, don't get any ideas about being a hero.'

Charlie frowned back, his grip tightening around himself, but he did not move.

'Carroway's smarter than that,' Mikhail said, his eyes on Charlie. 'He remembers what happened the last time he stepped out of line.'

At Mikhail's words, Charlie's hand shot to the small of his back, his shoulders tense. He caught sight of Marko's simpering face and forced himself to look anywhere else. He focused on steadying his breathing as he reminded himself of what he needed to do.

He needed to stay out of trouble. He was responsible for more than just himself now. What he had was not quite a family, but it was the closest thing to one that he could ever hope to have.

He took a step backwards, away from the group of prisoners, a tight knot in his stomach.

'If Carroway's so smart,' Marko said, as Charlie started to grind his teeth, 'how come he hasn't realised he can make some money out of those three kids he keeps around him?'

'Maybe it's because you're so much *smarter* than I am,' Charlie began, his voice trembling as a wash of icy rage surged through his body, 'but I don't think I get what you mean.' He met Marko's eyes and refused to look away. 'You want to make it clearer for me?'

'I'll make it crystal clear,' Marko said, approaching him, his face alight and hungry. 'You have three brats to sell. We know plenty of people out there who would be happy to buy. We'd get our share, of course, but you'd get a cut too.'

'How generous.'

'You should be thanking me.' Marko's voice was rising. 'I'm giving you a way to get them off your hands and make something out of them while you've still got the chance.'

'It's as simple as that, is it?' Charlie's hands were shaking now.

'Nothing's sacred in Penumbra,' Marko said. 'Possession is nine tenths. We've had eyes on your place for months. You think you can protect them from us forever?'

Charlie leapt towards him, his face so close to Marko's that they were almost nose to nose. But Mikhail forced his way between them before either of them could make another move.

'Enough,' he said, shoving Marko away. 'You have a job to do. Get it done.'

Faulkner sighed, and pushed his coiffed, ash blonde hair out of his eyes. 'I would take you back, you know,' he said, turning to address Charlie as Mikhail and Marko returned to the Witchtrap Wall. 'If you would only apologise to me for what you did … and make it right.'

Charlie forced himself to remain calm. 'And how would you like me to make it right?'

'You know what I like.' His eyes never leaving Charlie's face, Faulkner's arm snaked its way around Charlie's body. The tips of his fingers found the raised words branded on the small of

Charlie's back and brushed over them, one letter at a time. 'I still owe you for running out on me three years ago ...'

'Don't touch me,' Charlie spat, his voice low, his skin crawling.

'You'd like to hurt me, wouldn't you?' Faulkner whispered, his lips at Charlie's ear. 'Try it and see what happens next. Or ... are you planning to run away from me again tonight?'

'I said don't *fucking* touch me,' Charlie snarled, shoving Faulkner off him.

Without a backwards glance, Charlie turned and headed towards the slums of the inner city. He was moving as fast as his legs would carry him without breaking into a run. He needed to put as much distance between himself and Faulkner as he could, as fast as he could.

He untied his black sweatshirt from around his waist and pulled it on, feeling the immediate relief of having his skin covered. Shoving his balled-up fists into his pockets, Charlie kept his head down, concentrating on trying to force himself to stop shaking.

Faulkner's furious voice rang out behind him. 'I *own* you, Charlie Carroway. Never forget that! You should spare a thought about what's best for that little family of yours before you think about turning your back on me again.'

'Stay away from my family.' Charlie refused to stop, or chance a look over his shoulder. 'Or you'll regret it.'

His shoulders hunched, his jaw set, Charlie made his way through the dark city streets of Penumbra, back to his family, and the home they shared in the Karbher Quarter. Once he had put a healthy amount of distance between himself and Faulkner and the Witchtrap Wall, some of the tension gradually started unknitting from his body. Slowly, he unclenched his fists.

A thin sheen of rain was falling, the light of the moon making the uneven pavement glitter beneath his feet. Wisps of cloud drifted across the pitch-black sky. From overhead, the low rumble of helicopters somewhere in the distance sent Charlie further into the shadows. Pulling the hood of his sweatshirt over his head, he gritted his teeth, and waited until they had passed him by. The last thing he needed was to attract the attention of the military police.

It was long past curfew, and he could not afford to get himself arrested.

Once the noise had faded away, he stepped out into the middle of the street again, scowling. With a sigh, he kicked a stone through a small puddle of water. He paused, staring over his shoulder, his thoughts still on the little girl he had seen by the Witchtrap Wall. Try as he might, he could not get her tear-streaked face out of his mind.

The wind whispered behind him. Under the collar, the burning sensation beneath his skin was stronger and fiercer than he had ever felt it before. He released a sigh and turned away, shoving his hands deep into the pockets of his sweatshirt.

He was needed at home.

CHAPTER 2

'For what we receive, and for another day free from the threat of the covens, no matter our hardship, let us all be content and grateful to our Great Protector for keeping the Wall standing strong for us.'

They ate dinner in the gloom once June had finished leading them in expressing humble thanks for the meal. It was a somewhat rushed affair, as they had to finish while there was still enough light from the guttering candle to see the food on their chipped plates.

Nikolai Ignatiev, the First Hunter General of Matya, looked down on all five of them from his faded portrait on the cracked wall by the staircase. He was always watching from the High Throne, always seeking out the evil of witches.

'You're not eating much this evening, Charlie,' June said, sipping a cup of weak tea.

Charlie stabbed at his potato stew with his knife. 'Not hungry.'

When they had finished eating, June and the children cleared the table. A comfortable hush enveloped them all as the candle in the kitchen burned low. Charlie went to stand by the draughty window, staring out into the distance.

His eyes were drawn to the lights on the mountain where the stronghold of the Elysian Castle stood. He let out a long, slow sigh, and ran his fingers through his uneven hair. Parted sharply, the longer section fell to one side of his head, its tips brushing his ear. He had been meaning to get around to shaving the shorter side at some point; it was starting to get fluffy.

'You were home later than usual tonight.' June stood beside him, following his gaze.

Charlie closed his eyes and exhaled through his nose. 'It's been a long day. I'm tired.'

The old lady adjusted her glasses and blinked. 'Is there something you want to tell me?'

'No.'

'I thought you weren't going to come back, Charlie.'

By now, it was too dark to see who had spoken clearly. But Charlie recognised Ruby's tentative voice below him, coming from somewhere around his knee. He ruffled her hair. 'I'll always come back, you know me.'

'Charlie, please may we have another candle?'

Ruby had balled a fistful of his narrow black jeans into her hand and was holding onto him fiercely. Charlie did not attempt to extricate himself. It took a lot for Ruby to feel afraid, and more for her to admit it.

'What does Granny June say?'

Leo's big voice piped up from near the kitchen. 'She says we can't yet.'

'I like the dark.' This was Dima. 'I'm down in the mine, like Charlie. Oh no, oh no, I'm trapped – *cave in!*' Charlie smiled ruefully and rolled his eyes as the little boy let out a shriek. 'I'm dying!'

'Boys, be quiet!'

At the sound of the old woman's stern voice, the scrabbling movements at the end of the bed stopped at once. Satisfied, Granny June returned to washing up the plates from dinner. Her hunched figure was bathed in the soft, twinkling light lent by the only candle in their home.

'Were you aware, Charlie,' she called from the kitchen, her voice even, 'that Dmitri has been skipping his reading lessons this week?'

Charlie rubbed his shadowed eyes. 'Is that true, Dima?'

'It *is* true,' Leo said, in a tone that suggested there could be no other answer.

'Only a few times,' Dima said, pushing Leo aside. 'I was … doing something else.'

Charlie pressed his fists against his closed eyes, attempting to smother the sharp throbbing that had been building in the centre of his head since the start of that morning.

Before he spoke, he took another deep breath, making sure to speak calmly. 'I'd like to hear exactly what you've got to do that's more important than working with Granny and learning how to read.'

'I'm not supposed to …' Dima mumbled, before tailing off.

'Well?' Charlie did his best to bite down on the edge in his voice. 'Can you tell me?'

Another few seconds passed by in silence. Then he heard Ruby's voice again. 'Charlie, *please* can we have another candle?'

'You should stand beside Granny while she washes up,' Charlie said, as he gently stroked her hair. 'She's got a little candlelight left. I bet she'd be happy if you helped her check everything is clean.'

A snort from the kitchen told him what the old woman thought of that idea.

'I want to stay with you,' Ruby said in a small voice. Charlie thought he heard a sniff.

The boys, Leo and Dima, both about a year younger than Ruby, still found the dark nights exciting. At six years old, she had already experienced enough of life in the Karbher Quarter to know that there was good reason to be afraid when the lights went out and the darkness stole in. Nevertheless, they were all still too young to understand why their candles had to be rationed, why there was never enough food – why they lived like this.

It happened before Charlie had time to react.

In the distance, there was the sound of a furious rumble, like thunder, as though from somewhere deep underneath the ground. The whole basement began to shake violently, the rotten floorboards beneath Charlie's feet creaking. From the kitchen, he heard the rattle of the just-washed knives and forks as they bounced around on the draining board. The candle had toppled over and gone out, plunging them all into darkness. His ears were filled with the sound of screaming and crying children. Ruby was no longer beside him.

'Where are the kids?' Charlie yelled, wheeling around in the direction of the kitchen.

June's voice rang out in answer, strong and clear for a woman of her age. 'They're with me. Don't worry.'

'Keep them safe!'

Gripping hard onto the windowsill to keep himself upright, Charlie's eyes found the Elysian Castle, and his gaze lingered there. There was a single moment when everything was perfectly still and silent. Then a blinding white light cast everything into total illumination, and he had to shield his eyes against the piercing light flooding their home. The children's screams grew louder as the violent shaking started up again, much worse than before.

Fighting against the brightness, painful after such a long time in the dark, Charlie's eyes were drawn immediately to the source of the disturbance. In the distance, a column of intensely bright light illuminated the sky over the Elysian mountains. It pulsed and swirled as though it were alive. Charlie watched it, mesmerised, unable to pull himself away. The next moment, it had vanished, and the tremors faded to nothing.

'What in the nine hells ...'

Charlie spoke softly, his fingers white from holding onto the windowsill so tightly. Though they had been plunged back into darkness, he could still see the pillar of light burnt into his eyelids when he blinked, like a distant glow on the horizon. The lights of the Elysian Castle twinkled as before. The children's crying had faded, but for the occasional whimper.

'Is everyone all right?'

'We're all safe,' came June's voice, as she struck a match and re-lit the candle.

'Granny, what was *that*?' Ruby asked, her voice trembling.

'I think it was a witch,' Leo said, sounding confident. 'It was hungry and mad.'

'Don't say such things.' At Leo's words, June's eyes had darted to the portrait of the Great Protector, still swaying slightly on the wall. 'You will bring the covens down on us.'

'Does the witch eat people?' It sounded as though Dima was torn between feeling afraid and excited. 'Will it eat us?'

'The Great Protector keeps the Wall standing strong for us,' June said, her voice firm, her hand at her heart. 'While he sits on the High Throne in Elysia, we are safe.'

'It can't eat us if it can't find us,' Leo said to Dima. 'Let's build a fort to hide in!'

'It's … rather late for that, boys,' June said. 'I think we had all better –'

'Charlie, will the witch *really* eat us?' Ruby asked, coming to stand beside him again.

Charlie grinned, and placed his hands on his hips. 'Are you serious? Any witches that come looking for trouble around here had better watch out if they run into me. Trust me, I can handle anything the covens throw our way.'

Ruby nibbled at her lower lip. 'But what if –'

Charlie stifled an exaggerated yawn. 'I don't know about you, Rubes, but I'm feeling tired. It must be almost time for bed.' Carefully, he unhooked Ruby's fingers from his jeans and, taking her hand in his, gave it a squeeze. 'Come and sit by the window with me,' Charlie said, 'and I'll tell you a story. Leo, Dima, you two come over here as well.'

With a cheer, the boys raced over at once. Charlie caught the flash of a smile on Granny June's lined face as she turned to give him an appreciative nod. As the moon broke free of a patch of cloud, a silvery beam rippled through the window and lent enough light to reveal the smiling faces of the three children sitting by his feet. Charlie felt a surge of happiness course through him. The pain in his head was fading at last.

'Once, in a place far, far away from here,' he began, having cleared his throat, 'there lived three small children, and their names were Ruby, Leo and Dima.'

A wave of excitement spread through his audience, along with a dramatic whisper of, 'That's *my* name!'

'Now, these three children lived a happy life,' Charlie said. 'They went to school, then they came home and played together. They always had enough food to eat. They had their Granny June to look after them. Life was good.'

18

'But wait!' Leo interrupted, his eyes wide. 'What happened to Charlie in the story?'

'How do *you* know about Charlie?' Charlie asked, feigning surprise. 'Wait … I haven't told you this story before, have I?' As the children giggled, he settled back against the window and continued with his tale. 'But life wasn't always so good for these three children. There used to be a lot of scary monsters lurking around.'

'Like the witch covens,' said Leo at once.

'And the gangs,' added Dima, sounding nervous.

'And the bad men,' Ruby finished, nodding with a solemn expression.

'Luckily for these three kids, though,' Charlie went on, as the children squealed happily on the floor, 'there was a brave knight who lived nearby called Charlie, and he saw how frightened they were by the monsters, and it made him sad.'

'Charlie is my *favourite*,' Ruby said to the boys, a gap-toothed smile on her face.

'He knew he wanted to help the three children somehow,' Charlie said, smiling too. 'So, one day, he went out with his sword, and he fought for them. He fought off all the witch covens and the gangs and the bad men. Then they were gone, forever, and the three kids were happy.'

'What happened to Charlie?' Dima asked quickly. 'You never tell us.'

'He was happy too,' Charlie told him, 'because he knew he had saved the children.'

'What happens at the end?' Ruby asked. 'You never tell us that part either.'

'Yeah, you never tell us!' Leo insisted. 'You never tell us how he kills everyone!'

Charlie shrugged. 'You can make up the ending yourselves, I guess.' He paused, his hands making fists on top of his knees. 'One day, I –' He swallowed, his mind returning to the darkness of the never-ending tunnels, and the ruthless, searing heat of the Pit. 'I promise, I'll come home from work on time, every day … and I'll tell you a story, every single night.'

'Wow,' Dima breathed.

Leo was watching him with a serious expression. '*Every* night?'

'You promise, Charlie?' Ruby's eyes were wide.

'I promise,' Charlie said, drawing a diagonal line across his heart with his index and middle fingers. 'Someday, everything will be different. I'll make it all better. I promise I will.'

The creak of a rotten floorboard overhead broke the silence, and Charlie felt a frisson of anxiety spiral through his body. His eyes darted to the top of the staircase, the children's gaze following his. Their faces had fallen at the sight of his expression.

Through the open shaft, Charlie could just make out a group of dark figures moving along the hallway passage above them. Then there came the unmistakable sound of heavy boots slowly descending the stairs, the creaking of wood underfoot shrieking through the silence. His stomach was churning.

A pleasant, dangerous voice drifted out of the shadows. 'What a beautiful thought. I hope you don't mind the boys and I interrupting your little bedtime story, Charlie.'

Charlie's blood went cold. He recognised the shapes of three men looming out of the darkness by the foot of the stairs, all of them dressed in smart black suits. Marko and Mikhail followed in the footsteps of their master, Faulkner, who had led the way down into the basement.

Charlie leapt to his feet, pulling Ruby, Leo and Dima behind him. In the same instant, he realised that they had not come alone. Two other figures followed in the wake of the three members of the Pen gang. Although Charlie could not see their faces, the way they carried themselves told him that they were no ordinary street thugs. The urge to scratch the itch under the metal collar at his throat was growing again.

'From what I know about you, I would have thought you'd know better than to believe in fairy tales, Charlie. Praying for a miracle only makes accepting reality that much harder.'

Faulkner strode out of the shadows first, the thump of his boots making the floorboards groan. It felt surreal – obscene – for him to be there, in this sanctuary that Charlie had carved out for himself and his little family. Faulkner towered over everyone else in the room, a jeering smile stretched across his face.

Charlie was keenly aware that he was defenceless. He had left his knife upstairs by the door, hidden inside one of his sneakers. His eyes darted to the kitchen. June had forbidden him from keeping weapons in the house when she took him in, and he would never be able to reach the dull knives by the sink without abandoning the children. Not that they would be of much use, even if he could get to them.

The amused glint in Faulkner's eyes gave Charlie the uneasy feeling that his thoughts were obvious on his face.

At Charlie's stony silence, Faulkner went on. 'Boys, let's have some light in here.'

On his command, Marko and Mikhail each switched on a high-powered torch, shining their lights directly into the eyes of Charlie and the children. Shielding his eyes from the sudden glare, Charlie scanned the other faces in the room. They belonged to two young men he had never seen before.

The two strangers were both dressed in black too, but their clothing was of a much finer material than Charlie was used to seeing in Penumbra. Unlike the gang, they wore dark red cloaks over their uniforms. He did not fail to notice that they were both armed with rifles. Slowly, he reached out behind him, ensuring that the children were all still there. Dread was stealing over him. He did not understand why Faulkner would have brought soldiers with him.

'I couldn't let you simply walk away, Charlie,' Faulkner said, adjusting the heavy gold rings on his fingers. 'It's time for us to have a proper heart-to-heart talk. It's been far too long.'

CHAPTER 3

Charlie's mind was racing. There was a good possibility that he could take on any one of the members of the Pen gang who now stood before him on his own. But with the three of them together, alongside these two capable-looking strangers – and all of them certain to have come heavily armed – he knew he stood no chance.

'What are you doing here?' June demanded. 'How did you get in?'

Faulkner considered her with a lazy look, as Marko turned the beam of his torch in her direction. 'Don't waste my time with questions you already know the answers to, old woman.'

'Get out of my house,' she said, drawing herself up to her full height, 'at once.'

'All in good time.' His voice measured, Faulkner ran his hands over his knuckles. 'Now, I can see you certainly have a ...' He ducked under an exposed beam in the roof as he stalked towards Charlie and the children, gingerly testing the floorboards with his weight as he went. 'Yes, you have a fine establishment here. But it's strange ... you don't seem to have troubled yourselves with protecting it particularly well. Isn't that right, Mikhail?'

Without hesitation, Mikhail lashed out at the wooden table with his boot, turning it over and sending the chairs crashing to the ground. One of the boys started to cry. Charlie had balled his hands into fists to try to stop himself from shaking. His head was full of half-crazed ideas about what he should do next, each more useless than the last.

He caught sight of the two soldiers, still standing back from the fray. Both of them were watching him closely. One of them, dark-haired and sombre, seemed to almost be looking straight through him, as though barely even aware of the scene unfolding in the basement. The other soldier's hard face held something cruel, and the glint in his cold eyes convinced Charlie that this was someone to be wary of.

Faulkner had come to a halt with his face so close to Charlie's that when Faulkner tipped his head down they were almost nose-to-nose. 'You don't know why we're here?' he said, his voice soft and dangerous. 'The money, you old crone.' His face snapped towards June. 'The money I lent to you. The money you swore to repay me. The money I still *do not have.*' The scarred part of his mouth was curled into a sneer. 'Where is it?'

The colour had left June's face. She opened her mouth to speak. 'I –'

'I don't have it,' Charlie said, keeping his voice low and his eyes fixed on the floor.

'You don't have it,' Faulkner repeated softly, his gaze boring into Charlie as he reached into his suit jacket. 'I see. No odd jobs come your way recently, Charlie? Well, in that case …'

'You can see we have nothing, Faulkner,' June said, indicating the sad-looking basement around them. 'If we had the money, we would give it to you. You know how hard this last winter was. The children were sick. We had nothing to keep them warm. We needed food and medicine.'

Faulkner rubbed his stubbled chin with a shake of his head. 'You realise I'm not running a charity here, don't you, Granny?'

June's voice wavered, and she blinked furiously behind her broken glasses. 'The foreman knows that Charlie is a good worker,' she said. 'He will be paid again soon, and then we can start repaying the money we owe you. I swear to you, you will get your money as soon as we have it …'

Faulkner considered Charlie carefully. From his pocket, he withdrew a silver cigar case. He handed it to Charlie, who opened it wordlessly, holding it out for him to choose one. A smile playing around Faulkner's mouth, the cigar between his teeth, he crouched down. Taking a silver lighter from the pocket of his jacket, he offered it to Ruby.

'I need your assistance, my little beauty. Would you do me the honour?'

Charlie felt himself trembling with fury as Ruby tentatively flicked the lighter and held the flame up to the end of the cigar. Faulkner trailed a finger along Ruby's jaw and straightened up. Charlie could feel her burying her face in the back of his leg.

'Don't touch her,' he breathed.

Faulkner appeared to be deep in thought as he took a long drag on his cigar and breathed the smoke out into Charlie's face. 'If it's the kids that are the problem, Charlie, there are other ways we can settle this.' From his other pocket, Faulkner withdrew a small notebook and an ink pen. 'The girl, for instance, would be worth enough to my associates in Elysia for me to consider your debt settled. In fact,' he checked his figures, and cast Charlie an evil grin, 'you'd be in credit.'

'You should be ashamed of yourselves.' June seemed caught between horror and disgust. 'We are all Penumbrans, aren't we? How can you speak of such a thing?'

'We all know the penalty for harbouring witches,' Faulkner murmured, and the soldiers behind him stirred. 'I heard some troubling rumours … a young girl, perhaps her age … living somewhere around here, perhaps in this very house …' Faulkner's grin widened at Charlie's expression. 'You may be my friend, Charlie, but I had to do the right thing. I had to inform the Hunters. We cannot allow the safety of our families to be threatened, now, can we?'

'You monster!' June shrieked at Faulkner. 'What rumours? Why are you doing this?'

There was a ringing in Charlie's ears again. Ruby was hanging onto his leg so tightly he thought she might never let go. His teeth gritted, he stepped firmly in front of the children, meeting Faulkner's eyes. Whatever happened next, he would not run away.

'Charlie, I'm losing my patience,' Faulkner said. His voice was calm, but his eyes flashed with simmering fury. The cruel-faced soldier had sloped towards them, followed immediately by his serious-looking partner. Faulkner lowered his voice so that only Charlie could hear his next words. 'We all have our skills. If you really want to help your family, you should go back to doing what you do best.'

'Go to hell.'

'Your old bedroom is still waiting for you, exactly as you left it,' Faulkner said, brushing his hand through Charlie's hair. 'I know the boys will be more than happy to throw you a welcome party. You didn't think you could hide from what you are forever, did you?'

'I'm never going back,' Charlie whispered, frozen beneath Faulkner's touch.

'Think about it, Carroway.' Mikhail's voice was clipped with impatience. 'Is all this trouble worth it? And you two!' He pointed at Leo and Dima. 'I'm still waiting to hear your answer. If you really want to help your Uncle Charlie, you know where to find us.'

Charlie threw a confused glance at the boys, who looked miserable and frightened.

'I'm not leaving empty-handed, Charlie,' Faulkner warned softly. 'I promised my new friend here that there would be a reward in it for him. He will not be satisfied otherwise.'

Charlie caught sight of the hungry look on the face of the cold-eyed soldier standing beside Faulkner. He knew what he had to do. Without a word, Charlie gathered Ruby up into his arms and motioned for Leo and Dima to follow him into the kitchen. The boys held onto either side of June's stained dress, its colour faded from years of wear, while Charlie passed Ruby to her. Then he turned to face Faulkner, standing between the Pen gang and his family.

'Stay here,' he told them. 'I'll handle this.'

Something like surprise flickered for a moment in the depths of Faulkner's eyes, before he let out a bellowed laugh. 'Charlie Carroway, always playing the hero. Boys, you know what to do.'

His henchmen moved as one. Marko and Mikhail each took hold of one of Charlie's arms, their hands on his shoulders, trapping him between them. Though he tried to stifle it, Charlie could not prevent the strangled yelp of pain that escaped from him as Marko put the pressure of all his strength on Charlie's old injury. The children were screaming and crying. June was trying to stop them from running after him. The Pen boys did not pay any of them a moment's attention.

The sombre-faced soldier left first, leading the way silently up the stairs. Faulkner went next, the smoke from his cigar wafting into Charlie's face as he, Mikhail and Marko followed behind. The cruel-faced soldier brought up the rear. Charlie was sure he heard the sound of wooden furniture being smashed before the soldier's heavy footsteps caught up with them. He tried to crane his neck back to see if June and the children were safe, but Mikhail slammed the palm of his hand into the back of Charlie's head, and his eyes returned to his feet.

Charlie was almost dragged down the hallway, his toes brushing the floorboards due to the height of his captors. They passed the front door, left wide open and hanging off its hinges, and moved out into the night. From over his shoulder, he saw that the serious-looking soldier had walked off alone in the opposite direction. Charlie felt a strange kind of satisfaction at the sight. He guessed the soldier did not have the stomach for what was going to happen next.

They marched on in silence down the deserted streets. Soon, the network of low-lying shacks began to disappear and grow into the jungle of slums that made up the larger part of the Karbher Quarter. They had brought him to the Spike, the centre of the city.

Charlie recognised the Ration Station standing closed for the night, its doors sealed with heavy chains. It looked eerily deserted without the crowds that usually surrounded it. From his portrait above the door to the Station, the pitiless eyes of the Great Protector seemed to have a way of finding him in the dark to bear witness to the scene. The lack of emotion in his haughty face was oddly comforting.

Only now did Marko and Mikhail release him. They pushed Charlie back against the wall with such force that the back of his head slammed into the brickwork. The number of stars in the sky above him doubled. Before he had time to react, a flurry of punches had been landed to his stomach and ribs, and he was knocked to the ground. Groaning, Charlie rose to his feet, leaning against the wall to let it take his weight.

The silent slums towered above him on all sides of the square. Cascades of faceless windows and washing lines strung between buildings loomed out of the darkness. The Pen boys had backed off, watching him closely. Charlie felt suddenly lightheaded. To his dismay, he realised that he was still shaking, but no longer with anger.

'Let's get this over with.' He forced his voice to stay steady. 'I won't try to stop you.'

'You're not playing by the rules, Charlie.' Faulkner sounded amused. 'I told you before you left our organisation that I could offer you much better terms than your foreman at the mine. It's easier work, too – even you would have to admit it.'

Charlie spat out blood and stared up at Faulkner. 'I told you, I'm done with all of that.'

'You can't tell me you actually *want* to spend the rest of your life slaving away underground, digging up rocks to decorate rich Elysian whores?' Faulkner's voice was mild as he readjusted his rings. 'All for, what, a life spent chained to slum rats?'

'I'd rather be chained to them than to you!'

Rage coursing through him once more, Charlie lunged at Faulkner. But he was caught around the neck by the cruel-faced soldier, who forced him to the ground with a knee to the stomach.

'Try that again, you worthless piece of filth,' the soldier murmured. 'I dare you.'

Curled up on the ground and fighting to catch his breath, Charlie froze as he heard Faulkner's soft voice in his ear. 'Now you're playing the game, Charlie. Make it fun for my boys – they've earned it. I know you remember how. And I'm still waiting for my money – don't forget it. You keep holding out on us and we'll make sure it's the kids who pay for it next time.'

Someone grabbed him under the arm, wrenched him to his feet, shoved him roughly back against the wall again. They had formed a tight semicircle around him and were slowly advancing on him from all sides, like a pack of stray dogs at the end of a hunt.

'You can't fight us all, kid,' Mikhail said. 'Don't think we'll go easy on you.'

'You think I'm scared of you?' Charlie snarled. 'Get on with it, you fucking cowards.'

His breathing shallow and rapid, Charlie wiped the blood out of his eyes and braced himself. He gritted his teeth as a fist came swinging towards his face. The pain consumed him almost instantly. He was lost to the darkness, hands swarming across his body. The last words he heard before he lost consciousness were spoken by a deep voice that he did not recognise.

'That's enough, all of you. Leave him to me.'

*

The next time Charlie opened his eyes, he was on his own, lying on his side underneath a tarpaulin. His memory of how it had got there was hazy. He guessed that he must have pulled it over himself at some point during the night to use as a makeshift blanket.

It was not yet sunrise. He did not know how much time had passed, or how long he had been lying in the street. Grimacing against the pain lashing through his body as he moved, he forced himself to stand, his legs unsteady beneath him.

The taste of copper was on his tongue, and he spat out blood. There was more of it crusting under his nose and around his mouth. He cradled his head in his hands, a low moan escaping from him as a burst of agony lanced through his skull. His eyelid was swelling beneath his fingers. Tears burnt behind his eyes, but he refused to let them fall.

The kids.

They would be waiting for him at home. He would not let them see him like this.

'Saints' mercy,' June whispered when she saw him. 'What did they do to you?'

She was standing at the threshold to their home. The front door was back on its hinges.

'You didn't have to fix that.' Charlie winced as he spoke. It was painful to talk. 'I would have done it.'

He could sense the old woman's eyes watching him closely as he struggled along the hallway. He was breathing heavily, and had

28

to lean against the wall for support. His legs felt as though they were about to give way. The searing ache in his head was still just as fierce as before.

June said nothing until they reached the top of the flight of stairs that led down to their rooms. Charlie paused, his knees threatening to buckle underneath him. Everything around him seemed to be swaying. Then he became aware of June gently draping his arm over her shoulders. He felt her arm around his waist supporting him as they descended the stairs.

'I won't have you breaking your neck and waking up the children,' she said, and Charlie thought he saw the ghost of a smile playing around her mouth. 'Besides, we can't afford to fix the damage.'

Caught between a laugh and a hiss of pain, Charlie inhaled sharply. He made his way unsteadily to the window, and rested against the sill, breathing deeply through the ache in his side. The frosty night air was soothing after the effort of walking for so long.

June had laid out his blanket on the floor, in the space between the bed and the wall. The kids were all lying beneath a blanket of their own, in the narrow bed that they shared with June. Their eyes were closed, their breathing steady, but Charlie did not believe for a moment that they were asleep.

'I'm back,' he said, 'so you can all stop pretending.'

The three children sat up at once, staring at Charlie with wide, frightened eyes.

'What happened?' Dima asked.

'I fell down the stairs.'

'But they —'

'I have a question for you two, as well,' Charlie said, his voice sharp. 'Mikhail said he was still waiting for your answer. What did he mean by that?'

'I don't know,' Dima said in a small voice.

'I'm telling you now, Dima,' Charlie warned, his teeth gritted against the pain, 'if you don't start talking —'

'They want us to go gloaming for them,' Leo piped up, after throwing an apologetic glance at his brother. 'Mikhail told Dima to tell me and Ruby that they want us to join the Pen gang.'

29

'They said because we're small, we won't get into trouble even if we do get caught,' Ruby added, nodding. 'They said the soldiers won't even suspect us because we're kids.'

'They said if we wanted to help you, it was the right thing to do,' Dima finished, his voice barely audible. 'We just wanted to help. They said we'd make you happy if we did it.'

Charlie dragged his fingers through his blood-soaked hair and sighed. He looked at the three children, still staring at him with concern. He felt immensely tired. He had tried his best to protect them from this. It had not been enough.

'The best way you can help Charlie is to work hard on your reading and your numbers,' June said firmly, easing the children back down to sleep and pulling the blankets back over them. 'That way, you'll be ready for school when Charlie gets us all out of this place.'

At her words, Charlie swallowed hard and rubbed his eyes fiercely. The children shared excited whispers amongst themselves for a few minutes, until, exhausted, their eyes gradually began to close. Charlie drank in their sleeping faces, feeling oddly separate from himself.

'If Faulkner thinks he's getting his filthy hands on these kids …'

June turned to him with a stern expression, like he was one of the children. 'Don't you go looking for trouble, Charlie.'

'I didn't,' Charlie said, his jaw clenched. 'It's found me. You heard what Faulkner said about Ruby. They've got a score to settle with me, and this is how they plan to do it – by threatening the kids. You know what he'll do to them if the Pen gets hold of them. I won't let that happen.'

June shook her head with a heavy sigh. 'Something like this was bound to happen eventually. Saints know how life goes for kids like this in Penumbra. But those Hunters …'

'They're not interested in Ruby, they just wanted some action,' Charlie said darkly, wincing as he touched the wound at his head. 'It's the Pen boys we should be worrying about.'

'What do you imagine you can do? If Faulkner wants them, then–'

'Not these kids,' Charlie said, venom in his every word. 'Not while I'm around.'

CHAPTER 4

C harlie arrived at the Pit soon after sunrise that morning. He had not bothered sleeping or changing clothes before leaving the house. Ignoring the furtive looks and outright stares he was getting from the men around him as he weaved his way through the crowd, Charlie kept walking towards the mine face. His whole body was stiff and aching from the attack, but he was used to the pain. It did not take him long to find who he was looking for.

He was following the sound of Marko's raucous voice, which he could hear clearly, a little way ahead of him, mingling with chesty coughs and harsh male laughter. Eventually, he caught sight of a group of men warming themselves around a blazing fire pit. The scent of rain-soaked wood combined with smoke hung in the air. The men were gathered in a circle between two cabins, which were used to store tools and equipment for the miners. As usual, Marko was holding court.

'Tell you what, I am *shattered* after that quake last night.' He yawned widely. As a known member of the Pen gang, most of the other men were wary of Marko, so he was afforded a certain level of indulgence at the Pit. 'I barely got any sleep after that. I'm surprised I managed to get out of bed at all this morning.'

Grinding his teeth, Charlie drew himself behind a large barrel, his thoughts racing. The familiar touch of the knife concealed by his ankle was reassuring against his skin.

One of the older miners, Ivan, snorted. 'It doesn't take a power surge for us to hear that from you, Marko. When was the last time you arrived for a shift on time?'

A roar of laughter followed these words. Closing his eyes, Charlie caught a snatch of conversation drifting over from the circle of men.

'Is that what they're saying it was – a power surge?' a younger miner asked.

'That's what I heard,' said Ivan, as Charlie peered around the barrel. 'They'll be working us harder than ever if it's true,' he added, groaning as he stretched. 'Ah, but remember, lads, it's not for us to question why ...'

Marko frowned. 'What about that weird light in the sky, then?'

'That was the power surge, of course. That light was the power escaping.'

Ivan shook his head slowly. 'Never seen anything like it ...'

'Do you think it could have something to do with the covens?'

'Don't talk nonsense! Isn't the Great Protector still on the High Throne?'

'But –'

Steeling himself, Charlie rounded the corner of the cabin. He came to a halt a few paces outside of the circle, his arms folded tightly across his chest, his face set. One by one, the men noticed his presence, the smiles sliding from their faces as they took in his injuries. He watched in silence as they hastily drained their mugs of watery coffee and sloped off.

Ivan was the only one to meet his eyes. 'Keep a look out for the foreman, Charlie,' he said, his voice low. 'You know he doesn't like trouble.'

'I'm not here for trouble,' Charlie said. 'I just need to make something clear.'

The grizzled older man narrowed his eyes and shook his head. 'I know trouble when I see it,' he said, clapping Charlie gently on the shoulder before Charlie shook him off. As he began to walk away, he added, 'Looks to me like you're bringing plenty.'

Marko had not moved. His eyes were wide with shock. 'Carroway, you ...'

Charlie did not look away. He let Marko take in the patchwork of bruising that covered the whole of the left side of his face, from his eye to his jaw, and the dried blood that had set across his nose and right cheek.

'You think you can make a move on me because the others aren't here?' Marko's fists were clenched. 'What do you want?'

'To give you a final warning.' Charlie winced. His lip was split. It still hurt to speak.

'I – I don't –'

Before Marko could say another word, Charlie had shoved him bodily against the wall of the cabin. Marko cringed away from Charlie, who could feel him trembling under his grip. The colour had drained from Marko's face.

'I've got a message for Faulkner,' Charlie said, a soft growl in his throat. 'You tell him that Charlie Carroway's kids are off limits. If I hear that your cousin – or any of the other vultures in your pathetic little gang – have said another word to those kids, they are all dead. You got that?'

'You need to get wise, Charlie.' Marko pushed Charlie away from him. 'The Skoto Gate tunnel is wide open. We've got another group of brats going through tonight. There's space for yours too. If they're quick, there's no risk of them getting nailed. We've got candles in position to watch out for the screws from Elysia. It's just business, Charlie. There's money to be made for all of us, even if we *are* Penumbrans.'

Charlie squared up to Marko, forcing him back. 'You're not playing the game.'

'What do you care, anyway?' Marko's voice was becoming shrill. 'It's not like they're even *your* kids. You'd be better off on your back with the Pen protecting you than martyring yourself for those brats and that old hag. Who d'you think you are? All you're good for is –'

The familiar scream of fury was whistling in Charlie's ears. He did not even think about the knife. The next thing he knew, he and Marko were both on the ground, fists flying, and the screws that patrolled the Pit were wrenching them apart.

'What's all this? What do you two animals think you're doing?'

Charlie forced himself up onto his feet as the foreman came marching towards them. Beside him, Marko was looking sorry for himself, but Charlie was certain Marko did not feel the same surging fear that he did. He did not know what the foreman might deem reasonable punishment for fighting at work. Marko had his connections with the Pen boys to fall back on. Charlie had four mouths depending on him for the meagre wage this job brought in.

One of the guards pushed Charlie forward. 'These two were fighting, sir.'

The foreman's brow furrowed as he took in Charlie's injuries. 'This is a place of work,' he said. 'I will not tolerate brawling. You,' he jerked his chin at Marko, 'get to work, now.' He turned to look at Charlie, running his teeth over his lower lip as his eyes travelled over Charlie's bruised face. 'How long have you worked here, Carroway?' he said at last.

'Three years, sir.'

The foreman nodded. 'Three years, and I've had no complaints about you in all that time. You're a good worker. I need good workers. But this,' he made a vague gesture in Charlie's direction, 'this isn't acceptable – not when you work for me.'

'No, sir.'

'I'm not interested in what you get up to outside of this mine, but when you pick a fight with one of my employees on company time …' The foreman shook his head with a sigh. 'I'm sure you know about the connections Marko has. I can't have that kind of trouble here, not when I have hundreds of men and their families relying on me to keep this operation running.'

'I understand, sir,' Charlie said quickly. 'I'll stay away from him. Just don't kick me out. Please – give me another chance.'

The foreman considered Charlie for some time before he replied. 'I will give you one more chance. This is your first and last warning, Carroway. If anything like this happens again, you're out. Now get back to work.'

'Yes, sir. Thank you, sir.'

Charlie kept his eyes fixed on a patch of gravel by his feet until the foreman had walked away. He was alone. At their boss's last words, the guards had slunk off too. They only took pleasure in having the opportunity to escort former employees off the premises, and had no interest in second chances. Charlie made a mental note to do his best to keep out of their way for the rest of the day. They would be itching to take out their disappointment on him, and he had no desire to add to the collection of bruises already covering his body.

His head was throbbing painfully again.

The tool cabins were deserted. By now, most of the men would already be at the mine face. He collected a hammer and chisel, stuck them in his worn tool belt, slung a shovel and pickaxe over his shoulder, and headed out towards the entrance to the mine. The sky that morning was a solid sheet of grey, and it was threatening to pour down. Charlie held the feel of the wind on his skin and the smell that promised the coming of rain close to him as he descended the shaft.

Then he was sent deep underground, into the heat and the never-ending darkness.

It was pitch-black down there, and Charlie immediately felt the tightness in his chest returning. Beads of sweat had formed on his forehead before he had even started work. He moved carefully, wary of scraping his head on the sharp rocks above him. He knew they were there, even if he could not see them. The roof of the tunnel was so low that he needed to shuffle along in a crouched position to move forward.

The ache in his legs was terrible at first. But, as he began to chisel and pick away at the tunnel walls, he eventually became numb to it. He sensed rather than saw where he had left off at the end of the previous day, always listening intently for any sign of danger. It was too narrow in the tunnel to turn around and go back to the shaft easily, so Charlie proceeded slowly, only moving on when he was certain he would not need to return.

As the hours wore on, time slipped away from him. In the darkness, there was no way to distinguish between morning, afternoon, or evening. He would be down there until he heard the bell signalling the end of the shift for that day. Pain stole through his body. It throbbed and hummed in his back and his arms and his shoulders as he worked. That was nothing new. What caught Charlie's attention was the burning sensation in his chest. When the coughing started, he found that it would not stop.

He could not catch his breath.

It was like he was being stabbed between the ribs each time he tried to breathe in.

There seemed to be even less space in the tunnel than usual. Trying desperately to stay calm, even as he struggled to breathe, Charlie forced himself to focus on making his way backwards along the tunnel. He edged his way towards the shaft, his lungs on fire.

When he reached it, he wrenched down on the rope connected to the emergency bell at the surface. Then he collapsed onto the wooden boards beneath him, still unable to stop coughing. They were only supposed to use the bell when they had been caught in a tunnel collapse and needed to be pulled back up out of the shaft to safety. But Charlie did not know what else to do.

Please, someone hear it, he prayed, as memories of hands forcing him into a shadowy place, bodies smothering him, swamped his mind. *Someone, help me. Don't let me die down here alone in the dark.*

He was rising. The light was comforting, like home. Maybe his brother would be …

'Max …'

'Get him some water – now!' He could hear Ivan's strained voice. 'Come on, Charlie, sit up. Saints, what's happened to you?'

Ivan pressed a metal cup into Charlie's hand and helped guide it to his lips. As the worst of the panic subsided, Charlie found that he was able to breathe a little deeper. The stabbing pain in his chest began to lessen slightly. He could feel himself shaking, and hurriedly brushed the tears out of his eyes. With Ivan's help, he got to his feet, his skin crawling at the touch.

'How are you feeling, Charlie?'

Charlie could only manage a weak cough in response. He shook his head.

'What's going on here?' The foreman was striding towards them, flanked by six guards. He looked harried, and a muscle worked in his jaw as he laid eyes on Charlie. 'You again, Carroway?

What did I tell you this morning? I was informed that there had been a collapse.'

'Carroway is ill, sir,' Ivan explained. 'He was coughing so bad that he couldn't breathe. He just needs to rest, then he'll be fine to go back down again.'

'Carroway is ill?' the foreman repeated, eyeing Charlie intently. 'Is that so?'

'I'm fine, sir,' Charlie insisted, though his chest was heaving, and he had to hold his hand in front of his mouth to stop himself from coughing. 'I don't need to rest. I'm fine.'

The foreman was not listening. He had removed a notepad from his pocket and was using a pen to hurriedly fill out a blue form. 'You know the rules, Carroway,' he said, tearing the piece of paper from the pad and thrusting it towards Charlie. 'I do not have the luxury of being able to employ liabilities at this pit.'

Charlie froze. 'But, sir,' he began desperately, careful not to cough and splutter in the foreman's face. 'I'm not due to attend a health inspection for months.'

'I need that fitness to work certification signed and stamped by a doctor and returned to me before you even think about going back down that mineshaft. The Infirmary Station will still be open. I suggest you go there.'

'But I can't take the time off. I can't lose this job.'

'And what about the time I'm losing?' The foreman's face was reddening. 'You may not take this work seriously – brawling and getting into fights at the slightest provocation – but it is essential to the survival of our nation. Those pretty stones you dig up fuel the weapons the Great Protector uses to defend us from the covens. You think you're worth more than that?'

'But it's not just me I'm thinking of! I have three kids at home and –'

'Your personal life is none of my concern,' the foreman said, his voice turning cold as he held his hand up to prevent Charlie from saying anything more. 'Each of us makes his own bed in this life, as they say. I am telling you for the last time, Carroway: until I have that fitness to work certification signed, stamped, and back in my hands, you are not permitted to step foot on my property. Guards, see him out.'

*

By the time he reached the Infirmary Station, Charlie's cough had subsided. He hesitated at the threshold of the rundown building, one hand on the door handle, the other still clutching the piece of paper the foreman had given him. He usually tried to avoid this place at all costs, and hated the annual health inspections because they meant a day less paid work.

But the foreman was right. Now he had been served with the little blue form that was currently scrunched up in his hand, he would not be able to find another steady job anywhere in Penumbra. Not until he found a doctor who was willing to vouch for him being fit to work.

With a sigh, he pushed the heavy door open. One short blare of an alarm greeted him as he stepped into the Station, reigniting the pain in his head as he joined the back of the queue of people waiting to be signed in at the front desk. The Great Protector glared at him from his portrait, which hung in a wooden frame on the wall behind the desk. Charlie smothered a cough and tapped his foot on the floor, his hands thrust deep in his pockets as he tried to stay calm.

While he waited for the white-haired old man in front of him to be processed, Charlie scanned the holding area absentmindedly. It was as overcrowded as usual, but oddly quiet for a room containing so many people. His eyes lingered over an exhausted-looking young mother, whose eyes had glazed over while her baby lay limply in her arms. Another small child rolled around on the floor by her feet. With a wan smile, Charlie ran his fingers through the longer section of his unkempt hair and gazed around the rest of the room. When he looked down at his hands, there were flakes of dry blood underneath his fingernails.

Sensing someone's eyes on him, Charlie looked up. It was only then that he noticed he was being watched. A tall young man with wild black hair, about his own age, wearing military fatigues and carrying a rifle, was staring directly at him from the other end of the room. He looked somewhat familiar. The soldier was standing beside the archway that marked the entrance to the examination ward, where the doctors and nurses worked. The dark scowl on his face was enough to make Charlie wilt. He was relieved when he was called over to the front desk by a girl he recognised. He decided he would do his best to avoid making any trouble with this serious-looking stranger.

The nurse at the desk had thick dark hair, which she had braided over her shoulder. She wore a long-sleeved black cotton shirt underneath her light blue uniform.

'I didn't expect to see you back so soon, Charlie.' Nika smiled as she took the blue form from him. He watched as she checked the details before adding it to the top of a pile of papers in a variety of colours. 'I thought your last inspection was only six months ago?'

Charlie grinned at her. 'You make a point of remembering the last time you saw all your patients, or am I just special?'

Nika laughed. 'You're very special, Charlie.' She paused, taking in the cuts and bruises on his face and the layers of dirt and dust covering him. 'I see you're still getting into as much trouble as ever.' She frowned. 'Did the Pit shut down early today?'

'Why are you on front desk duty, anyway?' Charlie asked. He did not like the look of concern in Nika's warm eyes.

'You know how it is,' she said, shrugging. 'We're short-staffed, so I'm processing everyone until we close up. I'll stay until all our patients have been treated.'

'Saint Nika, always putting everyone else before herself.'

Nika snorted. 'You're one to talk! How are Granny June and the kids?'

'Fine,' Charlie said. 'Tell me this, though,' he added, unable to restrain his curiosity as he leant in closer and spoke in a softer voice. 'When did Elysian soldiers start patrolling the Infirmary Station?'

CHAPTER 5

Nika's face fell, and she stole a frightened glance towards the soldier at the far end of the holding area. 'He just showed up this morning. We hadn't heard anything to suggest they would be deploying anyone here … but then, no one ever does, I suppose.' She glanced at the soldier, looking uncomfortable and anxious. 'Everyone's on edge because of him. Some people were even saying it might be …' She trailed off, biting her lip.

Charlie frowned. 'Has there been any trouble here in the last few days?'

Nika shook her head. 'Nothing.' She paused before lowering her voice further. 'You don't think it might have something to do with that earthquake, do you? Could that column of light over the mountains have been –?'

Charlie shook his head. 'Has no one tried asking him what he's doing here?'

Nika raised her eyebrows. 'Would *you* want to be the one to ask him? Look at him. No, he just went and stood by the entrance to the ward, and he's stayed there all day. He hasn't said a word to anyone so far.'

'What's so special about today?' Charlie wondered aloud. The soldier was still staring directly at him, his expression fierce, and Charlie did not blame the patients in the holding area for feeling unnerved. 'Has anything else happened that could explain it?'

'Nothing out of the ordinary,' Nika said with a shrug. 'You can go through to the ward now, Charlie. Patients with employment get priority,' she added, seeing his confused look. 'Oh, and we have a new nurse starting today. She's shadowing Doctor Zhang. Try not to frighten her off.'

'If she can handle Doctor Zhang then she doesn't need to worry about me.'

'What am I going to do with you?' Nika smiled, rolling her eyes as he left.

The soldier was still staring at him, his brow furrowed. His dark eyes followed Charlie as he approached the far end of the holding area, and Charlie was keenly aware of how close the soldier's finger was to the trigger of his rifle. Neither of them said a word, and Charlie kept his eyes downcast. Even as he walked through the archway leading into the ward, he could feel the soldier's gaze burning into his back.

The examination ward was a long, narrow room with plain white walls. Metal cot beds lined both sides of the room, each separated from the other by screens of thin white material for privacy. A walkway through the middle of the room led up to an unoccupied desk at the far wall. Charlie could hear the low moans of patients behind screens, but otherwise the room seemed completely empty. The sensation that he had entered somewhere he should not be prickled through him, and he cleared his throat loudly.

'Nurse Woods, set Carroway up in Bay Nine, please,' a clipped male voice said.

'Yes, Doctor.'

The young woman who had answered the doctor appeared from behind a screen in the middle of the room and strode straight towards Charlie. She was golden brown, like him; half a head or so shorter than he was; and slim, with straight, chestnut brown hair that fell past her shoulders. Her deep brown eyes were darker even than his. A huge, warm smile spread across her face as they regarded each other. Charlie swallowed, his mouth suddenly dry. Her eyes widened as she stared at his injuries, her smile faltering as her mouth fell slightly open. But she did not look afraid.

'Are you Mr Carroway?' she asked, smoothing her navy-blue scrubs.

Charlie nodded. 'I need a fitness to work certification. My boss sent me.'

'I'm Nurse Woods,' she said, looking straight into his eyes. 'This is my first day here.'

Charlie nodded again. 'Yeah, I heard.'

There was a look of curiosity in the young woman's face that Charlie did not understand. 'Please follow me, sir,' she said. 'Doctor Zhang will be with you soon.'

Charlie blinked. He was sure he had never once been called 'sir' in his whole life. Lost for words, he followed her into a free bay.

'You should sit down,' the nurse said, indicating the bed. When she joined him there, Charlie instinctively shuffled away from her a little. 'That must hurt,' she said, seeming not to notice. 'Have you been icing your face, sir? When did you last take any medicine for the pain?'

Baffled, Charlie watched her hand race across a small notepad, which she had drawn from the pocket of her dress. He did not know where she expected him to find the money to buy pain medication in Penumbra.

'It's fine,' he said, hastily rubbing his hand on his jeans before offering it to her. 'You can call me Charlie.'

She regarded his outstretched hand for a moment, before meeting his eyes and smiling. 'Alice,' she said, shaking it. 'It's a pleasure to meet you, Charlie.' Her skin felt feather-soft under his calloused fingers. She wore a delicate gold chain around her neck, weaved around red stones of varying sizes that glinted in the lights from above their heads.

'On your feet, Carroway. You know how this works.'

Doctor Zhang burst through the screen. Middle-aged, with thinning hair, and wearing round glasses, Charlie had been examined by this doctor during his last three annual health inspections. He braced himself for what he knew was coming next.

'Nurse Woods, watch carefully,' the doctor snapped, busying around with a number of complicated-looking machines that stood beside the bed. 'You'll be doing this for our next female patient.'

Charlie removed his t-shirt. He was aware of Alice's eyes widening as they fell on the patchwork of vicious scars that

43

covered his right shoulder. The sprawling spiderweb tattoo that had marked him as property of the Pen gang had been there once, but he had got rid of it himself, years ago. Charlie drew one hand behind his back to keep the base of his spine hidden. Then he allowed his mind to drift as the doctor prepared his other arm. A long needle pierced his skin. Charlie swayed on his feet as his blood was drawn, wincing a little as the doctor prodded and probed his chest and torso with rough fingers.

From the corner of his eye, Charlie had the sense that Alice was watching him closely, a troubled expression on her face. He thought he saw her motion to the bruising around his ribs. He watched as the doctor pointed at her in a way that made Charlie think he was giving her a warning. But there was no reason for the doctor to do that. He guessed that the loss of blood must be making him see things.

He was so tired. His body felt heavy. The machines whirred and beeped, the noises smothered as though he was hearing them from underwater. Charlie felt himself gradually sinking, growing steadily weaker. The thought crossed his mind that, if he were to simply close his eyes now, he might never have to wake up again.

*

'He still hasn't woken up?'

'It's been far too long. I've told the doctor, but he doesn't seem to care at all.'

Charlie's head shifted against the pillow. He recognised both of those voices.

'I still don't understand why you wanted to come here. The risks involved are –'

'I can't keep living my life like a bird in a cage,' he heard Alice say. 'I want something more than that, Vasco. I need to experience what's really out here while I still have the chance.'

'What do you mean by that?' Vasco asked. 'I tried my best to warn you about this place, didn't I? I need to return soon. We've been gone far too long already. We *must* leave, Alya.'

'I know, I know. You should go. I'll find you when he wakes up.'

Charlie heard the sound of heavy footsteps fading away and felt soft skin on his.

'Can you hear me, Charlie? Try to squeeze my hand if you can manage it.'

Blinking in the bright lights above his head, Charlie slowly opened his eyes, and found himself looking directly into Alice's face. Her expression softened from concern to relief, and she withdrew something rectangular from the pocket of her dress.

'Here, you need to eat some of these,' she said, opening the packet and offering it to him. 'Apparently, there's not a single biscuit in this entire building. But luckily for you, I don't go anywhere without a snack. I need to find the doctor about the readings on your chart.'

Wary, Charlie took a biscuit and nibbled the corner. He had never tasted anything like it before.

'I couldn't find any juice either, so water will have to do. I'll get you some now.'

She made to get up from the bed, but Charlie grabbed her wrist and held it tightly. He did not know what she meant by 'juice', but that was not important at the moment. 'Please don't leave me,' he said, his voice low and weak. 'I don't want to be alone. I don't feel right.'

Alice paused, regarding him with the same warm expression she had worn when they had first met. She sat down again. 'I won't leave,' she said, her voice so gentle that it sent a shiver along his spine. 'Finish that biscuit for me – and you should have another one after that, too. Your blood pressure went so low that I was worried you wouldn't wake up.'

Charlie managed a weak laugh. 'Didn't they tell you? I'm indestructible.'

Alice rolled her eyes and shook the packet of biscuits in his face. 'Eat.'

At her insistence, Charlie took another biscuit and chewed it thoughtfully. 'You know, I think you're the first Elysian I've ever met,' he said, before correcting himself. 'Like this, I mean.'

With a frown, Alice got to her feet. 'What makes you think I'm from Elysia?'

Charlie snorted, wincing a little at the pain the movement caused. 'I could tell the second you opened your mouth,' he said, as Alice's face fell. 'Besides, us Pennies don't carry around packets of biscuits in our pockets,' he continued, as she sat back down on the bed. 'Or wear rocks like those around our necks. These are more our style,' he added, indicating the metal collar that he, like all Penumbrans, was always required to wear as protection against the witch covens. It was the Great Protector's gift to his people.

Alice's fingers strayed to the delicate gold chain she was wearing. Without a word, she removed it and handed it to Charlie, who examined the red stones intricately woven into the gold band.

'These are dragonstones, aren't they?' he said. 'They're my speciality. I wouldn't be surprised if it was me who dug these out of the ground for you. I thought they were for – I don't know – weapons against the witch covens, or something.'

'You work in the mines? I thought that was the most dangerous work there is here.'

'I have to think about my family. They're all depending on me.'

Alice did not say anything more. They sat in silence for a few moments, her eyes on Charlie, as he continued to examine her necklace.

'No one in Penumbra could dream of owning something like this,' he said, turning it over in his hands. 'I've never seen anything like it before. It's beautiful.'

'It was a gift from my father,' Alice said flatly. 'I've never liked it all that much.'

'It's a dead giveaway for an Elly in disguise,' Charlie said, grinning, and Alice shook her hair back over her shoulders imperiously. 'So, d'you come here often?'

'If you must know, you're the first Penumbran I've ever spoken to,' she said, a defiant edge to her voice. 'Or – the first one that I've spoken to like this, at least.' She held his gaze for a moment, a slight crease between her brows. 'It's been … interesting.'

They both jumped when Doctor Zhang pulled back the screen and strode into the bay. He stood over Charlie's bed, ignoring Alice completely, his eyes darting to the chart in his hands before he spoke.

'I have your test results here,' he said. 'You will need to prepare yourself, Carroway.'

At the doctor's words, a fist seemed to clench in Charlie's chest. He glanced quickly at Alice, who was frowning at Zhang. Charlie felt her reach for his hand and squeeze it tightly with her own. He shivered.

'The tests we carried out showed abnormalities,' Zhang said. 'Whatever it is, there's no hope for you. Your body is turning against itself. Have you experienced any coughing yet?'

Charlie froze. There was a ringing in his ears. Everything seemed to be falling away.

'None of this is surprising, given the age you started working at the Pit,' the doctor continued evenly, shaking his head. '*Thirteen* … I don't know what you were thinking. Surely they must have warned you of the risks? Our choices always have consequences, you know.'

'I didn't have –' Charlie managed to croak.

'I understand you came here hoping for a fitness to work certification,' Zhang continued, ignoring him. 'Obviously, I cannot provide you with one now. There is nothing more I can do for you. You may see yourself out – as quickly as possible, please. I still have many more patients to get through today.'

'This isn't right,' Charlie heard Alice protest. She sounded as though she was somewhere far away from him.

Doctor Zhang paused before leaving the bay. 'I suggest you go home and get your affairs in order, Carroway. Time is not on your side. In fact, I would be surprised if you have much of it left at all.'

Then he was gone. The silence that followed in his wake seemed to stretch on forever.

Finally, Alice spoke. 'Charlie,' she said, whispering his name before shaking herself and staring at him with her large, impassioned eyes. 'I'm so sorry. I'm so sorry for how he spoke to you. That wasn't right.' She fell silent for a moment, her eyes downcast, before raising her free hand to his chest. 'Maybe I could … there might be something that I can –'

Charlie flinched away from her as though burned. 'Don't touch me!' he snarled.

Alice's face fell, but she nodded. 'Talk to me. Tell me what you're thinking.'

'What's going on?' The curtain was ripped back. Charlie looked up to see the dark-haired soldier scowling down at him, before shooting a glare at the floor as Charlie pulled his t-shirt back over his head. 'Aren't you needed elsewhere, *Alice*?' he added, his face colouring.

'Not yet.' Alice sounded desperate. 'He's ill. Charlie, what are you going to do now?'

'I'm going back to the Pit,' Charlie said. He was not quite sure what he was saying. Someone else seemed to be in control of his voice. 'I'll forge the papers myself if I have to. It's the only way. There's nothing else I can do.'

'You can't work if you're sick,' the soldier said, his voice harsh and a bad-tempered look on his face. 'You shouldn't be doing that anyway. You're just a kid. You need to rest.'

'No.' Charlie heaved a sigh. 'I've got too many people depending on me to do that.'

'Isn't there anyone else you could ask to help you?' Alice was chewing her nails.

Charlie let out a feeble laugh. 'Now I know for sure that you're not from around here.'

'But you can't deal with this all on your own ...' Alice's eyes were misty as she turned to appeal to the soldier. 'Vasco, tell him! There's got to be something else we can do to help.'

Charlie's jaw clenched. 'Listen, I never asked for your help!' he snapped. 'It's my problem and I'll deal with it myself ...'

He raised his hand and drew it back, his fingernails aiming for the burning itch at his throat. He saw Alice's eyes widen in fright. He understood what she was afraid of a split second before Vasco's hand encircled his wrist in an iron grip. Then he was forced back against the headboard.

'Try that again and you're dead,' Vasco said, his voice taut. 'Get it together, already.'

'This can't be happening to me,' Charlie murmured, his hand dropping to the blanket as Vasco released his wrist. 'This ... this can't be happening to me.'

'Vasco, he's in shock,' Alice said, giving the soldier a reproachful look. 'I'm so sorry this is happening to you, Charlie.'

Charlie drew his knees up to his face, bracing his fist against his forehead as he began to rock backwards and forwards, his hands shaking. 'What am I going to do?' he said, in a whisper that steadily grew into a strangled howl. 'What am I … what should I –?'

'What's wrong with him?' Vasco asked, his voice sharp. 'What do we do?'

'We need to help him, Vasco,' Alice said at once. 'I don't *know* what to do.'

'We need to leave – quickly. Before anyone realises you're gone.'

'But we've got to do *something*!'

Fury erupted in Charlie's body. 'There's nothing you *can* do!' he roared, staggering out of the bed, and facing them with clenched fists. 'You Elysians have done enough already!' With a kind of savage joy, he realised that the fact the soldier was carrying a rifle meant nothing to him anymore. 'Get out of here and stay the hell away from me!'

'Charlie …'

He saw tears shimmering in Alice's huge brown eyes, grief tugging her lips down, before he was knocked sideways by a vicious punch to the head from the Elysian soldier. He fell to the floor with an anguished cry of pain.

'Vasco, don't! It's not his fault –'

'Alexandra, they're coming. Forget about him. We need to get out of here *now*!'

The sound of racing footsteps soon faded into the distance. Curled up on the floor, Charlie cradled his aching head in his hands and felt the cool brush of metal against his temple. He unclenched his fist. The dragonstones set into the Elysian girl's necklace danced like flames in the light reflected off the silver frame of the cot bed. She had left it behind. A familiar dry cough was threatening to burst from his throat.

He was alone.

CHAPTER 6

Charlie did not remember returning home from the Infirmary Station. He was only dimly aware of finding himself standing in front of the open door leading to their basement rooms. June was there too, sweeping the threshold, a broom in her hand and a look of surprise on her face.

'Are you making up for last night, getting home so early?' She continued sweeping.

Charlie blinked, and raised his head up to the bright, cloudless sky, tracing the path of a solitary bird. 'Granny, are the kids around?' He swallowed hard. 'Something's happened.'

'They aren't back yet.'

'What?' Charlie's heart began to hammer in his chest. 'Where are they?'

'They're late. You're setting a bad example for them, you know.'

'When did you last see them?'

'Well, it must have been hours ago …' June paused. 'Why, is something wrong?'

Charlie had already turned and started to sprint away. 'Stay here. I'll be back later.'

'Where are you going?'

'I'm going to find the kids,' Charlie said, without looking over his shoulder. 'And I'm going to make Faulkner sorry he ever thought about threatening my family.'

The Pen gang's hideout was located deep in the slums of the inner city. Charlie wandered through the twisting cobbled streets, avoiding the eyes of anyone who looked as though they might be heading in his direction. He had to fight to keep his breathing steady. There was a small part of him that knew he was about to do something extremely foolish. But then again, he had little left to lose anymore.

He ducked down a winding alleyway full of tall, narrow buildings, the roofs of which sloped into one another, giving the impression that they were about to collapse in on their neighbours. He had not been back to this part of the city since he had escaped the clutches of the Pen gang three years ago.

The entrance to the hideout was an innocuous wooden door set into a stone archway. He had hoped that he would never have to set eyes on it again. He had certainly never planned on stepping back across that threshold willingly. But they had left him with no other choice.

Taking a deep breath, Charlie stepped out of the chilly evening air and entered an uncomfortably warm, low-lit room, heaving with bodies. Groups of men and women were gathered together, pressing against one another due to the limited space, drinking from tall glasses and laughing beneath clouds of cigarette smoke. Countless gang tattoos flashed at him across exposed skin, marking the members of the Pen boys and their allies. Charlie felt his scarred shoulder prickle beneath his black t-shirt.

There was too much noise inside the hideout for anyone to notice him coming in. His hands deep in his pockets, Charlie kept his shoulders hunched and his eyes on the floorboards. He forced himself to edge his way through the crowds towards the bar. Once he was there, he would be able to sneak into the back rooms to search for Ruby, Leo and Dima.

He was sure it would not take long for him to find them. The layout of the Pen hideout had not changed at all during the seven years he had been imprisoned there. He knew where the new arrivals were kept isolated until they lost their will to fight back. Until they were considered ready to be trained. His stomach twisting, he forced away the memories of dark rooms and long nights that came surging into his mind. He lengthened his stride.

He must not be caught here.

'You've been in the wars, haven't you? Want me to take care of you for a while?'

Charlie stilled at the sound of a familiar lilting voice. 'I thought we were past all that?'

He looked up, finding himself face to face with a teenage girl he had not seen for three years. She wore an extremely short strapless dress that plunged below her neck. In her high-heeled shoes, she was close to his own height. Her straight, silver-blonde hair was longer than he remembered, and her face had sharpened in the time he had spent away from the gang.

'It's you ...' Maya's bright blue eyes widened, and she took a step back, glancing around, her brows knitted. 'What are you *thinking*, showing your face around here again?'

'I'm here to see your boss.' Charlie went to move past her. 'Get out of my way.'

Maya put a hand on his chest. 'Have you lost your mind? If anyone recognises you –'

'Faulkner,' Charlie said, just about managing to keep his voice calm. 'Where is he?'

'*Saints.*' Maya grabbed his hand and pulled him into the shadows of an alcove. She pushed him back against the wall and pressed her body close to his as he tried to edge away from her. 'Why have you come back?' Her words rushed out in a desperate whisper, her face drawn. 'You got away ...'

'I'm looking for three kids. Two boys and a girl, about five or six years old.'

'Kids?' Maya frowned. 'Wait, you mean –? Don't tell me you're this stupid, Charlie.'

'They would have been brought in today. Have you seen them?'

Maya narrowed her eyes, worrying the corner of her mouth. 'No, I haven't seen them.'

'But you know where they are.'

'They're not here,' Maya said, shaking her head. 'You won't be able to reach them.'

'There's nowhere in Penumbra I won't be able to find them.' Charlie paused, understanding what she meant. 'Unless ...'

'Anyone seen the boss's girl?' came a rough voice from somewhere behind them.

'You need to leave,' Maya said, backing away from him. 'Now – before they find you.'

Charlie stepped forward, his voice urgent. 'Maya, what do you know about this?'

'Don't ask me about this, Charlie.' She stole a look over her shoulder before facing him again, gripping her arms. 'We were friends, right? I'm trying to look out for you.'

'If you were my friend then you would help me.'

Maya considered his words for a while. 'Elysia,' she said finally. 'They will have been taken to Elysia. The fortress at the top of the mountain.'

'You know that for sure? How? Why?'

'Faulkner is heading up the operation on this side of the Wall,' Maya explained. 'Shipments cross over into Elysia every single night. They bring them in from all over the country. There are people disappearing everywhere, even here in Penumbra. Women. Kids.'

'What do they want with them?' Charlie asked, frowning as he thought back to what he had seen at the Skoto Gate the previous night. 'What's Faulkner up to?'

'I don't know. It's true!' she added quickly, throwing a scowl at him when he rolled his eyes. 'None of us know what happens to them once they get to Elysia.'

'Faulkner knows,' Charlie said, as he strode past her. 'And I'm about to find out.'

'I can give you a name,' Maya said. 'He's one of the leaders on the Elysian side.'

Charlie paused. 'What name?'

'Ivanov.'

'Got it.'

Maya touched his elbow. 'You're getting into something dangerous.'

'I am no stranger to dangerous things,' Charlie said, pulling his arm away from her.

'You talk big, but whatever Faulkner is up to in Elysia, you need to stay out of it.'

Charlie glanced at her, his hands in his pockets. 'What d'you mean by that?'

'These aren't people you should take on if you're planning to live long enough to see your next birthday,' Maya said, a troubled expression clouding her face. 'Let's put it that way.'

Charlie smirked. 'I guess we'll have to see, won't we? It was good seeing you, Maya.'

'Just think carefully before you do anything crazy for once, yeah?'

'Thanks for the advice.' Charlie did not look back at her as he walked away.

'Why thank me?' he heard her mutter behind him. 'I know you won't take any of it.'

Charlie stalked off towards the bar. He could not afford any more delays. Keeping close to the wall, he slipped behind the bar and along the narrow wooden passageway that led into the bowels of the gang's hideout. The corridor was not quite wide enough for two people to pass side by side, and he felt an unpleasant constricting sensation bearing down upon him.

His heart hammering, he kept walking, his fists clenched at his sides. He was trying to fight the terrified voice warning him that at any moment he was about to run straight into Faulkner.

The hideout was built like a labyrinth, with rickety wooden staircases set between every few doorways. They led the way up and down, this way and that, deeper into the maze. It was as though the building had been purposefully designed so that anyone who was not certain of their route would find it impossible not to lose their bearings. Once they were disorientated, they were easier to catch. As a child, Charlie had experienced that horrifying sensation of being snared in a trap many times, until he had finally managed to escape.

His feet had come to a halt in front of a familiar wooden door. His knees were trembling. He reached out one hand for the wall, his shoulder collapsing against it as he just about managed not to fall. Panicked, Charlie stared at his hands, which were shaking in front of him.

He could not think straight. The passageway was closing in on him. Something in his mind was dredging up memories he had fought for years to keep buried. The sights and sounds of those long, dark nights mingled with what he now saw before his eyes. He forced himself to keep moving. He had to get out, but he did not know the way.

'I assume this means you're up for it again?' an amused voice behind him said. 'I heard there were only two things that you were ever good at: fighting and – *don't let him get away!*'

Charlie wheeled around, trying to dodge out of the grip of the men surrounding him. But the corridor was narrow, and he was blocked in. They forced him down, a firm hand on each of his shoulders keeping him on his knees, as his hands were secured behind his back with a length of thick rope. Unable to break free, Charlie glared up into Marko's smug face.

'Well, well, well,' Marko sneered. 'Look who's back. Couldn't stay away, Carroway?'

Charlie ground his teeth, his anger flaring. 'What have you done with my family?'

Marko laughed. 'Wouldn't you like to know ...' He examined his fingernails, looking bored. 'You've wasted your time coming here, you know, and now that you're back, there's no way Faulkner is letting you out of here alive. I doubt he'll even let you out of that bedroom.'

Charlie mastered himself quickly. He refused to let any emotion show on his face.

'What do you want us to do with him?' one of the men restraining him asked.

'Where's Mikhail?'

'He's got business at the Wall tonight.'

'Then take him underground,' Marko answered, tapping Charlie's face with the side of his gun, 'and get a message to the boss. Let him know his lost puppy has found its way home. I'll be seeing you real soon, Charlie,' he added, as the men dragged Charlie to his feet.

Struggling fruitlessly against the rough hands on either side of him, Charlie was led down a dark flight of stairs into a cold, empty cellar. It was lit by a solitary bulb hanging from the low ceiling. They shoved him inside with such force that he lost his balance and fell sideways onto the concrete floor, his shoulder taking the impact of the fall.

'Remember how he likes it?'

Laughing amongst themselves, one of the men switched off the light. The door closed, plunging him into total darkness. Charlie was left alone, with only the sound of his ragged breathing for company.

By the time the door opened again, Charlie was soaked in his own cold sweat. As the light flickered back on, he edged himself up onto his knees, his eyes narrowed as he watched Marko close the door and approach him.

'They're all excited to have you back,' he said, leering at Charlie with a malevolent gleam in his eye. 'No one up there has forgotten about your particular talents, I promise you.'

'Don't sell yourself short,' Charlie shot back. 'You're the real cocksucker here.'

Charlie's head snapped to the side and he spat out blood as Marko's fist connected with his face. He heard his own laughter, empty of emotion, as Marko seethed in front of him.

'Offended? Come on, why else would Faulkner be keeping you around?'

'He sees something in me,' Marko hissed. 'You lost your place. You're just jealous.'

This only made Charlie laugh harder. '*Jealous?* This is a fucking house of horrors.'

Marko was regarding him with a curious expression. 'I heard you always fought back, every single time, no matter how many of them there were,' he said, his voice dropping to a low murmur as his eyes trailed down Charlie's body. 'Is it true, what they say he did to you?'

Charlie recoiled, uncomfortably aware of the ropes binding his hands behind his back.

'I guess I can always see for myself,' Marko continued, his lip curling. 'Can't I?'

'What are you doing down here?' The door creaked open. Maya stood there, furious.

'Guarding the prisoner,' Marko answered, casting her a sullen look.

'He's no prisoner, he's the boss's property,' Maya said, leaning against the doorframe and throwing Marko a look of open disdain. She spoke to him in a way that only one of Faulkner's favourites could get away with. 'Faulkner won't want him damaged. Get out of here and go pick a fight with someone else.'

'Who do you suggest?' Marko asked, drawing far too close to her for Charlie's liking.

'Oh, well, you'd have to tie me up first,' Maya said, completely unruffled as she regarded him with her cool, steady gaze. 'I know how much you hate a fair fight. Sorry, honey, but I'm not in the mood for that tonight. Maybe some other time – if you can afford it.'

'He needs to pay for daring to show his face around here again.'

'Sure, if you want to be the one to explain that to the boss when he gets back.'

Charlie watched as Marko glared at Maya, who returned his gaze with a pleasant smile and a little shrug. With a last look in Charlie's direction, Marko barged out of the cellar, slamming the door behind him. Maya's nonchalant expression fell from her face at once and she rushed to Charlie's side, untying the ropes that bound his hands and helping him to his feet.

'What are you doing?' Charlie demanded, his voice low, his eyes on the door.

'You always had my back when we were kids,' Maya muttered, her cheeks glowing.

Charlie massaged his wrists where the ropes had cut into them. 'If they find out –'

'They won't.' Maya strode over to the door. 'Get out of here and don't come back.'

Charlie stood there without knowing what to say as Maya left the cellar, leaving the door slightly ajar behind her. He waited until the sound of her footsteps had disappeared, planning to head up the stairs once there was no risk of her being seen with him. It was then that he heard the sound of muffled banging and shouting coming from somewhere behind him. He hesitated, his brow furrowed, then followed the noise to a small door near the far corner of the cellar.

Charlie tested the handle, only to find that it was locked. Inside, the banging and shouting grew louder. He pressed his ear to the door and heard cries for help. A wild, desperate hope soaring in his chest, he abandoned any thought of leaving the cellar before he discovered who was trapped inside the hidden room. He shoved his shoulder against the door a few times, to no effect, then lashed out at it with his foot. Finally, he managed to kick it open.

The light from the cellar cast the smaller room into sharp relief, and Charlie felt his eyes widen as he took in the scene in front of him. Wire cages were stacked on top of one another, filling the room almost entirely. Most of the cages were empty, but a large one close to him drew his attention.

Fingers were poking through the wire mesh, the sight of which made his skin crawl. When he crouched down, the faces of four girls stared back at him. He swore softly under his breath as mingled fury and nausea churned in his stomach.

'Help us,' the girl closest to the wire mesh said, pointing to the lock at the front of the cage. She fixed her fierce eyes on him, her jaw clenched. 'Please. Get us out of here.'

'Don't talk to him,' a younger, frightened-looking girl whispered. 'He's one of them.'

'No. I'm not,' Charlie said, his voice firm. 'How long have you all been kept here?'

The older girl seemed to be sizing him up. 'I hear you're looking for your family.'

Charlie paused. 'How do you know that?' Then, he understood. 'What are you?'

'You don't want to take a guess?' Her heavy-lidded eyes glittered. 'I have information.'

For a split second, Charlie was torn. It was treason to help a witch. Then he thought of Ruby, Leo and Dima, and all his doubts melted away. 'I'm looking for three little kids – two boys, one girl,' he said in a hurried voice. 'What do you know about them?'

'Get my sisters and I out of these cages and I'll tell you everything I know.'

Charlie narrowed his eyes. 'What's stopping you from getting out yourselves?'

'We're not strong enough,' the girl said at last. Charlie thought it cost her some pride to admit that to him, and he noticed that she was the only one among them not wearing a collar. 'They're keeping us underground, away from the sunlight. We're getting weaker every day.'

One of the younger girls let out a quiet sob. Charlie looked at each of them in turn. The girl who appeared to be their leader was probably close to his own age. She was wearing some kind of uniform. The others were much younger, perhaps not even into their teens. He remembered being trapped like this.

Charlie drew a bobby pin from the longer section of his hair. 'Start talking.'

'The Volya Research Facility,' the girl said, following his movements as he began to pick the lock at the front of their cage. 'It's part of the Elysian Castle compound. The mountains. That's where they will have taken your family.'

'How do you know that for sure?'

'It's where all the prisoners are sent, sooner or later.'

'Why there?'

'That's what I'm trying to find *out*,' the girl said, a touch of impatience in her voice. 'My coven sent me to learn more about what's going on at the Facility, but I won't be able to protect myself in this state. I need to get my sisters out and regroup with the Lilith coven first.'

Charlie hesitated, his fingers slowing. 'You're one of *them*? One of the … terrorists?'

'I am Jasmine Darkwood, the last daughter of a ruined clan,' the girl answered, her face hardening. 'The Witchkillers have taken everything from my people. Someone has to fight back.'

'The Great Protector keeps the Wall standing for us,' Charlie found himself saying.

Jasmine cast a pitying look over his face. 'The only difference between the Lilith coven and Nikolai the Merciless is that he has the law on his side. Why don't you wake up and open your eyes? Can't you see what's going on here?'

The lock clicked free, and Charlie tossed it aside, opening the wire door of the cage before standing back to let the four girls out. The three younger ones inclined their heads, avoiding his eyes. They bunched together at the door to the cellar, waiting for Jasmine to join them.

'Thanks for your help,' she said, levelling him with her cool gaze. 'The four of us are in your debt.'

'Try not to get caught again,' Charlie replied. 'I won't be here next time.'

Jasmine blinked, before her face split into a dark smile. 'What's your name?'

'Charlie Carroway.'

'You're not worried about us giving you up as soon as we get out of this place?'

Charlie raised his eyebrows, making no attempt to hide his scorn. 'I can take care of myself. Tell whoever you want.' He stared around the room of wire cages. 'Besides, I want Faulkner to know exactly who's responsible for this. I don't plan on sneaking out of here.'

Jasmine's malicious smile broadened, her eyes flashing. 'Good, because neither do we.'

'We need to get armed up,' Charlie said, as they headed up the stairs out of the cellar. 'I know where there's a weapons cache. First we take what we need, then we escape together.'

'Not necessary,' Jasmine answered at once. 'Stay with us. We'll cover you.'

'It's this way,' one of the girls called to her. 'Jasmine, it's almost time.'

At these words, Jasmine surged to the front of the group, the three younger girls behind her, and raised one unarmed hand out in front of her face. Charlie thought he saw a bright blue light appear in the centre of her palm, flickering red, orange, and yellow. He no longer felt cold.

'As soon as you get the chance, run,' she said, turning her stern gaze on him. Her dark skin was bathed in a warm light that seemed to emanate from her own body. 'I won't be able to control it after so long under the ground. It's got to be all or nothing.'

She turned away from him, and Charlie felt a burst of heat on a sudden gust of wind. A wall of flame rose in front of his eyes.

Then the explosions began.

CHAPTER 7

Charlie did not stop running until he reached the edge of the slums. The sun had set behind him as he fled the heart of the Spike, and darkness was now stealing in around him on all sides. He had lost sight of the four witches almost immediately after they had made their escape.

Deep purple clouds scudded across the starry sky, and waves of thunder rolled ominously overhead. A storm was approaching fast. His skin prickled with goosepimples under his thin, short-sleeved t-shirt, as a strengthening wind began to pick up behind him.

But he did not feel cold. He did not feel anything at all.

June was waiting for him in the doorway. She looked frantic.

'Thank goodness you're all right,' she said, pulling him into a tight embrace. 'You were gone for so long. Where have you been?'

'I –'

'I didn't know what to think. Those three haven't come home yet either. I'm going to stay up and wait for them, and then they're *really* going to be sorry.' Charlie let her keep talking as she went inside. 'Is that one new?' she added sharply, before turning back and indicating the fresh bruising around his eye.

Charlie found himself unable to cross the threshold. 'Granny, I need to talk to you.'

'You're not in trouble again, are you?' She was eyeing him suspiciously.

'It's –' He swallowed, his fingers in his hair. 'I need to tell you something.'

The old woman regarded him closely. 'What's happened? You know more Pen boys were here again this evening?'

Charlie lowered his hand and gritted his teeth. 'Oh yeah?'

'They were looking for you this time. I was told to give you a message.'

'Let's have it, then.'

'They told me to tell you that stray dogs get put down.'

Charlie smiled darkly, his insides hollow. 'Just let them try.'

June's watchful eyes scanned his face. 'There's something different about you tonight, Charlie. Why do I get the feeling that you're not quite here with me?'

'There's something I have to do. Take this,' Charlie said, pulling the Elysian nurse's gold necklace from his pocket and handing it to the old woman. June's mouth fell open, but before she could say anything, Charlie plunged on. 'You can sell it on the black market to settle your debt with Faulkner, or you can trade it to one of the other gangs for food and protection.'

'What are you —?'

'What you're holding in your hand right now is worth more than you need to pay off everything you borrowed from them,' Charlie said, regarding her seriously, 'as well as provide for you and the kids for a good few years.'

June's expression was unreadable. 'Charlie, where did you get this?' she asked, as disappointment furrowed her brow and clouded her face. 'Tell me who you stole it from.'

Charlie gave her a sad smile. 'After all this time, do you still think so little of me?'

'Something happened today, didn't it? Why won't you tell me what's wrong?'

'I've made up my mind,' Charlie said. 'I'm going to get the kids back from the Pen.'

June blinked. 'You've lost your mind,' she said quietly. 'If Faulkner has them, then —'

'They're out there on their own, Granny,' Charlie murmured. 'I know what Faulkner is capable of. I have to save them. They're the only family I have left.'

'The only family you have left,' June repeated, nodding. 'Is that what you think?'

'You know that's not what I meant,' he said, pressing her to him in a half-embrace. '*You're* the one who took me in when I had no one else, remember? You took care of me. Did you think I'd forgotten? Why would I have spent the last three years in the mines if I didn't care about you and the kids?'

'I did what was right,' June said at once, shrugging. 'Our people … we need to stick together.' She met his gaze, her lined face set. 'When you were a little boy, you told me you ran away from Faulkner and the Pen gang because you wanted a different life. Don't roll your eyes at me! You promised me you would stay away from them, no matter what happened.'

'This is different! This isn't about me. If I don't –'

'You know how Faulkner does things, Charlie.' She shook her head with a deep sigh. 'What hope is there of even finding the children now, let alone rescuing them?'

'I can't give up,' Charlie said, his hands deep in his pockets and his gaze averted.

The old woman gestured to the tumbledown building behind her, blinking back tears. 'Do you have any idea how many children I've cared for over the years, Charlie?' she asked. 'They come and they go, but do you want to know something I've learnt? There are always more lost children out there who need help. There will *always* be more, and those – those children will need you.' She looked up at him, her eyes brimming with tears. 'I – I need you.'

Charlie shook his head and took a deep breath. If he allowed himself to show any weakness in front of her now, he would never be able to let himself leave. 'I've made my decision. Nothing is going to stop me getting into Elysia tonight. I need to find those kids.'

'You know the law. You *know* it's forbidden for us to cross the Witchtrap Wall.'

'Yes.'

June reached up, grasped him by the shoulders, and shook him roughly. 'You won't be protected from the covens in Elysia. You know what the military police will do to you if they catch you. And you still –' She paused, shaking her head. 'You intend to go anyway.'

Gently, Charlie removed her hands from his shoulders. 'You can't protect me anymore, Granny,' he said. 'Keep looking after the kids. They need you.'

'Please don't do this, Charlie. You're making a big mistake.'

Something painful was straining within him. For the briefest moment, he wanted to tell her everything. But how could he? Where would he start? What good would it do?

'I can't spend the rest of my life living like this. I want to be – something more than that.'

'This world doesn't care what you want,' June said, her voice hard. 'For people like us, there are few choices. There is only one thing that matters: that we do what is right.'

'I've spent the last three years trying to do what's right,' Charlie muttered. 'From now on, I'm going to do what I need to do, and I'd like to see anyone try and stop me.'

She sighed. 'What will be, will be. You must make your own decision, Charlie.'

June took his hand in hers, eased open his fingers, and pressed the gold necklace into his palm. Then, without a word, she turned her back on him. Charlie did not look away as she edged slowly down the hallway towards the staircase that led down to their basement home. She suddenly seemed so much older than the woman who had helped support him to get down those stairs without falling. That had only been one night ago. So much had changed since then.

She had left a candle on the spindle leg table that stood beneath the cracked and cloudy mirror hanging on the wall. Illuminated by the flickering light, Charlie caught sight of his own reflection for the first time since he had been beaten up by the Pen gang.

So, this was what a dead man walking looked like. It was no wonder people had been avoiding him. The stranger glaring back at him looked as though he had been dragged through the seventh hell backwards. A fierce desperation burnt in his dark eyes. Charlie no longer recognised himself.

He braced himself against the table as a roiling wave of grief threatened to engulf him.

A gust of wind from the gathering storm outside snuffed out the candle, plunging him into gloomy half-light.

He needed air.

He wandered around aimlessly for a while, pacing back and forth in front of the doorway, his arms crossed tightly in front of his chest. His head was pounding again. Dead leaves rustled at his feet, caressed by the wind, and cast into the air by unseen hands.

Perhaps it was his imagination, but he was sure he could feel his own blood pulsing through his body. The body that was failing him. Even now, he was already running out of time. Every moment he delayed was another moment he would never get back.

The first spots of rain speckled the ground, and a rumble of thunder sounded overhead. Far away, the lights of the Elysian Castle glowed in the hills. Ruby, Leo and Dima were somewhere in those mountains. It was possible that they might be looking down at the dark shadows of the Penumbran slums even now, thinking of him, wondering if he was coming to rescue them. If there was even the slightest chance of finding them, Charlie had to take it, before it was too late.

He descended the stairs silently. June had laid out his blanket on the floor as usual. She was curled up on the bed and was already fast asleep, her breathing deep and even. Charlie covered her with his blanket.

Unable to look at her face any longer, he lowered himself onto his stomach and reached under the bed. Careful not to wake her up, he stretched his arm out as far as he could, his shoulder pressed right up against the bedframe. At last, his fingers closed on a familiar shape.

He dragged the battered metal box out from under the bed by the handle and opened the lid. Some notes and a few coins lay scattered on top of remnants from his childhood: curiously-shaped rocks; stones with interesting patterns; a marble; a toy soldier. He had never been able to save much money over the years. Everything he had earned from going into the mines he had willingly given to June to support the family. Occasionally, though, there had been enough left over that he could add a little into this box, and now, three years of savings stared back at him.

Another roll of thunder rumbled like a distant explosion far above them. A flash of lightning forked through the sky, lighting up the room. Without hesitation, Charlie removed all the money, closed the lid of the box, and pushed it back under the bed.

He got to his feet, and found himself staring straight into Ruby's eyes, heavy with sleep. The memory was so vivid that he felt as though it was happening right in front of him.

'*Charlie,*' she had whispered, her mouth quivering, '*I'm frightened.*'

'*It's just a little rain,*' he had said, perching on the edge of the bed and brushing away a tear from her cheek with his thumb. '*I'm here. You're safe. Everything's all right, I promise.*'

Ruby had smiled. '*I love you, Charlie,*' she had told him, as her eyes closed gently.

Charlie felt something catch in his throat as he remembered stroking her hair. Steeling himself, he got to his feet, rubbing his eyes vigorously with the back of his arm as a prickly heat began to spread through them.

He set all the money and the gold necklace down on the table, before pausing, his hand travelling to the collar at his neck. He could not remember ever being without it. But if he walked into Elysia still wearing it, he would be a sitting target.

He crouched down, removed the flick-knife from his shoe, and brought it to his throat.

No Penumbran is ever permitted to remove their collar, he thought, reciting the law in his head. *The collars are the touch of the Great Protector defending us against the witch covens.*

Bracing himself, he tore the collar from his neck and threw it down onto the table with the money and necklace. His skin felt oddly bare without it.

His old black sweatshirt was hanging over one of the kitchen chairs. That was all he would need. His gaze was drawn reluctantly back to the bed as a ripple of doubt crossed his mind. He shook himself, pulling on his sweatshirt and returning his knife to his sock.

He allowed himself one last moment to memorise every detail about the one place he could remember living where he had not spent his days in fear. Then he headed back up the stairs. He deliberately ignored his reflection in the hallway mirror as he strode passed it on his way to the door.

Once outside, he pulled his hood up against the rain and shoved his hands into his pockets, bracing himself against the wind. He knew what he had to do, and he knew exactly where he had to go.

*

The Skoto Gate tunnel was one of the many well-kept secrets in Penumbra. It was one of a series of tunnels that ran underneath the Witchtrap Wall, connecting the outskirts of Penumbra with the supply tunnels under the Elysian mountains. Soldiers from Elysia were always on the hunt for gloamers. They were usually orphaned or abandoned kids from Penumbra who were desperate enough for food or medicine to risk breaking into Elysia and smuggling supplies back through to the other side.

The official portions handed out at the Ration Station were pitifully inadequate to feed the city's population, so there was always high demand for whatever those who went gloaming brought back with them. As fast as one tunnel was shut down, another sprang up, and, as Charlie had been reliably informed, the Skoto Gate tunnel was wide open.

The Pen boys had run out of the Skoto Gate tunnel for years. They always made sure to have numerous candles stationed nearby to keep an eye open for Elysian soldiers. It was their job to warn anyone in the tunnels of the presence of danger. Charlie could not help but feel a little smug that none of them had noticed him approaching. He supposed he had not lost all of his old tricks in the time he had been away.

Mikhail was standing by the mouth of the tunnel. About a dozen small children, all of them skinny and dressed in ragged clothing, were grouped around him. He was gesturing with a handgun. As Charlie approached, he heard the last of Mikhail's instructions.

'Whatever you do, stay out of the path of the Witch Hunters. They don't need an excuse if they catch anyone from Penumbra sneaking into Elysia. They get their hands on you and you'll never see the light of day again.'

Charlie shuddered, shook himself forcefully, and cleared his throat. Mikhail jumped back at the noise. With some satisfaction, Charlie saw that his eyes widened in shock when he recognised that it was Charlie walking towards him from out of the shadows. He tried to keep the tension from his shoulders, reminding himself that Mikhail had not been there when the hideout was attacked. He was not in any danger of being caught.

'You,' Mikhail sneered, 'are the last person I expected to see tonight, Carroway.'

'I've been thinking things over,' Charlie said coolly. 'I'm going through.'

'Were you followed?'

'Give me some credit.'

Mikhail eyed him appraisingly, before turning back to the group. 'We have a contact in Elysia. He'll be waiting to meet you all on the other side,' he said, his voice low. 'I have two pieces of advice for you: stay sharp and stay quiet. It might save your life. Now get going.'

One of the smaller boys shifted nervously. 'I – I don't want to go …'

'You'll get in there now if you know what's good for you,' Mikhail snarled, advancing on the child as he raised his gun.

'I'll get him in,' Charlie said, stepping in between the two of them quickly. While Mikhail turned around, grinding out a curse and kicking at the ground, Charlie bent down to the little boy's eye level. 'Don't be scared,' he said, smiling at him. 'We'll be in and out before you know it. There's nothing to be frightened of. It'll be an adventure.'

'Is – is it dark down there?' the little boy asked, tears spilling over his cheeks.

Charlie ruffled the boy's hair and took his hand. 'Don't worry, I'll look after you.'

'Are you done playing house, Carroway?' Mikhail sneered.

Charlie ignored him and smiled at the little boy again, giving him a nod of encouragement and leading him towards the entrance to the tunnel. Many of the other children had already started to make their way through it. The roof of the tunnel was so low that even the smallest of the children had to crawl on their hands and knees to get through. Charlie waited until they were the only ones left, before following the others in behind the little boy.

He had to flatten himself right down onto his stomach to get inside. But he was relieved to find that the tunnel was wide enough for him to stretch out his arms and use his elbows to ease himself along the rough ground. The tunnel floor was littered with stones and sharp rocks, and he had to duck occasionally to avoid exposed tree roots above his head. It reminded him uncomfortably of being in the mine.

They had only been in the tunnel for a few moments when a girl further along the route came to an abrupt halt.

'Listen – what was that?'

Charlie had heard it too. From above ground, someone was whistling a warning.

'What's going on?' the little boy in front of him asked, his voice wobbling.

'Everyone out of the tunnel – now,' Charlie said, his voice sharp. 'Come on, move!'

Once they had all scrambled back to the surface and stood gasping for breath in the night air, it became all too clear what was happening. The unmistakeable, rhythmic beating of jackbooted feet racing towards them, and the sharp staccato barking of oncoming dogs, told Charlie everything he needed to know.

'Elysian soldiers,' he muttered, his heart plummeting horribly. 'They've found us.'

One of the girls rounded on Mikhail. 'You told us we'd be safe – you lied to us!'

'Don't you talk like that to me, you little brat.' Without hesitation, Mikhail shoved the girl who had spoken to the ground. 'One of you tripped the Wall detectors. Who's a new face here? Who's the witch?' He stared wildly around at the children, his eyes popping.

'You're scaring them,' Charlie said, forcing him away from the children. 'Where d'you get off, accusing kids like you're some kind of Hunter?'

'*You* must have had a tail, then!' Mikhail yelled, glaring at Charlie.

'Like I said, if I was followed, I would've known about it,' Charlie said, helping the little girl to her feet. 'These guys are good. They knew we'd be here. I bet one of your lot broke and told them everything.'

'Say that one more time.'

Charlie gritted his teeth. 'None of that matters now. If we don't move fast, we're all going to end up in an Elysian prison cell, or worse.'

'Are you cracked?' One of the older boys was staring at him incredulously. 'We're in deep shit, mister. Don't you know who leads these raids? Those bastard Elysian Lieutenants, Arron Dragomir and Vasco Kovalev. They're both Witch Hunters, too.'

A collective shiver seemed to run through the children at the mention of the two soldiers' names. Charlie's brow furrowed. He was certain that he had heard one of those names somewhere before.

'It won't be a prison cell we'll end up in if they catch us, it'll be a shallow grave.'

'And if any of you brats mention my name, I'll make sure your families join you there!' Mikhail said savagely, pointing his gun in the faces of each of the children in turn. Without another word, he raced away from them and was swallowed up into the darkness.

'What do we do now?' the smallest boy asked, looking around in desperation.

'You kids get out of here!' Charlie ordered. 'Don't stop running 'til you're safe.'

At his words, all of the children nodded. As the sound of barking dogs drew nearer, they sprinted away down the alley, and peeled off into the shadows in different directions.

The little boy paused, turning back. 'Mister, come with us!' he shouted.

'They have to find one of us,' Charlie answered. 'Don't worry about me – *go!*'

The glare of searchlights flooded the tunnel mouth, blinding him as he turned. Dread coursing through him, Charlie heard the unmistakeable sound of the slide of a gun being pulled back and released.

'You're in Elysian custody now, boy. You move an inch, you're dead.'

Charlie froze, his hands behind his head, his eyes narrowed against the light. The soldier who had spoken strode forward. His close-cropped hair was parted sharply on one side of his head and he had a clipped, light-brown beard. He was taller than Charlie, broad-shouldered, and was dressed in military fatigues and combat boots. A dark red cloak fell from his shoulders. A rifle was strapped across his back, and there was a pistol gripped tightly in his hand.

A large group of soldiers stood behind him. Some of them had their guns trained on Charlie, while others fought to hold back huge dogs that were straining to break free of their leashes. Charlie thought they looked as though they would like nothing more than to sink their teeth into his neck.

'Looks like we've trapped a big rat this time, lads,' the soldier said, his flint-like eyes boring into Charlie's as a derisive smile twisted his face. 'It's about time – I was starting to get bored of catching pups. I can't stand the squealing.' He let out a single, mirthless laugh.

Mingled fury and horror rippled through Charlie's body as he realised that he recognised the man standing in front of him. This was the cruel-faced soldier who had smashed up his family's home and beaten him up the previous night.

Charlie had come across monsters before, but he knew at once that this man was something different. Every muscle in his body was screaming at him to run, but he remained motionless, tensed like a coiled spring.

He needed to give the kids enough time to get away.

The soldier approached him leisurely, pressing the muzzle of his pistol into Charlie's temple. 'So, what are you doing out of your hole, you lowlife Pen scum?' he murmured. 'Were you too afraid to run away with the others from your nest, or were you just too stupid?'

'I'm not afraid of you, you piece of shit,' Charlie spat viciously.

A flicker of surprise crossed the soldier's face before it split into a jeering smirk.

'You'll regret that,' he hissed. 'Get on your knees. I'm going to make you crawl.'

Stars burst in front of Charlie's eyes as the butt of a rifle connected with the side of his head. He fell to his knees, the world spinning around him.

'That's enough, Dragomir,' a familiar voice said sharply. 'He's coming with us.'

Dragomir grabbed a fistful of Charlie's hair and yanked his head back. A knife was in his other hand, the point of its blade tracing the skin across Charlie's bare throat. 'Where's your sense of fun, Kovalev?' he said silkily. 'The night is still young, after all.'

On his knees, Charlie watched as Kovalev stepped into the light. A pale-faced Elysian soldier about his own age, his rifle was slung over his shoulder, while his dark red cloak and messy black hair rippled in the cold breeze. Charlie knew he had been right, back at the Infirmary Station, to think he had seen this soldier somewhere before.

Kovalev looked just as he had done when they had first crossed paths, even before everything that had happened when Charlie had learnt he was living on borrowed time. He had been there that night, standing beside his cruel-faced partner. He had been there when Charlie had been taken away by Faulkner and beaten up. Even the dark scowl on his face was the same.

Charlie opened his mouth to speak, but the ferocity that burnt in Kovalev's eyes was enough to make him close it again.

'Don't tell me you've taken a liking to him yourself, Vasya?' Dragomir purred.

'We have our orders,' Kovalev said shortly, his eyes flicking up to Dragomir's face. 'You'll have time to play with your toys later. Get him on his feet. We're going back to Elysia.'

His head spinning, Charlie had just enough time to register the look of abject hatred Kovalev threw his way, before Dragomir forced him roughly to his feet.

A hood was pulled over his head and tightened painfully around his neck. For a fleeting moment, Charlie had the sensation that he was drowning. The image of his old bedroom in the Pen gang hideout flashed in front of his eyes.

Then he was lost to the darkness.

CHAPTER 8

I n his dream, he heard the voice of a woman singing softly. The words she sang were indistinct, as though they were travelling towards him from some distant land. He was not even sure that they were in a language he could understand. But they stirred something within him that he had not felt for as long as he could remember.

Charlie's eyes flickered open. He was lying on a cold flagstone floor that was sprinkled with straw. His eyes were dim, and the air was clammy, as though he was underground and far from natural light. With a groan, he forced himself into a sitting position, leaning on one knee to support his weight before he got to his feet and took in his new surroundings.

Wherever he was, one thing was certain – he was in prison. Heavy iron bars separated him on both sides from the cells connected to his. The walls of the dungeon were solid stone, slick with damp and cold to the touch. As he craned his neck to see through the bars set into the steel door of his cell, which was heavily locked and bolted, Charlie's heart sank.

He could make out a couple of flaming torches pulsing in brackets along the far wall of the cellblock, leading to another steel door at the end of the row. He was trapped. There was a close smell in the air, and his breath rose in a mist in front of his face when he exhaled. He shivered, and rubbed his goose-pimpled arms, before tapping his fingernails on the bars of the cell.

'Those bastards took my sweater, damn them …'

'Oh, so you *are* alive.'

Charlie started in shock. The girl's voice had come from the cell to his left. She had been so still and quiet that he had not even noticed she was there. Sitting in a cross-legged position about an arm's length beyond the iron bars that connected their cells, she was watching him intently. Her warm brown eyes glowed in the light from the torches.

She was wearing a ragged grey shift dress with black horizontal stripes. She looked thin and exhausted, her face ghostly white. Thick waves of red hair, bright as autumn leaves, tumbled down her back and in front of her shoulders, brushing the floor of her cell. Her full lips were pursed in a thoughtful expression as she eyed him watchfully.

'Seems that way,' he said. 'Was that you singing, before? I thought it was a dream.'

The girl's eyebrows arched slightly, an amused expression quirking the corners of her mouth. 'Perhaps.' A frown clouded her face. 'You look awful. Did they hurt you too?'

'Who, the soldiers? Trust me, I'm used to worse than them.'

'No, I meant the doctors. Weren't you –?' She broke off, a wary look in her eyes.

'Wasn't I what?'

'The Hunters … I thought you were –' She frowned, shook her head, and fell silent.

'What are you talking about?' Charlie muttered. He ran his fingers through his hair, scratching at the overgrown buzzed side as he tilted his head back and forth. His whole body was aching. 'I haven't seen any doctors. When did –? Wait.'

He had noticed an angry red scar, the stitching still visible in her skin, running from the girl's temple down to her collarbone. Most of it was hidden by her cascades of thick hair.

'What in the nine hells have they done to you?'

'Nothing that affects you,' the girl said, moving awkwardly as she made to edge back to the far wall of her cell. 'I only wanted to see if … but you're not, so …'

'Not yet,' Charlie murmured, guessing her meaning as he noticed that her wrists and ankles were bound with restraints made of a soft black material. He reached through the bars connecting their cells, gesturing to her. 'Come over here, I'll help you get those things off.'

The girl stayed just beyond his reach, a suspicious look in her eyes.

'I'm not going to hurt you,' Charlie said gently. 'I promise, I won't hurt you.'

Hesitantly, the girl shifted towards him, hobbling on her palms as she dragged her bound legs behind her. When they were face to face on either side of the iron bars, she held her wrists up in front of her, and Charlie caught the scent of burning wood in her hair.

Her eyes never left his face as she rested her hands in his. Charlie felt the blade of his knife against his ankle. For some reason, whoever had locked him up had taken his sweatshirt but left him armed. However, he had the feeling this girl would not appreciate him pulling a blade on her.

His brow furrowed in concentration, Charlie tinkered with the restraints, gradually loosening them, before unravelling them one section at a time. It was obvious from the torn fibres across the black material that she had tried to use her teeth to free herself more than once. Finally, the restraints slackened, and the girl let them fall to the floor, shoving them away from her into a far corner of her cell.

'Thank you,' she said, swinging her legs in front of her and hastily tugging at the restraints that bound her ankles. 'I don't know how long it's been since –'

'Try to be patient and go slowly,' Charlie said. 'Whoever put you in those things knew what they were doing. There's no way you could have freed yourself without help.' He moved to assist her with undoing the ankle restraints. 'Let me –'

'Don't!' the girl cried, her voice harsh, wrenching her legs out of his reach.

'I'm sorry,' Charlie said, watching as the girl began to pick at the restraints more carefully. Soon, she had managed to remove them completely. Charlie could not help but notice the collection of scars that littered the skin around her ankles and feet. 'I'm sorry.'

'Don't be,' the girl said, shrugging as she started massaging her wrists and ankles. 'I just don't like … I don't want people touching me, that's all. Like I said, thanks for your help.'

'Who did this to you?' Charlie asked. 'Why have they treated you like this?'

'I don't know, but …' She regarded him in silence for a few moments, as though weighing her words carefully. 'I am far from being the only coven daughter imprisoned here.'

Charlie's eyes widened and he drew back instinctively. His fingers reached for the metal collar at his neck, finding only his own bare skin as he cursed himself for removing it. 'You're a – you're one of them?'

'Why?' The girl spoke calmly, even curiously. 'Are you afraid of me?'

'I …'

Charlie paused, then frowned. He was imprisoned in Elysia with a self-professed coven terrorist, trapped in a cell in touching distance of a witch. He had even helped free her from her restraints. Yet … he did not doubt for a moment that he had made the right choice to help her. He shook his head, bewildered at his reaction, and raked his fingers through his hair, trying to find an answer to her question.

The fact was, he was not afraid.

He opened his mouth, and found himself asking, 'What's your name?'

'It's Seren … Seren Casimir,' the girl said, and Charlie thought she spoke her name with the same care that one might hold a new-born baby. 'That's all I know for sure.'

'What d'you mean?'

'Ever since they took me to that place, I –' Seren shook her head, her face falling. 'Apart from my name, I don't … I can't …' She dug her fingernails into her palms, balled her hands into fists, and pressed them fiercely against her eyes. Her shoulders were shaking.

'Your name is enough for now,' he said. 'I'm Charlie Carroway.'

'Do they have your family too?' Seren asked, looking up at him urgently.

'I don't …' Charlie felt himself go cold. 'Why would they have my family?'

'I'm not the only one they've been doing this to,' Seren said through gritted teeth, motioning to the jagged scar on her head. 'There must be hundreds of people being used by the Facility in their experiments.'

'Witches?'

'*People.* Yes, witches, but not my people alone. I was the only one who escaped.'

'You escaped? Wait – what do you mean, *experiments?*'

'But I had to come back. I had to find my sister. I have to save her.'

'Your sister is here in this place somewhere too?'

Seren nodded. 'I found my way back to the Facility, but there were too many of them. The soldiers were there, and the doctors.' She braced her forehead in her hands. 'I … I pushed myself further than I thought I could … further than I ever had during the experiments. It felt like … like the entire world was shaking … there was so much light … and when I woke up, I was here, in this place.'

Charlie swallowed hard, remembering how he had stood by the windowsill, watching the Elysian Castle at the top of the mountains. 'You mean … *you* caused that earthquake? That pillar of light – that was you? But how did –?'

Seren shook her head, waving her hand to dismiss his questions as she raised herself gingerly to her feet. At first she seemed unsteady, as though she had forgotten how to use her legs. But once she stopped swaying, she marched straight over to the door of her cell and rapped her knuckles smartly on the steel in front of her. It was almost as though she expected someone on the other side to open it for her.

'I haven't had much to do with your kind, but I owe you for getting me out of those restraints,' she said, throwing him a roguish smile that made him blink with surprise. 'What d'you reckon, Charlie Carroway – are you ready to get out of this dump?'

'I reckon you're forgetting that we're trapped inside these cages,' Charlie replied, fixing her with a stony look. 'What're you planning to do – bust us out?'

A mischievous grin spread across Seren's face, lighting up her features. 'That's exactly what I'm planning to do.'

Charlie laughed, despite himself. 'Sure, and then what? You think you can take on all those soldiers out there singlehanded?'

'I could, but I thought you might want to help. You look like you'd be good in a fight.'

Charlie raised his eyebrows. 'I tend to come off worst.'

It was Seren's turn to laugh. 'I did wonder. But in that case, it's a good thing you're with me. Just you watch this.'

Her arms outstretched, she brushed the air in a single graceful movement to the right, like an artist wielding two invisible paintbrushes. As though responding to unspoken orders, the heavy steel bolts on the outside of their cell doors scraped to one side.

Lowering her arms, Seren stepped up to the door of her cell, raised a knuckle to the steel, and flicked it open with her index finger. A moment later, Charlie's cell door was also standing wide open. Seren was leaning against it with her arms folded, a satisfied expression on her face.

Charlie blinked rapidly. 'What exactly,' he murmured, 'did you just do?'

Seren turned to him, grinning wickedly. 'If you liked that, wait 'til you see this.'

With one careless twist of her hand, the steel door at the far end of the cellblock was ripped right out of the wall. Seren giggled and ran straight towards the debris, waving for Charlie to follow her.

Amongst the dust and crumbling stonework, a single guard, who appeared to have been sitting on a chair beside what was now a gaping chasm in the wall, had leapt to his feet. He was fumbling with his rifle and looked petrified.

Seren strode past the wreck of the steel door without so much as a glance at him, and Charlie followed her, speechless.

'Hey!' the guard cried, pointing at them. 'What are you two prisoners doing out of your cells?'

'Are you bulletproof as well?' Charlie asked, searching hopelessly for a way out.

'I don't need to be,' Seren answered, laughter in her voice. 'Watch this.'

'I said,' the guard repeated, his voice shaking, 'what are you two prisoners doing out of your cells? Stop right where you are!'

Charlie's body tensed, preparing to attack. The guard was younger than he was and did not look as though he would have much chance of beating Charlie in a fight, if it came to that. He still had his knife. What worried him was the rifle in the guard's hands.

Charlie had just stepped forward, when, from beside him, Seren made a small swiping gesture with her hand. The guard was lifted off his feet and slammed headfirst into the stone wall. He lay crumpled on the flagstones, a trickle of blood oozing from the side of his head.

'Is this another one of your talents?' Charlie asked her, sure he was dreaming.

'Child's play,' Seren said, shrugging. 'There's nothing to it.'

'He's still alive,' Charlie said dubiously, after checking the guard's pulse.

'Don't worry, by the time he wakes up we'll be long gone,' she said, tossing her long hair over her shoulders and flexing her fingers in front of her and above her head.

'Which way should we go?' Charlie asked. 'Do you remember the way out?'

'Let's go this way,' Seren answered, jutting her head to the right.

'Stay sharp,' Charlie muttered. 'This place will be crawling with soldiers.'

'Soldiers are nothing.'

'Hunters too.'

Seren paused, then nodded wordlessly, a dark expression settling on her face.

Together, they began walking along the stone passageway. Charlie noticed that Seren kept sneaking glances at his face, although she made sure to look away the instant he returned her gaze. He decided not to say anything about it. She was not hurting anyone, and he had no desire to irritate or offend a witch while he was still in Elysian custody.

After a while, Seren broke the silence. 'I can't stop thinking … I have the strangest feeling that I've met you somewhere before.'

'Trust me,' Charlie said with a small smile, 'if we'd met, I would remember it.'

'You definitely remind me of somebody,' she said, looking him up and down. 'I'd like to see you on a good day, then I'd be able to know for sure.'

Charlie raised an eyebrow. 'On a good day?'

She nodded. 'You know what I mean. When you hadn't just been beaten up, when you'd done something with that crazy hair, and decided to wear something a bit smarter.'

'What's wrong with what I'm wearing now? And what's wrong with my hair?'

She eyed him closely. 'Have you considered letting that short side grow in a bit more, or even growing it all out properly? You'd suit long hair, I think. You have the right kind of face for it. Noble. Mysterious.' She winked. 'You could look good if you wanted to, you know.'

Charlie, whose hand had leapt to his hair at her words, did not quite know what to say. 'How do I look to you now?' he asked carefully. 'Compared to typical coven tastes, I mean.'

He was quickly becoming familiar with the playful smile that quirked her mouth in response to his question. 'If my mother were here she would say you look like a – well …' She paused, smiling ruefully. 'She'd tell me to stay far away from you, let's put it like that.'

Charlie grinned, despite himself. 'I'm glad to hear I could meet a witch's standards if I wanted to,' he said. 'Maybe some glasses to complete the look, what d'you think? But your mother doesn't need to worry, in any case, since – hey, is something wrong?'

The smile had slipped from Seren's face. She was frowning now, staring beyond him into the middle distance as though she was seeing something that he could not. 'He …' she murmured. 'He wore glasses.'

'Who?'

'The scientist,' she said, her voice barely audible. 'He was there when I escaped from the laboratory. He was the one who showed me how to get out of the Facility. He was always kind to me.'

'What happened to him? D'you think he'd help us – if we found him again?'

'There were too many soldiers.' Seren was still frowning as she looked right at him. 'I thought it was my imagination. But now you're here and … you look so much like him.'

Charlie was staring at her, wide-eyed. 'This scientist – do you remember his name?'

Seren appeared to be deep in concentration, as though trying to recall a fading dream. 'They called him … Maxim.'

CHAPTER 9

'M'ax ...' Charlie's mind was racing. Inside his head, a hundred questions battled to be asked first. Then, the full weight of what Seren had said hit him like a tonne of bricks. 'You said something about soldiers. What happened to him? How is my brother involved in this?'

'I just saw the soldiers surrounding him. I didn't see what happened afterwards.'

'And you didn't stop them? He was trying to save you, and you didn't help him?'

Seren narrowed her eyes. 'I wasn't exactly in control of what I was doing at the time.'

'Where did they take him?'

'How am I supposed to know? I came back for my sister, not your brother.'

'We need to find him,' Charlie said, looking around wildly, as though expecting his older brother to materialise out of thin air. 'You said you escaped from some lab. Could you find your way back there again? Maybe we'll find a clue there, or –'

'I'm never going back to that place again,' Seren said, her voice as sharp as a knife.

They fixed each other with furious stares, before Charlie rolled his eyes and began to walk away. 'Whatever. I don't need your help. I'll do this on my own.'

'You've thought it all through, have you?' she called after him. 'Ready to be a hero?'

Her words brought him to a halt. 'Listen, I'm grateful to you for getting me out of that cell, but you should consider our partnership officially over. You can go off and find your sister, and I'll rescue my family, and that'll be the end of it. There's no reason for us to work together anymore.'

'Fine,' Seren said with an ice-cold glare. 'Good luck facing those soldiers without me.'

Charlie let out a humourless laugh. 'I *hope* I see them again. Just let them try to –'

'*Breakout from the High-Security Cells!*' a piercing, tinny voice shrieked. '*Witch Hunters – red alert!*'

With a cry of shock, Charlie and Seren leapt towards one another. They each grabbed hold of the other briefly before immediately breaking apart again, both of them reddening slightly. There was no one else in the passageway with them. The voice was coming from a loudspeaker above their heads.

'*Escaped prisoners still in the Volya Research Facility. All available units, these orders come from Lieutenant Dragomir: locate and contain the prisoners! Maintain radio contact.*'

'Perfect,' Charlie sighed, scratching his throat with his nails. 'Just what we need.'

'I see something over there,' Seren said, pointing. 'Let's check it out.'

They had reached a circular antechamber, from which eight passageways led off in different directions. A large, detailed map of the Volya Research Facility was fixed to a far wall. Charlie hastily went over to inspect it, his heart falling. It only took one look at the pictures for him to realise that he was in worse trouble than he had thought.

What he had supposed was a prison appeared instead to be one single part of an enormous complex, spanning countless floors and multiple separate buildings. Some of the larger buildings were named, while others were marked with numbers and letters. There was a key at the bottom of the map, but Charlie could not decipher most of the words.

Seren was watching him closely, making him nervous. 'Can't you read it?'

'Can't *you* read it?' he snapped back.

'I can *speak* Matyan, I can't read it! I thought you were from around here?'

Charlie looked around desperately, his heart hammering in his chest, and headed down the nearest passageway, motioning for Seren to follow him. 'Let's go this way.'

The passageway was empty, but Charlie could hear the thunder of oncoming footsteps in the distance, coupled with the sound of his own heart thumping horribly fast. The noise of the soldiers echoed all around them, confusing him as to which direction their pursuers were coming from.

'This way!' he shouted to Seren.

With each new connective passageway that they reached, Charlie was convinced they were about to run straight into a wall of gunfire. A terrible shooting pain was lancing through his side, making him feel as though he was being stabbed between the ribs.

'Why are you stopping?' Seren asked, coming to a halt beside him. 'What is it?'

Charlie leant against the wall, his hands braced against his thighs, trying to catch his breath. As the pain gradually began to subside, he glanced up at Seren. She was wearing a strange expression.

Set into the wall beside him was a heavy wooden door. Seren stood in front of it, one palm pressed to the wood, her brow knitted in concentration. It was as though she was listening intently to something he could not hear. She met his eyes and withdrew her hand from the door.

'We need to get inside. It has something to do with the other prisoners.'

'Are they in there?' Charlie asked, pressing his ear to the door but hearing nothing.

Seren shook her head, the furrow in her brow deepening. 'I don't think so.'

'Then we should keep going. It won't take them long to catch up with —'

'*Third level is clear,*' a nearby voice declared. '*Sweeping fourth level now.*'

'But they *were* here,' Seren murmured, her hand returning to the door almost longingly as she looked at Charlie. 'Maybe there'll be a clue to help us find my sister, or your family.'

'Let's get inside,' Charlie said. 'It should be a safe enough place to hide, at least.'

He shouldered the door and forced his weight against it a few times, even kicking at it, but it would not budge. Seren watched without comment before she stepped in front of him and threw her arm out towards the door. It flew open. They both hurried inside and Seren closed the door behind them, plunging them into complete darkness.

Charlie immediately had the sensation that he was trapped, surrounded by countless shadowy figures. He could feel their hands on his skin. His breathing began to turn harsh and shallow. His hands were shaking. He closed his eyes against the nauseous feeling rising up his throat, and, in an attempt to find something familiar to hold on to, gripped Seren's wrist tightly. She shifted slightly but did not pull away from him.

'I'm here,' she said, her voice unexpectedly calm and gentle. 'You're safe.'

'It's – too dark.' He forced the words out through gritted teeth. 'I can't –'

'I'll take care of it.'

The next moment, Seren's face was illuminated by a warm, flickering light, emanating from a small ball of flames that she held cupped in her hand. Charlie felt relief wash over him and dropped her wrist quickly. He nodded his thanks to her, and she smiled back.

'My sister is afraid of the dark too.'

'I'm not *afraid* of –!' Charlie snarled at once, before deflating at her knowing smile, which, even in his distress, he could see held no malicious intent. 'Anyway.' He avoided her eyes and looked around, squinting through the low light provided by the flames. 'What is this place?'

'I don't know, but …' Seren began to walk forward, the flickering light travelling with her, and Charlie made sure to keep as close to her as he could cope with. 'I've been here before.'

The room was much larger than Charlie had first assumed. The door they had come through appeared to be one of many side-entrances that led into a sort of theatre hall. Behind him, the floor rose upwards on a sharp incline, and there were countless empty wooden benches ranged around the room in the shadows. In front of them, the floor sloped steeply downwards. There were more wooden benches on either side of a central gangway, allowing access down to a viewing platform.

'Why did they bring you *here*?' Charlie murmured. 'Hey, where are you going?'

Charlie followed Seren as she continued walking towards the platform until she reached an iron railing. It seemed to have been erected there to prevent anyone leaning over the edge from falling into the space below. Many more wooden benches were set up on the lower level of the hall, all of them empty. He guessed that hundreds of spectators could easily be packed into the theatre. The benches were all facing the front of the room, towards a raised area on which a steel table was set up. It was large enough for a grown man to lie on.

Charlie squinted. 'Am I imagining it, or is there something on that table down there?'

He leant further forward over the railing, straining to make out the shapes in the semidarkness. Without a word, Seren increased the size of the ball of flames in her hand. By the stronger light, Charlie saw that heavy manacles were hanging from the corners of the steel table. Strong chains rested across it, positioned appropriately for chests and torsos.

A shiver of horror rippling through him, Charlie stepped back from the railing. He half-expected somebody to be standing right behind him in the darkness. Seren was still staring at the restraints as though in a daze. Charlie's eyes were drawn to the enormous portrait of the Great Protector, Nikolai Ignatiev, hanging above the steel table, his eyes cold.

'Is this where –?' Charlie began, picturing the scars he had seen on Seren's head.

'I knew it was real …' Seren whispered. 'They tried to make me forget, but –'

'Why are they doing this?' Charlie clenched his fists. 'How many people have they done this to?'

Seren shook her head, the flames in her hand guttering. 'I need to get out of this place. If my sister is —'

She broke off, her head snapping towards the steel table. For a moment, Charlie caught sight of the fear in her eyes. Then the ball of flames disappeared, and they were plunged back into darkness. At the sound of voices below them, he forced Seren down onto the floor with him, hissing at her to be quiet.

'Yes, but can you commit to more shipments?' a sharp voice demanded. 'I don't care about whatever messes you have to clean up. The project cannot be delayed any longer.'

'No worries. Keep the payments coming, and we'll keep sending them straight to you.'

'That's *him*,' Seren whispered, her hands gripping her head, her eyes huge.

Charlie gritted his teeth, risking a glance through the iron railings. That had been Faulkner's voice, he was sure of it. It was too dark to make out what was going on beneath them through the gloom. However, the theatre hall was so huge that the conversation from the floor below carried up to them, even when their owners kept their voices low.

'You will have whatever you need. We are close. I must have more specimens.'

'And you will, Doctor Ivanov, you will.' A new voice, soft and faintly mocking, sounded from under the railings. 'The four of us share a dislike for empty cages. But do not let us keep you. I know how committed you are to your work.'

Silence fell once more, and Charlie frowned as he attempted to piece together the fragments of information he had learnt. Whatever Faulkner was doing with the people he had captured, it had something to do with a project being run out of an Elysian research lab. He knew the kids would have been taken here too. Seren had said there were already over a hundred people imprisoned in the Volya Facility. But the doctor — Ivanov — still wanted more.

Charlie blinked. *Ivanov.* Wasn't that the name Maya had shared with him before the Pen hideout had been destroyed? His mind was racing. Jasmine Darkwood and the other prisoners he had freed from the cages … he had assumed the explosion had been accidental. But he remembered Jasmine's triumphant expression before she ran off into the slums. Was it possible that she –?

'What do we do now?' Seren mumbled, her face a pale shade of green.

'I think they've gone,' Charlie said, tearing his mind away from his thoughts and trying to sound braver than he felt. 'We should get out of this place. It's not safe here.'

Seren nodded, pointing to the way out. 'Stay close to me. Let's do this.'

They both eased themselves onto their feet, silent shadows in the darkness. Then, there was a horrible groan from underneath their feet. The sound of a creaking floorboard reverberated around the enormous theatre hall. Charlie closed his eyes, holding his breath.

'Did anyone else hear that? Sounds like your muscle was right, my lord.'

Charlie froze at Faulkner's words, his eyes wide open, his heart hammering in his chest.

'Oh, no …' Seren whispered, her hands in front of her mouth. 'It's –'

'Perhaps our conversation was not quite as private as we had intended,' the Great Protector said, his voice low and dangerously relaxed. 'Where is our uninvited guest?'

'You have to get out of here *now*,' Charlie whispered. 'Don't argue with me.'

Seren frowned, her mouth tight. 'What about you? I can't just leave you behind.'

'Just go already!' Charlie urged. 'You need to find your sister, don't you?'

'But if they catch you, they'll –'

Charlie tried to keep his tone light. 'Don't worry about me, I'll be fine.' Seeing that she was still hesitating, he ground his teeth. 'Damn it, *go* – while you still have the chance!'

Biting her lip, Seren nodded, then turned and raced back up the walkway. She was heading straight for the door through which they had first entered the theatre. Charlie raised himself onto his haunches, readying himself to chase after her.

'There's someone up there!' he heard Faulkner yell from below him.

'Bring them to me – alive.'

The Great Protector's order echoed around the cavernous theatre hall, ringing in his ears as Charlie sprinted after Seren. He needed to give her enough time to escape. If he followed roughly the same route she had taken through the wooden benches, he might convince them that there had only ever been one person hidden in the shadows. That it had only been him listening to their plans for trafficking human beings and experimenting on living people.

He was closing in on the door now, but Charlie had no intention of leaving the hall. Instead, he flung himself to one side and raced further up the gangway, deeper into the upper section of the room. If he made it obvious that he was still there, they would not try looking for anyone else beyond the theatre hall. Breathing hard, Charlie raced ahead, glancing over his shoulder to gauge how far behind him his pursuers were.

Then his foot connected with something solid. With a yell, he tripped over and crashed onto the floor. Gritting his teeth, pain tearing through his knees and elbows, Charlie attempted to force himself to his feet. He managed to raise himself onto his knees but stopped dead in his tracks when he felt the muzzle of a gun pressed into the back of his head. When he heard the amused voice of Arron Dragomir from behind him, he went completely still.

'You should really watch your step. You could've gotten hurt.'

Charlie closed his eyes, bracing himself. He heard the whistle of air as Dragomir drew back his arm. There was a jarring crack as the butt of the soldier's gun smashed into the back of his head. He slumped forward, the world spinning in front of his eyes. Then everything went black.

*

'Will this take much longer, Lieutenant? I don't have all day.'

'It would be my pleasure to hit him again for you, sire.'

'I have no doubt that it would, but I hardly think that it will get us what I want …'

His head throbbing, Charlie groaned, blinking to clear away the stars in his eyes. He was on his knees on the lower floor of the theatre. As the scene before him stopped swimming, he instinctively drew back. Something tore into his wrists as he shifted position.

He tested his hands. They were bound behind his back with zip ties, secured so tightly that they dug painfully into his skin. Looking up, he caught sight of the chains and manacles on the steel table in front of him. This close, he could see that the floor beneath the table was covered in dark red stains.

'Finally, you are awake.'

Charlie looked up to find a tall, middle-aged man standing above him, an expression of mild interest on his sun-kissed face. Though narrow-framed, he had a commanding presence. He was dressed immaculately in a navy-blue, formal military uniform, adorned with medals. His thick, dark brown hair was brushed back into neat waves, and his light green eyes burnt with an intensity that made Charlie feel like he was being pinned down. They were the same pair of eyes that had been watching him out of faded portraits for as long as he could remember.

He could not believe it was real, yet there was no mistaking the man standing before him.

'Come now, do you have nothing to say in my presence?'

Charlie felt his whole body begin to shake with terror as the Great Protector knelt down on one knee in front of him. Charlie lowered his head, his eyes on the blood-stained floor, as he heard a soft, mirthless laugh. He felt one of the Great Protector's sharp fingernails dig into the skin underneath his chin. Unwillingly, Charlie lifted his head, his eyes wide and horrified as he came face to face with Nikolai Ignatiev for the first time in his life. The older man's wide mouth curved in a way that made Charlie think he looked as though he was preparing to bite.

'You have caught my attention, my little thief,' he said, an almost tender smile twisting his mouth as he studied Charlie's face.

'I congratulate you. I must confess, I am rather interested in what a piece of filth like you is doing on the wrong side of the Wall.' His eyes narrowed as they fell to Charlie's throat. 'And without a collar, no less. Is this the best the covens have to offer?'

'I – I'm not –' Charlie did not recognise the sound of his own voice, hoarse with fear.

'But we have more than enough time to find out,' the Great Protector said, stroking his fingers through the longer section of Charlie's hair and getting to his feet. 'I am sure you will enjoy our hospitality. I imagine you will find your stay here to be a memorable one. Take him away,' he added, waving a lazy hand as he turned on his heel and disappeared into the shadows.

'Get on your feet, scum,' Dragomir said, grabbing Charlie under the arm and wrenching him up. 'You're coming with me.'

CHAPTER 10

'Which coven sent you?'

'*No one* sent me.'

The interrogation cell was a small, windowless, low-ceilinged room, the walls and floors of which were stained with blood that had long since dried.

'Why did you attempt to infiltrate the Castle?'

'I *didn't.*'

Charlie hung suspended from a beam. His arms had been shackled above his head, so that his toes just touched the ground. Dragomir stalked around him in slow, leisurely circles, slapping the flat of a hunting knife against his open palm as he went.

'You'll need a muzzle if you're planning to go anywhere near his mouth,' Faulkner warned. A wicked smile played around his lips as he surveyed Charlie from where he stood, leaning against the wall nearest the door. 'Consider me the voice of experience – this dog bites.'

'Is that so?' Dragomir made an unconvinced noise in his throat. 'Where is the witch?'

'I don't *know.*'

Charlie hoped she was far, far away by now.

'It doesn't have to be like this, kid,' Faulkner said, his smile fading as he resettled himself against the wall with a sigh. 'You don't have to protect her. Why not save yourself all this trouble and tell us the truth? Don't you remember? You always have a choice.'

Charlie barked out a hollow laugh. 'Like you always gave me a choice, you mean?'

Dragomir's eyes narrowed. 'Who *are* you?'

When Charlie did not answer, Dragomir backhanded him across the face. 'Don't feel like talking?' he asked, a lazy smirk shifting his features, as Charlie tasted blood in his mouth. 'Let's see if I can change your mind.'

Charlie sensed Dragomir approach him from behind, and his shoulders tensed. He heard the sound of chains jangling above him. A moment later, he dropped to the floor. His knees hit the ground hard as his hands were wrenched behind his back and zip-tied together at the wrists. Dragomir had unshackled him from the beam, and was now crouched over him, one hand on the back of Charlie's t-shirt, the other on the waistband of his jeans. Faulkner made a noise of mild interest.

'I'm sure you can guess what I'm planning to do if you don't give me what I want ...'

'Fuck you!' Charlie snarled, thrashing desperately as he tried to kick out behind him.

'I'd much rather fuck *you*,' Dragomir growled into his ear, his hand coming to rest on the small of Charlie's back. 'And what's this?'

'Get your hands off me!'

Charlie fought to edge out of Dragomir's grip, but it was useless. Dragomir sat back on Charlie's legs, keeping him still. When he fell silent, Charlie knew what he was reading.

'*To the victor, the spoils.*' Dragomir traced the raised letters of the brand along Charlie's skin as he spoke, sending a violent shudder along Charlie's spine. 'Your handiwork, is it?'

'Get *off* me!'

Twisting around in fury, Charlie knew from the look of raw excitement on Dragomir's face that he had not imagined the pleasure in the soldier's voice. Faulkner appeared to have gone up in the Witch Hunter's estimation.

'*Now* I know who you are ...' Dragomir grabbed a fistful of Charlie's hair, wrenching his head back as he pushed down on the brand with his other hand. 'I can see you're used to putting up a fight.' He reached for the hunting knife, lying on the ground beside him.

'Get the *fuck* off me,' Charlie whispered, his body seizing up. 'I – I don't want this …'

'I know.' Dragomir let out a low chuckle in his ear. 'That's what makes you so hot.'

'Don't disappoint him, Charlie,' Faulkner murmured. 'You know you can take it.'

'What in the nine hells is going on here?'

The door burst open, banging off the wall, and Charlie saw Vasco Kovalev standing on the threshold. His dark eyes travelled from Dragomir to Charlie as a look of understanding passed over his pale face. His rifle was strapped to his back. One of his hands was clenched around a bundle of black material, while the other rested on a gun holstered at his waist. When he saw Faulkner, Kovalev grabbed him by the neck and slammed him against the door.

'Get out, you damn hyena,' he snarled. 'You don't have the authority to be in here.'

Faulkner's eyes found Charlie's as he rearranged the collar of his shirt and massaged his neck. With a cough and a shrug, his gaze on Kovalev's weapons, he slunk from the room. When he was gone, Kovalev turned to Dragomir, and Charlie flinched at the fury in his eyes.

Still sitting upright on top of Charlie, Dragomir regarded Kovalev steadily. 'Do you have something to say, Vasya?' He spoke calmly, a note of laughter in his voice. 'Or are you just feeling curious today?'

Charlie lowered his eyes to the floor, heat rising in his cheeks, and shifted beneath Dragomir. Humiliation burnt in the pit of his stomach. He knew the brand was still visible.

'Get up,' Kovalev said at last, his words dripping with venom. 'We have work to do.'

'Is it so urgent?' Dragomir sounded bored now. When Charlie continued to struggle, Dragomir brought his hand casually around Charlie's throat. '*Shh,*' he said, squeezing with practised care. 'I know you're desperate for it, but you'll have to be patient – unless you want an audience? Sounds like you're no stranger to that sort of thing, if what I've heard about you is true.'

Charlie had gone completely still. 'Get your fucking hands *off* me,' he managed to wheeze, as Dragomir's grip slowly tightened around his neck. 'I can't –'

'That's *enough*.' Kovalev's voice was so sharp it made Charlie flinch. 'Stop right now, or I'll make sure you regret it.'

It took a few seconds for Dragomir to react, during which time Charlie watched as the two Witch Hunters sized each other up. Kovalev's expression had darkened to the point that he looked murderous. Finally, with another soft chuckle, and after sending his hand trailing down Charlie's back all the way from the nape of his neck to his tailbone, Dragomir got to his feet.

'Don't you worry, I'll be back for you soon enough,' he said to Charlie, landing a vicious kick to his ribs before he strode towards the door. 'Make sure you keep me in your thoughts, then we can pick up right where we left off.'

He shouldered past Kovalev, hunting knife in hand, and disappeared out of sight. His cruel laughter echoed in Charlie's ears long after he had left the room.

Kovalev stared after him in silence for a few moments, his eyes oddly glazed. Then he drew himself up to his full height and, with a sigh, pushed his wild black hair out of his eyes. He turned towards Charlie, frowning.

Charlie watched with deep unease as Kovalev approached him, drawing a pocketknife from out of nowhere and unfolding it as he went. He bent down beside Charlie and gripped his right shoulder to hold him still.

'*Don't* fucking touch me,' Charlie hissed, flinching at the pain from his scarred flesh.

Without a word, Kovalev cut the restraints binding Charlie's wrists in one swift movement.

Then he let him go.

Before Charlie had a chance to gather his thoughts, Kovalev had dragged him to his feet by the front of his t-shirt. 'Who did that to you?' he demanded, his voice harsh, his fathomless eyes flicking down before returning to Charlie's face. 'When did –?'

'Shut up!' Charlie pulled the back of his t-shirt down, trying to cover his branded skin. 'It's none of your business.'

'Fine. Have it your own way,' Kovalev said, his voice turning cold. He shoved Charlie towards the door and threw his sweatshirt after him, which Charlie caught, confused. 'This is your one chance to escape,' Kovalev continued. 'If I find out you've told anyone about *this* –' he folded the pocketknife closed '– it's your funeral.'

Charlie frowned, edging towards the door. 'But –'

'Get out of my sight, before I change my mind.' Wild-eyed, Kovalev glared at him.

Charlie did not need to be told twice. He stumbled across the threshold and ran in the opposite direction to Dragomir, leaving Kovalev behind in the interrogation cell. Pulling his sweatshirt back over his head, he caught the scent of pine forests as he raced along unfamiliar passageways, all of which looked identical. Adrenaline was coursing through his body, rising up the back of his throat.

His situation was so desperate that Charlie almost felt like laughing. He had no idea where he was, and no clue as to where he was going. All he could do was keep running. It was the only way to prevent himself from thinking about what had just happened to him in the interrogation cell. What had almost –

He hurtled left along the next passageway, only to come face to face with a familiar redheaded figure. Halting in his tracks, he shook his head, unable to believe that he had run straight into Seren Casimir again. She was staring at him with one hand on her hip, her eyebrows raised. A faintly impressed smile was playing around her mouth.

'You actually did it,' she said, looking him up and down with some pride, before glancing over her shoulder.

Charlie followed Seren's gaze. Standing behind her was a girl he recognised, although he had not expected to see her ever again. She was dressed differently than when they had first met – almost all in black, from her leggings to her lace-up boots. Her glossy brown hair hung in loose waves over her navy-blue knitted jumper. She carried a black rucksack on her back and kept running the straps of it through her fingers.

'Hello, Charlie,' she said, sounding nervous. 'Do you remember me … from before?'

Charlie nodded, and swallowed hard. 'I – I remember you.' He ran his fingers through his hair and spoke to the floor before looking up again. 'It's Alice, right?'

'Alya is fine,' she replied, biting a hangnail, and not quite meeting his eyes.

'What are you doing here? Why are you two,' he frowned at Seren, 'together?'

'Oh, she's been a big help.' Seren cast an appraising eye over Alice, who bit her lip. 'She's the reason we were able to find you. She has a …' Seren paused, a mischievous smile spreading across her face. 'She has a good sense of direction, shall we say … *right*, Alya?'

'I don't get it,' Charlie said, noticing the look of obvious discomfort that clouded Alice's expression. 'Why are you here, with her?' he asked, turning his frown on Alice now. 'What d'you want? Do you know what she is?'

'Yes,' Alice said, her voice soft and uncertain. 'I know all about what she is. I was there when she escaped from the Facility.'

'Why were *you* there?' Charlie asked, his voice sharp. 'How are you involved in this?'

'I was only coming to speak to someone I know,' Alice said. 'But then I saw what she did. I saw her powers.' She gazed at Seren, wonder sparkling in her black eyes. 'I promised myself that if I ever saw her again, I would try to talk to her – learn from her. There are so many questions that I want to ask …'

'She needs a mentor,' Seren added, the same playful look on her face. 'A teacher.'

'Seren, *please*,' Alice murmured, a pained note to her words. 'Don't say anything …'

Seren's smile faded. 'We've got to go,' she snapped, grabbing Alice's hand, and breaking into a sprint. 'Hurry!'

'Where are you going?' Charlie shouted after her. 'There are still soldiers out there!'

'*There* they are!' a triumphant voice called out. 'You, block their escape route at Point C! You, with me!'

'We need to get out of here – *now*,' Alice urged them. 'If they catch us, it's all over.'

Seren whirled around. 'I'm not leaving without my sister! I'll kill them all first.'

Charlie breathed deeply, his fists clenched. 'Seren, you've got to listen to me! You think I want to leave? My family are still somewhere in this place too, remember?'

She scowled at him but did not argue.

'This guy tracking us down – Dragomir,' Charlie continued, his voice low and rushed, 'he and I have history. He's one of the soldiers who arrested me. He's a Hunter – a professional witch killer – and if he finds us, we won't have another chance to rescue your sister or my family because we'll both be dead. We need to listen to her.'

Seren cast Alice a withering look. 'What do *you* suggest we do, then, little cuckoo?'

'First, we get ourselves out of here alive,' Alice said. 'Then we help everyone else.'

But a team of soldiers was already racing down the passageway towards them, their guns raised.

'They're here, sir!' one of them shouted. 'We've found the prisoners. Orders?'

'*We need the witch alive!*' Dragomir's voice crackled through the radio. '*Recapture the girl. I don't care what you have to do to that Penumbran scum who's with her, just bring him to me!*'

Everything seemed to slow down in front of his eyes. Charlie looked in front of him and saw the guns aimed straight at his chest. He heard Alice screaming at the soldiers to stop. He looked at Seren by his side and saw the rage blazing in her eyes.

Seren had extended her arm towards the soldiers, and her fingers were curling through the air as though she were trying to catch smoke. The next thing he knew, the soldiers were groaning in a heap on the floor. Some of them had slammed bodily into one another before being knocked unconscious. Others had smashed straight into the walls and lay without stirring, their eyes closed.

Charlie was lost for words as he stared open-mouthed at Seren, whose legs were shaking beneath her. 'That was really something,' he said finally, while Alice nodded in agreement. 'Hey, what's wrong with you?' Seren had collapsed to the floor and was not moving.

'*Requesting status update on the prisoners.*' Dragomir's voice was coming through the radio again. '*Do you have the witch in custody? Report in. What is your current position? I'm bringing backup.*'

'We've got to get out of here,' Alice moaned, hopping from one foot to the other.

Charlie crouched beside Seren. 'Do you need me to carry you?'

'No – don't want –' Her voice was so weak he could barely make out what she said.

'You're going to have to run, then,' he said, pulling her to her feet. 'Alya, let's go!'

Charlie had no idea where he was leading them. He plunged down passageway after passageway, each one somehow mercifully empty. They zigzagged this way and that, trying to throw any pursuers off their scent, with Charlie dragging Seren behind him as he ran. Alice kept up without complaint, the heels of her boots clacking along the deserted passages.

At last, off a narrower corridor to their left, he noticed a hidden alcove, and pushed Seren inside it. Alice followed them in. Charlie closed his eyes, gasping for air as he leant against the wall, his knees trembling. The pain in his chest felt like someone was twisting a knife between his ribs.

Seren had slid down to the ground, panting. 'Did we lose them?' she asked.

Charlie peered cautiously around the alcove. 'For now,' he said, keeping his voice low as he turned back to her, 'but I don't think it'll stay that way for long. At least we're well-hidden here, so we can rest for a while.'

'We need to move as soon as we can,' Alice said, scanning the passageway. 'It's not safe for us to stay in one place.'

'Something's wrong with Seren,' Charlie said, his voice cold. 'She needs to rest.'

Alice fixed him with a hard stare, then shrugged. 'Don't say I didn't warn you.'

'I'm sorry for dragging you into this,' Seren said quietly, her eyes downcast.

'If it weren't for you, I'd still be in that cell,' Charlie said, running his fingers through his hair as he tried to think. 'Besides, you didn't drag me into anything.'

'I really thought I could find them,' Seren said, her voice thick as she spoke to her knees. 'I thought for sure that she would be here … Saga … my little sister. But I'm not strong enough, and if the soldiers find us … What if –?'

'Hey,' he said, bending down and meeting her eyes. 'We won't let that happen, all right? From now on, whatever happens, we're in this together.' He squeezed her hand with a smile.

Seren looked up at him, her bright eyes shining, and rubbed away her tears. 'Together.'

'I have an idea,' Alice said, turning to them with her arms folded across her chest. 'If it works, it will at least buy us some time. But first, we need to get out of here and back to Penumbra.' She held out her hand towards Seren. 'Can you stand?'

Seren was breathing heavily. 'I'm feeling a little better now. I … I think I'm all right.' She grasped Alice's hand and got to her feet. 'If we can rest soon, I'll be all right.'

Charlie scratched at his throat. 'Come on then, let's get out of here, before –'

He took a step forward, crashed into something solid, and staggered backwards. He had been looking at Seren instead of staying focused on checking whether the coast was clear. Someone had been waiting for them just beyond the entrance to the alcove.

Charlie's words died on his lips, his heart sinking as he realised who had discovered them. He recognised the dark scowl on the face of the furious-looking soldier who was blocking their path at once.

It was Vasco Kovalev.

CHAPTER 11

'Going somewhere, Carroway?'

Before Charlie had time to think, Kovalev had grabbed two fistfuls of his sweatshirt and thrown him straight against the opposite wall of the passageway. He heard someone scream as the back of his head hit hard rock. A racking cough surged through his body at the impact.

'I knew you would lead me to her,' Kovalev said, glaring at Charlie as he strode towards him. 'All I had to do was give you enough rope. You're all coming with me – *now*.'

'Seren, run!' Charlie yelled. 'Alya, get her out of here!'

He had no time to react before Kovalev had pulled him to his feet and pressed one forearm tightly across his chest, pinning both of his arms against the wall. He brought his face close to Charlie's, his teeth gritted.

'I'm starting to think that keeping you alive is more trouble than you're worth.' Kovalev's dark eyes flitted across Charlie's face as though in search of something. 'I'm warning you, you're *this* close to making me lose my patience.'

'I've got some good news for you, then,' Charlie gasped, struggling for breath. 'Because I'm telling you right now – if you want Seren, you're going to have to kill me first.'

Without easing up on the pressure against Charlie's chest, Kovalev used his boot to force Charlie's legs further apart and placed one foot on Charlie's shin. 'Your loyalty to your new witch friend really is quite touching,' he said, his voice low and dangerous. 'I wonder, would you still have the same resolve to save her if you had to crawl on broken legs to do it?'

'Let him go.'

Both Charlie and Kovalev's heads snapped to the side, to where Seren stood by the entrance to the alcove. Her breathing was ragged. The arm she was using to lean against the wall to steady herself was shaking. She had fixed Kovalev with a look of such vicious loathing that Charlie found he could not meet her eyes. It was only now that she seemed truly frightening.

'You're not in any condition to fight me,' Kovalev said, his voice losing some of its harshness. 'Stay out of this, witch. I'll deal with you later.'

'I said *let him go*!' Striding forward, Seren flung out her arm in front of her, and Kovalev was thrown back against the opposite wall of the passageway. He fell to the floor at Seren's feet, and she dropped to her knees beside him. 'If you ever threaten to hurt Charlie again,' she said softly, '*I* will hurt *you*. I know how to hurt you, Vasco Kovalev.'

'Wh-What are you –?'

Charlie watched as Kovalev clutched a hand to his head. His eyes grew wide and horrified as he seemed to become aware of something that Charlie could not see. Seren released her hold on him and wrapped her arms around her knees, her entire body trembling. She offered no resistance as Charlie helped her up, draping her arm over his shoulders to support her weight.

Breathing deeply, Kovalev got to his feet. Charlie could not help the grim smile that came to his face when he saw that Kovalev took a few steps back from them all.

Alice cleared her throat. 'Please listen to me,' she said, casting Kovalev a grave look before turning her large eyes to Charlie, her hands clasped at her heart. 'He didn't come here to fight you. I don't want to fight *either* of you,' she added, glancing at Seren before returning her gaze to Charlie. 'You may not believe this, but Vasco has been trying to help you.'

'*Help* me?' Charlie repeated, looking incredulously from Alice to Kovalev and back again. 'You're not serious? Did you miss what he just did? Besides, it was *him* and that cracked-out headbanger Dragomir who arrested me in the first place.'

'Who was it that stopped him from slitting your throat right there by the Gate?' Kovalev shot back, his fists clenched at his sides. 'Who do you think gave the order for you to be placed in the isolation cellblock so he couldn't finish what he started that night with those lowlife hoods in Penumbra?' At these words, his shoulders sagged, and some of the tension seemed to leave his body. He gazed at Charlie, a strange, unreadable expression on his face. 'You crazy kid, you seriously act like you've got a death wish or something.'

'*Vasco*,' Alice muttered, looking pained. 'Can't you at least *try*?'

Kovalev crossed his arms and scowled, scuffing the floor before continuing. 'Arron Dragomir wants you dead, and I'm the only thing standing in his way.' He glared at Charlie, some of the edge gone from his voice. 'Believe me when I tell you that if it weren't for me, you'd be six feet under right now – or worse, back in that interrogation cell with him.'

'You hate me,' Charlie said. The words came out of his mouth without emotion. 'I've known that from the very first time we met. Why would you stick your neck out for me?'

Kovalev cast him a dark look. 'Not owing to anything especially virtuous on my part, I assure you.' He put his hands in his pockets and scowled at the wall. 'You have a friend in Elysia, Carroway.' Kovalev glanced at Alice, and when he met his eyes again, Charlie flinched at the loathing raging in them. 'I'm simply doing what I'm told. That's all there is to it.'

'A friend in Elysia?' Charlie murmured. 'You mean … Alice?'

'My real name is Alexandra Ignatieva,' Alice said. 'Please, call me Alya.'

A muscle worked in Kovalev's jaw. 'I *had* planned to bring her to speak with you in the isolation cells, where there would be no risk of anyone learning anything about it. But since *you two* decided to take matters into your own hands so spectacularly …'

Charlie's lip curled. 'Oh, well, forgive us for not sitting around waiting for you to deign to brighten our stay in the dungeon with a personal visit,' he spat back. 'I'd guess people like Seren aren't

too popular with Hunters like you and Dragomir. Wait –
Alexandra *Ignatieva?*'

'We don't have time for pleasantries,' Kovalev snapped. He
took a deep breath and pinched the bridge of his long nose with
his thumb and forefinger. When he continued, his voice was
clipped, but calm. 'Look, she's in no condition to fight,' he said,
indicating Seren. 'I don't know what's happened to her, but I'd like
to know how she managed to get inside my head like that. I'm no
stranger to witches. She shouldn't be able to do that.'

'From what she's told me, you Elysians imprisoned her and
turned her into your own personal lab rat,' Charlie answered
savagely. 'That's how.'

'I don't know anything about that,' Kovalev said dully,
shrugging. 'I just hunt them.'

'What do you mean, Charlie?' Alexandra frowned. 'What have
you found out?'

'What game are you two playing?' Charlie demanded. 'Look at
the scar on her head. Do you expect me to trust you? You can't
think I'm that stupid?'

Kovalev threw a quick glance over his shoulder and began to
speak more urgently. 'You've got to listen to me. The soldiers are
coming. They will find you, and when they do, they will kill you.
You want to keep her safe?'

Charlie glanced at Seren, whose body was slack against his. Her
head was lolling on his shoulder and her eyes were closed, a pained
expression on her face. He nodded.

'Then follow me – and do *exactly* as I say.'

In one curiously graceful movement, Kovalev swung the rifle
strapped across his back into his arms. Charlie watched him stride
quickly to the end of the passageway and scan the one adjoining it
in both directions.

Without looking back, Kovalev indicated for the others to
follow him. Once they had all caught up with him, he began to lead
the way back down the passage towards the large antechamber, his
sharp features set in a grim expression.

'We already came this way, genius,' Charlie said under his breath, recognising the route they were taking. 'You realise you're leading us back towards the soldiers?'

Kovalev tapped his left ear, and Charlie noticed for the first time that a black, bullet-shaped object was sitting in it, camouflaged against his thick, wavy hair. 'I know exactly where the soldiers are,' he said quietly, 'and, if we can avoid drawing attention to ourselves, we won't need to worry about them.'

'Where are we going?'

'Library.'

'I'm not a big reader.'

'You surprise me.'

'Remind me again why I should trust you?' Charlie asked, smarting. 'How do I know you're not leading us straight into a trap?'

Kovalev heaved a deep sigh. With a shake of his head, he turned to look at Charlie, a bemused expression on his face. 'You heard me say her name, didn't you? Don't tell me that name means nothing to you, or have all those punches you've taken done a number on your brain?'

'Then he and Alexandra ...'

'The Great Protector is my father,' Alexandra said softly.

Charlie was silent for a few moments, allowing this information to sink in. A painful wave of shame washed over him, twisting his insides, at the thought that the First Daughter of their country had seen him at his lowest point. It made him cringe to think of the way he had spoken to her at the Infirmary Station, and what he had said to her in his anger.

Besides that, there was a more pressing matter he would now have to deal with. The hard fact was that Alexandra Ignatieva knew things about him that he had no intention of sharing with anyone else. She knew he was living on borrowed time. He had not once thought about her since he had learnt he was dying. He had not thought he would ever see her again.

'I still don't understand how you fit into this, mustang,' Charlie said.

'What does *that* mean?' Kovalev snapped. 'Besides, there's nothing to understand.'

'Every other soldier in this place is running around trying to recapture Seren and me,' Charlie said. 'You're the only one who managed to find us, and instead of turning us in, you're acting as our personal escort. She's got to be the most heavily guarded woman in the country.'

'Do you intend to come to your point any time soon, or can I stop listening to you?'

'Your priorities seem a little off, that's all I'm saying.'

Kovalev had come to a halt and was scowling at him again. 'What was that?'

'Vasco, don't.' Alexandra stood between them, her hands outstretched. 'Charlie, stop.'

Kovalev backed off, glaring at Charlie. 'This punk kid needs to watch his mouth.'

'You brought him with you to Penumbra, to the Infirmary Station,' Charlie pressed on, a reckless smirk twisting his mouth as he rounded on Alexandra. 'You were pretending to be a nurse, right? What was that – some kind of wish fulfilment fantasy? I thought this guy was supposed to be a renowned Witch Hunter. Seems more like you're her own personal guard dog ...'

Kovalev's hands had curled into fists again. He raised one to Charlie's face. Then, without breaking eye contact, he lashed out to the side, his knuckles connecting with the wall instead. 'I swear to you, Carroway,' he said, his voice soft, 'once this is over, you had better keep away from me if you like having your head on your shoulders. If you *ever* –'

'Lieutenant Kovalev, is that you? Have you apprehended the prisoners? I must have missed the comms update.'

Charlie's stomach dropped as a slight Elysian soldier hurried eagerly towards them. He caught the warning look Kovalev threw at him. Against his better judgement, he stayed still and silent, merely tightening his grip around Seren's waist. Alexandra had ducked behind them.

'My equipment is out of action,' Kovalev said. 'I'm bringing them in now.'

'Would you like my assistance, sir?' the soldier asked, beaming with enthusiasm.

Kovalev looked from the young soldier to Charlie, a cold smile curling one corner of his mouth. 'Take the witch. Leave the Penumbran mutt to me.'

'Yes, sir, right away!'

The young soldier turned towards Charlie, who flashed Kovalev a look of mingled confusion and anger. He pulled Seren closer to his body. Kovalev waited, motionless, until the soldier had passed him by.

Then there was a flash of movement. With a sickening crunch, the butt of Kovalev's rifle connected with the soldier's head, and he collapsed to the ground, clearly unconscious. It had happened so fast that Charlie had had no time to react.

Grudgingly impressed at the speed and ferocity of the Elysian lieutenant, he looked up from the prone body on the floor. 'Uh ... remind me not to turn my back on you in future.'

Something close to a real smile flitted across Kovalev's features. Slinging his rifle to the side of his body, he bent down and pulled the young soldier across his shoulders before carefully getting back up to his feet.

'We can't risk him being found like this,' he explained, noticing Charlie's doubtful look. 'He won't remember what happened, but it won't take Dragomir long to put two and two together if he's discovered. I'm still planning to get through this without being court-martialled myself. Come on, we're almost there.'

They moved on in silence, until they reached a steel door in the wall. Beside the door there was a plaque, on which a single word was written, although Charlie could not read it.

'Get in,' Kovalev ordered, holding the door open for Charlie, who was still supporting Seren, before following Alexandra into the room. Once they were all inside, he closed the door and bolted it behind him.

The library was illuminated by soft lights hanging from a chandelier set into a vaulted ceiling. Specks of dust glinted in the air above them. Rows and rows of wooden shelves were crammed tightly into the available space, each one of them packed with books. There was an antique mahogany desk near the door, chipped and worn with age, around which four wooden chairs were arranged. Carefully, Charlie eased Seren into one of them, fighting to contain the fear that had been building in his mind since she had first started to seem ill.

Her eyes fluttered open and a tired smile passed across her face. She nodded at his unspoken question. 'I'm fine,' she said, her voice small and weak.

Kovalev had eased the unconscious soldier off his shoulders. He was busy propping him up against the wall in a corner between a bookshelf and a wastepaper basket. 'So, Alexandra,' he said, folding his arms across his chest as he leant against the locked door, 'what was it you wanted to talk to him about so badly?'

Alexandra fixed him with a stony glare, one eyebrow raised. 'Is it any of your business, Lieutenant Kovalev? I wasn't aware that I now required a chaperone to hold a conversation.'

'Ouch.' Charlie raised an eyebrow too, smirking again. 'She sure told you, hey, *Vasya*?'

Kovalev scowled. 'It is when it involves Penumbran prisoners and escaped witches.'

Alexandra sighed before turning back to Charlie. 'I'm sorry for all this secrecy,' she said, 'and I'm sorry for anything the soldiers did to you when you were arrested.'

'How did you know about that?' Charlie asked, perplexed.

Alexandra chewed on her lip before answering. 'Because I ordered it. At least,' she added quickly, at Charlie's furious expression, 'I ordered Vasco to find you and bring you to Elysia to see me. Arresting you was the only way to get you into the Castle compound without arousing suspicion. I needed to speak with you. There was no other way. I hope you can forgive me,' she added, in a small voice, 'and Vasco too.'

Charlie glanced at Kovalev, who was watching him intently, his expression unreadable.

'He was only doing what I told him to do,' Alexandra continued. 'I don't blame you if you're angry with us. But I hope that now you're here, you'll listen to me.'

Charlie frowned, but said nothing. Her black eyes were shining, and there was a look of desperation in her face that she did not betray in her voice. 'I'm listening,' he said slowly.

Relief seemed to wash over her at his words. 'I want to help you,' she said, her voice returning to its usual confidence. 'Both of you,' she added, her eyes lingering on Seren.

'Alexandra,' Kovalev said quietly, 'what are you talking about?'

'And I know someone who can,' Alexandra pressed on, ignoring him. 'I have a plan for how to get us out of this place, and I know somewhere we can go where we'll be safe.' She turned back to Charlie, an almost frantic gleam in her eyes. 'There's just one thing I want you to do for me in return.'

'Oh yeah?' Charlie did not attempt to hide his suspicion. 'And what's that?'

Alexandra met his gaze fiercely and did not look away. 'Take me with you.'

'What?' Charlie blinked. Of all the things he had expected her to say, that was not it.

Kovalev's arms had fallen to his sides. 'I can't believe I'm hearing this.' He strode towards Alexandra, his jaw clenched. 'Come on, I'm taking all of you straight to your father, right now. I'm not indulging this anymore.'

'Stop!' Alexandra cried, throwing out her arm, her eyes tightly shut. 'Listen to me!'

As though caught in a strong wind, Kovalev was slowly forced back against the door. His mouth open, Charlie tore his eyes away from Kovalev's bemused expression and took in Alexandra's determined face. Beads of sweat had formed on her forehead, and her hands were shaking.

'You can't be serious,' Kovalev murmured.

'How can you do that?' Charlie asked, astounded.

Alexandra raised her head, her fists clenched. 'Because,' she said, 'I'm a witch.'

CHAPTER 12

'*What?*' Charlie and Kovalev both reacted to Alexandra's revelation in unison.

'You heard me,' Alexandra said, addressing Charlie with her face set and her hands on her hips. 'I want to help my people. I can get you out of the Facility, and I know someone in Penumbra who will be able to help Seren. I'm certain they'll be able to help mount a real rescue to save everyone else who has been imprisoned here, too.'

Charlie looked at Seren, chewing the corner of his mouth. 'What's the catch?'

'I want to come with you,' Alexandra said, swallowing hard. 'That's all. I think that's a fair return on your freedom and your lives, how about you?'

'Alexandra, do you realise what you're saying?' Kovalev had gone pale. 'I don't care how good this *friend* of yours is. What you're talking about is impossible. There's no way you can all make it past Dragomir and get out of here alive, let alone help anyone else escape.'

'You don't know my friends,' Alexandra said at once, dismissing his words with a wave of her hand. 'I know they'll help us, I *know* it. Trust me, Charlie – please.'

Charlie shook his head, drawing his nails across his neck. 'My family are still here …'

'This is the *only* way,' Alexandra said, her voice clipped with urgency. 'Believe me, I've had a long time to think about this. You want to see your family again, don't you?'

'Can't *you* just –?'

She shook her head immediately. 'You think I have any real authority in this place?' she said, a sour look clouding her face. 'I can't risk my father finding out that I've been snooping around asking questions or giving orders.' She tossed her hair over her shoulders, a roguish smile curling her lips. 'We simply need to make a fast, inconspicuous getaway.'

Kovalev's jaw had dropped. 'Alexandra, how long have you been planning this?'

Once again, Alexandra ignored him. Folding her arms, she looked directly at Charlie. 'If we came back here with my friends, we could rescue your family like *that*.' She snapped her fingers for emphasis. 'Without them …' She trailed off with a shrug of her shoulders.

Charlie groaned. 'All right,' he said at last. 'All right, all right. Let's do it.'

Alexandra beamed and punched him playfully on the shoulder before extending her hand towards him. 'It's a deal? Remember, if you shake on it there's no backing out.'

Already beginning to wonder whether he was making a mistake, Charlie took her hand in his and shook it, smiling at her eager expression despite himself. 'Fine. You've got a deal.'

'And you're planning to walk right out of here, are you?' Kovalev asked. He was scowling at both of them now. 'I'd love to hear how you thought that was going to work out.'

Alexandra clasped her hands behind her back. 'Well, we may need to complete a little extraction mission first,' she said, her warm eyes sparkling as she twirled a strand of her hair.

Charlie stared at her, unable to believe what he was hearing. 'Say that again?'

'There's someone who works here in the Facility that I need to speak to before I leave.' She was racing to get her words out, Charlie thought, as though she was desperate to explain everything as quickly as possible. 'He's the best! We've been meeting in secret for months – and don't look at me like that, he's been teaching me about *medicine*,' she added, noticing Kovalev's outraged expression. 'He's always been there for me, especially since I started having …'

Alexandra heaved a sigh, pinching the bridge of her nose. 'I just need to see him.'

'How long have you been dealing with this on your own?' Kovalev asked, his voice much gentler now. 'Why did you never talk to me about it?'

'Why did the First Daughter of Matya never tell a Witch Hunter that she's a witch?' Charlie let out an incredulous laugh, ignoring the furious look Kovalev threw his way in return. 'Are you for real?'

'Besides, I wasn't alone,' Alexandra said. 'He helped me. More importantly,' she added, turning to Charlie, 'he kept detailed notes of all his observations. If we can bring him with us to the people I know in Penumbra, I *know* I'll be able to gain their trust.'

'Where is he?' Charlie asked.

'He'll be in his lab. It's a few floors above us. He should be there right now.'

'That's awfully convenient, isn't it?' Kovalev sneered, still leaning against the bolted door. 'And how are you planning on getting past Dragomir and his soldiers to reach him?'

Alexandra pulled a grey pistol from underneath her jumper in one sharp movement, making Charlie leap back in surprise. She held it up in front of her, her eyes fixed on Kovalev, who only blinked, looking supremely unmoved.

'I'm more than capable of looking after myself if necessary,' she said, before she returned the gun to her waist. 'Let me make this perfectly clear. I'm getting out of Elysia today, and before I do, I'm going to get what I need to make sure I never have to come back again.'

'And were you planning to give me a choice in the matter of whether or not I betrayed my country?' Kovalev asked. 'Or did you assume that I would go along with all this simply because you asked me to?'

'I thought,' Alexandra said, all the frustration gone from her voice now, 'that you might forget your duty to your country for one moment and help *me* instead.'

'Saints, Alya ...' Kovalev groaned, all the tension leaving his shoulders as he exhaled deeply, his eyes fixed on the ceiling. 'Fine.

You win. I'm with you.' At Alexandra's huge smile, his lips quirked slightly, and he looked away, clearing his throat. 'So, what's your plan?'

Alexandra pulled a scroll from a shelf behind her, eased off the band, and unrolled it. She spread the scroll across the desk, careful to avoid disturbing Seren. 'What happened to her, exactly?' she asked, her brow furrowed. 'Did she get hurt somehow? What should we do?'

'She's just resting,' Charlie said, in what he hoped was a convincing tone.

'These are blueprints of the Volya Facility,' Kovalev said, frowning.

'That's right.' Alexandra was smiling proudly. 'I took them from my father's study a few days ago. I've already marked the lab, two floors above, and this is his office next to it,' she explained, indicating two rooms on the map, both of which were circled in pencil.

'We'll have to stick together, but moving in a larger group will be difficult,' Kovalev murmured, talking more to himself than to the others.

Alexandra pointed to another circle. 'This is where we are now, and *this*,' she tapped another circle at the top of the map, 'is the roof, which is what I suggest we use as a rendezvous point when the mission is complete. Then we can break out of this place for good.'

'What's on the roof?' Charlie wondered aloud.

Alexandra looked expectantly at Kovalev, who was staring back at her with a mixture of dismay and wonder on his face. 'The helipad …' He sounded grudgingly impressed. 'You want us to fly out of here?'

'I know you can pilot one,' Alexandra said, grinning at Kovalev's stunned expression as she jangled a set of keys in front of him. 'Don't tell me you don't want to see the look on his face.'

'You really have thought of everything, haven't you?' Kovalev said, his eyes softening as he looked at her. His expression soon darkened again, however, as he studied the map. 'We won't have long before the soldiers catch up with us.'

'We'll be out of here before they even know what's hit them.' Alexandra looked smug.

'We can't rely on Dragomir overlooking something or making a mistake,' Kovalev warned. 'He's too sharp for that. He knows Penumbra as well as Elysia.'

'We should stay close,' Charlie said, thinking back to his childhood. 'He'll expect us to run. We should find somewhere quiet and stay hidden until the heat is off us. That way we'll be safe.'

'No one's ever safe around Dragomir.' Kovalev glanced from Alexandra to Charlie, his jaw clenched, and shook his head. 'I don't like it. There's too much risk in staying put.'

'You think this is the first time I've had to hide from Elysian soldiers?' Charlie asked.

Kovalev stared back at him with a furious scowl that made Charlie wilt. Alexandra rolled her eyes. Charlie was about to open his mouth to retaliate, when Seren lifted her head from the table. Her face was pale, and her fists were clenched on top of the wooden surface.

'If we're going to have any chance of escaping this place,' she said, 'we need to start trusting each other. Believe me, I've tried getting out of here before. None of us stands a chance alone, but together, it might actually be possible.'

Charlie crouched down beside her. 'How are you feeling?'

Seren regarded him with a weak smile. 'I'm a little better now. Thanks.'

'She's right,' Alexandra said, addressing Kovalev with a wary look in her eyes. 'If you're coming with us, I need to be able to trust you.'

Kovalev seemed almost to flinch at these words. 'You can trust me with your life. You know that.' He crossed his arms in front of his chest, glaring at Seren. 'I don't like this plan, and I don't trust *her* ... but whatever you choose to do, I'll be right behind you.'

'If you trust me then there's no reason not to trust her,' Alexandra said smartly, rolling up the map and tapping it against her open palm. 'You only dislike her because she's a witch.'

pounding feet approaching them. Furious voices echoed off the walls, surrounding them, so that it was all but impossible to tell which direction they originated from.

'Take your team right down to ground level and start a sweep up!' At the sound of Dragomir's voice, Charlie froze, horrified. 'They're here somewhere! Maintain radio silence.'

'Charlie ...' Seren's eyes were wide with fright. 'I won't be strong enough ...'

'This way,' Kovalev said, motioning with his hand to urge them forwards.

Grabbing Seren's hand, Charlie charged up the last few stairs, outstripping the others as the sound of the oncoming soldiers grew louder and louder from above them. There was a tiny alcove in the corner space before the staircase that led to the next floor. Desperate, Charlie pulled Seren towards it.

'Get in, and don't make a sound!'

He shoved her into the alcove first and pushed himself in after her, forcing them both as flat against the wall as they could manage. Alexandra and Kovalev squeezed in behind them. They were packed in so close and tight together that Charlie's arms were trapped at his sides, leaving him unable to move an inch in any direction.

A hot wave of revulsion washed over him at the memory of bodies smothering him, hands holding him down. He screwed up his eyes, forcing himself not to make a sound. None of it was real. He was not there anymore.

'Vasco, what if –?' Alexandra began, before she broke off.

Judging by the pounding footsteps, it sounded as though the soldiers were passing right by them. Charlie could not have turned around to see what was happening even if he had dared to. His chest was horribly tight. He swallowed, desperately trying to resist the urge to start coughing.

He forced one hand up and clamped it over his mouth. Any second now, he was sure he would feel a rough hand gripping his shoulder, certain that they were about to be discovered and dragged back to the prison cells – or worse. It was only when he heard the last of the footsteps fading away that he dared to breathe again.

'They're gone,' Kovalev murmured. 'Everything looks clear. Ready to keep going?'

Seren and Alexandra nodded, breathing deeply, while Charlie tried to stop shaking.

The next flight of stairs was eerily quiet after the raucous noise of the soldiers searching for them. Once they had reached the top, they edged along the corridor. Charlie glanced left and right at each of the closed doors along the passage, looking for some sign that they were close to the room they were searching for. His fingers found the gun in the waistband of his jeans and encircled the grip. Its touch steadied him.

Alexandra picked up speed. 'We're here,' she called to them. 'This is his office.'

'You all go in and take a look around,' Seren said. 'I'll stay here and keep watch.'

Tentatively, Charlie pushed the door open an inch or two, drawing his gun. There was no sound from inside the office, so he moved to open the door fully. Kovalev gripped his wrist, shaking his head, and stepped in front of him.

With a motion towards his eyes, he encouraged Charlie and Alexandra to watch him, then kicked out at the door with such force that it slammed against the wall. He entered the room first, with a sharp turn to the right, trailing his gun around the office from right to left.

'It's clear,' he said, his eyes scanning the ceiling and windows as they followed him in.

The sight that greeted Charlie's eyes made him do a double take. The first thing he noticed was the blood on the windows and carpeted floor. His mind flooding with questions, Charlie returned the gun to his waistband.

'Someone got here before us.'

The floor was littered with pieces of paper. Broken glass from a shattered lamp crunched under their feet. Chairs that had been tipped over backwards lay strewn in the middle of the room. A shelving unit had even been pulled down from the wall and lay across the floor on its side, its drawers half-open.

'They must have been looking for something,' Seren said, following them inside.

'But how do we know what they were looking for?' Kovalev asked, glancing around.

'More to the point, how do we know if they found it?' Alexandra added.

Charlie reached the desk first. Papers were scattered haphazardly across it. To occupy his hands, Charlie scanned through them. His eyes were drawn away from the reams of scrawled handwritten notes and blocks of complicated-looking text to the many diagrams and images that accompanied the writing. Most of these were detailed drawings of human bodies, sometimes including close-ups of a head or a torso. Occasionally, a document would have a black and white photograph clipped to it, and these pictures showed things that made Charlie's stomach turn over.

'Take a look at this,' he said, motioning uncertainly for the others to join him.

Kovalev kept his gun trained on the door. Meanwhile, Seren and Alexandra took some of the papers from the pile Charlie had gathered together on the desk and started leafing through them.

'What *is* all this?' Alexandra asked, frowning as she returned to Kovalev's side.

'I don't know,' Charlie murmured. 'But whatever it is, I don't like it one bit.'

Seren shivered as her eyes travelled over the papers that included the diagrams of human bodies. 'These pictures are giving me the creeps,' she said. 'We should get out of here.'

'Something's not right,' Charlie said, his gaze drifting across the overturned chairs, the papers littering the floor. 'We should keep looking while we still have the chance.'

'But what if –?'

'Well, well, well.' Charlie's eyes snapped towards the door. Arron Dragomir was standing at the threshold, blocking their escape, his rifle trained directly at them. 'I had a feeling I would find you two here.'

Charlie's fingers itched for the gun at the small of his back. But at the sight of Dragomir's expression, he knew better than to reach for it. Dragomir's eyes seemed to follow his every movement, as though he could read Charlie's mind. A nasty smile was playing around his mouth. He had not yet noticed Alexandra or Kovalev, who were frozen still, their backs pressed against the wall. Kovalev had flung one arm out in front of Alexandra, his gun trained on Dragomir, his face set.

Dragomir edged further towards Charlie and Seren, staring fixedly at them through the sight of his rifle. 'I hope you've been enjoying yourselves. You've certainly led my men on a wild goose chase. You almost succeeded in making me look very foolish.' His teeth were gritted, his voice dangerously soft. 'But the fun ends here, I'm afraid.' In one sharp movement, he swung the barrel of his rifle towards Charlie's face. 'You first, gutter punk.'

With a shriek of effort, Charlie saw Seren lash out wildly from beside him, just as he heard the crack of gunfire. The soldier's rifle was wrenched from his hands and hit the wall. Dragomir himself was thrown into the air and flung to the side. He smashed headfirst into a desk with a sickening crack and lay on the floor without moving. He was bleeding from his head and right arm. Seren had collapsed to her knees with a cry of pain.

'Seren, what's wrong?' Charlie was at her side, shaking her by the shoulders.

Kovalev nudged Dragomir with the toe of his boot. 'Someone will have heard that.'

'You need – to run,' Charlie heard Seren whisper. 'Get out of here – now.'

Charlie gathered her up into his arms, the papers they had found shoved tightly between his upper arm and his chest. Without a backwards glance, he raced out of the room towards the stairwell, his footsteps echoing through the corridor. Kovalev and Alexandra followed close behind him.

'Just leave me,' Seren moaned, her eyes clenched tightly shut, 'or they'll catch you.'

'Don't talk,' Charlie snapped. 'You just rest. We'll be fine.'

He flew up the stairs, losing track of how far he had climbed, Seren cradled in his arms. Then a blinding stab shot through his ribs. He staggered towards the wall, biting back an agonised scream as the papers scattered to the ground.

Somehow, he managed to keep hold of Seren. But he was in too much pain to move. His knees were trembling beneath him as Alexandra and Kovalev caught up with them. Charlie was aware of Alexandra beside him, gathering up the documents.

'What's wrong?' Kovalev demanded, easing Seren out of his arms as Charlie slid down the wall and lay on the ground, his arms wrapped around his sides. 'Hey, come on, talk to me!'

Charlie heard Alexandra saying his name, her eyes wide with fear, but he could not speak. 'Vasco, what do we do now?' she asked, her voice shaking. 'They're coming!'

Kovalev was silent for a few moments. Peering up, Charlie realised that he was looking at each of them in turn. 'I'll take her up to the roof with you first, then come back for him,' he said finally, before crouching down beside Charlie. 'Stay here, all right? I'll be back for you.'

Bracing himself against the shards tearing through his chest, Charlie curled up on the floor. Sweat dripped from a sheen across his forehead as he kept his eyes screwed up tight, weathering the pain. He was vaguely aware of the sound of racing footsteps fading away above him, as well as of those approaching him.

'Oh, dear. What sort of trouble have you got yourself into this time, then, Charlie?'

Charlie's eyes shot open at the sound of Faulkner's sweetly mocking voice. He was standing so close to Charlie that the toes of his boots were almost touching Charlie's face.

Jerking back, Charlie reached out behind him, his hand finding the rough brickwork of the wall. With great effort, he managed to drag himself into a hunched sitting position, his legs sprawled out to one side. Breathing hard, he glared up at Faulkner's smug face, his teeth gritted.

'You don't look so good, kid,' Faulkner said, scuffing Charlie's leg with his boot.

One hand clenching his ribs, Charlie fought to keep his voice level. 'Where are they?'

'I'm not entirely sure who you're referring to ...'

'Those three kids, you bastard – *my* kids! What – the hell – have you done with them?'

Faulkner bent down beside Charlie, his eyes lingering on his face. 'Wouldn't you like to know, little one? You don't have any ideas? Go on, take a guess ...'

Charlie forced himself as far against the wall as he could, his body stiffening, as Faulkner lowered his face to Charlie's and brushed his lips against his forehead.

'I missed you,' Faulkner whispered against his skin.

'Don't touch me.' Frozen, Charlie ground the words out.

'You look like you want to sink your claws into me,' Faulkner murmured, his fingers tracing his scarred cheek. He paused, and Charlie heard the sound of footsteps hurrying towards them from above. Faulkner gazed at him, smirking. 'Catch me if you can, Charlie ...'

Charlie attempted to force himself onto his feet, but his legs collapsed beneath him. A feral howl escaped him as Faulkner retreated down the corridor and out of sight. A moment later, Kovalev had appeared, his hair wild and his eyes alive with concern.

'Be careful, don't push yourself,' he said, supporting Charlie's weight as he helped him get to his feet. 'You're a real fighter, aren't you, kid?' he added, studying Charlie's face as though for the first time. 'You don't know when to give up.'

'Don't *call* me that,' Charlie snarled, pushing Kovalev away and leaning against the wall to prevent himself from falling again. 'Listen, you need to take the others and get out of this place. I came here to find my family. I can't leave without them.'

'That's suicidal,' Kovalev said, shaking his head as he reached for Charlie's arm. 'We're running out of time, and I can't protect you in this state.'

'I never asked you to,' Charlie said, wrenching himself out of Kovalev's grip. 'I'm fine on my own.'

Charlie turned to follow Faulkner, but Kovalev's hand on his left shoulder stopped him.

'What are you –?'

'If you care about them so much, you wouldn't throw your life away like it's nothing,' Kovalev said, his voice even. When Charlie looked at him, he saw that the soldier's dark eyes were blazing. 'You're worth more than that, Charlie.'

CHAPTER 13

'Y ou don't know anything about me,' Charlie muttered, shrugging Kovalev's hand off his shoulder. 'Just get out of here. I don't need any of you.'

Without hesitation, Charlie staggered down the corridor after Faulkner. He did not stop to check whether the soldier was following behind him. He was better off alone. His mind fixed on his target, Charlie drew the gun from the waistband of his jeans and aimed it in front of him. He would not let Faulkner get away this time.

He roamed deeper into the Facility, thinking of nothing but saving the children, until, with a sickening feeling, he realised that he did not recognise his surroundings. He was lost. Then Charlie noticed movement in the shadows.

'Stop right there, you piece of shit.' He ground out the words, his sights set on Faulkner.

Faulkner strode out of the gloom, his hands raised to his shoulders. A nasty smile was hovering around his scarred mouth. 'So, you made it. You're just full of surprises, aren't you?'

'I'm not afraid to use this,' Charlie said, pulling back the hammer of the gun.

'Yes, you are,' Faulkner said, his voice soft, his eyes on Charlie's. 'You have always been afraid. Did you think three years apart would be enough to make me forget? Remember, I know you better than anyone.'

'I remember everything,' Charlie whispered. His fingers were trembling. 'Everything.'

Then he heard Kovalev's voice shouting his name and saw him sprinting towards them.

'I see you're as popular as ever,' Faulkner sneered, and Charlie gripped the gun tighter. 'Is your new friend here to save you, Charlie? What could possibly have motivated him to do such a thing?' His gaze moved to the muzzle of Charlie's gun. 'Walk away, or you'll regret it.'

Charlie sensed Kovalev beside him. 'Come on, let's go,' he said, a clipped edge to his words. 'Leave him, Charlie.'

'Have you told him what you are yet, Charlie?' Faulkner murmured, his eyes glittering. 'D'you think he'll still want to –'

'Shut the *fuck* up!'

A moment later, Faulkner was on the floor, bleeding from one forearm. Charlie did not remember making the shot. His arms went slack at his sides, his shoulders sagging as he breathed deeply. The pain in his chest and ribs was finally starting to ebb away.

'The roof,' Kovalev said, his eyes on Faulkner's body. 'We're getting out of here.'

They surged along the corridor and up the stairs. As they approached the last flight, Kovalev paused. He looked back at Charlie, watching him intently.

'You're not a bad shot, are you?'

'I've had experience,' Charlie muttered.

'I've seen him skulking around the Facility before. Who is he to you?'

'Old friend.'

'You make a habit of shooting your old friends?' Kovalev frowned. 'Who is he?'

Charlie did not reply, and Kovalev did not ask again. Once they reached the roof, Charlie followed the soldier past a row of helicopters, towards a small shack at the top of a flight of rickety steps. It appeared to be an abandoned watchtower.

Inside, the room was bare, but for a mouldy-looking wooden desk and shelving unit. Shafts of late afternoon sunlight pooled in through the dusty windows. The rotten floorboards creaked underfoot. Alexandra looked up at them as they entered, cradling Seren in her lap.

'She's not awake yet?' Kovalev's dark expression softened with concern as his eyes travelled over Seren's pale face, while Alexandra shook her head. 'We can't stay here long.'

'We're almost free, Seren,' Charlie said, staring into her face as she lay with her eyes closed in Alexandra's lap. 'Just rest. You'll be all right. Everything will be fine.'

Kovalev raised an eyebrow and regarded Charlie with a dubious look on his face, before turning to gaze over the mountains through the grimy window. 'Somehow, I doubt that.'

Seren's eyes flickered open. A relieved smile broke over Charlie's face, but she did not return it. She was staring at him as though she did not even recognise him.

'Where am I?' she asked, her voice uncertain, as she put one hand to her head.

'You're safe,' Charlie said. 'We're on the roof of the Facility now, in one of the watchtowers. We'll be safe here.'

He tried to help her to sit upright as he spoke, but she flinched away from him, pushing herself out of Alexandra's lap and drawing away from them all.

'Did I escape from the prison?' she asked, her brow furrowed. 'How did ... did I ...?'

Charlie watched her wordlessly, taking in her wild, wide-eyed expression, and the way her hands shook as her eyes darted to each of them in turn. He sensed Kovalev's gaze on them from behind him. Alexandra was stiff with tension and seemed to be holding her breath, her eyes flicking between the other three.

'We escaped together,' Charlie said, treading carefully. 'You saved me ... remember?'

The frown creasing Seren's forehead deepened as her eyes scanned Charlie's face. She looked as though she was trying to force herself to recognise him but was coming up empty-handed. Her lips were parted slightly, and she was twisting her hands together in front of her chest. Long moments passed, during which none of them broke the terrible silence.

Then, in a small voice, she asked, 'Who are you?'

'Saints ...' Kovalev breathed. 'Don't tell me –'

'Oh, no,' Alexandra whispered.

Charlie said nothing. He stepped back a few paces, noticing as he did so that Seren relaxed a little at the increased distance between them. He stared at his feet, his mind completely blank. The familiar feeling of nausea in his stomach had returned.

'Perfect,' Kovalev said under his breath.

'What should we do?' Alexandra asked, tugging at the straps of her rucksack.

'Well, unless Carroway has any bright ideas, I'm done playing babysitter.'

Kovalev gripped his rifle in his hand and left the watchtower, slamming the door behind him. Charlie watched him prowl back and forth in front of it at the bottom of the stairs, scowling.

Charlie's fingernails dug into the skin of his palms as he looked at Seren. She had wandered over to the dirty windows, her eyes on the slums of Penumbra beyond the wire of the Witchtrap Wall. Shivering in her thin dress, she wrapped her arms around her body.

'Where am I?' she asked, suddenly sounding much younger than she was.

'You must be cold,' Alexandra said to her. She handed Seren a thick, dark green woollen jumper, which she had managed to extricate from her rucksack. Now that he looked at it, Charlie saw that it was packed with belongings. 'You can keep it. I also have some shoes here,' she continued, as Seren pulled on the jumper and white sneakers without hesitation, giving her a shy smile. 'I have more clothes than I need, really,' Alexandra added sheepishly. 'That colour really suits you. Can I stand here with you for a while?'

'Thank you,' Seren said, tugging the sleeves of the jumper up over her hands. 'I'm Seren. I don't know if … do I know your name?'

Alexandra's face broke into her warm smile. 'I'm Alya. That's Vasco, and this is Charlie.'

'I know Charlie,' Seren said, her voice bright. She turned to look at him and flashed him a dazzling smile before twirling around playfully. 'Look, Charlie – Alya gave me a new jumper. Isn't it great? I've never worn anything this nice before. Isn't she so kind?'

Charlie opened his mouth, only to close it again. He ran his fingers through his hair and smiled ruefully back at her. 'Yes.'

Kovalev had returned. Charlie was uncomfortably aware of how closely the soldier was watching him, and of the pointed expression on his face. Charlie said nothing.

'She's given me some shoes, too. That makes life easier, doesn't it?'

'If you're all done with the fashion show,' Kovalev said grimly, looking away from Charlie at last, 'perhaps we can discuss what we're supposed to do next.' He was surveying the line of helicopters and the mountains beyond them with a distinctly unimpressed look on his face.

'What are we doing here?' Seren asked in a small voice.

'Do you want to take this one, Carroway?' Kovalev asked, his arms folded.

Charlie glared at him. 'I'll explain later, Seren,' he said. 'For now, though, it's probably best if you don't use your powers. You've been through a lot,' he added, seeing the questioning look on her face. 'Just rest. Let me take care of everything for a while.'

An exasperated noise escaped from Kovalev's throat, but he said nothing. For a moment, Seren looked as though she wanted to say something herself, but she seemed to decide against it. For a while, none of them said anything. Instead, they stretched their legs around the watchtower, the two girls taking in their surroundings with a mixture of interest and apprehension.

'Alya says you live down there, Charlie,' Seren said, wary curiosity etched on her face.

Charlie nodded, staring at the slums in the distance. 'All my life,' he said, and he fixed Alexandra with a humourless smile. 'And, if we're going down *that* road ... Before, when you were pretending to be a nurse at the Infirmary Station, what was the deal there? Was it some kind of fantasy of yours? You wanted to see what it was like to spend time around poor people?'

'What?' Alexandra looked horrified. 'Why would you say something like that?'

Charlie scowled back. 'I'm just interested in what you thought you were doing, before you went home to your palace and your father and your servants, and congratulated yourself on being such a good person – before you forgot all about the people living so far beneath you.'

Kovalev had gone white with rage. 'Do you even realise who you're talking to, you smartass lowlife?' he snarled. 'How dare you speak to her like that? She's worth a hundred of you! You'll pay for that, you –'

'No,' Alexandra said softly, which was all it took to make Kovalev halt in his tracks. 'No, Vasco. He has the right to be angry.' She let out a deep, sad sigh. 'I don't know what you'd like me to say, Charlie.'

'Why are you apologising to him?' Kovalev demanded. '*He's* the one who –'

'No, listen to me,' Alexandra broke in, twisting her hair over her shoulder. 'We've all been through a lot. We have a long journey ahead, and we won't make it if we're at each other's throats all the time.' Kovalev made to argue, but she waved a hand to silence him. 'Charlie was right to say that we would be safe here, Vasco. No one's following us. We should all take some time to rest, while we still have the chance.'

'I agree with Alya,' Seren said, her hands on her hips. 'Let's agree to cease fire for a while, shall we?' she added, fixing both Charlie and Kovalev with a hard stare, the intensity of which surprised them both.

Alexandra returned Seren's reassuring smile with a small, sad one of her own, and walked away from them without another word. Kovalev watched her go without moving from the spot where he stood. Charlie thought he saw genuine concern and distress on his face.

'What's the deal with you two?' he asked. 'Do you like her, or something?'

All the colour drained from Kovalev's face in an instant before he shot Charlie a furious glare. He appeared to be struggling to hold back some choice words. Finally, he managed a cold smile, his dark eyes burning. 'Ceasefire, Carroway, remember? I need some time to think.' He turned on his heel and strode away, his head bent and his hands in his pockets.

Once they were alone, Seren turned to Charlie with a meaningful expression, and nodded her head in Alexandra's direction. 'Well?'

'Well what?'

'That girl is the reason we're free,' she said. 'And you just bit her head off.'

'We would have been fine on our own. I could've handled it myself.'

Seren smirked, looking distinctly unimpressed. 'I thought you were better than that, Charlie,' she said, as she turned her back on him and began to wander over towards the window again. 'But maybe I was wrong.'

Charlie watched Seren go, an unpleasant mixture of guilt and resentment churning in his stomach. With a sigh, he made his way towards Alexandra. She was sitting on the dusty wooden floorboards, leafing through a black notebook. She seemed to be concentrating hard on ignoring him as he approached her.

Clearing his throat, Charlie launched into his apology before he lost his nerve. 'Alexandra, I'm sorry for the way I spoke to you, and the things I said. I don't know anything about you, and it was wrong of me to make assumptions. I'm grateful for everything you did to get me and Seren out of the Facility. I know I owe you a lot.'

Alexandra looked up at him, the same sad smile on her face. 'You weren't wrong to say what you said. People don't tend to speak that way to me, but maybe I needed to hear it.' As he sat down beside her, she continued. 'I know you're angry.' Her eyes bored into his. 'And I know why. Charlie, when are we going to talk about –?'

'Not now,' Charlie said flatly, shaking his head. 'Listen, Alya … Seren doesn't know about – about what's wrong with me. So, please … please don't –'

'It's your secret,' she said at once. 'I have enough of my own. Trust me, no one's going to hear about it from me. You don't need to worry about Vasco, either,' she added. 'All he knows is that you're sick, and he won't even mention it unless you do. That's just the kind of person he is.'

Charlie smiled darkly. 'I get the feeling your bodyguard doesn't like me all that much.'

A pained look crossed Alya's face. 'Don't blame him. He's just trying to keep me safe.'

'Who d'you need to be kept safe from?' Charlie asked, and Alya looked away.

'What are you two looking at?' Seren had appeared out of nowhere. 'Can I help?'

'This is my friend's journal,' Alya explained, showing it to both of them.

Charlie took one look at the tiny handwriting squashed into every white space on the pages of lined paper and lost all interest at once. His head was hurting again.

'I found it sitting on his desk in the lab while we were in his office,' Alexandra said. 'I've been looking through it and trying to make some sense of his notes.'

'Why do you look so worried?' Charlie asked, noticing her drawn expression.

'Some of the things he's writing about here,' Alya said, running her index finger along a couple of lines. 'It almost sounds as though ... but there's no way they could be ...'

Seren tapped Charlie's shoulder. 'Did you give Alya the documents we found in his office?'

Charlie hastened to gather all the sheets of paper together and spread them out over the floorboards. Soon, they were surrounded by a sea of white pages. The three of them leant in over the documents, scanning the writing, photographs, and drawings for any clue as to what the researcher had been working on.

Seren unclipped one of the black and white photographs and brushed her thumb slowly along the unmistakable image of a human brain. 'I remember what they did to me,' she said, her voice distant.

The hand that was not holding the photograph traced along the incision that ran from the crown of her head, behind her ear and down her neck. Her eyes were unfocused as she stared into the middle distance.

'There'll be soldiers everywhere, so watch your backs,' Kovalev said, scowling at Alexandra. He withdrew a black handgun from a holster underneath his shoulder and placed it firmly in Charlie's hand. 'You know how to use one of these, Carroway?'

Charlie's lip curled as he stuck the gun in the waistband of his jeans. 'What do *you* think?'

Kovalev looked at Seren, removing another weapon from a holster at the small of his back. 'How about you? You ever used one of these before?'

Seren regarded him silently for a moment, before shaking her head. 'I don't need one.'

A grim smile passed across Kovalev's face as he returned the gun to its holster. 'No, I suppose you don't.' He glanced at both Charlie and Alexandra in turn. 'Is she ready to go?'

Seren raised herself shakily to her feet. 'I can speak for myself, Witchkiller.'

Charlie took in her pale face and trembling hands. 'Are you sure you're fine?'

'I'm going to have to be, aren't I?' Seren said, rubbing her palms together and flexing her fingers.

Charlie was considering arguing with her. But, seeing the determination in Seren's fierce expression, he thought better of it. They went to join the others by the door. Kovalev drew the bolt away before cautiously opening it a few centimetres and peering through the gap, his back flat against the wall. A moment later, he jerked his head to indicate that the others should follow him.

Together, they made their way out of the library, towards the stairwell. When they reached the foot of the stairs, Charlie peered up to the levels above them, straining his ears to catch any sign of movement. The staircase zigzagged back and forth, rising as high as he could see.

'Just how big is this place?'

'I'll go first,' Kovalev said. 'It's only two floors. We'll be fine. Stay right behind me.'

They began to creep up the stairs. Charlie was trying his hardest to walk both as quickly and as quietly as he could. They had almost reached the top of the first flight when they heard the sound of

'They hurt me. And they – the others ... there were so many others ...' She braced her head in her hands, wincing as though in pain, while Alya rubbed her back to soothe her.

'So they really are experimenting on people?' Charlie shivered as he spoke. 'But why?'

'It's most likely a weapons programme.' Kovalev was standing behind them, his hands still in his pockets. 'Prisoners would be seen as expendable, their deaths easy to cover up. It's news to me, I should add.' The familiar scowl was back on his face as he watched Seren brush tears away from her eyes. 'They're the ones who did this to her, who made her this way. I don't like anything about this.'

'Prisoners ... human beings ... turned into weapons?' Alya frowned. 'But who intends to use them, and for what purpose?'

An uncomfortable thought was forming in Charlie's mind. He forced it away.

'Nothing here is conclusive,' Alya murmured, turning to the next page in the journal.

'Wait, what's that?' Seren asked, pointing.

Charlie followed her gaze. A small square of paper had fallen out of the notebook and was lying on the floor. He picked it up, unfolded it, and paused.

'What is it?' Seren was looking over his shoulder.

'I don't know,' Charlie answered honestly. The piece of paper was covered in numbers. As far as he could see, there were no words on it at all. 'It could be anything.'

'In that case, it could also be nothing,' Kovalev said, his voice like flint. 'It could easily be a piece of scrap paper he was using to add things up on, or something like that.'

'I don't think so,' Alya said quietly, running her finger down the list of numbers, which continued onto the other side of the piece of paper. 'This isn't random. These numbers have been separated into columns. Do you see here – on this left-hand side? Every single one of these numbers contains seven digits. I can't see a pattern, but –'

'They all either begin in zero or one,' Charlie suggested, scanning the list.

'That's true,' Alya agreed, nodding. 'And beside each number, in the middle column, there's another six-digit number. These ones seem more random, but it looks as though they go from smallest here,' she tapped the top of the list, 'to largest here,' she concluded, resting her finger on the final number of the middle column.

'Wait …' Kovalev crouched down beside Alya and eased the piece of paper out of her hands, checking both sides of it before continuing. 'Yes – do you see? These are dates. This last one – here, at the bottom of the page – that was only a few days ago.'

'Then each number is associated with a date,' Alya said, checking along each line to make sure their theory stood up to scrutiny. 'What about the final column?'

Charlie looked again. The right-hand column did not contain numbers, as he had first assumed, but short words, scrawled in terrible handwriting, as though the author had been in great haste while writing them down.

'The words keep repeating, but there's no logic to the pattern,' Kovalev murmured, stroking his jaw thoughtfully. 'This isn't written in Matyan. *Viv. – mort. – demen.* – it's the same words, again and again, at random.'

'But what does it mean?' Seren asked. 'What do those words mean?'

'Let me see it again,' Alya said, holding out her hand. She read the whole list through carefully, growing paler with every passing moment. When she finally looked up, her face had taken on a greenish tinge. 'It's written in a dead language,' she explained. 'Not many people know it. He was using a code.'

'Why would he use a code?' Seren asked. 'Unless …'

'Unless he had something to hide,' Kovalev finished, meeting her eyes with a dark look.

'Do you know what it means?' Charlie asked, looking from Kovalev to Alya.

'These words refer to …' Alya took a steadying breath. 'Life, death and … madness. I think …' She swallowed hard and looked around at them all. 'I think that each of these numbers in the left-hand column refers to someone who was experimented on, on the date indicated in the middle column. It's a record of experimentations and the raw results. They're experimenting on prisoners – prisoners of war, witch prisoners.'

Charlie was lost for words. Seren shuddered and began to scratch absentmindedly at her wrist. Kovalev was shaking his head.

'That's insane,' he said flatly. 'It's impossible. It wouldn't be allowed to happen. Your father wouldn't allow it to happen, not even to witches.'

'You've seen with your own eyes what they've done to Seren,' Alya countered. 'Why should this be so impossible to believe?'

'Even if you're right about the code and the dates,' Kovalev argued, 'where's your evidence that the numbers in the first column refer to humans – I mean, to witches? Isn't it more likely they were experimenting on animals, and that piece of paper was just used for recording the results? Why are you so determined to assume the worst of your father?'

'Seren, don't hurt yourself,' Charlie said quietly, taking her hand gently but firmly in his, and easing it away from her wrist. Then he saw something that made his breath catch in his chest. 'Seren … what's that?'

Alya and Kovalev were looking now too. Without a word, Seren pulled back the sleeve of her jumper and showed them her wrist. Stamped across her pale skin in spidery black ink was a seven-digit number, beginning with the number one.

'Nine hells,' Charlie breathed. 'They did this to you, didn't they?'

'We all had them,' Seren said softly. 'We were kept underground. At least, I think it was underground. We never saw the light, except for the Chamber. That was the punishment. We were forced to stay awake. I don't know for how long … and my sister was –' She looked straight at him, worrying at her lip as she wrapped her arms around her knees. 'Charlie, there are so many children down there …'

Kovalev was scanning the list of numbers again. He showed them the final number on the list, where, in the last column, instead of a word, there was a star. '1740904,' he read out.

The number matched the one tattooed on Seren's wrist exactly.

'And the star must be because Seren escaped,' Alya said. 'They still don't know the outcome of the experiment. That's why there's no code word beside the date that the procedure on her was carried out.'

'This … can't be right,' Kovalev muttered. He seemed to be talking more to himself than to the others, but Charlie felt rage flare up inside himself at Kovalev's words.

'What is it going to take for you to believe what you're seeing with your own eyes?' he demanded. 'She's been branded, tortured and experimented on. How many other innocent people are imprisoned here? Her sister is still in that place somewhere, and my family are too!'

Kovalev regarded him steadily. 'There are no innocent people imprisoned here.'

'What about the people being trafficked in across the Wall?' Charlie yelled back. 'What happens to the missing children? When Penumbrans are arrested and never seen again, is this what happens to them? Is this what it means to be Elysian? You *must* know *something*!'

Kovalev seized Charlie by the front of his t-shirt and slammed him against the wall. 'You need to choose your next words carefully, Carroway,' he warned. 'You may have a witch insurgent to help fight your battles for you now, but we both know you're no match for me.'

The anger was draining away from Charlie as quickly as it had come, only to be replaced by a terrible, dawning fear. 'You really don't know anything about this, do you?'

Kovalev was regarding Charlie with that same, strangely unreadable expression on his face again. Alya and Seren were watching them both closely. No one moved or said a word.

'We have to go back,' Charlie said, starting to thrash desperately. 'What if they –?'

'Quiet!' Alya said suddenly, leaping to her feet. 'I heard something …'

'I hear it too.'

Kovalev shoved Charlie away from him and moved to stand at the front of the group. His rifle was at his shoulder immediately, trained on a target beyond the door that none of them could see. He looked back at them all, his jaw set.

'We've got company.'

CHAPTER 14

They all stood frozen to the spot, straining their ears for any sound from the other side of the door. Charlie was tensed for the slightest sign of movement, hardly daring to breathe. When he listened carefully, he could make out a strange crackling noise. It seemed to be coming from somewhere just beyond the watchtower.

'Where are you going?' Kovalev hissed at him. 'Get *back* here, right now.'

Hesitantly, Charlie picked his way past the others, towards the sound. He sensed his way down the stairs as though blind, following the noise as it grew stronger and clearer. It was coming from a megaphone fixed to a wooden post beside the tower. He could hear muffled voices mingling with static as a radio clicked on and off.

'No sightings so far – move on to – no place left to hide.'

'False alarm,' Charlie called back to the others, breathing a sigh of relief as they came to join him at the foot of the stairs. 'It was just a comms update over the radio.'

No sooner had he finished speaking when there came the wailing of sirens, earsplittingly loud, sounding from all directions. Instinctively, they all drew close together, shielding their ears from the onslaught as they searched in every direction for the source of the noise. As the piercing sound faded and the crackle of static replaced it, Charlie noticed them. Every few metres along the edge of the rooftop, for as far as his eyes could see, there was a wooden post. Fixed at the top of each post, there was a megaphone, and from each megaphone a message was now blaring:

'*Attention, all citizens of Matya! This is an emergency announcement from the Elysian Interior Police. The heart of our nation has been attacked by political terrorists. They have kidnapped Alexandra Ignatieva, the daughter of our Great Protector, and are holding her hostage. She is sixteen years of age, five feet four inches tall, with dark brown hair, of slim build, and is known to wear a necklace of red dragonstones. We have not yet received any demands from the terrorists.*'

Charlie and Seren glanced at each other, their dumbfounded expressions mirroring one another's. Then they turned to look at Alya, who was staring at the megaphone, transfixed with horror as it went on.

'*Members of the Interior Police are close to identifying the criminals responsible for this outrageous act against our beloved state. We urge all loyal citizens to be on the lookout for Charlie Carroway, a Penumbran gang member, approximately sixteen years old and five feet eight inches tall, of slim build, with brown hair worn in a distinctive style. His accomplice is a teenage witch from the Kalnelys Border Region, slightly shorter, thin, with recognisably long, curly red hair. When last sighted, Carroway was badly bruised and was not wearing his identification and protection collar.*'

'You're not serious?' Kovalev glanced at Charlie's neck, and braced his head in his hands, shaking his head in utter disbelief. 'How could you be so recklessly idiotic? They could kill you just for that!'

Charlie had no time to respond; the voice was still coming from the megaphone.

'*The terrorists are being aided by the traitor Vasco Kovalev, a former Elysian Lieutenant, who is also wanted for the crime of desertion.*'

Kovalev paled at this, and turned to gaze, dumbstruck, at the megaphone.

'*He is eighteen years of age, six feet two inches tall, and of athletic build. Be aware that these three criminals are all highly dangerous. On no account should they be approached. If spotted, alert the nearest member of the Military Police. Information leading to the capture of any one of these individuals will be justly rewarded by the Great Protector. Know that harbouring or aiding these terrorists is an act of treason, and anyone believed to be guilty of this crime*' *will face swift and severe punishment. I repeat, this is an emergency announcement from the Elysian Interior Police …'*

'Well, I guess I really am a criminal now,' Charlie heard himself say. Beside him, Seren let out a nervous laugh.

'What have I done?' Kovalev murmured. He was still staring up at the megaphone, his eyes oddly glazed. 'Everything … everything I've sacrificed … everything I worked for … I've lost it all.'

Alya approached him cautiously, and tried to take his hand in hers, but he flinched away from her touch. He turned to face her, looking as though he was seeing her clearly for the first time. When he spoke, it was not with anger, but with a sombre kind of resignation.

'Why did I ever listen to you, Alexandra Ignatieva? My position, your father's trust, the chance of gaining his respect … it's all gone.' He covered his face with his hands. 'Why did I do this? He is just and – and fair. Maybe if we go back and beg for his forgiveness …'

Alya blinked slowly, her expression hardening. 'You know better than to rely on my father's mercy, don't you?'

'That was –'

'You may regret the choices you've made, Vasco, but I don't,' Alya said. 'I'm tired of obeying my father's laws and living my life as a prisoner, no matter how gilded my cage may have been.' She stepped away from Kovalev, and regarded him fiercely, her face set. 'I refuse to go back. I need to find the place where I belong. I need to protect my people.'

'I won't let anyone take us back to Elysia by force,' Seren said, moving to stand beside Alya. 'They can try, but I don't like their chances,' she added, looking pointedly at Kovalev, who scowled back at her, but did not move.

'You have a choice to make, Vasco,' Alya said, her arms folded across her body. 'I want you on my side, but if your rank and your reputation mean that much to you, you know what you need to do.'

Kovalev was frowning at her. 'Have you forgotten who – *what* I am, Alexandra?'

Alya took a deep breath. 'Then you're going to turn me in to my father as well?'

A humourless smile tugged at the corners of Kovalev's mouth as he shook his head, rubbing the back of his neck with his hand. He seemed to be looking everywhere but at Alya. 'Of course not. I could never do that. I …' He sighed. 'I just want to protect you.'

'I need answers,' Alya said. 'Not just about who I am – *what* I am – but about what's happening here, and in Penumbra. My father must know something, but he won't tell me anything about it. So, I've decided to find the answers out for myself. I know where we need to go.'

'I can't believe that there are children involved in this,' Kovalev muttered, his expression darkening as his eyes met Charlie's. 'The only people imprisoned here are our enemies, people who pose a real threat to our country …'

'I don't understand why you see us as a threat to you,' Seren said, her voice soft.

Kovalev frowned at her. 'Well, you wouldn't, would you? You're one of them.'

'Does anyone else hear that?' Charlie said, suddenly becoming aware of a noise in the distance. 'Sounds like they're already on the stairwell.'

'It's Dragomir,' Kovalev said grimly. 'He's coming.'

'We need to find a place to hide,' Alya said, looking around desperately, as though hoping a hiding place would reveal itself helpfully at that very moment. The thump of boots on metal was growing louder, along with the noise of indistinct shouting.

'No, we need to get out of here,' Charlie said. 'Come on, which of these helicopters are those keys for? We don't have any more time to waste.'

'It's this one,' Alya said, unlocking the door to the cockpit of the helicopter closest to them. She threw a nervous glance at Kovalev. 'Do we have our pilot on board?'

Kovalev looked from Alya to Charlie and Seren and back again, frowning, and said nothing. Alya pressed the keys into his hand. With a groan, he climbed into the pilot's seat, his fingers skimming over the controls. 'Everyone in – quickly. They're almost on us.'

Charlie followed Seren into the back seats of the helicopter, and Alya went around the front to clamber into the seat beside Kovalev. From the white edges poking out of the black notebook in her hand, Charlie realised Alya had collected all of the papers and documents from the lab and slotted them into the research journal. They would be leaving no sign that they had been in the watchtower at all.

Once Kovalev had checked that all the doors were closed, he started busying himself with the switches, valves and displays that surrounded him. As the soldier looked back, Charlie caught sight of an expression on his face that he had never seen there before. He almost looked lost.

Finally, there came the unmistakable crunching of jackboots on uneven, gravelled ground. Charlie caught the sharp snap of orders and updates as they were barked across the crash site by the soldiers.

'No one here!'

'Check the tower!'

'No sign of them so far!'

'No one make a sound,' Kovalev breathed, his fingers clenched around the stock and action of his rifle. His eyes were fixed on the door that led out onto the roof of the Facility. 'Dragomir will try to goad us into revealing our position. He's not stupid. No matter what he says, do *not* retaliate.'

Inside the helicopter, everyone was holding their breath. Charlie saw Kovalev's eyes narrow as a figure came into view in front of them. Charlie followed his eyeline, and recognised Arron Dragomir immediately. He was striding leisurely to and fro in a wide figure of eight around the space in front of the helicopters, supporting a rifle over his shoulders with one hand. A bandage was wrapped around one of his biceps. His head turned from side to side lazily as he observed the progress of his men. Then, he cleared his throat, and addressed the area at large.

'I'm speaking to you now, Charlie Carroway,' he began. He did not need to shout; his voice thundered effortlessly, and there was malice dripping from every word he spoke. 'You have stolen valuable Elysian property. Believe me, we are going to have a lot

142

of fun together when I find you, and then I will put you down like the mongrel dog you are.'

Seren had shuffled over so that she was sitting right next to Charlie.

'I *will* find you,' Dragomir continued. 'I can promise you that. I know you're close by. The Great Protector is enraged. To have stolen his daughter, and his prototype ...' He shook his head, an unnerving smile of relish spreading across his face. 'It won't be quick, that's for sure. I know how to make a death drawn-out. I know how to make you suffer ...'

'I've had enough of listening to this cretin.' Seren was seething. 'Get us in the air.'

'Got it.' Kovalev's knuckles were white. 'Everyone, make sure you're strapped in.'

Kovalev's finger reached for a switch, but he stopped dead at Dragomir's next words.

'I suppose you're out there too, Vaska, you traitorous rat.'

In front of him, Charlie saw Alya glance fretfully at Kovalev, but Kovalev did not seem to notice. His eyes were fixed on Dragomir, his face devoid of all emotion.

'I bet you never even considered the possibility that I might outrank you someday,' Dragomir went on, his boastful drawl clear for all those present to hear. 'Well, the day has come, brother. To think that you were weak enough to betray Elysia, to become a traitor to your own country, your commander, your men.'

'Vasco,' Alya whispered, but he silenced her with a shake of his head.

Dragomir's voice took on a cold fury as he continued. 'You are a coward and a deserter. If it were up to me, I would shoot you on sight, right between the eyes, like the common criminal you are ...' He exhaled deeply. 'But I need to set an example to my men. I will enjoy seeing the punishment that is coming to you, Vasco Kovalev. I intend to be the one standing before you at dawn as you face the firing squad.'

Alya's hand had found Kovalev's, and she was gripping it tightly. A small smile lifted the corner of Kovalev's mouth, and Alya nodded wordlessly, as though reassured.

Dragomir was still speaking. He seemed to be warming to his theme. 'I swear to you now, Kovalev, when they tie you to the post and place the target over your heart, I won't turn my back on you for a second. I will look you straight in the eyes as I see you damned to the frozen depths of the ninth hell. It seems that in the end you can't outrun bad blood, doesn't it?'

'Is anyone else starting to get bored?' Kovalev asked, still perfectly calm.

'What d'you mean, *starting*?' Charlie muttered, and Kovalev flashed him a smile.

'And once *he's* out of the way,' Dragomir continued, adopting a silky tone that made Charlie shudder, 'I'll be able to take care of you properly, Miss Alexandra, just as I always promised you I would ...'

Charlie noticed that Alya had drawn herself closer to Kovalev at Dragomir's words. She was gripping his arm so tightly her knuckles had gone white, her whole body visibly shaking as she buried her face in his shoulder. Kovalev was grinding his teeth. The look of pure loathing on his face as he watched Dragomir's amusement was like nothing Charlie had ever seen before. Kovalev made a sudden movement towards the cockpit door, but Charlie seized his arm to stop him.

'What are you doing?' Kovalev demanded in a furious whisper.

'Following your orders. Maybe even saving your life.'

'I can handle him. You stay here and –' He broke off, as a whirring sound started up from all around them. 'What in the nine hells did you just do?'

'You're going to want to stay where you are,' Charlie said, drawing his index finger away from the switch Kovalev had been about to press. 'Get us out of here in one piece, flyboy.'

Through the glass in front of him, he watched the soldiers massing around the helicopter, drawn by the commotion, their rifles raised. Dragomir stood before them, staring right at him. Charlie glared back, refusing to let himself look away.

'What's happening?' Alya shrieked over the noise, her voice high-pitched.

'Hold on!' Kovalev yelled back, his hands on the cyclic control between his knees.

Charlie's stomach lurched sickeningly as – slowly, steadily – they began to rise up into the air. It felt so unnatural that he had to shut his eyes just to stay calm. Alya was screaming, and Kovalev was shouting something that sounded like a frantic prayer. Seren was laughing gleefully. Over the sound of their voices and the whirring of blades above their heads, Charlie could hear the panicked clamour of the soldiers on the rooftop below.

Peeling one eye open at a time, Charlie strained to see what was going on. From his position just behind the cockpit, he had a clear view of the scene on the rooftop. Some of the soldiers had dropped their weapons and were pointing and staring up at the helicopter with open-mouthed astonishment. Others were fleeing to a safe distance, yelling incoherently. Dragomir alone remained where he was, his hands at his hips, his head cocked slightly to one side, his eyes narrowed.

'Bring them out.'

Dragomir shouted the order to his men, but his eyes were fixed on Charlie. Charlie frowned, his eyes drawn to a flurry of movement by the door leading to the roof. A group of soldiers had appeared, each of them guarding a single prisoner. As the small figures drew closer, Charlie recognised them, and a terrible scream started building inside his head.

Dragomir laughed. 'I even brought the old woman here just for you, Charlie …'

The soldiers led Charlie's family out onto the roof, lining them up and forcing them all down onto their knees. Their hands had been tied behind their backs. With a nod from Dragomir, each of the soldiers pointed a gun to their prisoner's head. Even from this distance, Charlie could hear the frightened cries and whimpers of the children as they cowered at the feet of the soldiers.

'Look away,' Kovalev told him, his eyes shuttered. 'You don't want to see this.'

They were still rising. Charlie's whole body had gone rigid. 'I have to save them.'

'He can't – he *can't*.' Seren was gripping her head, her eyes wide, her body shaking.

'Vasya, just go – get us out of here!' Alya urged. 'There's nothing we can do for them!'

The helicopter began to hover higher, drifting over towards the edge of the building. Charlie released the buckles and straps securing him to his seat. He stood up. One of his hands was on the roof of the helicopter, while the other had found the handle of the passenger side door.

'What the *hell* d'you think you're –?'

Kovalev had turned right around in his seat, his face softening from anger to fear as he looked at Charlie. Whatever he had been about to say seemed to die on his lips as Charlie met his gaze. They continued to stare into each other's eyes for a few moments, as something unspoken passed between them.

'Get Seren out of here,' Charlie said, opening the door, 'and don't come back for me.'

'Wait!' Horrified understanding dawned on Vasco's face. 'What are you –?'

'Give yourself up and they won't be harmed, Carroway,' Dragomir drawled.

'Charlie, don't jump!' Vasco shouted, steering them away. 'Alya, don't let him do it!'

Alya stretched as far as she could, grabbing Charlie's t-shirt. 'Vasco, go – *now*!'

Charlie tore himself out of her reach. 'Get off me! I don't need your help!'

'Charlie, *no*!' Vasco's voice cracked as he reached out a hand. 'What are you *doing*?'

Steeling himself, Charlie leapt from the helicopter, his bent knees cushioning his fall as he hit the roof and rolled over, again and again. Dizzy and shaken, but seemingly without any broken bones, Charlie got to his feet. The world was spinning around him. He winced, breathing hard. His skin felt like it was on fire. His wrist was bleeding.

He heard the whir of the helicopter behind him but refused to look back. The sun was beginning to set, dying the sky over the mountains orange and red. Ruby, Leo and Dima were crying out for him. Cold rage blazed inside him, right down to the bones, as the breeze lifted his hair. He took a step forward, his legs trembling, and pulled the gun from his waistband.

'You've got me,' he said, pointing it at Dragomir. 'Now let them go.'

'Drop the gun,' Dragomir shot back, 'and don't try anything stupid.'

Charlie's eyes darted to his family, each of them held at gunpoint by a soldier. He saw the fear in their faces. The whole world seemed to have stilled in front of his eyes. His hands shaking, he found his thoughts returning to the story he had told the children, only a few nights before. The memory of his own words replayed inside his head, drowning out everything else.

'Luckily for these three kids, though, there was a brave knight who lived nearby called Charlie, and he saw how frightened they were by the monsters, and it made him sad. He knew he wanted to help the three children somehow. So, one day, he went out with his sword and he fought for them. Then the monsters were gone, forever, and the three kids were happy ...'

'What happened to Charlie?'

'He was happy too,' Charlie murmured, 'because he knew he had saved the children.'

He threw the gun along the ground towards Dragomir.

Moving leisurely, Dragomir picked it up. His eyes remained on the helicopter as it drifted higher into the sky, pulling swiftly away from the building. 'No way out now,' he purred, his face alive with a savage hunger. 'Still sure you made the right choice, Carroway?'

'I surrender,' Charlie said, fighting to keep his voice steady. 'Let them go.'

'What are those brats whining about?' Dragomir snapped at one of the soldiers as he returned to stand beside the children. Charlie could not hear the soldier's reply, but Dragomir threw back his head and burst out laughing.

Charlie's hands curled into fists. 'What's so funny?' he asked, his voice low, his teeth gritted.

'These little brats think you're going to save them,' Dragomir cried, shaking his head with a malevolent grin. 'Go on, indulge me – how are you going to save them, Charlie?'

Three gunshots rang out in quick succession, echoing across the rooftop before Charlie had even opened his mouth to reply. June, Leo and Dima's bodies sagged in the hands of their captors, then slumped to the ground. Charlie blinked, totally numb, watching as their blood pooled around them over the gravel.

'You said you wouldn't hurt them …'

'Did I?' Dragomir's eyes gleamed. 'I don't remember saying anything about that …'

Towering above her, he aimed his gun between Ruby's eyes and pulled the trigger. But nothing happened. He had run out of bullets. Charlie watched, frozen to the spot, his throat too dry to speak, as Dragomir tutted to himself. He checked the magazine of the gun Charlie had thrown to him, then placed the muzzle against Ruby's temple. His eyes remained on Charlie's face, his grin widening.

'Charlie …' Ruby whispered, staring at him with huge, terrified eyes. 'Please …'

'I'll do whatever you want!' Charlie screamed. 'Please! *Please*, just let her go!'

He felt his legs give way as Dragomir fired the last shot and flung Ruby's twitching body to the ground. As Charlie fell to his knees, a hollow sensation began to spread through his heart. He blinked through tears, his knife somehow in his hands, his arms shaking as he held it out towards Dragomir.

As Dragomir strode towards him, Charlie turned the point of the blade towards himself. The next moment, he felt agonising pain lance through his arm as Dragomir lashed out, his boot connecting with Charlie's hand. The knife flew from his fingers and skidded away. Charlie cradled his hand to his chest, his head bent as uncontrollable sobs wracked his entire body.

'Did you think I'd let you have it so easy?' Dragomir hissed into his ear. 'I already told you – there's no way out for you now.'

He straightened up, his fingers digging into Charlie's scarred shoulder so hard it made him yelp with pain. Charlie struggled, fighting to get free, but Dragomir only tightened his grip.

'Give him something to make sure he behaves himself,' Dragomir ordered, his voice hard and cold. 'I have big plans for him later.'

Before Charlie had time to react, one of the soldiers had crouched down beside him and stuck a needle into the crook of his arm. Charlie felt hands across his body. Something told him he should resist, but his limbs were too heavy. He could barely lift his fingers. As the world grew dim around him, he slumped to his side on the ground, a deep fog clouding his mind.

Blinking slowly, his gaze settled on the dead faces of his family, their eyes open but unseeing. He fought to stay awake, but his eyelids felt like lead.

The sun was about to dip behind the horizon. The last rays of the sunset burnt everything before him away into shimmering golden light.

A single tear tracked its way across his nose and down his cheek.

'That's right. I like you better this way.' The same menacing voice. 'Take him away.'

CHAPTER 15

H alf-formed torments swam through Charlie's clouded mind.

He could not see. He could not move. His throat was raw. Someone kept screaming.

'Administering another dose.' The sound of a bored, vaguely familiar voice.

'Let's see you try and fight me now.' His scarred shoulder burning under a fierce grip.

The pinprick of a needle at his neck, his heart thumping far too fast, then empty space.

*

Ruby was staring up at him, blood dripping from her mouth. 'Charlie?' Her eyes were bleary, as though she had recently woken up from a dream. She patted the bony arm of the elderly woman beside her. 'Granny, it's Charlie. Charlie's here.'

'I'm here.' Charlie gathered them both into a tight embrace, holding them to his chest, determined that nothing would ever make him let go of them again. 'I came back for you.'

'I knew you'd save us, Charlie,' Ruby whispered, smiling.

Charlie looked around wildly, his insides burning. 'Where are Leo and Dima?'

'The soldiers came and took them away,' June said. 'They're already gone.'

'We'll be fine.' Charlie's eyes travelled over the chains that were tangling around all of their limbs. He tried to force away the twisting feeling in the pit of his stomach. 'I'll get you out of here first, then I'll find the boys.'

'It's too late for that, Charlie.' Something red was blossoming at June's temple.

'Granny, don't –' Charlie stared into her eyes as they rolled back in her head, blood pouring down her cheeks from the gaping wounds. 'Don't say that. I – I'm going to save you, all right?'

'You couldn't save us, Charlie.'

'*No.*' It escaped his throat as a guttural moan, something almost feral. He tried to pull at their hands, his teeth gritted. But they were so heavy that he could not move them even an inch. 'Come *on*! Why won't you come with me?'

'There's nothing you can do.' June's mouth lolled open, her head slumped to one side.

Tears began to spill out of Charlie's eyes, running down his cheeks in a steady flow. 'I left you,' he choked. 'There was so much I … I only wanted …' The raw panic inside him was starting to spiral out of control. 'Why can't I *do* anything? Why can I never do *anything*?'

'Will you play with me now, Charlie?' Ruby whispered. 'You won't leave, will you?'

'I'm sorry,' Charlie sobbed. He covered his face with his hands as the skin disappeared from her face, leaving behind a small skull and two hollow, empty eye sockets. 'It should have been me. I wish I could … I'm so sorry …'

'Charlie …' the wide, yawning mouth of the skull moaned. 'Will you tell me a story?'

*

'Can't you do something to shut him up? All this screaming is killing my head.'

'I'm not going near that mouth of his again – he almost bit my hand off last time.'

'He will wear himself out eventually. Be patient. This is all part of the process.'

'And how long can we expect this process to take, Doctor Ivanov?'

'It's highly individual, sire. There's really no way to say for sure.'

'Trust me, I know just what he needs.'

His jaw was prised open, a foreign object forced into his mouth. His screams were muffled. His eyes were wide underneath a black cloth. The world was dark and fathomless.

'I remember when he used to make noises like that all the time. I missed that sound.'

Soft laughter. The brush of a proprietary touch along bare skin. 'This look suits you. No one's coming to save you. You know that, don't you? You're all on your own now.'

*

What felt like much later, though in truth he had no idea how much time had passed, Charlie returned to his senses. He found himself sitting on a familiar bed, his hands twisted in his lap. He did not know how he had gotten there. Perhaps someone had thought it was the best place to put him for now. Maybe they had decided it was a good idea to leave him to sit in silence on his own for a while. He remembered he had done something bad again. They had made him do it.

A length of rope ran from his wrists to the iron bedframe. His prison. Sitting on the edge of the bed, his feet did not yet touch the wooden floorboards. The last thing he remembered was his brother's face, but why he was thinking of his brother, he did not know.

The door creaked open, and he caught sight of the lower half of an adult man's body, followed by another, and another, until the room was full. He did not let himself look up. He had buried it all deep within him, long ago. Nothing would ever be enough to dredge it back up. His skin felt too tight. Somewhere beyond the padlocked window, someone was screaming.

'Have you thought about what you did?'

'You know what we want.'

'You'd better not fight us this time.'

*

'Another.'

'Out of interest, Doctor, how do you know when you've pushed too far?'

'He hasn't broken yet, has he? He can take it.'

'He looks kind of … not all there.'

'Well, that is to be expected.'

A needle pierced through skin near his throat. The dim shapes before his eyes started to swim in front of him as his vision began to blur. He felt strangely light and empty. A numb sensation was creeping through his veins, starting at his heart. He felt it coursing its way down his bones, all the way through his body, to the ends of his fingers and into his toes.

'Don't fight it.'

The feeling threatened to consume him. He glanced across to the bedstead again and frowned. It was still there, the frame no longer made of iron, but of wood. He reached out to touch it. It felt wrong. His fingers moved, yet his wrists were blocked by something solid. There was the familiar touch of cold metal against his skin. But it was only a vague feeling, somehow just out of reach, like a day-old dream.

A little skeleton with red hair was running around beside him, like it wanted him to come and play.

*

He was in the dormitory of the orphanage where he had lived before the nightmares began. He looked up and down the rows of beds, each of them covered with the same rough brown blanket and single pillow, and slowly got to his feet. The tall, narrow windows at the end of the room let in the weak winter sunlight, which shone on the dust particles drifting through the air.

The room was exactly as he remembered it from a decade ago. The walls were bare, and the single shelving unit at the end of the room closest to the door was empty. There was not a single toy or game to be seen. As he crossed the room towards the door, he caught sight of the battered trunks lying underneath each bed that he passed. They contained all the meagre possessions that each boy who occupied a bed in that room owned. It was daytime, so the dormitory was empty.

Tentatively, he reached out to grasp the rusted doorknob on the splintered wooden door and pulled it open. He stepped out into the dark, narrow corridor, its walls cracked and chipped, finding his way by instinct towards the dayroom. He knew that this was where he was supposed to go. When they were not in lessons, the boys were put to work in the kitchen or required to do yard work or to scrub the floors. But Charlie somehow knew that this day was different for him, and that he was supposed to be in the dayroom.

This was by far the most welcoming room in the orphanage. It was the only room the boys were ever allowed into whose walls were painted. There was a box of toys in the corner that they were encouraged to play with. In the middle of the room, there was a small table, where they would find a box of crayons, and papers to colour on. The boys always looked forward to the times they were allowed into the dayroom. It meant that they would get a break from the cross words, rough hands, and hard work, at least for a while. For some of them, it even offered the opportunity to escape from the orphanage forever.

When he stepped through the stone archway into the dayroom, Charlie saw what he had expected to see, but it still caught him by such surprise that he faltered. He found himself torn between a desire to see and not to see, to remember and to forget. Two boys were sitting in comfortable silence by the small table in the middle of the room, their dark heads bent over their own tasks.

Charlie approached them. His six-year-old self was drawing a bird, while his older brother was colouring a picture of a house. As he examined his brother's drawing more closely, Charlie identified four clumsily-drawn stick figures. There was an adult man and a woman, and two young boys, all with smiling faces. He watched his younger self push the crayons away before getting to his feet and hurrying straight past him on unsteady legs.

'Where are you going, Charlie?' His brother did not look up from his drawing.

'I'm going to get my book,' his childhood self replied, pointing towards the dormitory.

Charlie felt his breath catch in his chest as a painful memory pierced him. That was right, he had once loved to read. He had been learning how to do it in the orphanage, and he had been good at it. There was a teacher there who used to smile at him and tell him she was so proud that he was reading by himself already …

Charlie shook himself and made to follow his younger self back to the dormitory. He wanted to know what book he had been reading all those years ago. The desire to watch this childhood version of himself doing something that he no longer had any ability to do gnawed at him like hunger.

'But we were told to stay here,' his older brother reminded him. 'The people will be here soon. It might be a mama and papa.'

'I don't want another mama or papa,' his younger self said simply, and walked away.

Charlie felt hot tears prick the corner of his eyes as he mouthed the same words at the same time. He remembered saying those words. He remembered how he had thought nothing of going back to the dormitory that day. He had never even had a chance to say goodbye.

'No,' he strained to say, his voice echoing faintly inside his own head. 'Don't go.'

He reached out a hand helplessly, as though he could do something to stop his younger self from taking those fateful steps back to the dormitory, back to his books. He stayed rooted to the spot as he heard movement behind him. When he looked over his shoulder, the scene was becoming oddly hazy, the light from the windows into the playroom over-bright.

Two adults had appeared in the room – a middle-aged couple, well-dressed and smiling, though Charlie could not make out their faces clearly. He had never seen them, but he had imagined them often enough. The man would have kind eyes and would want to teach him things. The woman would have warm arms and would feel like home.

The scene began to dissolve in front of his eyes, vanishing like smoke in the air. He was left with nothing but a hollow space in the pit of his stomach. Then the terrible sound of his childhood self discovering that his brother – his only family – was gone forever screamed through his head. Charlie covered his face with his hands, his whole body racked with sobs.

There was so much pain in that sound that he thought he would die from it. It was too much for him to bear any longer. He knew

155

where that little boy had run away to next, and what had happened to him once he got there. He could not take any more.

His eyes shot open.

He was not alone.

*

'Charlie? Are you lucid yet?'

Charlie blinked slowly, his gaze unsteady and unfocused. With some effort, he raised his eyes. A slight, pale young man was standing in front of him, his bright eyes gleaming. He wore round glasses, and his hands were hidden in the pockets of a long white lab coat. Sharp-featured, with high cheekbones and a jutting chin, his curly hair was the same shade of brown as Charlie's. They shared the same slightly crooked nose.

'Max,' Charlie wanted to say, but though his mouth moved, no sound came out.

'Can you hear me?' his brother asked, tilting his head to one side. Drawing closer, he removed a needle from one of his pockets. 'You've worn yourself out, haven't you? I'm going to draw some more blood now. Don't struggle!' he added, as Charlie seized up at the sight of it and tried to jerk away. 'Just relax. This is something different. It won't be like before ...'

Exhaustion creeping through his body, Charlie allowed himself to go limp, his eyes drifting to the needle stuck in the crook of his arm. His sweatshirt was gone. He felt strangely light, and his head was spinning. He shifted his hands, feeling metal against his bare skin. Both of his wrists had been secured to the arms of a chair with a pair of handcuffs. He glanced up, and saw his own fear and confusion mirrored in his older brother's eyes.

'They needed to restrain you to keep you from hurting yourself.' The needle was withdrawn.

His voice raw, Charlie managed to rasp out a single word. 'Why?'

'I need to check something again,' Max said, as though talking to himself, 'before ...'

Charlie swallowed, his throat dry and ragged. 'Why is this happening to me?'

'It's not going to kill you.' Max shrugged. 'You've survived worse.'

'How do you know that?' The question escaped him in a whisper.

'Well, you weren't exactly being quiet about it.' A thin smile shifted his brother's delicate features. 'Even that animal of a lieutenant eventually got tired of your screaming, which, believe me, is something I never thought I would witness.'

'What is this place?' Charlie asked, shifting towards the edge of his chair.

Max regarded him steadily, stroking his sharp chin as he did so. He seemed deep in thought. 'Whatever you're imagining,' he began, relishing the words, 'it's a whole lot worse.'

'We could get out of here,' Charlie said desperately. 'We could escape – together.'

A soft furrow appeared in Max's brow. 'Why would I want that?' he asked, sounding genuinely confused. 'I'm exactly where I want to be.'

'Do you even know what they're doing to the people they've got imprisoned here?'

'I'm learning more here than I ever have before. I want to be part of this discovery.'

'You do realise there are children trapped here? Someone's got to do something!'

'Do I need to give you another dose,' Max warned, sharp-edged, 'little brother?'

Charlie felt a hairline fracture crack somewhere in his mind, as a terrible realisation threatened to break upon him. With some effort, he pushed it away. He would not – he could not – believe it.

'But the things they're doing – the experiments,' he said. 'It's – it's not right.'

Max's eyes narrowed, lending his youthful face a hard, dangerous look. 'Whatever is going on in that thuggish mind of yours, I suggest you put a stop to it, for your own sake.' He backed away, his hands returning to the pockets of his lab coat. 'Nothing you do will make any difference. You may have been an urchin prince out on the streets, but you are powerless here.'

'I always believed that I would find you,' Charlie found himself saying. He saw Max, who had turned on his heel to leave, pause at his words. 'There was a window in my bedroom. They always kept it locked. I couldn't reach it, but I could see the sky from the bed. I used to count the stars every single night – it was the only thing that kept me from losing my mind. On each one, I made a wish. Always the same one. I wished I would get back to you, someday.'

Max did not turn around. 'If you had just listened to me, none of it would have happened.'

Charlie watched his brother leave the cell, his words ringing in his ears. He let his head hang low, his neck stiff and aching, and closed his eyes. He breathed through the feelings that rose up, swirled around, reached their peak, and gradually began to fade. What remained, he forced deep down inside of himself.

There had been no sound of a key turning in a lock. Perhaps Max had forgotten about it, or perhaps they had thought that – with Charlie drugged and restrained – there would be no need for one. He opened his eyes, his heart beating fast in his chest. He knew what he had to do.

Craning his neck down towards his shoulder and upper arm, he drew a mouthful of the material of his t-shirt between his teeth, gathering as much of it into his mouth as he could. He pressed his knee against the arm of the chair, pushing up the handcuff and keeping it taught.

He brought his thumb back under his palm, twisting it as far as it would go. Then he wrenched his hand through the gap, his agony muffled as skin shredded beneath metal until, at last, his hand was free. He allowed himself to heave in one ragged breath. He swallowed the bile that rose in his throat at the sight of what he had done to himself.

Then he did it again with his other hand.

His shoulders trembling, a sheen of sweat covering his forehead, Charlie staggered towards the door to the cell. His knuckles were ruined, and both his thumbs were twitching horribly. The taste of adrenaline still at the back of his throat,

Charlie knew he still had some time before he would feel the full extent of the pain. He collapsed against the frame, edging the door open the slightest fraction, enough to see that the passageway was dark and empty.

'Powerless, am I?' he muttered, kicking the door open, his breathing heavy as his chest rose and fell rapidly. 'Think I can't make a difference, huh? Just wait – I'll show you ...'

He was on his own. His family were gone. No one was coming to save him.

But he was alive – and he was not the only person imprisoned in the Volya Facility.

Charlie knew then what he had to do next. No matter what it took, no matter what the cost, he was going to make sure the other prisoners were set free. He was going to get them out.

Every last one of them.

The passageway was lined on both sides with countless locked doors. Charlie took a step forward, unsure where to begin. Then he halted in his tracks, drawn by movement a few doors down from his cell. He caught a snatch of unpleasant laughter and narrowed his eyes. As the door opened outwards, Charlie heard the sound of two male voices, neither of which he recognised. This was likely to be his only chance.

Without hesitation, Charlie flattened his back against the wall and stalked closer towards the guards. He made sure to stay in their blind spot, hidden behind the open door of the cell. He knew, after what had been necessary to escape the cuffs, that his hands would be useless in a fight. He braced himself for a quick, brutal scuffle, calling on all the experience he had ever learnt in his time spent fighting on the streets.

When the guards made to close the door behind them, he launched himself forward, catching them both unawares. He was faster than they were, and they had no warning. He brought one of the guards crashing to the ground with a roundhouse kick to the head. Spinning through, carried by his own momentum, Charlie smashed his knee into the second guard, bringing him down as well. He took the set of keys that one of the men had let fall from his hand, as well as a handgun, which he stuck in the back of his jeans.

'What d'you think is happening out there?' he heard a girl ask, as he entered the cell.

Charlie's eyes fell on a group of about thirty children, all of them female. Most of them looked around the age of ten, and he guessed that none of them were as old as he was. Their hands were not restrained, and some of the older girls had their arms around the younger ones, who looked terrified. Charlie realised, rage pounding in his head, that all of them had their ankles shackled. They were chained together on a much longer chain that was fixed into an iron hook set into the floor. While most of the girls wore collars, a few of their throats were bare.

'Please,' one of the older girls said hesitantly, 'don't take us back to the machines …'

'Don't worry, I'm a friend,' Charlie said, his fury rising at the images that sprang to the forefront of his mind at her words.

He knelt beside them and, one by one, unlocked the shackles keeping them prisoner. The pain in his hands steadied him.

'Come on, I'm getting you all out of here, right now,' he said, picking up two of the smallest girls and leading the way out of the cell. 'Follow me. Quickly.'

It was with some relief that Charlie found the girls were willing to follow his orders. He stood at the door as they all hurried out into the passageway, looking around them with anxious expressions. The younger girls clustered around the older ones, but they seemed to know without being told that they must be quiet.

Once he had checked that the cell was empty, Charlie headed to the front of the group, leading the way. Then, as he looked back, his eyes scanning the girls' faces, a thought hit him.

'Wait,' he said, and the others stopped at once. 'Has anyone seen a little girl with red hair? Saga?'

'You mean the little Casimir coven girl?' one of the older girls asked, pushing her glasses up her nose as she pointed along the passageway. 'She's in one of those cells back there. It's the one with the red door.'

Charlie eased the two girls he was carrying out of his arms and set them on their feet. 'You older kids look after the younger ones, all right?' he said. 'Don't let them fall behind.'

'You're not coming with us?' the girl with glasses called after him as he tore away.

Charlie threw the set of keys to her. 'Take these and get out of here. You come across any guards, don't hold back. Kill them all. Don't stop running 'til you find somewhere safe.'

'What about you?'

'I'm not leaving this place without her.' He glanced over his shoulder to see them all still standing beside the cell. 'What are you waiting for?' he demanded. 'Don't look back – *go*!'

'Hey!' the girl shouted, as the others started running. 'What's your name?'

'My name's Charlie,' he said. 'Now go, and don't let them catch you. Don't you ever let me see your faces around here again, you hear me?'

He planted his feet in front of the cell with the red door, and, aiming the gun squarely at the keyhole, shot the lock off. Inside the room, there stood a single wire cage. And inside the cage, there was a little girl with a tear-stained face. Her hair was the colour of fire.

CHAPTER 16

'You're Saga, aren't you?' he said, as he approached the cage. He did not need to ask. It was as though he were looking at her older sister in miniature.

The little girl had shrunk back to the far end of the cage. Her huge, dark eyes darted between his face and the gun in his hand. 'L-Leave me alone,' she said, her small voice wobbling.

With deliberately slow movements, Charlie placed the gun on the ground, so that it was as far away from the cage as his reach would allow. 'Don't be scared,' he said, softening his voice as he held his hands up to the wire to show her they were empty. 'I'm not going to hurt you.'

She watched him with wide eyes, her body still frozen with fear. 'Who are you?'

'I'm Charlie, and I'm here to rescue you.'

'You *are*?' She whispered the last word a little breathlessly, her eyes filling with tears.

'It's all right to cry,' Charlie said, keeping his voice even, as he fought to steady his emotions. 'I promise you, this feeling won't last forever.' He drew the bobby pin from his hair and fitted it into the lock at the front of her cage. 'I'm going to get you out now,' he told her.

Saga kept her gaze fixed on him as the lock clicked free. Charlie opened the door to the cage and offered her his hand. She had shuffled forward a little but seemed unable to force herself to move any closer towards him. Crouching down, Charlie held out his arms inside the cage, their faces level with one another.

'Is it all right with you if I pick you up?' he asked. 'I want to take you to a safe place.'

Saga reached out for him with a tiny nod of her head, her tears still falling. 'Please?'

Charlie gathered her into his arms, protecting her head with one of his hands as he drew her out of the cage. Once she was out, he straightened up, holding her close to his chest and gently rocking her to and fro. The warm weight of her in his arms was a familiar sensation. She stared up into his face with long-lashed eyes, her thumb in her mouth. She was smaller than Ruby had been.

'I forgot to tell you,' he said. 'I'm friends with your sister. Did you know that?'

'With Seren?' Saga shifted a little in his arms, her face brightening up at once.

'That's right,' Charlie said, nodding as the sight of her toothy smile sent a grin spreading across his own face. 'She's a good friend of mine. Did you know she's been looking for you, all this time?' He brushed a tear from her cheek. 'Seren loves you very much, Saga.'

Huge tears welled up in the little girl's eyes, falling silently. 'I want my big sister ...'

Charlie held her closer to his body. 'You'll see her again soon,' he said. 'Believe me?'

Then he heard a gun being cocked behind him, followed by the sound of a cool, drawling voice. 'It didn't have to be like this, Charlie,' Faulkner said. 'Turn around – slowly.'

Charlie did as he was told. Faulkner stood a couple of paces away from him, his gun pointed directly between Charlie's eyes. Charlie's gaze flitted from his own gun, discarded on the floor, to Faulkner's triumphant sneer, to Saga's frightened face. With a gentle touch, he tilted her face towards his chest, away from the sight of the gun.

'Close your eyes,' he told her.

Faulkner lowered his gun, pointing it at Saga. 'My aim is better than yours, you know.'

Charlie stared back at him, statuesque, his blood boiling.

Faulkner raised an eyebrow. 'What is this obsession you have with waifs and strays, Charlie? I'm beginning to see a pattern …'

'What do you want?' Charlie managed to ask, as Saga bunched his t-shirt in her fist.

Faulkner's smug smile twisted the scar across his mouth. 'I want you to put her back.'

His body stiff with tension, Charlie turned, placing Saga back into the cage. 'Your sister is coming, Saga,' he told her, as quietly as he could, while she stared up at him desperately, her eyes brimming with tears. 'She'll get you out of here, I promise. She hasn't forgotten about you. Don't give up, all right?'

'Lock her in,' Faulkner ordered, making no attempt to mask the pleasure in his words.

Charlie snapped the lock back in place and met Saga's eyes. Something pierced his heart at the sight of the little girl's anxious expression as she stared back at him.

'Don't be scared,' he said to her – he begged her, his voice cracking on the words. 'Everything's going to be fine.'

'Get on your knees with your hands behind your head,' Faulkner said, his voice flat as he watched Charlie follow his orders. 'You even think about trying anything, and she's dead.'

'Leave her alone,' Charlie snarled, as Saga whimpered in the cage. 'It's me you want.'

'And now I've got you,' Faulkner said. He approached Charlie, lifting his chin with the muzzle of his gun, so that Charlie was forced to raise his eyes to Faulkner's arrogant face. 'It's a shame. That's another person you've let down, isn't it? The list must be getting fairly long by now.' He shook his head, his smile broadening. 'You are such a disappointment.'

'I hope I never stop disappointing you,' Charlie said, relishing the words, his face set.

Faulkner heaved a sigh. 'You're going to wish you had just done as you were told.'

Charlie caught the flash of movement as Faulkner drew back the hand holding his gun. He heard the crack of metal against bone as Faulkner pistol-whipped him straight across the face. Saga was crying out his name.

He was on the floor, his head spinning. There was blood everywhere. His hands throbbed dully with pain. He had not noticed how much it hurt until now.

Then there was only darkness.

*

'Rise and shine, sleepyhead.'

'Wh-Where am I?'

Charlie became aware of himself in stages. He was on his feet, lashed to a steel support pole in the middle of a dimly lit room. Heavy chains bound his chest, legs, and ankles. His restraints were tight enough that they rubbed painfully against his skin when he shifted his body to test their strength. His arms, chained above him, felt like lead. There was blood on his skin where it had dripped down from his hands. With his wrists shackled, he could barely move.

He was trapped.

With difficulty, Charlie's eyes focused on the shape before him. Hunting knife in hand, Dragomir was watching him with a dangerous, almost elated look in his bright, cold eyes.

'It's been a while,' he said, smirking. 'No kiss good morning? Didn't you miss me?'

'You ...' Charlie gritted his teeth, fury blazing inside him as he strained against the chains holding him still. 'You *motherf–*!'

His head snapped to the side as Dragomir struck him. Skin burning, icy rage slowing his movements, Charlie turned his face back towards his captor, glaring at the man who stood leering in front of him.

'You've been busy, haven't you?' Dragomir sounded amused. He took a step forwards, his muscular arms folded, his eyes trailing along Charlie's body. 'I'm told you even went on a little playdate after our last encounter. Did I leave you wanting more?'

Charlie froze at the sly, knowing look on Dragomir's face. He refused to think about what it meant. 'Where is she?' he demanded, a low growl in his voice. 'What the fuck have you done to her?'

Dragomir placed his hand on Charlie's scarred shoulder and pushed him back against the metal pole, smirking at the whine of pain that Charlie could not help but let escape. It was only then that Charlie realised he had still been straining his body against the chains. His neck was stiff with tension, the skin around his wrists already rubbed raw. Dragomir took in Charlie's furious expression with a brief chuckle, as though he was mildly entertained by it.

'Now, whatever happened to my obedient little prisoner from up on the roof?' he asked. His tone was playful as he placed the point of his knife to Charlie's chin and nicked the skin, tipping his face to one side. 'Although, I have to admit,' he added silkily, bringing the blade up to brush Charlie's eyelashes, 'I do have a soft spot for your aggressive side. Not planning to fight me, today?'

Charlie held himself very still, forcing himself not to blink. His heart was trembling.

'You haven't realised yet, have you?' Dragomir continued, trailing the flat of the blade down Charlie's cheek and delivering a sharp smack against his jaw with it. 'That traitor Kovalev isn't here to protect you this time. No one's coming to save you.' He stepped even closer, his breath hot against Charlie's neck. 'If anyone cared about you, don't you think they would have got here by now? You're alone.'

'No.' Charlie felt every muscle in his body lock into place as Dragomir strode casually behind him. 'Don't.'

'Which means,' Dragomir continued, his voice a low rumble in Charlie's ear as he brought his hand around Charlie's throat and began, almost tenderly, to squeeze, 'we can pick up right where we left off …'

It had begun when Dragomir had stepped out of his line of sight. Charlie had gradually started to feel somehow separate from himself. It was as though his body belonged to someone else, and the real Charlie was elsewhere, watching everything that was happening to him unfold from a distance. If he saw his body as a stranger, closed himself off, he knew he could survive this.

But, almost as though he were dragging Charlie on the end of a chain, Dragomir's voice forced him back to himself. Charlie knew then that the soldier would refuse to allow him any kind of escape. There were hands on his hips, moving him into position. Terror flooded him, along with searing pain.

'You thought you could kidnap the First Daughter?' The words were laced with violence. 'You thought you could humiliate me? Look at the state of you now, you worthless punk.'

'You're – wrong,' Charlie managed to grind out the words. 'She's a –' He fought not to say the word. He would not betray his friend. Not for anything. 'She – uh – she wanted to leave.'

'Why would she want that?'

'To get away from *you*? How the hell should I know?'

Dragomir had gone dangerously still. His grip tightened around Charlie's throat, his fingers pressing down on Charlie's windpipe, choking him. 'Lady Alexandra is of great value to me,' he murmured, as, wide-eyed and panic-stricken, Charlie fought for breath under his grip. 'I guess there's something in particular you wanted from her ... and I'm going to make you pay for that.'

'Huh?' Charlie wheezed, as Dragomir released his throat. 'I didn't want anything ...'

Dragomir had stopped. He strode back into Charlie's eyeline, his shoulders rising and falling with exertion. Charlie watched, hardly daring to breathe, as Dragomir removed a length of chain, and what looked like a metal pipe, from a hessian sack lying by the door.

'I brought some toys for us to play with.' Charlie watched a vicious smile spread across the soldier's face as Dragomir took in his expression. 'Don't you worry,' he said, prowling back towards Charlie, his voice almost becoming a purr as he added, 'I'll make sure you enjoy this too.'

Dragomir brought his face close to Charlie's, his twisted smile broadening, his eyes on Charlie's lips. There was a rushing in Charlie's ears. When he felt Dragomir's fingers pushing into his mouth, instinct took over.

Without thinking, he crunched down on them. He heard Dragomir's yell of surprise and pain, and was promptly rewarded with a backhanded slap, tasting copper in his mouth. He felt the cold metal of the chain as Dragomir wound it around his neck and pulled.

'You like it rough, you little whore?'

With a strangled moan, Charlie brought his eyes back up to meet Dragomir's. He was going to die here. That much was obvious. A reckless smile sliding across his face, he drew on all the reserves of strength and impotent rage he had left. Arching his neck, he sucked up all the blood that was swirling around inside his mouth and spat directly into Dragomir's face.

Dragomir let his grip on the chain around Charlie's neck go slack. His face darkened, his eyes flashing as he wiped away the blood. 'You're going to regret that, you damn hustler,' he growled, his fingers reaching for the knife at his belt.

'Touch me again and I'll kill you.' The taste of blood was thick on Charlie's tongue. 'I'll fucking kill you.'

For a second, Dragomir seemed not to know how to react. He blinked in surprise, ran a hand over his face, then threw his head back and laughed.

'Honestly, Carroway, sometimes you're too much,' he said at last, wiping away a tear as he mastered himself and smirked at Charlie's livid expression. 'But really, I think it's about time to shut you up.'

Charlie, who had been struggling hard against the chains binding him to the steel pole, stilled as Dragomir returned to the hessian sack. When he turned back, Charlie saw he was holding a metal ring in his hand, two leather straps trailing between his fingers. As Dragomir strode leisurely back towards him, Charlie fought harder, but it was no use. The chains would not give even an inch.

'I may not be able to kill you – yet.' Dragomir gripped the back of Charlie's head and yanked at his hair, forcing the metal ring between his teeth as he cried out in pain. 'But I don't have to. I'm going to break you instead.'

Through watering eyes, Charlie sensed the soldier moving behind him again, felt Dragomir securing the leather straps of the gag behind his head. The metal ring between his teeth not only forced his mouth open painfully wide but prevented him from closing it either. A strip of metal kept his tongue in place, so that any sounds he made were muffled and unintelligible. Drool was already beginning to spill down his chin. He shuddered and, bracing himself, kept struggling.

'You think this is bad?' Dragomir murmured, and Charlie froze as he felt Dragomir's knuckles brushing down his spine. 'Trust me, I haven't even begun yet. You don't have to hold back this time. Scream as much as you want. No one's coming to save you, remember?'

Charlie stiffened as he felt Dragomir's breath on his lower back. His tongue began to lick across the words of the brand stamped across Charlie's tailbone, caressing each letter one by one. Certain he was going to vomit, Charlie bucked and twisted against the chains keeping him still, his desperate sounds muffled by the gag in his mouth. He wanted to rip his skin off.

A cascade of memories collided with one another as he was wrenched, inextricably, back to his years of captivity. Hands on his skin; moans in his ear; the warm, inescapable weight of bodies crushing him – and then the white-hot agony and smell of burning flesh as he screamed himself hoarse, certain he would not survive, that he could not withstand the pain.

'I wonder if I might drag you away from your pleasure for a moment, Lieutenant?'

Charlie looked up, horrified at the idea that someone else would be witness to this.

'Sire. What are you doing here?' Dragomir stopped quickly. 'I hadn't expected –'

'You know how seriously I take my responsibility for the welfare of my possessions.'

The Great Protector spoke in a lazy drawl, an edge of cruel humour in his voice as he came to stand within touching distance of Charlie. His hands clasped behind his back, Nikolai Ignatiev bent his spine slightly, surveying Charlie with a thoughtful look on his face. There was a gleam in his eye that sent Charlie hopelessly, desperately straining against the chains that bound him.

'What a sight,' he murmured. He hooked a long finger around the metal ring in Charlie's mouth and started manoeuvring his head from side to side, as though examining a captured animal. 'After all these years of searching, you are finally mine.'

'Sire …' Dragomir, who had come to stand beside his master, threw a confused frown at Charlie. 'What are you saying?'

'The results are conclusive,' the Great Protector said, letting go of Charlie's head and trailing his fingers along the chains binding his chest to the steel pole. 'He is the one.'

'*What?*' Dragomir's lip curled as he took an involuntary step backwards.

Nikolai Ignatiev smiled as he moved his hands behind Charlie's head, releasing the straps that held the gag in place. Their eyes met, and Charlie found himself unable to look away. The Great Protector's eyes were unusually bright, the colour of grass in late spring.

'It looks to me as though you could use a helping hand,' he said, with a pleasant smile.

With some hesitation, Charlie opened his mouth wider, allowing the middle-aged man to remove the metal ring from between his teeth. The Great Protector turned it over in his hands, one eyebrow raised, something close to amusement on his face. Then he cast it aside, wiping the drool from his fingers on the sleeve of Charlie's t-shirt.

'Let me ask you something,' he said, his voice soft and polite. 'When you close your eyes and picture yourself, what do you see? Do you perhaps see yourself as I see you now?'

Burning with shame, Charlie blinked back furious tears. As though tired of waiting for his answer, Nikolai Ignatiev curled the chain that was still wound around Charlie's neck through his fingers. An almost fond smile brightening his sharp features, he jerked Charlie's head forward with one powerful movement.

'Nothing to say?'

'Please stop.' Charlie heard his own voice, small and exhausted. Broken. 'It hurts …'

Charlie felt his limbs begin to shake as Nikolai Ignatiev grasped his chin between his thumb and forefinger, tilting Charlie's face up to his own. 'My prize …' he murmured. 'You do not know how long I have waited for this day to arrive.' The gleam in his bright eyes and the fanatical edge to his smile made his face take on a mask-like appearance. 'And to think, they said you were a common thief …' His eyes roved over Charlie's face, now beaded with sweat. 'Who could have known you would turn out to be such a special prisoner?'

Dragomir looked faintly nauseated. 'You don't mean …'

Charlie yelped with pain as Nikolai Ignatiev grabbed a fistful of his hair and shook his head in Dragomir's direction. 'You don't see the family resemblance?' he asked mildly.

Releasing his grip, he stroked his fingers through Charlie's hair, a cruel smile lifting the corner of his mouth, as though his mind had lighted on a particularly pleasant memory.

'I was acquainted with your mother for a time, did you know that?' he said, still in the same conversational tone of voice, with only a hint of threat. 'Sweet, gentle Erin … I don't see much of her in you.'

'*Don't.*' Charlie jerked his head away. 'Don't talk about – about my mother …'

'Tell me, is she still alive? I hope she remembers our time together fondly – I certainly do.' Nikolai Ignatiev let out a soft laugh. 'I did so enjoy having her as my plaything, even if it was only for a brief *spell.*'

Charlie felt himself growing cold, his ears ringing. 'No …'

'She managed to twist out of my grasp in the end, regrettably. She ran off as soon as she managed to get my property out of her. Well, you never can trust a witch, I suppose.'

'*Stop.*' Charlie screwed up his eyes, fighting back the tears that burnt behind them.

That same laugh again. 'You're emotional. Good. I have high hopes for you.' He flicked idly at the chain hanging from Charlie's neck with his long, slender fingers. 'Perhaps you will prove to be even more interesting than she was …'

Clenching his fists, Charlie stared up at the cold face in front of him. 'Get the *fuck on with it*, then!'

Dragomir lunged forward with a strangled curse but halted in his tracks when Nikolai Ignatiev raised a hand. He was now looking genuinely entertained.

'A promising start,' he said, stifling a chuckle with one hand in front of his mouth. 'If I can be honest with you, I am curious to discover how long you will be able to hold out.' He looked between Charlie and Dragomir, a dangerous smile spreading across his face. 'I hope you two have had enough fun – playtime is over.'

'Don't come near me!' Charlie snarled, shifting helplessly against his restraints.

He let out a cry of pain as Nikolai Ignatiev lashed out with a knife, which he had drawn from his sleeve without warning. Charlie saw his own blood dripping down his forearm from a long, shallow cut. When he looked closer, he recognised the knife that was grasped in the Great Protector's hand. It was the same knife Dragomir had kicked out of his hand on the rooftop after executing his family. His own.

Charlie watched as the Great Protector whirled the knife in his fingers, examining it with interest before holding the blade against Charlie's cheek. With a smirk, he applied the slightest bit more pressure, and drew a light cut along Charlie's cheekbone. Charlie glared back at him, flinching, but forced himself not to betray any other reaction.

'You seem to have an unusually high tolerance for pain,' Nikolai Ignatiev murmured, seeming only vaguely interested in this observation. 'So you will have to be patient with us, while we see if you are fit to be put to any real use.'

'Sire, might I?' Dragomir had stepped forward, hunting knife in hand. His eyes were fixed on Charlie, who had to fight not to be physically sick at the look on his face.

'I would hardly deny you that pleasure, Lieutenant,' the Great Protector said, smirking. 'But we must make sure to take our time with him.' He drew his fingers along Charlie's cut face and brought them to his mouth, his tongue tasting Charlie's blood. 'This prisoner of ours is unlike any of the others. He deserves our closest attention, our finest treatment.'

Charlie, who had closed his eyes, trembling, felt one of his eyelids being prized open. He found himself unable to look away, horrified at what he saw. Nikolai Ignatiev's face was hovering right in the corner of his vision, his grin wide and terrifying.

'I wonder,' he mused, as he twirled the knife in his other hand, 'how much of your blood will we have to shed before you show us your true face?'

CHAPTER 17

The door to the Shadow Cells slid open with a terrible, high-pitched creak that echoed off the bare walls. Charlie, accustomed by now to who – and what – that noise announced, felt himself growing cold. A creeping sensation that spread slowly throughout his body told him he was starting to seize up. His mind was preparing itself to survive by beginning the process of shuttering itself from what he knew was to follow. There was no taunting laughter yet today.

He could feel himself fading. He would not be able to hold out much longer. He wondered how long it had been since they had chained him up and started working on him. Unbidden, his eyes drifted towards the door, wondering if he was imagining things again. There was a tall, familiar figure standing in the shaft of light. But it was not who he had expected it to be.

'Max?' He rasped out his brother's name. His voice was almost entirely gone.

'Charlie ...'

Someone rushed over towards him, someone he had thought he would never see again.

'Have you found him?' That was Seren's voice. No – she couldn't be here ...

'He's here! Vasya found him.' Alexandra. There was no way that this could be real.

'Is he –?' Someone's fingers touched his skin, and he flinched back, chains jangling.

'We need to get him out of these shackles.' Vasco's voice – controlled, dangerous.

'I'll handle it.' The sound of another girl's voice, one he had heard somewhere before.

'If you hurt him …' Vasco's words were edged with threat, sharp as a blade.

'Stop distracting me, I need to concentrate. Stand back – unless you want to get burnt.'

'But what if you –?' Vasco's question was strangled, his desperation loosed from him.

'I'll be able to heal him,' Seren said, her voice calm and gentle. 'Leave her to work.'

Charlie felt heat prick his skin like a knifepoint at his wrists. He jerked back, panicked, but the chains limited his movement, keeping him in place. Then the shackles on his right wrist broke, causing his weight to collapse towards his other side as he fell onto his shins.

Still half-suspended from the beam above his head, he hung by his left wrist, swaying slightly. Someone was unwinding the chain from around his throat, their fingers brushing his skin with a shocked intake of breath.

'What are …?'

His eyes flickered open. Charlie became dimly aware of Vasco beside him, bracing his body so that his shoulder did not take all his weight as he hung suspended by one wrist.

Seren and Alexandra hovered behind Vasco, and Charlie had a vague impression that a girl with braided dark hair stood over him. She was reaching up towards the wrist that was still chained above his head.

Heat prickled his skin. He heard something heavy hit the floor just as he felt himself drop, but Vasco caught him before he fell. He slumped against Vasco's arm, his head resting on Vasco's shoulder.

'Thank you,' he heard Vasco say, although Charlie did not understand what he meant.

'Look at his arms,' Alya murmured. 'They've – they've mutilated him. Will he –?'

'I can help him,' Seren said, her voice firm and steady. 'I know what to do.'

Charlie felt the touch of her fingers tracing along his bare arms, all the way up to his neck. She paused at one of the places where he had been injected with the drug, taking a deep breath.

As she pressed down more firmly, Charlie heard himself make a small, whimpering sound. Someone squeezed his hand. A moment later, he felt a soothing warmth begin to spread through his body, calming him. It was a sensation he recognised.

His eyes shot open.

They had managed to fool him again.

'No,' he managed to protest, his voice a weak moan. 'Let go – don't want.'

'Hold him still,' Seren said, and Charlie felt Vasco's arm tighten around his shoulders.

As his limbs began to shake, Charlie forced his eyes to stay open, fighting the blissful waves tempting him towards unconsciousness. He knew what sort of nightmarish hallucinations would follow once he went under. He knew exactly what memories he would have to fight through before he woke again. He knew the kind of pain that awaited him when he finally returned to reality.

'Please don't make me,' he whispered, finding Vasco's dark eyes, and holding his gaze.

'I've got you,' Vasco said, his voice soft and hesitant. 'I'm here. You're safe now.'

With a groan, Charlie saw his vision tilt as he was lifted off his feet, feeling oddly weightless. He sank into darkness, and when he next opened his eyes, he was lying on his back on the floor.

He flung himself up as far as his aching muscles could take him, his hands bracing his upper body in a half-sitting, half-leaning position. Vasco sat cross-legged beside him, chewing on his thumbnail. Without thinking, Charlie tugged the hem of his t-shirt down, making sure the base of his spine was covered.

Vasco did not appear to notice. His eyes were fixed on Charlie's hands. 'You're awake,' he murmured, looking up into Charlie's face at last. 'She really did it.'

'It's …' Charlie frowned, his eyes darting to his newly bandaged hands, before returning to Vasco again. 'It's you?'

'It's me.' Vasco was watching him steadily, his expression pensive.

Charlie's frown deepened, his hands curling into fists. 'Are you really here?'

'Yes.' Vasco gave him the barest nod. 'Yes, I'm here, Charlie.'

'Why did you come back?' Charlie's teeth were gritted. 'I told you not to do that.'

A smirk crossed Vasco's face, and he glanced away. 'I don't take orders from you,' he said, his voice cool and even. He had started to wind a bandage around Charlie's upper arm.

'Will you –' Charlie shifted away, but Vasco continued. 'Just leave it, it's fine …'

'Are you always so cavalier? Stop fighting me and let me take care of you.'

At these words, Charlie went still, and allowed Vasco to bandage his many injuries.

'They really did a number on you, huh?' Vasco said, shaking his head, his voice low.

'It's fine. I'm used to it.'

'You're going to have some more scars to add to your collection.' He had finished with the bandages. With a slight sigh, Vasco brought his knees up to his chest and wrapped his arms around them, gazing at Charlie with a strange look in his eyes. 'You reckless kid.'

'Quit acting like you're my father,' Charlie snapped. 'We're practically the same age.'

'That one has healed badly,' Vasco said, pointing to his right shoulder. 'It still hurts?'

Charlie stared up at the ceiling, his voice flat. 'There used to be a tattoo there.'

'Aren't you a bit young for tattoos?'

'Now you sound like my mother.'

'So what happened?' Vasco asked, his brows arched. 'You regretted it that much?'

Charlie shrugged. 'I burnt it off with a hot spoon when I was thirteen.'

Vasco paled slightly at this. 'All saints … you're not afraid of anything, are you?'

Charlie stared into space for a few moments, his eyes growing unfocused. With a huge effort, he settled his face into an impassive expression and gave a little shrug of his shoulders. He was not going to open that door. Not for anyone.

'I told you not to come back for me,' he said again. 'You should have left me behind.'

'Yeah, well, I figured I wouldn't take you too seriously,' Vasco said, scratching his jaw, the barest hint of a smile on his face. 'That *was* just before you jumped out of a moving helicopter, after all.' His shadowed eyes returned to Charlie's face and rested there. 'Did you –'

'We can't stay here,' Charlie said, his stomach twisting. 'They'll find us.'

'Don't worry. We're in a safe place. Everyone is taking turns standing guard.'

'Everyone? You mean you dragged Seren and Alexandra back to this hellhole too?'

'I didn't *drag anyone back*.' Vasco scowled at him. 'They both wanted to help you.'

'And you just let them tag along with you?'

'You think I could stop them?' Vasco dragged a hand through his hair, making it stand on end. 'Even if I hadn't come back for you, they would have tried to rescue you without me.'

'Why would they – would you –?' Charlie's question died in his throat. 'Why?'

Vasco's eyes narrowed. 'You'd prefer to be back in chains still, would you?'

'*No*, I just don't want any of you getting hurt because of me.'

'*You're* the one who's hurt.' Vasco sighed, and pinched the bridge of his nose. 'You're testing my patient bedside manner.'

Charlie ground his teeth. 'I can still fight.' He forced himself to stand up.

Vasco was on his feet too, his arms folded across his chest. 'You need to rest.'

'Don't treat me like a child,' Charlie said softly. 'I am *not* a child. I'm not weak.'

Vasco weathered his furious gaze. 'Can't you let someone take care of *you*, just once?'

'Get out of my way.'

Rage strengthening him, Charlie made to storm past Vasco. Without even blinking, Vasco raised a palm to sit just below Charlie's left shoulder, entirely unmoved. Charlie froze, his eyes dropping to the floor.

'I know you don't like people touching you,' Vasco said. There was no malice in his words, no hint of a threat, or any promise of violence. 'You have to stay here until it's safe for us to move.' He almost sounded apologetic. 'I don't want to have to make you do anything you don't want to do.'

Charlie glared at him. 'I'd like to see you try.'

Vasco's face was set. 'You really want to do this with me right now?'

'What, scared you won't be able to take me without your best friend backing you up?'

Something flickered in Vasco's eyes, and his expression hardened as he lowered his hand. 'He's no friend of mine,' he muttered, as though the idea revolted him. 'Did he ...?' He had grown pale again, his fear writ large on his face as he reached out for Charlie's hand. 'Charlie, what did he do to you?'

'Nothing.' Charlie shook him off. 'Whatever. It doesn't matter. Leave me alone.'

'Charlie, listen to me. Your body has been through a lot. You need to –'

'I need to make them pay for what they've done to my family! I need –' His knees had given way.

Vasco caught him before he hit the ground. 'Lie down. I've got you.'

His back flat against the floor again, Charlie watched as Vasco curled himself up beside him. With a deep sigh, Vasco rested his chin on his knees, a sombre expression clouding his features.

'The girl who freed me – Jasmine,' Charlie murmured. 'I've met her before.'

A faint smile graced Vasco's grave face. 'Yeah, I heard about your exploits.'

'You did?'

'Why else would she be here? She told us what you did for her and her friends.'

'She didn't have to do that,' Charlie mumbled, looking away.

'Maybe not, but she wanted to,' Vasco said, gazing at Charlie with a fond look in his eye. 'She's one of Alya's *new friends*,' he added, unable to keep the bitterness from his voice.

'You managed to find them?' Charlie recalled the sound of the helicopter drifting off into the distance without him. 'That's good.' He was aware of how empty his voice sounded.

'Yeah, but I didn't stick around,' Vasco said, shrugging. 'I had to – I mean ...' he added hastily, and Charlie realised that Vasco had coloured a little, and seemed to be determined to avoid meeting his eyes. 'You know ... witches – it's not exactly my scene.'

Charlie raised an eyebrow. 'They didn't welcome you with open arms, then?'

Vasco rolled his eyes and smiled to himself. 'I didn't know you were involved in blowing up that scumbag's den,' he said, sounding both proud and grudgingly impressed.

'Faulkner's place?' Looking up, Charlie met Vasco's eyes, and they both grinned.

'He was furious about it. I had no idea it was you.' Vasco was still smiling at him.

'He had it coming,' Charlie muttered.

'You really have a grudge against him, don't you?' When Charlie did not answer, Vasco glanced at his right shoulder. 'Does it have something to do with –?'

Charlie sighed, and gazed up at the ceiling, his eyes tracing the patterns he found there. All the rooms in the Volya Facility looked the same.

'So, you're telling me a coven insurgent teamed up with a Witch Hunter, for me?'

'Did you forget about those prisoners you freed?' Vasco said, frowning. 'The witch said that some of them managed to meet up with her. They told her that a teenage boy with crazy hair and bruises helped them escape –'

'That's enough.'

'– but he never made it out –'

'Didn't you hear me? I told you to –'

'– because he went back to save a little girl.'

'Can you stop looking so pleased with yourself? Who says that was me?'

'Of course it was you.' An infuriatingly satisfied smile spread across the whole of Vasco's face as Charlie rolled his eyes. 'The witch knew it was you, as well. She said she'd make sure she got you out of here – something about owing you a favour.'

'What about you?'

Vasco shrugged, the smile slipping from his face. 'I was already on my way to find you. I'm glad they all came too, though. I wouldn't have made it far without their help.'

'You …' Charlie shook his head, laying the back of his palm across his forehead. 'I honestly don't get it.'

Vasco watched him in silence for a few moments. 'You spend all your time protecting the people around you,' he said eventually, his tone softened of its usual edge. 'Is it so hard to believe that someone else might want to do the same for you?'

Caught off-guard, Charlie made a derisive sound in his throat. 'I couldn't protect anyone – not when it counted. When it really mattered, I couldn't do anything.' He turned onto his side, away from Vasco. 'And now my family are gone … and I'm all on my own.'

From beside him, Vasco spoke quietly. 'I needed to get Alexandra somewhere safe.'

'I don't blame *you*,' Charlie said, turning back towards him at once. 'You didn't think that I –?'

Vasco was looking anywhere but at Charlie, picking at his fingernails. 'I watched it happen,' he said, his words stilted. 'All of it. You – in front of him. I couldn't get it out of my head.' Finally, he looked at Charlie. 'I had to come back for you. I had to know for sure if …'

'You were just in time,' Charlie said, scratching his throat. 'If you hadn't come …'

'I will always come back for you,' Vasco said, his dark eyes burning. 'I promise.'

Charlie covered his face with his hands. His entire body was aching. 'I'm so tired.'

'Try to get some sleep,' Vasco said, moving to stand up. 'I'll be right here.'

'Can you –?' Charlie began, and Vasco paused. 'Would you … for a bit … please?'

A slight frown creasing between his brows, Vasco lay down beside Charlie. He settled himself so that they were side by side, and yet not quite close enough to touch. 'Like this?'

Charlie nodded. 'I just …'

Vasco shifted his body and closed his eyes. 'Forget it,' he said quietly, lying very still as Charlie watched his chest slowly rise and fall. 'You don't have to explain yourself to me, all right? Not ever. It's fine.'

*

'Should we wake them up?' Alya's uncertain voice drifted into Charlie's awareness.

'*Oh* …' Seren sounded disappointed. 'But they look so cute like that …'

'Trust a Casimir to see a Witch Hunter with his guard down and think he's *cute*.'

'What's that supposed to mean, Darkwood?'

Charlie sat up to find Seren and Jasmine glaring at one another. Alya was looking between them with wide eyes as she chewed on her lower lip. Jasmine had a tiny ball of flames clenched in her palm, while ribbons of light curled themselves around Seren's arms. Beside him, Vasco stirred, settling himself into a cross-legged position and observing the stand-off with a smug smile.

'What're you looking at, Witchkiller?' Jasmine snapped, rounding on him, flames in hand.

'Nothing,' Vasco replied, shrugging. 'I was only thinking that if this is the best the coven insurgency has to offer, my men can relax. It seems as though we just need to sit back and wait for you to turn on each other. More than strength or tactics, discipline wins you wars.'

'You –!' Jasmine lunged forward just as Vasco's hand shot to the gun at his waist.

'Try me, witch.' His voice was soft, the flicker of her flames reflected in his brown eyes.

'Stop it, both of you!' Alya ordered, standing between them with her arms outstretched. She was no longer carrying her rucksack with her. 'Don't forget – we may have found Charlie, but that doesn't mean our mission is over. We still have to get out of here alive.'

'And destroy the weapons,' Jasmine added.

'And rescue my sister,' Seren finished.

'*If* she's still here,' Jasmine muttered, casting a dark frown at Vasco, who looked away.

'She is,' Charlie said. His voice was still rough, but it no longer hurt him to speak.

'How do you know that, Charlie?' Alya asked, looking troubled. 'Weren't you –?'

'I found her,' Charlie said, looking up at the three girls. 'I almost managed to get her out, but I …' He scratched his face, then his forearm, glancing away. 'I couldn't.'

'She's alive,' Seren murmured, her hands clasped in front of her heart.

'There's someone else trapped here that we need to take with us, too,' Charlie said.

'Who?' Jasmine asked, her expression grim.

'My brother.'

Vasco's head snapped towards him. 'You have a brother? *Here*?'

'It's my fault he's here,' Charlie said. He was aware that Vasco was watching him closely, his eyes searching Charlie's face, as though looking for something he had left unsaid. 'He's the only family I have left now.'

'And he *works* in this place?' Jasmine's expression told Charlie everything he needed to know.

'I know he'll come with me if I can talk to him,' he insisted. 'I … I have to help him.'

'Charlie …' Vasco looked as if he wanted to say more, but he only shook his head.

'Well, we should all get a bit more rest first,' Alya said. 'Then we can make a start.'

She touched Jasmine's arm, which was enough for some of the tension in Jasmine's shoulders to visibly disappear. Together, they wandered off into another corner of the room, their heads close together.

Seren approached Vasco, who stiffened. 'I'd like to speak to Charlie,' she said.

Vasco regarded her warily for a few moments before he turned his gaze to Charlie, who stared back at him, his expression mild. For some reason, this made Vasco scowl.

'I'll go stand guard,' he said, sloping off towards the door. 'I hope you two enjoy your precious reunion …'

'Thanks, we will!' Seren called after him, her tone pleasant as she waved at his back.

'I'm impressed you all made it back here without killing each other,' Charlie said, as Seren settled herself beside him on her stomach. She had folded her arms, and was resting her head on top of them, her face tilted towards his. 'I'm glad you're safe.'

'That's my line,' she said. A fond smile curled the corner of her mouth for a moment, before it slipped away again, and her gaze fell to the floor. 'So … you said you saw my sister.'

Charlie nodded. 'She looks a lot like you.'

Seren smiled weakly, her eyes shining. Looking away from him, she cleared her throat.

'I'm sorry,' he whispered, a painful catch burning in his chest. 'I couldn't … I really did try … I know it's my fault that she –'

'None of this is your fault, Charlie,' Seren said softly, managing a small, sad smile.

'I told her you were coming to save her,' he went on. 'She knows that you –'

'Thank you,' she said, brushing her index finger against her eyes. 'The more time passes, the more I worry that – that she might –' She sniffed. 'I don't want her to forget me.'

Charlie put his arm around her shoulders, his jaw clenched, and closed his eyes.

'We'll save her,' he said. 'No matter what it takes, we'll get her back. I swear it.'

CHAPTER 18

'Charlie, I need to talk to you about something …'

Charlie, who had been sitting alone against a far wall, was busy trying to parcel up his thoughts and feelings and store them somewhere safe and out of sight, deep inside himself. When he heard Vasco's voice, he forced himself up onto his feet. His legs still a little unsteady, he fixed Vasco with a hard stare. He had known that this would be coming at some point. He was prepared for it. In truth, he was impressed that Vasco had managed to hold himself back from chewing him out for this long.

'What d'you want? I thought you were on guard duty?'

'We need to get moving,' Vasco began, his voice stiff. 'Do you need –? Are you –?'

Charlie shrugged. 'You didn't come over here just to tell me that. Go on, say it.'

Vasco regarded him in silence for a moment before something changed in his face. 'Fine, I will.' He drew in a sharp breath. 'When I realised that you had decided to try to save your family without me, I was so worried about you that I thought I'd lose my mind.'

He said all of this in a clipped, rushed voice that seemed to leave him close to breathless by the time he had managed to get all the words out. He stared at Charlie for a second, wide-eyed, then scowled at the floor. His arms were crossed tightly against his chest, his shoulders taut.

Charlie, who had looked up sharply at the idea that Vasco had been worried about him, did not quite know what to say in response to this. It was not what he had expected at all.

'The thought of you here, in this place ... and knowing that I couldn't do anything to help you ...' Vasco shook his head, running both hands through his hair, making it stand on end. 'Don't *ever* do that to me again, all right?' he said fiercely, giving Charlie a gentle push below his left shoulder. 'No more lone wolf adventures – I'm not sure my nerves can take it.'

'You're right,' Charlie admitted, his voice sounding as hollow as he felt. 'Back then, it would have been better for everyone if you were there – on the roof – and I had just stayed out of it. You would have known what to do. You would have saved them.'

Vasco's face fell. 'That's not what I meant,' he said quickly. 'I meant that I –' His shoulders sagged as he exhaled with a little shake of his head. 'I just don't want you to leave me behind. I'd rather be in danger myself, by your side, than have to think about you coping with something like that on your own ...' He looked up into Charlie's eyes. 'You're not alone.'

Charlie, who had found himself only half-listening to what Vasco was saying, forced himself to speak. 'If you had been there, they might still be alive right now. Dragomir, he – he played me, and I was ...' He paused, breathing deeply, his throat burning as he felt the full weight of the terrible, irrefutable truth of his words in his heart. 'I was completely useless. I couldn't do anything to stop him. Now they're gone – forever. They're dead, and it's all my fault ...'

'You killed them, did you?' At the sound of Seren's voice, Charlie looked up. She was glaring at him, her hands on her hips and a fierce expression on her face.

'What did you say?'

'I asked you if you were the one who killed them.'

'No,' Charlie shot back, 'but I'm responsible. I'm the reason they're dead. If I had –'

'You need to stop thinking like that,' Vasco said, his voice quiet but firm. 'You're going to drive yourself out of your mind with those kinds of thoughts. No matter how hard you wish things had been different, you can't change what happened. You can't change the past.'

'You have to keep moving forward,' Seren added, nodding in agreement.

'Tell me this then, if you two are so smart – how am I *supposed* to move forward?' Charlie asked, his voice flat. 'If I could go back and die in their place, I would.' The words were out of his mouth before he had a chance to stop them. 'I wish I were dead. I don't deserve to be alive. It's not …' He felt a hollow smile curl his mouth as he realised how pathetic he sounded. The world had never been fair. 'I don't think I can do this anymore … something's different this time.' He closed his eyes. 'I can still feel it – *him* – inside me … under my skin. I feel –'

'You're right, it's not fair,' Seren said gently, taking his hand in hers as he looked away. 'You think I don't know how you feel? If I had the chance to switch places with my sister and trade my freedom for hers, don't you think I would take it? I think about her every day, you know – every single day. There's a hole in my heart and it's tearing me up inside.'

Charlie watched her brush a tear from her eyelashes and squeezed her fingers.

'But this is the way things are, for now,' Seren went on, after taking a deep, shuddering breath. 'We have to live with it. We have to keep going. We have to keep trying. What else can we do? Do you think *I* should give up?'

'No,' Charlie said softly, 'I don't. I don't want you to give up. I mean …' He looked from Seren to Vasco, and over to Alya and Jasmine, only fully processing his new realisation as he spoke the words for the first time. 'I need you.'

'Well, we need you too,' Seren replied immediately, as Vasco kept his eyes fixed on the floor, his cheeks colouring. 'That means *you* can't give up either, all right? No matter what happens, we stick together – all of us. We're here for you, you know … I'll always be here.'

Charlie nodded. The familiar sensation of guilt was twisting in his stomach again. At some point, what had started out as a secret he felt entitled to keep had swollen to the point where he felt like he was living a lie by refusing to share the truth with them.

He was dying.

There would never be a better time to tell them than this.

But as he looked into Seren's eyes, he found that the words simply would not come. He could not bring himself to cause her more pain. He forced himself to smile and said nothing, wincing as a searing pain shot through his chest.

'You didn't finish what you were saying ... before,' Vasco said, once Seren had gone to re-join the other two girls. He was watching for Charlie's reaction, a cautious expression on his face. 'When you were talking about how you were feeling, you said that – that you wished you were ...' He trailed off, his shoulders tense. 'I don't know what to say. But I can listen. I'm worried about you. I ...' His dark eyes met Charlie's. 'I care about you. You *do* know that I don't want you to die, don't you?'

'Oh, right, sure ...' Charlie tried his best to laugh it off, and Vasco lowered his eyes again with a small sigh. 'It's nothing. I'm fine. I was just going to say that I feel ... I don't know ... ruined, I guess.'

He caught sight of the sombre look on Vasco's face, his gaze calmly rising to meet Charlie's, and he smothered a cough before scratching at his forearm.

'But that's nothing new,' Charlie added, shrugging, knowing he should stop talking. 'I'll be fine. It's always ... always like this, straight after ... I'm fine. I'll be fine.'

Vasco blinked rapidly, his eyes shining. 'You don't always have to be so brave, Charlie.'

'You –' Charlie took a step backwards, his eyes narrowing. 'What would you know about it, anyway? Why can't you just ...' He let out a deep sigh, finding that he no longer had the energy left to pretend. 'Just leave me alone, all right?' He had attempted something sharp-edged, but it came out sounding exactly how he felt – hopeless, exhausted, pathetic.

Vasco's throat bobbed. 'If that's what you want,' he said, his voice soft and sad.

His stomach twisting at Vasco's downcast expression, Charlie swallowed. He was about to attempt an apology when Seren, Alya and Jasmine descended upon them. Clearly uncomfortable, Vasco was forced to shuffle closer towards Charlie as the girls joined them, and the five of them grouped together into a tight circle.

'Everyone, listen up,' Jasmine said. 'We've made our decision. We've got Charlie back, but we're not done yet.'

'What d'you mean?' Vasco asked, his voice sharp. 'Who said *you're* the leader here?'

'The three of us have put together everything we know, as well as the information from the prisoners Charlie helped to escape,' Alya answered, 'and we have a plan.'

Vasco closed his eyes and stifled a groan but made no attempt to argue with her.

'What's the plan?' Charlie asked.

'Sabotage, and an extraction mission,' Jasmine said. 'We're not leaving until we've rescued Seren's sister and destroyed whatever it is that they've been working on to hurt the witch covens.'

'You're pushing your luck,' Vasco warned, folding his arms as he cast a dark look at Jasmine. 'We came here to rescue Charlie. We got him. Now we need to leave. We stay here and we risk everyone getting captured.' Charlie noticed that Vasco glanced at Alya, who stubbornly avoided his gaze. 'If they get their hands on any of you, you're not getting out alive this time.'

'No one's asking you to join us,' Jasmine said at once, as she examined her nails. 'If you want to leave, you're free to do so. Honestly, I would feel more confident doing this without the help of a Witchkiller. That way, I wouldn't feel the need to constantly be watching my back.'

Vasco regarded her with a cool stare. 'You don't know where her sister is, or where the weapons are,' he said, his voice superbly calm. 'Do you even know what you're looking for?'

Jasmine dismissed him with a wave of her hand. 'Whatever it is, we know it's a weapon,' she said. 'We make our way towards the armoury. We destroy whatever we find there.'

'I should be able to locate Saga if I have Seren close by as a conduit,' Alya added.

'We need to get in and get out – as fast as we can,' Seren said. 'We've done a good job of avoiding Dragomir and his forces so far.' One by one, she fixed them all with a grim expression. 'Let's hope our luck holds out for a little while longer.'

With a shake of his head, Vasco led the way out of the room, his rifle in his hands. Charlie and the others followed, bunched together, moving as quickly and quietly as they could. Their eyes scanned the long corridors in all directions for any sign of movement.

Then, with a horrible sinking feeling, Charlie caught sight of someone coming towards them. Vasco came to a sudden halt, his rifle raised before him.

'Stop right there!' he ordered. 'Get your hands up.'

'Don't shoot,' a hesitant voice answered. A young man in a long white coat strode towards them, his hands raised in front of his chest. 'I'm unarmed. Please, don't hurt me.'

'Max!' Charlie pulled Vasco back and stepped in front of the rifle, staring at his brother in shock. 'What're you doing here?'

Max's eyes travelled across the faces of the three girls, to Vasco with his rifle, before they settled on Charlie. 'I thought about what you said.' There was a determined look on his face. 'I want to help you.'

Charlie grinned back at him. 'I knew you'd change your mind.'

'What are you doing?' Vasco hissed, as Charlie encouraged Max to join them with a wave of his hand. 'Don't you know he's –?'

'He's coming with us,' Charlie answered, meeting Vasco's eyes. 'He's my brother.'

'He may be your brother, but he works for the regime,' Jasmine said, her voice strained.

Alya shifted her weight, looking uncomfortable. 'He's been a good friend to me.'

'He was always kind to me, too,' Seren added, looking at Charlie. 'Besides, he's Charlie's brother. We can trust him.'

'We *can't* trust him,' Vasco retorted at once, his grip tight on his rifle as he glared at Max.

Max smiled politely back, pushing his glasses up his nose and placing his hands in the pockets of his lab coat. 'We are not so unalike, are we, Lieutenant Kovalev?' he said, his voice light. 'We both live to serve the Great Protector. By the way, he is a Witch

Hunter – were you aware of that?' Max glanced at Jasmine and Seren with a quizzical look. 'Surely, the question you should be asking yourselves is whether you can really trust *him*?'

'That's cute,' Vasco sneered, as Jasmine and Seren exchanged a look, while Alya began chewing on her fingernails. Vasco turned to Charlie, who felt his heart begin to beat faster. 'Charlie knows he can trust me,' Vasco said. 'Right, Charlie?'

'We should keep moving,' Charlie muttered. 'Get in and get out, right?'

Vasco, whose grip on his rifle had gone slack, was staring at Charlie with wide, bewildered eyes. 'Charlie, come on …' he began, his voice a little shaky. 'Tell me you can see through this? You know what he's trying to do, don't you? He's trying to turn us against each other. You know I'd never –'

Charlie clenched his fists as his teeth ground together. 'You want me to trust *you* over my own brother?' he snarled. 'He's the only family I have left. I don't even *know* you.'

At this, all the tension seemed to leave Vasco's shoulders. He shrugged and looked away, his eyes shuttering. 'It's your decision,' he said, his voice flat and distant. 'What would I know?'

He resettled his rifle against his chest and continued striding forwards, his features like stone.

'Come on,' Jasmine said, after clearing her throat and moving to the front of the group. 'Charlie's right, we need to keep moving. We can't afford any more hold-ups.'

She and Alya followed behind Vasco. After giving Charlie a nod of reassurance, Seren hurried to catch up with them, leaving him alone with his older brother.

'I'm glad I wasn't too late,' Max said, turning to Charlie with a tentative smile.

'What made you change your mind?' Charlie asked. His grin had returned.

'I remembered that I let you walk away once before, a long time ago,' Max answered. 'I wasn't going to let you make the same mistake again.'

Charlie took a deep, steadying breath. 'I remember. You told me to stay with you that day, and I ignored you. By the time I came back, you were gone.' His voice was beginning to shake. 'They – they wouldn't tell me where you were, only that I would never see you again.' He forced himself to continue. 'I ran away from the orphanage that night. I – I thought it would be so easy for me to find you ...'

Max was watching him steadily. 'You didn't have much luck, I take it?'

'I wish I had just listened to you. Everything went wrong for me after that.'

Max nodded. 'I wish you had stayed with me that day too,' he said, letting out a small sigh. 'But I suppose we have another chance now. From now on, the two of us stick together.'

Charlie nodded back with enthusiasm. 'That's right. We're brothers. No matter what.'

'We're here,' Jasmine said, as they came to a halt on a corridor lined with wooden doors. 'Everyone split up – and let us know if you find anything suspicious.'

Nodding to Max as they separated, Charlie went through the door closest to him. Immediately, he had the sense that he was not alone. Squinting through the darkness, he caught sight of a shape hidden among the shadows. He expected to feel fear, but he only felt empty. Steeling himself, he closed the door and switched on the light. At the sight of the person in front of him, he froze.

'You ...'

'Easy, Carroway.' Faulkner stepped towards him. 'I'm not here to hurt you – this time.'

Charlie launched himself forward and slammed Faulkner against the wall. 'You expect me to believe that?' he said harshly, one fist balled against the older man's throat. 'Do you know what that monster did to me when you handed me over to him? How stupid d'you think I am?'

Faulkner smirked back at him. 'Well, you tell me,' he said, spluttering a little, but still managing to maintain his lazy drawl. 'Don't think I hadn't noticed your little fraternal reunion.'

Charlie's eyes narrowed. 'My brother has nothing to do with this.'

'Are you really so sure about that?' Faulkner coughed as Charlie shoved him back against the wall, his hands clawing at Charlie's fist, which remained firm against his throat. 'You can't trust him, Charlie.'

'Why would I ever trust *anything* you say?' Charlie demanded, his teeth gritted.

'*Listen* to me,' Faulkner said, his voice urgent, as Charlie eased up a little on the pressure against his windpipe. 'Those three maniacs still have plans for you. I don't know what it is, but it's something big. You've made it personal. You should get out of here while you still can.'

Charlie laughed coldly. 'Thanks for the advice, but next time don't bother.'

'This is your last chance, Carroway,' Faulkner pressed on, righting his shirt and collar, as Charlie let him go and backed away from him. 'I'll take you back. You'll be welcomed back into the fold, I swear it. You could lead the whole gang someday. I always saw you as my successor, you know. You remember how it used to be between the two of us, don't you? Before you ruined everything.'

'*What* did you say?' Charlie whispered. Faulkner's words had made him go numb.

'You can have a good life,' Faulkner continued, holding out his hand. 'We'll make the best of this. We could be partners again. Everything can be forgiven.'

Charlie shook his head. 'Everything can be forgiven … can you even hear yourself?' He stumbled backwards against the closed door, his limbs shaking. 'You abducted me from off the streets when I was *six years old*. You kept me as your prisoner for *seven years*, and you –'

'I saved your life.' Faulkner shrugged. 'I took you in out of love. I gave you a home.'

'You raped me.' Though Charlie was trembling with fury, his voice remained cold and steady. 'And when you got bored of me, you hired me out to anyone who was willing to pay. And then, when I tried to run away from you, you let anyone who had ever wanted to put their hands on me rape me as well. Then you tied

194

me down and branded me, so that I would never be able to forget the words you said to me. What part of *that* has *anything* to do with love?'

'You survived, didn't you?' Faulkner was gazing at him with pride. 'It was all to make you stronger. I always told you that you were special, didn't I? You can't escape what you are.'

Charlie felt something slip inside of him. He felt his clenched fist connect with the side of Faulkner's face. The next thing he knew, Faulkner was sprawled, bleeding, on the floor.

'I'm going to have your words stamped on my skin for the rest of my life, you sick, twisted fuck.' Charlie was breathing hard, as though he had been running flat out. 'You didn't want to make me stronger. You wanted to destroy me. You wanted to see me broken into pieces, just so you could be the one to pick up the shards and put me back together.' Charlie straightened himself up to his full height, staring down at Faulkner, a strange calm stealing its way through him. 'But I'll never be like you. I got away, and I'm never going back. I'm free now.'

'Is that so?' Faulkner grimaced up at him, one hand to his cheek, his scarred mouth twisted. 'Fine by me. You've made your bed, so you can lie in it. Don't come crawling back to me when you find yourself with fleas. I never thought you'd be one to lie down beside your enemy – and willingly, at that.'

'What are you talking about?'

'You figure it out. I'm done. You'll regret making an enemy of me, Charlie Carroway.'

Glaring at him, Charlie's eyes followed Faulkner out of the room. He did not trust himself to think too much about what had just passed between them. When Faulkner was gone, Charlie braced himself against the wall, his hands shaking. It was only when his thoughts had stopped racing that he remembered the plan. When he returned to the corridor, Vasco was there.

'Where have you been?' he asked, his tone hovering somewhere between cold and concerned.

'What do *you* care?' Charlie snapped, making to push past him, only to find himself brought to a halt by the grip of Vasco's fingers around his upper arm. 'Get,' he breathed, '*off* me. *Now.*'

'I know you don't want to hear this, but please listen to me,' Vasco said, easing his hold on Charlie. 'I know he's your brother, but I don't trust him. His work here, it's —'

'Back off!' Charlie warned, wrenching himself free. 'It's got *nothing* to do with you.'

A hurt look flickered across Vasco's face, before his expression darkened. 'Charlie —'

'I don't *need* you, you understand?' Charlie almost shouted, shoving Vasco away. 'Why can't you —'

'Charlie, it's all right.' Max was beside him, one arm around his shoulders. His voice was calm in Charlie's ear as he stared at Vasco, who had staggered backwards, looking close to inconsolable. 'Listen to me. Let it go. He's not worth it.'

'I know you,' Vasco said to Max, his voice a low rumble, as Charlie attempted to master himself in his brother's grip. His head was spinning, and a bitter, acidic taste was rising in his throat at their enforced proximity so soon after his encounter with Faulkner. 'I *know* what you are. If you even *think* about hurting him, I'll —'

'What will you do? Kill me?' Max shot back coolly. 'That's all you're good for, isn't it?'

Before Vasco could reply, they heard a shout. 'Everyone, over here — we've found it!'

CHAPTER 19

C harlie followed the sound of Seren's voice towards a large chamber at the end of the corridor, Vasco at his side. As they crossed the threshold, Charlie's eyes ranged over the ghoulish collection of blades and knives that lined the walls, glinting in the low light. A shiver of nauseous fear curled up in his stomach at the sight. He forced himself not to take a step backwards. Already, it felt as though the room was closing in on him.

'We don't have to stay here,' Vasco said. 'If you need to leave, I'll come with you.'

'Would you stop treating me like you think I'm about to fall apart at any second?'

At Charlie's words, Vasco closed his eyes and walked away, raking his fingers through his hair as he went. With some effort, Charlie tried to focus his attention on what Seren, Alya and Jasmine were talking about instead. The three girls seemed to be discussing how they would go about attempting to destroy the weapons, their voices hushed. Charlie felt his body humming with tension. The whisper of their soft voices surrounded him, closing in on him, the silver blades along the walls catching his reflected fear.

He was starting to remember again.

Looking for a distraction, Charlie's eyes were drawn to Vasco. He had approached a desk in the corner of the room and picked up a sheaf of papers. There was something about the intense look on Vasco's face that held Charlie's gaze. He swallowed, his throat suddenly dry. As Vasco rifled through the papers one by one, Charlie saw his expression darken, and watched as his pale face steadily lost what colour it still had.

'Find anything interesting?'

Charlie's eyes lingered on Vasco's face as he scanned through the pages of scrawled handwritten notes. Vasco seemed drawn to particular sections of the papers, his brow furrowing as he re-read certain passages aloud, his words barely audible. Charlie noticed Vasco's eyes widen as he came across a stack of sepia photographs that had been clipped together in a folder. His skin was gradually taking on a greenish tinge. He seemed unable to draw his gaze away from what he was seeing.

His stomach roiling, Charlie left Vasco to his thoughts. He joined Seren, Alya and Jasmine instead. The three girls were clustered around a collection of machines and devices. They appeared unremarkable at first. There was a wooden table, a stool with a pointed seat, and an iron cap amongst them. But when he examined them more closely, Charlie saw the chains, the ropes, the spikes. He backed away, his skin crawling to be so close to them.

Everything in this chamber had been designed to inflict pain – intricate and excruciating pain. It was clear that time and attention had been spent creating inventions of supreme cruelty and humiliation. Just looking at them was enough to dredge up his most recently buried memories, so Charlie returned to Vasco's side. His breath was coming fast and shallow now.

'Are you all right?' Seeing how Vasco's eyes had glazed, Charlie drew closer to him. 'What are you reading?'

'You can read it yourself.' Vasco's words came out sounding forced and oddly stiff. His knuckles had gone white, his grip so tight that the papers and photographs in his hand were shaking. 'If you'd like to.'

Charlie shook his head. 'Your face tells me everything I need to know.'

'Have I been ...' Vasco's eyes ranged over the sepia photographs, his eyes lingering on the mutilated bodies of small children, their eyes closed as if in sleep, 'an accessory to this?' His eyes wide, he braced a trembling hand against his forehead, covering his face as his shoulders began to shake. 'Charlie, I … I swear I … I didn't know –'

'You're a Witch Hunter,' Jasmine said, her voice steady. 'You must have known.'

'I didn't know about *this*!' Vasco rounded on her, looking desperate. 'I would never have …' He shook his head, paling further. 'And never – never children …'

'And so?' Jasmine regarded him with a cool stare. 'What are you going to do about it, Witchkiller?'

'I'm going to make sure these children get the justice they deserve,' Vasco said, after a long pause. A look of steel-eyed resolve had settled over his face. 'Whoever is responsible for this, I will make sure they are punished. I'll …' He clenched the photographs in his fist, his head bowed. 'I'll give my life to make this right.'

Jasmine arched a dark eyebrow. 'Even if that means standing up to your master?'

'I became a soldier to protect people … to defend the people who needed me,' Vasco said, as Jasmine walked away. His voice was low enough that Charlie thought he might have been talking to himself. 'I only ever wanted to do what was right.'

Out of the stillness, a rough sound, as though of a blunt object smashing down on metal, sounded from across the room. Both Charlie and Vasco looked over to see the three girls standing before the weapons, their arms outstretched. It looked as though they had come to an agreement as to how they would destroy the machines. By the sound of it, they were already making some progress.

'Be careful,' Jasmine was warning the others. 'We need to make sure we don't push ourselves too hard.'

Alya shook her head. 'This is the only way,' she said, circling the machines with a frown, as Seren flexed her fingers. 'We have to do whatever is necessary if we're going to get what we want.'

'You need to think smarter than that, princess.' Jasmine crossed her arms, following Alya's movements with her eyes. 'You're only just beginning to understand your Gift, and if Seren reaches her limit it'll be up to me to protect both of you idiots.'

Seren appeared to be readying herself, rolling her shoulders and swinging her arms. 'She's right,' she said, nodding towards Alya. 'This is our only chance. We need to make it count.'

With a sigh, Jasmine inclined her head. Her acquiescence seemed to spur them all on to do what needed to be done. Moving their arms as though swirling water – seeming to draw strength out of the very air around them – the three witches brought all their ferocity down on the weapons before them.

Their progress was slow, and Charlie stared at his bandaged hands, ashamed of his own powerlessness. Meanwhile, Vasco watched them work with unseeing eyes, his thoughts still obviously elsewhere.

With a shriek of effort, Seren sent a wall of air towards the weapons. An intense wave of heat whipped around the rest of the room, its raw power making Charlie flinch. Eventually, the floor was littered with broken machinery and twisted metal. The weapons had all been destroyed.

Picking their way through the debris, the three girls approached Charlie and Vasco. Their shoulders were heaving with exertion and sweat lined all three of their faces. Alya's cheeks were flushed, while Jasmine's eyes were bright. The hint of a triumphant smile was creeping across Seren's face, although her eyes had a hollow look to them.

It was not clear who broke the silence first. It seemed as though all five of them burst into exhilarated, nervous laughter as one. At once, the spell was broken, and words started tumbling out of their mouths in joyful freefall as they began to talk loudly over one another.

'Nice work, both of you,' Jasmine said, grinning at Seren and Alya. 'We make a pretty good team.'

Alya was beaming. 'That felt incredible! I can't believe it – we actually *did* it!'

'I'm glad she's on our side,' Vasco said, giving Seren an appreciative nod.

It was only then that Charlie looked at Seren properly. He felt his stomach do an unpleasant somersault at the sight of her pained expression. Her eyes were squeezed tightly shut, and she was biting down on her lip so hard that she had started to draw blood. Her arms were trembling all the way from her shoulders to her hands. It looked as though she was about to collapse beneath the burden of an invisible weight.

Seeming to become aware that he was watching her, Seren opened her eyes. She fixed him with a look of such heartfelt desperation that Charlie felt her fear being poured straight into him.

'Seren's getting weaker,' he said. He rounded on the others, ignoring Alya's stricken expression, his voice urgent. 'We need to find somewhere safe – fast! If we don't –' He broke off, unwilling to countenance what would happen then.

'The only safe place now is Penumbra,' Vasco said, his eyes flicking to Seren as though already evaluating their next move. 'We won't be safe until we're far away from the Facility. We have to make it out and find somewhere in the city to hide. There's no other way.'

'How long until we get there?' Seren gasped, her shoulders hunched in pain.

'We'll be there soon, Seren,' Charlie said. 'Just hang in there, all right?'

'Mm-hmm.' Seren seemed to be struggling to speak. Her eyes were screwed up in effort, her brow furrowed as if deep in concentration. Her whole body was shaking now.

'Has anyone seen Max?' Alya asked, her eyes scanning the room anxiously.

Charlie looked around too. His brother was nowhere to be seen. 'Maybe he just …'

'We should get out of here,' Vasco said, tightening his grip on his rifle. 'Now.'

'Where are we supposed to go?' Charlie asked, as Seren moaned her sister's name.

'The Lilith coven hideout is our best bet,' Jasmine said, throwing a meaningful look at Alya, who was chewing on her lower lip. 'She'll be expecting you.'

Vasco followed Jasmine's gaze, his eyes hard. 'Alexandra, what is she talking about?'

'Well, I …'

'When are you going to tell him, Alya?' Jasmine demanded, as she supported Seren's weight.

'Tell me what?' Vasco looked between the two girls, an expression of dawning realisation on his face. 'Tell me *what*, Alexandra?' Then, 'Charlie, where are you going?'

Charlie was already at the door. 'I'm going to find Max. I can't leave him behind.'

'Charlie, wait.' Vasco was at his side in an instant.

'Don't try to stop me,' Charlie said. 'I know you don't trust him, but he's my family.'

'He can't have gone far. We'll find him.' Vasco's dark eyes met his. 'I'll help you.'

'You two take Seren and get out of here,' Charlie called back to Jasmine and Alya.

'No. Need to – find my sister.' Seren's voice was weak. 'I won't leave … without her.'

'Did you think I was planning to leave her here on her own?' Jasmine shifted Seren's body against her as she locked eyes with Charlie. 'Don't worry, I'll look after her.'

'Me too,' Alya said, pulling Seren's other arm around her shoulders. 'We stick together, no matter what,' she added, turning her bright smile on each of them in turn. 'We're a team, aren't we? Besides, isn't this what real friends do?'

They left the chamber together and headed straight down the corridor. They had not gone far, however, before Seren wrenched herself out of Alya and Jasmine's grip. She took a couple of tentative steps forward, looking as dazed and unsteady as a new-born fawn. Then she stumbled and fell to her knees.

'Get her up, Charlie,' Vasco said, looking around them. 'We don't have much time.'

'Seren!' In his panic, Charlie shook her more fiercely than he intended to. 'Seren, can you hear me? Open your eyes!'

She groaned, and her eyes flickered open. 'My head hurts,' she mumbled, lifting one hand to brace her right temple. 'What happened? Where am I? Have you seen my sister?'

'We should go – *now*,' Vasco muttered, scowling. 'I have a bad feeling about this.'

'Is she hurt?' Alya asked, crouching down beside Charlie.

At the sound of her voice, Seren glanced from Charlie, to Alya, Jasmine and Vasco, and back again. A wary frown creased her forehead. 'Who is she?' she asked, crawling backwards away from Charlie. 'Who are you people? Where have you taken me?' Anger flared in her eyes as Charlie gazed at her, at a loss for what he should do. 'Tell me!' she demanded, her voice becoming high and shrill. 'Where *am* I? *Tell me* – right now!'

'Seren ...' Charlie began, 'don't you know who I –?'

The crackle of gunfire up ahead silenced him, and he pulled Seren to her feet, forcing her behind him. She struggled against him, furiously trying to break free of his grip, but her legs seemed unsteady. Still clutching her head with one hand, she let out a low moan of pain.

'Someone's up ahead,' Jasmine said, one hand outstretched. 'Multiple threats sighted.'

'Back the way we came,' Vasco said, shoving Alya ahead of him. 'Go and hide – now!'

Charlie saw Alya give Vasco a brief nod before following his command without hesitation. The next moment, she was racing back down the corridor, away from them. He registered a sinking feeling in his stomach that he could only describe as betrayal, which confused him.

Before he could think too much about it, though, his eyes were drawn back in the other direction by Seren. She was staggering towards the group of people who were blocking the way ahead.

'Seren, *don't!*' he shouted, and went straight after her.

'Charlie, *where* are you *going?*' Vasco groaned, and Charlie knew without having to look that Vasco was following right behind him.

Ahead of them, their path was blocked by three men. Charlie recognised them at once. The Great Protector, Nikolai Ignatiev, stood in the centre. He was carrying something in front of him – something which, when Charlie got closer, he recognised as a small child. It was a little girl with red hair.

'Saga ...'

Now Charlie understood why Seren had raced ahead of them. She was on the floor on her knees, the muzzle of Dragomir's rifle hovering in front of her face. Standing on the other side of the Great Protector, Charlie realised, his mind suddenly blank, was his own brother.

He did not need anyone to force him to his knees this time. He went there himself, at Seren's side, all the strength leaving his body. Vasco was beside him at once, his eyes wide with concern, while Jasmine stood frozen behind them, the only one of them still on their feet.

'I have to admit, Doctor Ivanov, I was sceptical, but you have impressed me.' The Great Protector gazed down at Charlie as though he was eternally skirting the edge of boredom. 'I had expected your plan to fail. Then again, he is not the brightest subject we have ever had the pleasure of studying, is he?'

Charlie ignored him, and stared up at his brother, stricken. 'Max, what's going on?'

Dragomir snorted. 'Don't tell me he fell for it?' A cruel grin had spread across his face.

'I'm not letting you get near him again,' Vasco snarled. His dark eyes burning, he glared at Dragomir, reaching an arm out across Charlie's chest at the same time. 'Never again.'

'Max, come on,' Charlie said, his voice strained. 'Let's get out of here – together.'

'He always was a naïve fool,' his brother said, his voice as hard as stone, while Dragomir laughed. Max surveyed Charlie through impassive eyes, a smirk playing around his mouth. 'Did you really think I would forgive and forget, little brother?'

'Why?' Charlie managed to whisper, his voice cracking. 'Why would you –?'

'Don't look so surprised,' Max sneered, his eyes narrowing as he stared down at Charlie. 'You abandoned *me*, remember? I'm just returning what's owed to you.'

From beside him, Charlie heard the grind of Vasco's teeth. 'You treacherous rat,' he said, his voice rising steadily. 'How could you do this to him? He's your brother!'

'My brother died ten years ago,' Max replied. He spared Vasco a brief look of distaste, before he shrugged, and returned his gaze to Charlie. 'I am just exorcising myself of his ghost.'

'We destroyed your weapons,' Jasmine said. 'You can't hurt our people anymore.'

Nikolai Ignatiev's eyebrows rose, an amused smile curling his mouth. 'Are you referring to the mess you made of my playroom, witch?' He let out a soft, cold laugh at the confused look on Jasmine's face. 'Those were simply diversions. Those toys were merely –'

'You're a monster.' Vasco had gone very still beside Charlie, his eyes wide and unseeing. 'I see it now. Why? Why did you do it? They were *children*, you –!'

Vasco broke off as Dragomir kicked him viciously in the stomach, sending him straight to the floor. He lay still, curled up and coughing. At the sight of Vasco in pain, Charlie felt himself begin to tremble with rage the likes of which he had never experienced before.

'Merely a hobby of mine,' Nikolai Ignatiev continued, after politely clearing his throat. 'For fun, you know …' His smile broadened, showing two rows of gleaming white teeth. 'No, you have not begun to scratch the surface of my true weapons.' He adjusted his grip around Saga's neck, causing her to whimper in fright. 'I believe this creature is what you are here for?'

'Let her go,' Charlie said, grinding out the words, his eyes fixed on Saga's.

Nikolai Ignatiev tilted his head, one eyebrow raised, as he applied pressure to Saga's throat. 'I want something first.' His eyes fell on Seren, who had got to her feet and started to stagger towards him. Her arms were outstretched, her sister's name a dying whisper on her lips.

'No …' From his knees, Charlie watched her go, frozen with horrified understanding.

'Yes, that's right, witch,' Nikolai Ignatiev said, his eyes burning as he stared at Seren.

He extended his arm, holding Saga out towards her sister. Seren reached out one arm. Her fingers almost managed to touch her sister's face, before, with a smile, Nikolai Ignatiev drew the little girl away at the last moment. The movement caused another soft cry to escape from Saga's throat, and Seren echoed it.

The thought crossed Charlie's mind that the sound of their shared heartbreak was possibly the most painful thing he had yet endured, perhaps in his whole life. He watched, his own worthlessness a physical ache in his chest, as Nikolai Ignatiev handed Saga to Max. His brother lowered her to her feet and crouched down beside her, his hands gripping her shoulders. Saga looked from her captors, to her sister, to Charlie, pleading silently through wide, frightened eyes.

'Now, you be a good little girl,' Max crooned in Saga's ear, his eyes fixed on Charlie, 'and nothing bad will happen to your big sister. We always keep our promises – right, Charlie?'

'Let her *go*!' Charlie yelled, surging forward, before flinching in pain as Vasco gripped his scarred shoulder and wrenched him back. 'What are you *doing*?' he demanded, shoving Vasco's hand away from him. 'Why would you stop me? Don't get in my way! You don't –'

But Vasco only shook his head, his fathomless eyes silently imploring.

'Good, I see you remember your training, Vaska,' Nikolai Ignatiev purred, beckoning Seren towards him. He turned her around, so she faced the others, his fingers curling around her upper arm, gripping her pale flesh. 'And as a show of good faith, I will share a secret or two of my own with you.' His eyes fell on Charlie, who felt his stomach drop. 'Do you see this pathetic gutter rat squealing at my feet?'

And Charlie found himself crawling forward on his knees, his mind blank. '*No.*'

'Would you believe that this piece of vermin is my only son?'

'Charlie …' Vasco was staring at him, open-mouthed, before he shook himself and rounded on Nikolai Ignatiev. 'It's not true! I don't believe you! There's no *way* he could be –'

'It *is* true, Vaska, and I am most grateful to him for having returned my weapon to me.'

Shaking, Charlie raised his eyes to Seren's face, begging her to understand. 'I …' He had not wanted any of this to happen. It was all his fault. 'Seren, I didn't mean to –'

'I have a message for all those parasites, those coven witches crawling through my city like cockroaches.' Nikolai Ignatiev's voice rose with every word he spoke, drowning Charlie's out. He tightened his grip on Seren's arm, his fingers digging into her skin hard enough to draw blood. 'Thanks to my *true* weapon, your days of hiding in the shadows are over.' He threw out his arm, gave Seren a fierce shake, and delivered his command to her with a single word. '*Fire.*'

She was swallowed up in a ball of light. Golden-yellow flames, the colour of a dying star, consumed her. The whole building began to shake with violent tremors as the terrible sound of creaking steel rumbled overhead. Then everything was illuminated in a blinding flash of white light.

On his knees, Charlie was forced to brace himself as a burst of scorching wind whipped through the passageway. Open-mouthed, he stared up at Seren, cocooned in fire. Her eyes were wide, tears streaming down her cheeks, a silent scream trapped in a fiery cage. From beside her, the sound of the Great Protector's shrieks of cruel laughter rang through his head.

'Run.' Vasco had wrenched him to his feet. '*Run*, Charlie!'

Their feet thundering beneath them, Charlie, Alya and Jasmine fled down countless passageways. They were following Vasco, who never once let go of Charlie's hand as they raced away from the ball of burning light – away from their friends and their enemies. Charlie did not know when Alya had joined them, or where she had appeared from, and nor did he care.

'What are they going to do to her?' he managed to say at last, his voice empty.

'You know what they're going to do,' Vasco said. 'It's too late, Charlie. She's gone.'

'*No.*'

He might have whispered the word or shouted it, he did not know. But he had managed to pull his hand out of Vasco's grip, and he was turning on his heel at the gates of the Volya Facility, determined to get back inside. He would find the monsters who wanted to hurt innocent children, and he would stop them. He could not get the sight of Saga's face – or of her little body, hanging frozen with fear – out of his mind. Somehow, he would save them all.

'Charlie, stop! I won't let you do this!'

The world had slowed down. He would be able to catch up with them if only he could find a way to make himself go faster. His legs seemed to be struggling through mud, and his breath was ragged in his chest. He had to be the one to save them. He had to protect the children.

He paused. Someone had taken his hand and was holding him back. It was Vasco.

'I'm sorry,' was all he said. 'Charlie, I'm so sorry …'

'We can't leave her,' Charlie said, staring up at the building. 'We *can't* just –'

'Wh-What's that sound?' Alya asked, her voice shaking. She staggered towards the edge of the cliff, where the gloomy shapes of the city of Penumbra spread out below them in the deepening half-light. 'Can any of you hear it too?'

'I never knew there were so many of us living in hiding.' Jasmine had joined her and was leaning over the railing. She shook her head. 'It's the collared witches. They're screaming.'

'Look!' Alya was pointing to something in the distance, her hand trembling. 'It's …'

Eventually, Charlie stopped resisting long enough to allow Vasco to drag him over towards the edge of the clifftop. It was then that he discovered what had drawn Alya's attention. He caught sight of a wall of light where there had only ever been darkness before. Although he did not understand how it could be possible, he knew exactly what it was, and knew what it meant.

'It's the Witchtrap Wall,' he murmured. 'It's …'

It was on fire.

A ring of flames encircled the dark city below them. As they stood on the edge of the cliff, looking down at the hell seething below them, a dreadful song rose up to meet their ears. It raged throughout the city, down the shadowed alleyways and across the dingy tenements of the slums. Filling the night air, hidden in the shadows, came the endless, agonised screams of the witches of Penumbra.

CHAPTER 20

They kept to the shadows. Not daring to stop running, either to catch their breath or check if they were being pursued, they followed Jasmine deep into the slums of Penumbra. Narrow, dilapidated buildings towered above them out of the darkness. They raced down blind alleys and vaulted over high brick walls into a maze of tiny courtyards and back-to-back outbuildings. The sharp pain lodged in Charlie's chest and between his ribs was dizzying.

They crossed a patch of abandoned wasteland and entered the bowels of what at first glance appeared to be a bombed-out factory. Broken glass from the shattered windows littered the floor, crunching underfoot. The building looked as though it had been left to rot since the war. Somewhere close by, the drip of water echoed around them into the silence.

Gasping for breath, Charlie halted in his tracks. 'I'm – not going with you,' he said, as the others spun around to stare at him. 'You all can – go on – without me.'

'What are you talking about?' Alya asked, her mouth twisting into an anxious frown.

'Don't you get it? They're going to come after me,' Charlie said, one hand pressed against his forehead, trying to ward off a splitting headache. 'He's not going to let me get away that easily. Before … when I was – he said something about …' He pushed the memory away, furious at himself for allowing it in. 'It doesn't matter. You're all in danger for as long as I stay with you.'

Jasmine strode towards him and shoved him hard, making Charlie stagger backwards. 'Get over yourself. We were always in danger.' As Alya stepped forward, one hand reaching out for Jasmine's arm, Jasmine narrowed her eyes towards Charlie. 'I've lived my whole life in fear of Nikolai the Merciless and his Witch Hunters. Face him alone and you'll only get yourself killed. That's all you'll achieve with your childish attempts at heroism. So stop being a stubborn idiot and follow me.'

Alya cast Charlie a sympathetic look and followed Jasmine deeper into the rundown building. Vasco hung back, and Charlie saw that Vasco's gaze had come to rest on the place where Jasmine had put her hands on him. They followed behind the girls, walking side by side.

Charlie spoke to his feet. 'This is the part where you get to tell me you told me so.'

'I ...' Vasco raised his eyes to Charlie's. 'I'm sorry he hurt you.'

'I was wrong.' The pain in his head worsening, Charlie braced both his hands against his temples and closed his eyes. 'I was wrong about everything, wasn't I? I'm such a –'

'Hey.' One of Vasco's hands had come to rest between his shoulder blades. 'Talk to me.'

'My family are dead. My brother despises me. Seren is gone.' Charlie shook his head, the reality of those words sinking in at last. 'And it's all because of me. It's all my fault.'

'It's not.' Vasco moved his hand in a gentle circle. 'None of this is your fault.'

Charlie let out an involuntary, sceptical huff. 'It sure feels a lot like it's my fault ...'

'Charlie, come on ...'

'You ...' Straightening up, Charlie regarded Vasco carefully. 'You were one of *them*.'

The ghost of a mirthless smile flitted across Vasco's face. 'Don't give me too much credit,' he said, his hands burying themselves in his pockets. 'I still am.'

'You would go back to *him*, after ...' Charlie's stomach was a knotted mess. 'After everything?'

Vasco shrugged, and scowled at the grimy floor. 'Where else am I supposed to go?'

'You could –' Charlie began, without thinking, but he held himself back from going on.

'The Great Protector …' A muscle slid in Vasco's jaw. 'He said that you're his –'

'*Don't!*' Charlie snarled, fury ripping through his body as he fought to keep his fists clenched by his side. 'Don't *ever* let me hear you say that – that …'

With a huge effort, he cycled through a few deep breaths. When he spoke again, his voice was low and controlled.

'You try to talk to me about this ever again, and it'll be the last thing you ever do, you got it?'

Vasco had gone pale. 'Understood,' he said.

He had not dropped his gaze from Charlie's face for a second, but it was only now that Charlie noticed his brow had furrowed. They had come to a halt in the middle of an empty, shadowy corridor.

'It's too quiet. Where are –?'

Charlie caught sight of movement in the corner of his eye right before he saw stars.

The next time he opened his eyes, he was lying on his side, his knees tucked up against his chest. His hands had been secured behind his back with cable ties. Vasco was lying beside him in the same condition, his gaze resting on Charlie. When he saw that Charlie had regained consciousness, Vasco gave a minute shake of his head, warning him that he should remain silent.

'Stand further away from him.'

At the sound of a rough voice, Charlie flinched. He glanced up to see a middle-aged man wearing silver glasses grip Alya's shoulder.

Vasco forced himself to his feet. 'You get your hands off her!' he roared, before the man promptly smashed him in the face with his elbow and he sank to his knees. His nose bleeding freely, Vasco ground his teeth as the man in the glasses turned away from them with a mild expression on his face. 'Untie me and try that again,' Vasco said, his voice deadly soft.

'Next time, I won't hold back,' the man said, and he left the room without another word.

'You have to be more careful,' Alya warned gently, helping Vasco to his feet.

'I'm fine.' He was scowling, but he allowed her to dab at his nose with her sleeve.

'How does it feel to get a taste of your own medicine?' Charlie asked, pushing himself up onto his knees before gingerly edging himself into a standing position. 'Where are we, anyway?'

'Stop talking.' The sound of Jasmine's sharp voice came from outside the room, just as Vasco opened his mouth to retaliate. 'The Whisperer could be back at any moment.'

'Jasmine, where are we?' Alya demanded. 'Why did you bring us here?'

'You'll find out soon enough,' Jasmine answered, sliding the door open and entering the room with a knife.

She placed a hand on Charlie's shoulder and twisted his body around, so that his back was facing her. Then she split the cable ties binding his wrists with one sweep of the blade.

'Wait here,' she said, before turning back to the door. 'The High Witch will see you soon.'

'Hey, witch, aren't you forgetting something?' Vasco turned, showing her his bound hands. 'You're going to let *him* out of these things and not me?'

Jasmine regarded him with a sly smile. 'That's right,' she answered with a shrug, and left.

'Nine hells,' Vasco sighed, craning his head up to stare at the crumbling ceiling. 'How is this happening to me? Maybe I'll wake up and find out this has all just been a bad dream.'

'At least we're all together,' Alya said, managing a small smile. 'Even if they're planning to keep us imprisoned here, we're all still alive.'

'For now,' Charlie muttered.

'Exactly,' Vasco said. 'I get the feeling I'm not going to be too popular around here.'

'And what would make you think that, my young Witchkiller?' a delicate voice asked.

The voice belonged to a woman like none that Charlie had ever seen before. She entered the room carrying herself with a confidence that suggested years of authority, but she did not yet look as though she had reached middle age. Her face held an otherworldly kind of beauty, only somewhat hardened by a bitter edge around the corners of her mouth. Her ice-blue eyes were bright and piercing, and her golden hair shimmered almost like a mirror around her shoulders. Jasmine stood behind her, her eyes fixed on the others.

Vasco said nothing, his expression wary as his eyes travelled over the woman's face. No one seemed to want to break the silence. As she observed the three of them steadily, the older woman's full lips curled into what would have been a pleasant smile, were it not for the fact that its warmth did not even get close to reaching her steel-like eyes.

'Show our guests in,' she said, turning on her heel and leading the way out of the room.

Jasmine grasped Vasco roughly by the upper arm and dragged him out first. Alya followed meekly behind, her eyes darting across their surroundings with obvious anxiety. Charlie brought up the rear, relieved not to be the punching bag for once.

They were taken down another corridor, through a wooden door that led into a large room with walls of exposed brickwork. Wide, open windows were spaced around the walls, through which the first rays of sunrise were beginning to stream into the room. The morning sky was baby blue and cloudless.

'Well, then,' the older woman said, her hands behind her back as she surveyed them one by one. 'Let's see what we have here …'

Her blonde hair fell in loose, playful curls around her shoulders, and her face seemed to betray nothing, whether emotion or memory. Charlie flinched a little under her gaze, so controlled it was almost imperial. It was a feeling the likes of which he had never experienced before.

An entourage of young women had entered the room and amassed around her. They were all wearing the same uniform as Jasmine, and each of them carried a variety of different weapons.

All of them had the same serious demeanour and stern expressions on their faces. None of them were wearing collars.

'Welcome to our hideout,' the woman said. 'I hope you have settled in well.' When no one answered, she held out her hand expectantly. 'I suppose you will have some questions for me.'

'Who are you?' Alya asked at once. 'What is this place?'

'You have entered the Lilith coven,' the woman answered. 'My name is Eva Brightheart, and I am the High Witch of Matya.'

Charlie glanced at Vasco and Alya, looking to see if his confusion was mirrored in their own faces. However, he had the distinct impression that he was alone in his ignorance about this group of witches. Alya's breath had caught in her chest at the High Witch's words, and, from beside him, Charlie heard Vasco make a noise of clear distaste in his throat.

'The Witch Queen,' he snarled, his hands curling into fists. 'So, this is your lair?'

'You flatter me, Witchkiller, but my people recognise no kings or queens,' the High Witch said, before turning her cool gaze on Alya. 'I can see we each have some questions for the other,' she continued. 'It may save us some time, Miss Ignatieva, if you ask yours first.'

'What do you want with us?' Alya asked, without a moment's hesitation. 'Are we to be your prisoners?'

Eva Brightheart blinked, then let out a sweet laugh. 'Certainly not,' she replied. 'Do you consider yourselves prisoners? No, indeed, you are our guests.'

'You have an interesting approach to treating your guests,' Vasco said darkly.

The High Witch looked at him directly for the first time, and Charlie noticed with increased respect that Vasco did not quail for a moment under her icy stare. If anything, he seemed to become even more resolved, and glared back at her without breaking eye contact. Eva Brightheart took a couple of steps towards him, her cold gaze flickering across his face.

'You know, you remind me of him,' she murmured, her eyes boring into his. 'I think you could almost be handsome, but you carry the stain of violence with you, young Witchkiller. Ah, yes …'

She nodded as Vasco's eyes fell to the floor. 'I see I am right.' She turned her head back slightly, addressing Jasmine. 'He is the one?'

'Vasco Kovalev,' Jasmine answered at once. 'Elysian Lieutenant. Witchkiller. His name regularly comes up in our reports from the survivors. He is close to Nikolai Ignatiev.'

'*This* is him?' Eva Brightheart returned her gaze to Vasco, a quizzical look on her face.

'That's right,' he growled back, straining against the ties that bound his hands.

'Really? Hm.' Without another word, Eva Brightheart turned away from him. 'As to what we want with you, let me explain a little about our humble organisation. We are the Lilith coven, and for years, our sole aim has been to overthrow the tyrannical rule of the so-called Great Protector, First Hunter General Nikolai Ignatiev. He may be your father, Miss Ignatieva, but you and your friends are under our jurisdiction now.'

Vasco let out a cold laugh. 'I've heard of these witches.' His eyes flashed with rage as Eva Brightheart turned to look at him, a mildly curious expression on her face. 'They're terrorists, guerrillas mired in the slums, clamouring for an armed rebellion with no strength or support from any of the other covens or clans. You can't seriously believe that you have any chance of challenging the Great Protector?'

Jasmine approached Vasco without hesitation and, in a single vicious movement, backhanded him across the face with such force that Charlie flinched. 'You need to learn when to be silent,' she said, her voice flat. 'Speak out of turn again and you'll regret it, Witchkiller.'

'We must remember to treat our guests gently, Jasmine,' Eva Brightheart said evenly, the merest hint of a smile playing around her mouth. 'However, you would be wise to take her warning seriously, Witchkiller,' she added, as Vasco glowered back at her. 'We have more friends in this city than you do. You will find the people of Penumbra more than willing to turn a blind eye to the disappearance of a worthless war criminal such as yourself, should we deem it necessary.'

Vasco's fury burned in his eyes. 'Your threats don't scare me,' he said quietly.

'I never make threats,' Eva Brightheart said, her voice level. 'Only promises.'

Alya cleared her throat. 'Excuse me, ma'am, but I would like to suggest something.'

Eva Brightheart cast her a leisurely glance. 'Do you plan on keeping up this pretence,' she said, her eyes fixed on Alya with a curious hunger, 'or will you speak honestly, daughter?'

'Alexandra, what is she talking about?' Vasco demanded, looking warily between them.

'We have good reason to help each other,' Alya protested. 'That's not a lie.'

'But not yet the whole truth.' Eva Brightheart had been watching her closely, and her lips had grown thinner at Alya's words. 'We know you escaped Elysia with a certain weapon,' she continued. Her eyes travelled from Alya to Charlie, who frowned back at her, nonplussed. 'I believe you know what I am talking about, child of the Darkwood clan.'

'*What?*' Jasmine's head snapped towards Charlie, whose eyes had darted to his feet.

'We recognised you at once from our source's intelligence reports,' Eva Brightheart said. 'She provided us with regular updates from deep inside the heart of Elysia. Yes,' she added, nodding at the look of understanding on their faces that none of them could hide. 'We have known about the horrors that have been inflicted on our people at the Volya Research Facility for many months now.'

'What are you talking about?' Vasco asked, fuming. 'How could you know anything about that? In the condition they're kept, there's no way any of the prisoners could have —'

'We knew a daughter of the Casimir coven of Kalnelys had escaped.' The High Witch looked directly at Charlie. 'We have been on the lookout for anything suspicious taking place in the Volya Facility ever since. We knew it would only be a matter of time before we had you in our grasp.'

'If that's so,' Alya began hesitantly, 'then why didn't you —'

215

Vasco overrode her. 'Who was your spy?' he demanded. 'Who betrayed us?'

'Who was our source?' Eva Brightheart's voice was pleasant. 'Can you not guess?'

Charlie shook his head. 'There's no one who could have told you about me, except …'

'Alexandra Ignatieva Brightheart,' the High Witch said. 'With her burgeoning Gift, she reached out to me, and I learnt that my daughter was still alive – and much more, besides.'

'*These* are your friends in Penumbra?' Vasco said softly, staring at Alya in horror.

Alya's eyes widened. 'You mean you knew that I'm your – that you're my … my mother?'

Vasco was staring at Alya in shock. His mouth was open, but no words came out.

'What about *him*?' Jasmine asked in a strangled voice, her eyes still fixed on Charlie.

'Ah, yes, I almost forgot,' Eva Brightheart said, 'that we have another honoured guest present amongst us. Charlie Carroway, the son of Erin Darkwood – your mother's youngest sister, Jasmine.'

'Charlie's mother is a witch?' Alya asked, gazing at him, stunned. 'Charlie, why didn't you tell me?'

'Erin Darkwood was a rare talent,' the High Witch continued. 'She was also unusual for a witch in that when she gave birth, it was to a son. Male births are all but unheard of amongst our kind, you see. For years, there have been many who have searched for him,' she added delicately, looking directly at Charlie again, 'but most assumed him long dead, along with his mother.'

'Then she …' Alya's face fell, and she lowered her head. 'Charlie, I'm so sorry …'

His gaze still averted, Charlie could sense everyone's eyes on him. He shivered, a nauseous feeling creeping up his throat from the pit of his stomach. He did not want their pity.

'How do you know this for sure?' Vasco said sharply. 'If Charlie's mother –'

'There is no doubt,' Eva Brightheart answered immediately. 'I could smell Erin Darkwood in his blood the moment he entered the room. Along with another familiar scent ...'

Charlie glanced up, his heart racing horribly. It was under his skin. Somehow, he had known it all along. The truth of his own nature was inescapable. He revolted himself.

'Please,' Alya said quickly. 'Please help us save Seren and the other prisoners.'

'He has saved plenty of us before now,' Jasmine said. 'We should help him in turn.'

Eva Brightheart was looking from Alya, to Charlie, to Jasmine, with growing interest. 'We believe that Seren Casimir is being held in Elysia with an unconfirmed number of other prisoners of our kind,' she said. 'We have also had reports suggesting that large numbers of our people have been brought into Matya in regular shipments from smaller covens around the Elysian mountains. It appears they are to take part in some sort of ritual sacrifice.'

'*What?*' Charlie breathed. His head was spinning and pounding furiously.

'Why have they treated so many people this way?' Alya asked, shaking her head. 'What was the point to all this suffering? I can't think of any reason that could justify this ...'

'And I suppose your little gang is planning to do something about it?' Vasco sneered.

'We plan to free our people and overthrow Nikolai Ignatiev's rule,' the High Witch said, her eyes hardening. 'He has caused the witches of this land untold suffering.'

'By what right?' Vasco demanded, his voice dripping with venom now. 'Do you expect me to believe that the High Throne holds no appeal for you? We cannot be led by demons.'

'I do not deny that I also have a personal reason for wanting to liberate Matya,' Eva Brightheart said carefully. 'Nikolai Ignatiev has kept my daughter from me for many long years.' She turned to Alya. 'My little daughter, Alexandra ... my only child. I don't know what your father might have told you about me, but –'

'He didn't like to talk about you,' Alya said, her voice strangely flat. 'When I was younger I would try to ask him about you, but eventually I … I learnt not to.'

'I see,' Eva Brightheart said, her voice taut, before she took a deep breath. 'Well, that's all in the past now, my darling. With the two of us together again, we can make a fresh start.'

'What do you mean by that?' Vasco asked, his voice soft, but Alya waved him away.

'What are you planning to do next?' she asked. 'How can we help you?'

Eva Brightheart smiled, and strode towards the windows. 'For some time now, we have been planning to launch an attack on Elysia. And now, thanks to your support, we will be able to make our move sooner than I had anticipated.'

She regarded Charlie with a grim expression on her face, the sunlight reflecting off her hair. 'We have also received intelligence that an Elysian Witch Hunter, a lieutenant called Arron Dragomir, has been assigned to handle your friend's time in captivity. I imagine you are familiar with this name too, Witchkiller?'

Charlie's legs had almost given way beneath him at the thought of Seren in a cell with Dragomir. His whole body was shaking now, his chest uncomfortably tight.

'We have to go back,' he said at once, holding a fist in front of his mouth to smother a sudden cough. 'We have to save her.'

'I'm with you, Charlie,' Alya said. 'She'll be all right. We'll save her.'

'I'll come too,' Jasmine added. 'Don't worry, cousin. With the Lilith coven's support, we'll definitely be able to get them all out of there. We still have time. We'll save everyone.'

Vasco shook his head. '*Think* for one second – all of you,' he urged. 'How are you planning to save them when you've seen for yourselves what they can make her do?'

'We'll find a way,' Charlie said. 'This is all my fault. If it weren't for me, Seren –'

'Dragomir is trying to lure you back to Elysia,' Vasco said furiously. '*You*, Charlie! Listen to me. Don't be stupid. Don't fall for it. Trust me – if you do this, you're all going to be in danger!'

'Why should I trust anything you say?' Charlie murmured. 'You're still one of them.'

Charlie's words wiped Vasco's face free of any expression. His dark eyes shuttered.

'I think we should go,' Alya said. 'If my mother believes that the time is right, then –'

'Alexandra, *why* are you so determined to trust her?' Vasco asked, rounding on her instead. 'You hardly know her. She walked out on you when you were just a child!'

'I wonder if I might ask you some questions now, Lieutenant Kovalev?' Eva Brightheart said, her voice still pleasant, but softer now. 'Why are you so interested in my daughter?' She prowled forwards, her hands behind her back. 'What exactly is the nature of your relationship with her father? Why do you have such a strong conviction that the story your master has told you about me is the truth?'

'You don't have the right to question *me* when *you're* the one who abandoned her!' Vasco retorted, his voice harsh. 'No one in this room cares about Alexandra more than I do.'

Eva Brightheart regarded him with cold fury in her eyes. 'Vasco Kovalev, I name you as Witchkiller, a murderer, and place you under arrest, by the order of the Lilith coven.' A savage smile spread across her face as the man in glasses entered the room at her words. 'Take him to the cells and put him in chains,' she added, and the man strode forward at once to carry out her orders. 'This young man has a great deal to pay for. See to it that he does so in full.'

As he was forced from the room, Vasco turned back to Alya, appealing to her with his eyes. 'Alexandra, why are you just standing there?' he asked desperately. 'Aren't you going to stop her? It's – it's me.'

Alya bit her lip, her gaze falling to the floor. 'If my mother thinks that this is what is right …'

'Alexandra, don't do this! Don't trust her!'

With an intense effort, the spectacled man wrenched Vasco out of the room. Charlie could hear him struggling to break free as he was dragged down the corridor and out of sight.

'Well, then,' Eva Brightheart said, breathing a deep sigh and smiling, 'now all that unpleasantness is over and done with, I think you all deserve some rest. You must be tired.'

Charlie's eyes lingered on the empty doorway as he schooled his features into a neutral expression. He held himself still, forcing himself to remain calm. His heart was hammering in his chest. He was certain he had not imagined the look of satisfaction on Eva Brightheart's face when she had ordered Vasco to be punished. By now, he was all too familiar with that look.

They had taken Vasco. Charlie felt his absence keenly, like a wound. He did not understand why, but somehow, the matter of who Vasco had allied himself with no longer seemed as important to him anymore. All Charlie wanted was to have Vasco back by his side.

Nevertheless, he refused to allow any sign of his emotions to show on his face. He knew he would do Vasco no favours by charging through the Lilith coven hideout to save him right there and then. Vasco was more than capable of handling himself for now. Charlie would find him in the cells later.

It was a date.

CHAPTER 21

The blisteringly hot water of the shower was a blissful experience. At first, Charlie loathed the idea of ever turning the water off. But by the time Jasmine started banging on the door to be let in, he felt as though he had at least managed to scrub some of the worst of his time at the Volya Facility off his skin.

He dressed before leaving the bathroom, dumping his bandages in the bin, and borrowed a towel to dry his hair. This caused Alya to smile fondly at him when she saw him with it draped over his head. He still felt dirty. Not once had he ever been able to wash away the feeling of contamination.

Afterwards, while Jasmine showed Alya up the rickety wooden staircase to the dormitories, Charlie was directed to a small room off one of the gloomy corridors. It was a simple space, clean and sparsely furnished. The walls were of the same exposed brickwork as the rest of the hideout. There was a round window opposite the door that let in the soft glow of the sunlight.

A thin mattress had been rolled out across the wooden floorboards, and Charlie was relieved to see a pillow and blankets again after so long without proper sleep. Just looking at the makeshift bed was enough to make him feel exhausted. But he knew he would have nightmares.

The thought of Vasco crossed his mind, and his stomach twisted painfully.

Witchkiller.

When he could no longer hear voices nearby, Charlie tested the door to ensure that it was properly closed. There was a key in the latch, but he did not use it. He never wanted to be inside a locked room ever again.

Charlie removed his shoes and socks before placing them beside the mattress. He debated for a moment whether he would need to wear all his clothes to sleep in or not. The blanket looked thin, and there was no source of heat in the room. However, once underneath, he was pleasantly surprised at how quickly he warmed up, so he opted to remove his jeans and sleep in his t-shirt and boxer shorts. He was asleep as soon as his head hit the pillow.

'Charlie?'

He opened his eyes blearily at the noise. 'Ruby,' he murmured, 'go back to sleep.'

'It's me,' said the voice, and Charlie realised that it was Jasmine. She must have sneaked down from the dormitories to visit him. A huge grin had spread across her face. 'I couldn't wait until later to speak with you. I can't *believe* your mother was a Darkwood coven witch … I *knew* there was something about you I recognised. It's so exciting!' When Charlie did not return her smile, she tilted her head to one side. 'What's wrong?'

'Nothing.' He yawned widely, the back of his palm resting against his forehead. 'I just don't see what's so exciting about any of this.'

'You could be like me,' Jasmine suggested. 'That's exciting, isn't it?'

'How could I be? Witches are female.'

'You heard what the High Witch said. Sons of witches are incredibly rare. Besides,' she said, as she began to re-braid a section of her hair, 'haven't you heard of the Bloodwitch?'

'No.'

'Why are you being off with me?'

'I'm not being anything. I'm trying to sleep.' Charlie attempted to turn onto his side again, but she put one hand against his chest, stopping him from shifting over. He stiffened. 'Get off me.'

'Something's going on with you.' Jasmine narrowed her eyes, bringing her face closer to his. 'Why won't you tell me? We *are* cousins, you know. I could help you.'

Charlie shook his head firmly, frowning. 'I don't need your help.'

'When has that *ever* been true?' Jasmine demanded. 'I suppose you didn't need my help to get out of prison in the Volya Facility, just like you didn't need my help to get away from Dragomir?'

Charlie sat up, the blanket falling off him. 'I would have figured something out.'

'Or how about when you were almost caught by your own brother? You definitely didn't need my help then!'

'Can you stop shouting at me? You're making my head hurt.'

'Apparently, your skull is so thick that I have to shout to get anywhere with you.'

'I'm not a little kid, so stop treating me like one!'

'Stop acting like one and I wouldn't need to!'

Charlie ran his fingers through his hair and pressed his hands against his eyes. Taking a deep breath, he forced himself to speak calmly. 'You're right. Without your help, none of us would be here right now. It's at least partly thanks to you that we're safe.'

'Thank you, I'm glad you noticed that, *at least.*'

'But it didn't come without a cost, did it?'

'You're talking about Seren. You blame yourself for what happened to her.'

'Using her powers damages her – weakens her. I should never have contributed to that.'

'How noble of you.' Jasmine's voice dripped sarcasm, and her lips had curled into a sneer. 'I suppose you expect me to be impressed because you *care* so much about her wellbeing. But I think you should mind your own business from now on. She can make her own choices.'

'You'd prefer it if I didn't care about her, then, would you?' Charlie snapped.

'If you're going to be so sanctimonious about it, then yes, I would. You're no hero.'

'I don't understand why you're getting angry at me for caring that she might get hurt.'

'Because we're soldiers!' Jasmine said hotly. 'This is our duty. We *have* to fight back. Kindness is a luxury we cannot afford.'

Charlie opened his mouth, paused, and closed it again. For some reason, his thoughts had found their way back to Vasco once more. There was a knock on the door, and Alya came in, looking between them anxiously as she hovered on the threshold.

'May I join you?'

'Be my guest,' Jasmine answered, glaring at Charlie. 'I was just leaving, anyway.'

She stormed out of the room. Alya waited until Jasmine had slammed the door behind her before coming to sit cross-legged beside Charlie, next to the edge of the mattress.

Wincing against the pain in his head, Charlie mirrored her pose. He steeled himself for what he was sure she would want to discuss with him next. He was starting to feel nauseous again.

'We're almost the same age, aren't we, Charlie?' she said softly, her eyes downcast.

'I turned sixteen a few months ago, in the spring.' It had been a bright, cold day.

'It's my birthday in a couple of days,' she said. 'Then I'll be seventeen.'

'It's strange to think I've had a big sister,' he said, 'all … all this time …'

Alya looked up at him, nibbling her lower lip. 'Do you have any others?'

'Brothers or sisters, you mean?' Charlie shook his head. 'No, not anymore.'

'I never dreamed that Doctor Ivanov could be involved in any of this,' Alya said, her gaze rising towards the window, the sunlight reflected in her brown eyes. 'Even when I read his notes, I thought he was – trying to stop them, or something. I thought he was my friend …'

Charlie watched her, choosing his words carefully. 'Did you know him well?'

'I *thought* I did ...' Alya gathered her hair over one of her shoulders and began to braid it absentmindedly. 'He was the first person I told. You know ... about me being a – a witch. He said it was our secret.'

Charlie frowned. 'Why would he keep that information to himself?'

Alya shrugged back, shaking her head. 'He always seemed like such a good person,' she said. 'He always had time for me, no matter what else was going on. He listened to me.' She glanced up at him, biting at a fingernail. 'I'm sorry, I sound really stupid, don't I?'

'No, you don't,' Charlie said, his grip tightening around himself. 'I'm listening.'

'I think he knew that I wanted to get away from my father,' Alya said. 'He made me feel ... I don't know ... like I was *important* – does that sound weird? And he was always happy to answer my questions about medicine,' she added, when Charlie shook his head. 'I – I want to become a doctor,' she continued, her voice wavering a little, 'someday. If I can.'

'That's a good ambition,' Charlie said, smiling when she flushed a little at his words.

'The Doctor Ivanov I knew was always there for me,' she said. 'If I needed advice or support, or when it was all getting too much with Arron and my father ...'

At the mention of Dragomir's name, Charlie looked away, feeling physically sick, but Alya did not seem to notice.

'When I think that he's been a part of this – all along.' She shivered. 'I'm sorry ... I honestly think I'm finding it a little bit difficult to process all this. I don't know how I didn't see it.'

'It's not your fault that you trusted him.'

'It makes me feel ...' Alya seemed to be struggling to find the right words. 'Guilty by association, is that it? I mean, I *let* him take my blood and examine me and – what's wrong?'

'Nothing,' Charlie muttered, his hand over his mouth as he forced himself not to vomit.

'I know I was stupid, and it was wrong of me,' Alya said, 'but he said he was interested in what he could learn from studying me.

I thought … I don't know, I suppose I thought that I needed to repay him for – for being so kind to me.' She was staring at the floor, a confused, anxious expression clouding her face. 'I feel … *bad*. Like all of this is my fault, somehow.'

'Listen, you haven't done anything wrong, Alya,' Charlie said. 'D'you believe me?'

Alya shook herself. 'Oh, no! I'm so selfish, aren't I?' she said, her tone bright and forced. She was smiling at him, although her smile did not reach her eyes. 'I've been going on and on about myself and I haven't even asked you how *you're* feeling, Charlie.'

Charlie sighed, raking his fingernails across his throat. 'Look, Alexandra, you don't have to do this, all right? I don't want anything from you. You don't have to treat me like –'

'I always wanted a brother.' She was smiling at him. She looked almost hopeful.

He raised an eyebrow. 'A little brother?'

She laughed. 'Who's little? You're taller than I am …' When she saw the first hint of his smile, hers grew a bit brighter. 'I'm glad that it's you.'

This took Charlie by surprise, and he knew it showed on his face. 'Why? I'm not exactly someone you can be proud of. I –' He broke off, coughing, and fought to catch his breath.

'It's getting worse, isn't it?' She frowned. 'Charlie, we need to talk about this.'

'Alexandra, I would really like to be left alone right now.' It was a struggle to speak.

'That's the last thing you need,' she replied, shifting closer to him, and cupping her chin in her hands as she rested her elbows on her knees. 'Maybe that's what you want, but you need to be around other people.' She rubbed his back. 'You need to realise that life goes on.'

Charlie's eyes widened at her words, and he gripped his knees to stop his hands from shaking. 'Did you really just say that to me?' he asked, with a bitter laugh. 'Are you for real?'

'I'm trying to help,' Alya said softly. 'When are we going to talk about this?'

'What d'you want to *talk about*?' Charlie said sourly, knowing the answer.

'You're getting worse.' She was watching him closely, her face full of concern. 'You may want to pretend otherwise, but it's true.'

'What's your point?'

'When are you going to talk about – about what's wrong with you?'

'That's *my* business, not yours,' he answered. 'You *said* you'd let me deal with it.'

'But you're *not* dealing with it, Charlie, you're avoiding it.'

'This is me dealing with it. I'm sorry if it's not the way *you* would choose to deal with it, but it's not happening to you, it's happening to me.' Alya had sprung to her feet, but he was determined to give her no chance to interrupt what he had to say. '*I'm* the one who's *dying*, Alexandra, not you, so you don't even have to waste your time thinking about this, if it's getting you so concerned.'

'Who in the nine hells do you think you're talking to?' Alya demanded. 'I'm –'

'I know, I *know*,' he said. 'You're the First Daughter of Matya, *and* you're the daughter of the High Witch of the Lilith coven. You're the heir to the leader of the country and the leader of the resistance, and I'm just some orphan Penumbran criminal scum, right? How dare I –'

'Will you shut up for *one second* and *listen* to me?' Tears had sprung to Alya's eyes, but she blinked furiously to clear them. Sinking to her knees, she rounded on him with barely contained rage. 'I don't care what you are or where you come from! It doesn't matter who I am either – whether I'm your half-sister, or whatever else. Don't treat me like I'm your enemy. I'm your *friend*, Charlie – that's all I was going to say! I'm your friend …'

Charlie felt all the anger draining from him at her words, only for it to be replaced by a feeling that was far worse.

'I'm trying to help you. Why can't you *see* that?' Alya's fists were clenched as she got to her feet and began to tap her foot against the floorboards in a staccato pattern. 'All I've tried to do from the very beginning is *help* you!'

'I never asked you to,' he said, his voice small and empty.

'Do you want to die? Is that it? You want to punish yourself?'

He scowled and did not look at her. 'You wouldn't understand.'

'Why do you insist on refusing everyone's help?' Alya's voice had fallen almost to a whisper. 'Don't you realise that if you tried relying on someone other than yourself for *one single moment of your life* you might actually find yourself better off for having done so?'

'This is who I am,' Charlie said flatly, dragging his fingers through his hair, a desperately empty feeling in the pit of his stomach. 'I'm sorry. I wish I could be someone different, someone less –' He gestured vaguely to himself. 'But I can't. I can't change who I am.'

Alya shook her head and huffed out a sigh. 'Then I can't keep doing this with you,' she said. 'I've tried my best to help you, Charlie. But if you've decided you're going to give up, then there's nothing more I can do for you. Enjoy facing the end of your life alone, I guess.'

'*Speaking* of enjoying being alone,' Charlie said suddenly, unable to stop himself, 'are you planning to go down to the basement to pay a conjugal visit to Vasco any time soon?'

Alya, who had almost crossed the threshold on her way out of the room, turned back slowly. Her fingers were gripping the doorframe so tightly that they had gone white. There was an expression of such dangerous intensity on her face that Charlie almost quailed beneath it. Suddenly, he saw both the ferocity of Eva Brightheart, the High Witch of the Lilith coven, and the iron fist of Nikolai Ignatiev, the Great Protector of Matya, in every aspect of the young woman standing before him.

'Say that again,' she breathed, 'if you dare.'

'Forget it,' Charlie said quickly, shocked at the cold rage burning in her eyes. 'I'm sorry. I don't know why I said that. It's nothing to do with me, anyway.'

'You're absolutely right it's not,' Alya hissed in a furious whisper. 'I don't care what snide comments you throw at me, but you had better keep your mouth off Vasco. You know nothing at all about – about *either* of us. If my mother found out that I –' She broke off, running her teeth over her lower lip, the slightest trace of panic in her voice. 'Charlie, you *can't* –'

'I won't say anything,' he promised, holding his hands up in front of him in surrender. He hoped she knew that he was being sincere. 'Come on, you know you can trust me.'

'Yeah, I can always trust that *you'll* keep a secret,' Alya said bitterly, turning on her heel and striding from the room. Her dark hair whipped across her shoulders as she slammed the door behind her.

When she was gone, Charlie lay back down on the thin mattress, only to find that he was no longer tired. He stared up at the exposed beams of the ceiling, his thoughts returning to Vasco at once. A horrible feeling was gnawing in his stomach, burning away at him like acid. He was not sure how much longer he could keep lying to himself like this.

CHAPTER 22

Although he had not intended to do so, Charlie ended up sleeping through the rest of that day and long into the night. It was the nightmares that eventually woke him. When he crept from his room at last, he was resolved in his choice. The corridors of the Lilith coven hideout were silent and deserted in the moonlight. Shutting the door cautiously behind him, he paused, listening hard before making his move.

From much further away, he could hear the echo of laughter and chattering voices. The scrape of wooden benches on the flagstone floor rang along the walls, mingling with the clatter of knives and forks. He guessed that some of the girls were still up, perhaps eating a late meal. Otherwise, everyone else seemed to have already gone back to their dormitories. Charlie brushed a hand against his stomach, his wrist colliding with jutting hip bones. He could not remember the last time he had felt hungry.

Descending the staircase to the ground floor, he made his way towards the cells. He was working on the assumption that, in a building such as this, they were likely to be underground. After a little exploration, he discovered a flight of wooden steps located beneath a trap door, hidden in a corner.

Standing in the darkness, Charlie peered down into the gloom. There was no sign of movement on the stairs. He could already feel how the air turned colder below ground. The rising damp was cloying in his nostrils. No one seemed to be coming.

Glancing around, Charlie steeled himself, a strange fluttering sensation in his chest.

Vasco was down there.

He went as slowly as he dared, tentatively seeking out each new stair with the sole of his foot before putting his weight on it. The floorboards were rotten, some of them worn through completely in places. It would only take one misplaced step to give himself away. He had only made it halfway down the staircase, however, when the sound of a woman's voice made him pause.

Freezing where he stood, Charlie strained his ears to catch her words. But it was futile; he was too far away to have any chance of hearing anything she said clearly. Once satisfied that she had not heard him approach, he continued his careful descent.

When he reached the bottom of the staircase, he tiptoed hastily over to the door of a barred cell. Making sure that he was hidden from view, he pressed his back against the door and, his heart thumping wildly, began to listen.

'I do apologise for having kept you waiting so long, Lieutenant Kovalev. I did so enjoy our last conversation. I hope you are feeling a little less taciturn this evening.'

It was Alya's mother, Eva Brightheart, the High Witch of Matya. For a moment, Charlie was so taken aback that he almost thought he must be mistaken. But there could be no doubt that it was her. His heart began to beat even faster as he heard Vasco's voice answer.

'Not coming in to join me tonight, witch?'

'I'm afraid not. You will have to appreciate my visit from a distance, this time.'

'I'm sure I'll cope. It's just you this time, then, is it?'

A hundred questions flashed through Charlie's mind at once. The High Witch of the Lilith coven had gone to the makeshift holding cells in the basement to see Vasco, alone, late at night, when everyone else was busy eating dinner in the kitchen or sleeping in the dormitories. His shoulders tense against the wall, Charlie forced himself to listen harder.

'I see I have disappointed you. Tell me, were you perhaps expecting someone else?'

From his hiding place beside the barred door, Charlie frowned. There was no mistaking the cruel amusement in the High Witch's voice. A twinge of unease crept along his spine. It was a horribly familiar sound. He knew at once who it reminded him of, and that he was right to have come.

'You're right, it's true. I can't help noticing Alexandra isn't with you again tonight,' he heard Vasco reply, his words oozing cool defiance. 'Not quite confident that she'll be on board with how you treat your prisoners yet, are you? It's a reasonable concern, if you ask me.'

'You should consider the possibility that you are not quite as insightful as you think you are.' The High Witch's voice had hardened noticeably. 'To my eyes, my daughter has no interest whatsoever in seeing you.'

'Then your eyes need checking,' Vasco retorted at once. 'Your ears too, for that matter. If Alexandra has said anything at all to you, she'll have asked to see me.'

There was the sound of a scuffle, followed by a muffled yell. The noise of jangling chains echoed out through the bars to where Charlie stood listening. It stirred a memory within him, panic jolting through his body. His fingers had gripped the doorhandle before he even became aware that he had moved. But his better judgement halted him in his tracks, and he stopped himself before he could catch a look into the cell.

'I mean that with the greatest of respect, of course,' Vasco added, and Charlie heard the sound of something being spat onto the ground. 'But you'd never let her see me, would you? You don't even trust your own daughter not to betray you.'

'It's *you* I don't trust, Vasco Kovalev,' the High Witch hissed. 'You are the Witchkiller, the protégé of a monster – a tyrant. When I look into your eyes, all I see inside of you is him.'

'You don't know anything about me.' Vasco's voice was dangerously soft now. 'Or about Alexandra. She hasn't needed you for years, and now you show up pretending to be the concerned mother? I can see straight through your act. You're a bad liar, witch.'

'You common street dog, you have no right to –'

'Where were *you* when she was lonely, or scared?' Vasco demanded. 'She thought you were dead, and all this time you were here, plotting your glorious uprising.' Charlie flinched at the venom in his words. 'You're too late! While you were hiding here playing the queen in exile, you missed watching your own daughter grow up. Well, was it worth it?'

'I can see my husband has been feeding you the same lies as he has to my daughter,' the High Witch said slowly. Charlie noted the quiver in her voice as she struggled to regain her usual controlled manner. 'Tell me this – am I not entitled to care about her?'

'You don't care about her, you want to control her,' Vasco shot back. 'She's just another pawn in your game.'

'My daughter is an intelligent young woman and can make her own decisions.'

'And if she decided she wanted to see me? You'd let her see me like this, in this place, knowing I'd tell her everything about what you've said and done to me?'

'If she makes such a request, I will consider it at that time.'

'I know her. She'll have asked to see me by now – I know it.'

'Do you know, we spent almost the whole day together today, and she didn't mention you once.' The vengeful pleasure in the High Witch's voice was so pronounced that Charlie could picture the smile on her face in his mind's eye. 'Not even once.'

'I don't believe you,' Vasco said quietly.

The airiness of the High Witch's next words seemed to wave his words away. 'Believe what you like, but I have no great wish to spare you painful truths when it comes to my daughter, Witchkiller.'

'What do you mean by that?'

'I mean that you need to accept the truth when it comes to Alexandra.'

'What truth, exactly?'

The High Witch paused before replying. 'That I will never permit you to love my daughter.' Her tone had dropped lower, but her words were spoken with such furious animosity that they carried all the way to where Charlie stood listening. 'For as long as I live, I will prevent the two of you from being together. I will not allow you to covet her. You cannot have her. She is mi-' The High Witch cleared her throat. 'She is my daughter.'

At the sound of movement on the other side of the door, Charlie ducked into the shadows.

'You can't keep us apart forever, you old witch!' he heard Vasco shout after her.

Charlie flung himself behind a wooden post just as the figure of Eva Brightheart emerged from inside the cells. He peered carefully around the post and caught a glimpse of her unmistakable golden hair shining in the low torchlight. She did not lock the door behind her.

As he withdrew his head, Charlie heard her let out a deep sigh. He watched from the corner of his eye as she strode up the stairs, her cloak fanning out behind her. He waited, perfectly still, until he heard the sound of the trapdoor being closed.

Charlie approached the cell door without hesitation, telling himself that there was nothing for him to be afraid of. He would not be locked in. Vasco was in there, and Charlie had to get him out. Taking a deep breath, he forced his hands to stop shaking, and entered the holding cell.

'Were you not done?' Vasco lifted his head as soon as Charlie appeared, a sullen expression on his face. At the sight of him, the soldier's eyes widened. 'Saints, Charlie, I thought you were … What are you doing here?'

'I needed to speak to you,' Charlie said. 'I've got an idea. I –'

He broke off. Set against the far wall of the cell was a tall, locked cage. Vasco was chained up inside it. In the faint glow from the torchlight through the iron bars at the door to the cell, Charlie could just make out Vasco's face. It was covered in dried blood, as was most of his black sleeveless shirt.

His muscular arms were trembling in the cold and were raised high above his head. His wrists had been manacled with heavy chains that were fixed to the wall from an iron ring far above him. Every now and then, he jerked his head to the side to clear his vision, sending drops of water falling from his dark hair. His breathing was ragged, and a mist rose before his eyes each time he exhaled.

'It's bad, huh,' Vasco murmured, watching Charlie's face. 'It feels like it's bad.'

'You look terrible,' Charlie agreed. 'I don't think your nose is broken, though.'

'You've been a bad influence on me,' Vasco said softly, a humourless smile on his face. 'The last time anything like this happened to me, I was just a little kid.'

'You look ill,' Charlie said, his voice sharp, as he noticed the sheen of cold sweat across Vasco's forehead. 'Aren't you freezing? How long have they been keeping you like this?'

'They brought me down here as soon as I was taken away. They have an interrogator – the Whisperer – he likes to keep to a regular work schedule.' Vasco scowled, and looked away. 'And of course, the queen herself never misses an opportunity to drop by for a personal visit.'

'Are you saying they're torturing you?' Charlie heard the words rattle out of his mouth like gunfire. 'Tell me straight – don't play games with me. What do they want from you?'

Vasco shrugged. 'Information. They're amateurs, though.' His smile was devoid of all warmth, and his eyes were blazing. 'I could teach them a thing or two, given the opportunity.'

Charlie cleared his throat. 'Since you brought it up,' he began, making sure to bite back the anger he felt beginning to flare up inside of himself, 'I want to talk to you about something. I've been meaning to for a while now, but this is the first time you haven't been in the position to beat me up the second I say something you don't want to hear.'

Vasco looked straight at him, his eyes narrowed with interest, and said nothing.

'Why did you choose to become a soldier?' Charlie asked. 'You're a Witch Hunter – a lieutenant in Nikolai Ignatiev's forces. You knew him. You can't have been blind to his true nature. How could you not know what he was planning? How could you support a man who's been responsible for so much suffering? I can't ...' He let out a sigh. 'I don't understand you.'

Vasco was regarding him steadily. He seemed to be weighing up his answer. 'Maybe I'll tell you, one day,' he said eventually. 'You're not the only one who likes to keep secrets, you know. Maybe then you'll understand the choice I made.'

He spoke the words gently, and there was no sign of malice on his face. For a moment, Charlie suspected that he did not have an answer to give at all. But there was an intensity in Vasco's gaze that made him reject that thought.

'I *would* like to do something to help you and Seren now, though,' Vasco added quietly.

'What?' Charlie could not hide the surprise in his voice. 'Why?'

'Don't get me wrong. I'm not looking for redemption, or forgiveness, or anything like that,' Vasco said, his tone dry, his expression unreadable. 'I just think it's the right thing to do. I saw the photographs of those kids ... and Seren and her sister are still being held hostage. There are likely to be more witches imprisoned along with them, aren't there? More ... more children.'

'I didn't realise you cared ...'

Vasco cast him a scornful look. 'Don't even try to deny that you have a plan to rescue them – it's obvious. You need my help. You don't have a chance of saving them without me.'

'Then I have your word that you'll help me?'

'I'd shake your hand on it, but I'm a little tied up here at the moment.'

'Not for much longer.'

Vasco regarded him witheringly. 'Let me guess – you're stronger than you look?'

'No, just smarter.'

Grinning at the look of astonishment on Vasco's face, Charlie drew the bobby pin from his hair. One by one, he picked the lock at the door to his cage, then the manacles at his wrists.

'You keep managing to impress me,' Vasco murmured, massaging his wrists as they left the holding cell and headed towards the wooden staircase. 'Were you always this talented?'

'I've had a lot of experience.' Charlie was surprised to find that he was smiling a little, in spite of himself. 'I hope I can keep surprising you.'

As soon as they reached the top of the stairs, Vasco glanced quickly from side to side, before striding purposefully in the direction of the dormitories.

'Where are you going?' Charlie demanded, as forcefully as he could while making sure to keep his voice at a whisper.

Vasco stared at him as if the answer were obvious. 'I'm going to find Alexandra.'

Charlie shook his head firmly. 'No, she's not coming with us.'

'I can't just leave without her. I'm supposed to protect her.'

'Look, I'm not getting in the middle of whatever's going on between you two, but –'

'There's *nothing* going on between the two of us!' Vasco snapped. 'She's my *friend.*'

'But I can tell you this much,' Charlie continued, forcing himself to keep his voice calm and low. 'Alya is happy to be back with her mother. You may not like it,' he added quickly, as Vasco opened his mouth, looking furious, 'but she's made it perfectly clear that she doesn't want to go back to Elysia, or to her father. She as good as told me so earlier today.'

'That's not … she doesn't …' Vasco braced a fist against his right temple. 'I can't …'

'You're just angry because she wants to spend time with her mother, and her mother doesn't trust you because you're a Witch Hunter.'

Vasco rounded on him, looking desperate. 'Do you really think I'm so petty?'

Charlie held Vasco's troubled gaze, taking in the mingled sadness and confusion in his dark eyes. 'Maybe you should give her some time and space?' he suggested. 'At least for now.'

Vasco hesitated for a moment, before inclining his head a fraction. 'Maybe you're right. Besides, it's better if she stays as far away from Dragomir and her father as possible. They don't have limits. They don't know when to stop …' He glanced at Charlie, frowning. 'Is everything all right? You look like you're about to be sick.'

'We should get moving.' Charlie pushed ahead of him, his jaw clenched.

'Wait,' Vasco said, grabbing his hand to stop him going any further. 'What's wrong?'

'Nothing.'

'You think I'm blind? I know something happened back there. I *know* you're hiding something.' Vasco tightened his grip on Charlie's hand. 'What did they do to you, Charlie?'

'He –' Charlie balled his hands into fists, looking away. 'He *hurt* me – you understand?'

'What?' Vasco breathed, dropping Charlie's hand. He had gone very still. '*What?*'

'It's happened to me before,' Charlie said, his voice flat as he stared at his empty palm. 'I wasn't going to say anything about it, but you wanted to know. I'm not going to lie to you …'

'You've been dealing with this alone, all this time?' Vasco's voice sounded hollow.

Charlie scratched his throat and gave Vasco a playful shove to the shoulder. 'Come on, don't look so sad,' he said, forcing himself to sound exactly as he would if he were fine. When this only caused Vasco's expression to grow more forlorn, Charlie heaved a deep sigh and motioned for him to lead the way. 'I survived, didn't I? That's enough. If we're going, let's go.'

They made their way towards the perimeter of the hideout. Both of them were used to moving quietly and avoiding unwanted attention, so a comfortable silence had quickly settled between them. It was only when they had their exit in sight that Vasco spoke.

'There's something I still don't understand,' he began.

'Mm?' Charlie was focused on making sure they were not being followed. 'What is it?'

'Why did you set me free?'

'I needed your help,' Charlie said at once. 'I can't save Seren and Saga on my own.'

'But was I really the one best placed to help you?' Vasco asked. 'Why come to me?'

'Who else would I have asked? You know Elysia best out of all of us.'

'That may be true, but you could have got back into the Facility yourself if you wanted to. Seren would be a lot more help taking down the soldiers and helping you rescue the others than I could be.'

Charlie cleared his throat. 'I don't want to rely on Seren's help. Not with this, at least.'

'Why not?'

'Something's wrong with her,' Charlie explained. 'She's getting weaker every time she uses her powers. You've seen it happen.'

'That makes no sense,' Vasco said immediately. 'Witches gain strength from using their corruptions, they don't get weaker. I've never heard of anything like that happening before.'

'Well, it's happening to Seren,' Charlie countered. 'Maybe it has something to do with the experiments they performed on her at the Volya Facility – I don't know. But it's not just that she gets weaker, she also gets …'

'What?' Vasco pressed, as Charlie broke off.

'You've seen her …' Charlie struggled to find the right words. 'Disorientated. Confused. Afraid.' He drew his arms around himself. 'She doesn't remember who I am, or what happened to her before she used her powers, or how she came to be where she is now.'

'I see.' Vasco frowned. 'And you're worried it's going to get worse.'

'It *is* getting worse,' Charlie insisted. 'Every time she uses her powers, it gets worse.'

Vasco nodded. 'That's why you don't want to rely on her to help you. You're afraid of what might happen if she uses her powers again, in such a place.'

'Yes.'

'I understand.'

They walked on together in silence for a while before Vasco spoke again.

'I've been meaning to talk to you about something else, as well.'

Charlie's heart sank. 'Yeah?'

Vasco took a deep breath and ran his fingers through his hair. Charlie thought Vasco seemed to be looking everywhere but at him.

He frowned. 'What is it?'

'I want to tell you something,' Vasco began, his words stiff and uncertain, as though he was picking his way tentatively through what he wanted to say. 'Charlie, I know I haven't –'

He paused, a dark scowl hardening his face, his eyes narrowed into the night. With a snarled order to get down, Vasco shoved Charlie against the wall, his body pressed hard against Charlie's as the rattle of gunfire split the silence. Charlie found himself instinctively struggling against the feeling of having another body so close to his, but Vasco forced his forearm against Charlie's chest to keep him still.

'Don't move!'

'What are you –?'

Vasco nodded meaningfully to the broken window beside them, keeping the same vicelike grip on Charlie's upper body. Charlie followed his gaze, squinting through the gloom.

'See them?' Vasco asked, and Charlie nodded, realising what he was seeing. 'Military police. Soldiers. Witch Hunters. They've got this place surrounded. Someone sold us out.'

'Faulkner.' Charlie clenched his jaw as he caught sight of a blonde man at the head of his gang. 'He must have known about this place all along. The witches – they're all in danger.'

'You're right.' Vasco turned to Charlie, scowling. 'How long have you known him?'

Charlie made sure not to meet Vasco's eyes. 'Long enough.'

'Since you were a child?'

'Yes.'

At this, Vasco's eyes turned hard, his burning gaze fixed on Faulkner as though watching something repellent play out in his mind. 'Then *he's* the one who ...'

Below them, Faulkner was shouting orders to his men. 'Get me my property back!'

Charlie quailed as a menacingly serene expression settled on Vasco's face. 'What do we do now?' he asked. 'Should we try to take them right here, or get everyone else out?'

Vasco shook his head, blinking as if forcing himself to snap out of a reverie. 'We're both unarmed. We can't take them on alone, and it's too late to attempt a large-scale evacuation. We should get out of here while we still have the chance, and hope Her *Majesty* has a plan.'

Charlie considered these words, aware of Vasco's hard stare piercing him as he waited for Charlie's response. The faces of his family on their knees, surrounded by soldiers, rose in front of his eyes. He saw their bodies slumped forwards in death.

He stared at his hands, his mind playing over everything that had happened to him after he was imprisoned in the Shadow Cells. He could almost believe that it had only been a nightmare, were it not for the scars he now carried, inside and out.

'What do you think?' Vasco asked.

His thoughts skipping as though catching on something sharp, Charlie attempted to make some sense out of what had happened to him. It was, he realised, all because of Faulkner, and the advances of the Pen gang into the safe little world he had tried to create, that his family were gone.

If they had only left him alone, his family would still be alive. If Faulkner had never made Charlie his prisoner, kept him beaten down and humiliated all those years, Charlie would never have had a reason to start gunning for him in the first place.

'Do you agree with me, Charlie?'

It all came back to Faulkner. It was all his fault.

Charlie gritted his teeth, his decision made. 'I've got another idea.'

CHAPTER 23

'T his plan is insane,' Vasco muttered under his breath. 'I must have been crazy to come after you.'

'Leave, then,' Charlie shot back, slipping out of the shadows. 'No one's stopping you.'

'Charlie, *wait*,' Vasco whispered urgently, following him across the landing. They were heading towards a door that stood slightly ajar, spilling light and the rough laughter of soldiers. 'There's no way this is going to work. We'd be better off –'

'Shut up and let me listen!'

Charlie pressed his ear to the door and strained to make out any information they could use. When he heard a triumphant reference to the prisoners they had captured, Charlie turned to Vasco, nervous excitement coursing through his body.

'They're holding the witches in the courtyard,' he said. 'They've brought trucks to take them back to Elysia. Let's go, while there's still a chance for us to rescue them.' He strode forward, but Vasco held him still. 'What? What are you waiting for?'

'I don't like this,' Vasco said, his expression grim. 'Alexandra's mother is the High Witch of Matya. She's more than powerful enough to take down a force like this, especially with the rest of her coven backing her up. She would never surrender without a fight.'

'Look, I hate to break it to you, but this isn't the best time for you to lose your nerve,' Charlie snapped. 'Alexandra is down there too, or have you forgotten about that? We have an opportunity to rescue all of them – I'm not going to waste it because you've got a *bad feeling.*'

'And if you're walking straight into a trap?' Vasco was watching him pointedly.

'How could I be? Most of the soldiers are occupied out there with the witches.'

'There will be more.' Vasco shook his head, his face set. 'This is a bad plan.'

Feeling his last nerve beginning to fray, Charlie grabbed the front of Vasco's shirt, balling the material up into his hand. 'Are you going to help me or not?'

'Charlie –'

'Because I'm going to rescue them. I'm going in there with or without you, understand? If you're too afraid of getting caught then you should just keep out of my way.'

Vasco's face darkened. 'That's not what I'm afraid of. If you think I'm going to –' He broke off, paling, and Charlie saw Vasco's eyes widen sharply, drawn by movement over Charlie's shoulder. 'Charlie, behind you!'

'Whoever knew you'd be so hard to kill?'

At the sound of the familiar voice, Charlie turned his head, his grip tightening on Vasco. He found Marko standing behind him, and a gun aimed squarely between his eyes.

'I'm going to make sure I put you down for good this time, Carroway.' Charlie kept perfectly still as Marko lowered the gun to his knees. 'Or maybe I'll drag you back to Faulkner and let him have what's left of you, what d'you –'

Seizing his chance, Charlie sprang forward, knocking Marko off his feet. Forcing Marko's arm back and up, Charlie bent his other forearm against Marko's chest, keeping him on his back. Then he slammed Marko's wrist against the floorboards, over and over again.

It was only when Marko at last released his grip on the gun in his hand, and it span away into the shadows, that Charlie stopped. Flooded with power, he dug his fingernails into Marko's shoulders and shook him viciously. Charlie heard the sound of his own laughter, brittle and shaky. As his head smashed into the floorboards, Marko's shouts faded to groans.

'Charlie, stop.'

Above him, Vasco had collected the gun and disassembled it. Charlie became aware of him tossing the pieces to the floor. Then he felt a hand on his uninjured shoulder.

'That's enough.'

'It was all my fault, wasn't it?'

Charlie's whole body was trembling, his hands shaking before his eyes. Blood was speckled up his arms and trapped underneath his fingernails. He could not stop himself from picturing the bodies of children falling in front of his eyes, as though the memory was being played on a loop in his mind. For a brief moment, he brought his hands to his face, thinking of scratching his eyes out. Beneath him, he felt Marko shift, saw the glint of a knife in his hand.

'Vasco.' Charlie's world shrank until only one thing mattered. 'Watch out, he's –'

He reached out a hand, grabbed the knife, and the blade shattered beneath his grip. Charlie caught the handle and brought it down against Marko's head with a sickening crack, knocking him out in a single blow. He struggled to his feet, his head spinning. He was about to stagger forward when he felt a hand on his shoulder, gripping him firmly, preventing his escape.

'*What*,' Vasco began, his gaze on the shattered metal littered at their feet, 'was that?'

Charlie could not have answered him even if he had known what to say. He felt all the strength leave his body as his legs collapsed beneath him. It was only Vasco's quick movement to hold him upright that kept him on his feet. There was a ringing in his ears blocking out all other sound. He could hear his own racing heartbeat, his ragged breath.

His skin was on fire. He would surely not be able to withstand this pain. He wanted to hurt someone – anyone – simply to make them feel the slightest bit of what he felt.

The thought of hurting someone felt good.

It felt *too* good.

Someone was shaking him – hard. There was a pounding, screaming noise in his head that made him want to crack his skull wide open. Vasco was speaking to him in an urgent voice.

'Charlie, are you still with me? We've got to get out of here, Charlie.'

What happened next was a blur. He was vaguely aware of Vasco supporting him to walk, and of an intense burning sensation somewhere beneath his skin.

By the time Charlie knew where he was, they were lurking in the shadows off the courtyard, where the witches were being loaded into military trucks. His vision clearing, Charlie caught sight of Jasmine, Alexandra, and her mother. His legs were still shaking.

He was too weak to help anyone.

Vasco's face was set. 'I can't let him get his hands on her ...' He took a step forward.

'You won't get close,' Charlie said, grabbing Vasco's hand to hold him back, his mind clearing in the night air. 'You go out there now and he'll kill you the second he lays eyes on you.'

'I was supposed to protect her.' Vasco's teeth were gritted, his gaze on the trucks.

After a moment's pause, Charlie squeezed his hand. 'We'll get them back,' he said, with more confidence than he felt. 'We just have to be smart about it. We'll find a way – trust me.'

Charlie's eyes lingered on Vasco's expression as he watched Alexandra and the others being loaded into the trucks with a hungry, desperate look on his face. They stayed where they were until the trucks had disappeared across the wasteland into the darkness of the night. Soon, the sound of the rumble of their engines on the cobbled stones of the alleyways had faded away.

In the silence, Vasco heaved a sigh. Without a word, he strode determinedly out of the building, heading in the opposite direction of the trucks. His height was such that his stride was already long, but the speed at which he now moved meant that Charlie had to break into a jog from time to time to keep up with him. Once or twice, Charlie considered saying something to break the tension, but the look on Vasco's face made him think better of it.

'We can access the Vaults through here,' Vasco said, removing a drain cover to reveal a narrow iron ladder that plunged deep underground. 'If we follow the tunnels, they'll lead us back to Elysia. It's how the Hunters move around the city undetected,' he added, seeing the doubtful look Charlie threw his way.

'You'd better know what you're doing,' Charlie said, as he gripped the ladder and lowered himself down into the shaft. 'I'm not exactly a fan of the dark – or confined spaces.'

Vasco followed him down, closing the grate above him and leaving them in almost complete darkness. 'I suppose it's a good thing you've got me to look out for you, then, isn't it?' he said, causing Charlie to almost lose his footing on the ladder. 'Besides, I thought you worked in the mines.'

'Only because I had no other choice.'

When they reached the slimy flagstones at the bottom of the ladder, Vasco glanced at Charlie. 'That was quite a performance back there,' he said, the ghost of a smile flickering across his face. 'Do you think if we get out of this alive, we might even end up as friends?'

'I –' Charlie swallowed hard, taking a deep breath. 'Thank you, for taking care of me.'

'Don't thank me yet.' Vasco dragged his fingers through his hair. 'Come on, let's go.'

Charlie nodded and followed Vasco along the narrow passageway, which quickly opened up into a wider, vaulted space. Up ahead of them lay long tunnels interspersed with arched pillars, which rose high above their heads. Torches in brackets lit their way in the gloom.

'First, we need to get a couple of things straight,' Vasco said. 'We're heading into Elysia, understand? Once we cross under the Wall and make it up to the surface, you need to stay close to me and make some attempt to fit in.'

'What d'you mean?'

'Lower your shoulders and stop looking around all the time. No one's going to jump you.' Vasco gave his orders in a clipped voice that brooked no opposition, and Charlie felt his hackles rising.

'You always have an edginess about you, like you're expecting to be arrested or attacked at any moment.'

'I wonder why that might be.'

'If anyone says anything to you,' Vasco said, ignoring him, 'leave the talking to me.'

Charlie could not resist needling him. 'Is this your attempt at chivalry?' he asked. 'Don't you think you're being a little overprotective? I *am* capable of looking after myself, you know.'

'Hilarious.' Vasco fixed him with a disdainful scowl. 'I meant that you don't sound Elysian. You open that smart mouth of yours across the Wall, it'll give us away in an instant.'

'Anything else?'

'If you follow my lead and do exactly as I say, we'll be fine.'

'You got it, captain.'

'Good. I'm glad to hear it.'

They continued walking for some time without speaking to one another. It was Vasco who eventually broke the silence.

'We'll get her back,' he muttered, and Charlie nodded, unsure whether Vasco had intended for his words to be overheard. 'She'll be fine.'

'You two go back a long way, don't you?' Charlie said carefully, his curiosity getting the better of him at last.

'We grew up together,' Vasco said. 'I've known her for as long as I can remember.'

'You grew up in the Elysian Castle too?' Charlie asked. 'What about your parents?'

'I don't remember them,' Vasco said, with a slight shrug, his voice flat. 'The Great Protector was the closest thing to a father that I ever had – he was to Dragomir, as well.'

Charlie frowned. 'How is *he* involved in this?'

'Alexandra's father adopted us both,' Vasco explained, after a slight pause. 'We were raised as rivals, I suppose. Growing up like that, it wasn't exactly … easy. The Great Protector's discipline methods were …' Vasco paused for a moment, his hand coming to rest against his heart, before he shook his head, as though to clear it of an unspoken thought. 'But everything he did was to make me stronger. He made me who I am.'

Charlie snorted. 'He's a monster. You don't have to waste your breath defending him.'

'Maybe he never treated me like a son, but I never expected that,' Vasco said, his eyes hard. 'I was always going to become a soldier. I always believed that if I worked hard – if I did enough to win his respect – I could prove myself worthy enough to become part of their family.'

'No child should have to prove themselves worthy of love,' Charlie said quietly.

'Whatever he did to us, his actions had a purpose. And it meant that I could be close to Alexandra ...' Vasco trailed off with a sigh. 'She's like my sister, Charlie. She was the only friend I ever had. If I can't save her –'

'We'll save them,' Charlie said. 'All of them.'

Vasco frowned. 'I was raised to believe that witches were evil, and that the covens were a danger to our country and its stability,' he said. 'But I think I'm finally starting to understand. The ones in power – the people I've defended and fought for all this time – they're the ones in the wrong. I thought I did what was right, but I was part of it, all along. I've been so blind ...'

'It's not your fault that you were messed up by your childhood,' Charlie said, with a gentle touch on his arm. 'I had a warped father figure growing up, too. I know it's not easy.'

'Faulkner.' Vasco spat the name out with a murderous look on his face, before fixing Charlie with his steady gaze. 'I don't know what you've been through, Charlie, but I want you to know that I'm here for you. Whenever you're ready to talk about it, I'll listen to you.'

'You don't want to hear about any of that,' Charlie murmured, his hands in his pockets.

'I care about you, Charlie.' Vasco was still looking at him, his dark eyes full of sorrow.

Charlie made a strangled sound. 'I don't know what you want me to say to that ...'

'I don't want you to say anything – my feelings in this situation don't matter.'

'They matter to *me.*'

'Then …' Vasco's eyes widened, and his voice wavered. 'How do *you* feel?'

'I don't know anything about how I feel!' Charlie scratched his throat, suddenly full of nervous energy, and looked away to avoid the intensity in Vasco's face. 'I never have. What d'you want me to tell you? That I have …' He swallowed, his throat dry. 'Besides, even if I *did* –'

'Wait.' Vasco stopped dead in his tracks, flinging out an arm in front of Charlie to prevent him from taking another step forward. 'Watch out.' He gave the warning under his breath, with a meaningful nod. 'Someone's there – up ahead.'

'Charlie?' A familiar voice called to him, and his brother emerged from the gloom, re-settling his glasses on the bridge of his nose with a cold smile. 'Don't be afraid. It's only me.'

Charlie's blood had gone cold. '*You.*'

Ignoring Vasco's warning to stay away from him, Charlie stumbled forward, his knees shaking, towards his brother, who remained still.

'I didn't think you would actually go after them,' Max said, a note of hesitation in his voice. 'Perhaps a part of me was hoping that … but you can't stop him now.'

'What's he planning to do to them?' Charlie demanded, an icy chill enveloping him.

'This is how it has to be. There is no other way.' Slowly, Max drew a handgun from his pocket. 'Any great leap forward,' he continued, as he pointed the gun at Charlie, 'demands sacrifice.'

Silently, Vasco edged half of his body in front of Charlie's, into the line of fire.

'You think I'll hesitate?' Max asked, regarding Vasco with a cold look. 'I won't.'

'Vasco, what are you doing?' Charlie whispered, not daring to move. 'Get out of here.'

Vasco gave a barely perceptible shake of his head, his eyes fixed on Max. 'I won't abandon him to you,' he said. 'You're about to gun down two unarmed opponents in cold blood, Doctor. If you think you can become your own brother's murderer, go ahead and do it.'

249

Charlie's eyes roved around the shadows in the vaulted arches of the tunnels, desperately trying to think of a way that they could get out of this situation alive. He felt something prickle at the back of his neck. He had the strangest feeling that they were not alone. It was as though he could sense another presence somewhere nearby, although there was no one else anywhere to be seen.

Then he caught sight of movement in the darkness.

'Vasco, run!' he said, his voice sharp. 'Run away, leave me behind – I don't matter!'

'What?' Vasco swung around, a stubborn set to his jaw. 'Charlie, *no*, I –'

Charlie had a single moment to take in the bewildered expression on Vasco's face. Then the lights went out, and they were plunged into total darkness. Charlie sensed movement behind him a split second before his arms were wrenched behind his back. He heard the snap of steel handcuffs at his wrists. A strong hand gripped his scarred shoulder, keeping him firmly in place where he stood, despite his attempts to get free.

'The prisoners are secured, Doctor Ivanov.'

Charlie felt his heart plummet. They had been caught. Yet again, he had failed.

As the lights flared back into life, Charlie searched wildly for Vasco, and found him at his side. He, too, had been restrained with handcuffs, and was struggling against another grim-faced soldier, who stood behind him, unyielding.

'Jumping us in the dark?' Vasco let out a harsh laugh, sounding as though he could not quite believe what had just happened to them. 'You really are cowardly sons of bitches, aren't you? I guess they knew they couldn't take us in a fair fight, right, Charlie?'

'You appear to have forgotten your manners, Lieutenant Kovalev.'

Max approached Vasco and brought the butt of his handgun down against Vasco's forehead. With a groan of pain, Vasco raised his head, glaring at Max with a look of unreserved hatred as he blinked blood out of his eyes.

'Well done, both of you,' Max said, nodding to the soldiers as he surveyed Charlie and Vasco with some satisfaction. 'The Great

Protector will be more than grateful for your efforts, I have no doubt. With my little brother's arrival, the sacrifice ritual can proceed as planned.'

'Max!' Charlie shouted, trying to shake off the soldier. 'Max, what are you doing?'

'Don't fight them, Charlie,' Max said, smiling. 'I don't want you getting hurt – yet.'

'You stay the hell away from him!' Vasco snarled, almost managing to tear himself free of the soldier straining to hold him back. 'I won't let you hurt him ever again.'

'You have good instincts, Lieutenant Kovalev,' Max said, turning to Vasco with mild interest. 'But there is nothing you can do to help my brother now. Don't harm him,' he snapped at the soldier restraining Charlie. 'He has information we need. I can still extract it, given time.'

'What are you talking about?' Charlie spat, before the realisation hit him. 'Wait – you don't mean?' He watched in horror as the slight young man before him grinned, a menacing glint dancing in his eyes behind his glasses. 'It was you. You're the one who experimented on Seren … you're the one who hurt her.'

Charlie drew back as Max approached him slowly, a curious expression on his face. 'You're angry,' he murmured, 'but you are also afraid.' He pushed his glasses further up the bridge of his nose, a strangely intense smile gleaming on his sharp-featured face. 'Fear is good. I like to watch the fear in the eyes of the creatures I work with.' His grin widened horribly, and Charlie shuddered. 'You held out fairly well the last time we were together, but I don't like your chances this time.'

'I'll never give in,' Charlie whispered, a high-pitched whine in his ears as horrified understanding dawned on him at last. 'No matter what you do to me, I'll never stop fighting you.'

Max smiled placidly. 'Well, we'll soon see about that, won't we?'

'He's your *brother*!' Vasco almost managed to wrench himself out of the soldier's grip. 'How can you follow the Great Protector's orders if it means betraying your family? Where the hell is your loyalty?'

At Vasco's outburst, Max turned towards him, his head cocked to one side. There was a lopsided smile on his face. 'You have some very strange ideas about right and wrong, Lieutenant Kovalev,' he said, his voice dangerously pleasant as his gaze fell to Vasco's chest. 'Perhaps you need another lesson in loyalty yourself.'

A shadow of fear passed over Vasco's face before his furious scowl replaced it.

'However, I'm afraid to say that there is no time for that,' Max said. 'Lieutenant Dragomir's orders were quite clear when it comes to you, Vasco Kovalev.' He tightened his grip on the gun in his hand and aimed it squarely at Vasco, who stared right back at him, his face emotionless. 'No mercy for traitors.' He pulled back the hammer with his thumb and inhaled sharply.

'*No!*' Charlie yelled.

Everything seemed to slow down around him. With an intense effort, he managed to wrench himself free of the soldier restraining him. His arms still handcuffed behind his back, Charlie took a flying leap at his brother, kicking his legs out from underneath him, and leaving them both sprawled and brawling on the ground. Charlie's only thought was to keep fighting.

'Don't shoot him!' Max shrieked at the soldiers. 'We need him alive!'

He could not use his hands, so instead Charlie lashed out with his feet. He rained kicks down on Max's body for as long as he could manage. Then both the soldiers placed their hands under his arms, and he was dragged away from his brother. A fist connected with his face, and Charlie tasted blood in his mouth.

'Where is Kovalev?' Max demanded, staring around the shadowy passageway in fury.

'He escaped in the struggle, sir,' the soldier who had been restraining Vasco said.

Charlie smiled viciously through the blood dripping from his mouth as he saw that the soldier looked shamefaced and worse for wear. Vasco had apparently managed to get some kicks of his own in, too, before getting away.

'Find him!' Max ordered, getting to his feet, and wincing as he clutched his ribs.

Charlie glared at him, hoping he had broken some bones. 'You won't find him.'

'I suppose you think that was clever,' Max murmured, turning back to Charlie. 'Perhaps even now you are revelling in your bravery, congratulating yourself for your noble intentions.' He was watching Charlie closely, but Charlie said nothing. 'But you have merely prolonged your friend's suffering. He will be found. He will be killed. You will live on, and you will live with the knowledge that you failed to save him.'

'It looks to me like you're the only ones around here who have failed,' Charlie retorted, breathing hard against the pain in his chest and heart. Once again, he was alone. 'Vasco's going to escape. You won't find him. And I heard what you said – you need me alive. I'll be fine.'

'You may yet come to regret those words, little brother,' Max said, his voice soft. 'Oh yes, we will keep you alive, but believe me, you will wish that we had not. Soon enough, you will find yourself wishing that we had been merciful enough to kill you quickly. Soon, you will be begging for your death.'

'I surrender,' came a voice from the shadows, turning Charlie cold. 'I'll come quietly.'

'What are you doing, you idiot?' Charlie hissed, as Vasco was brought into line beside him and held fast by one of the soldiers. 'You escaped. You could have got away. I don't –'

'No, don't shoot him yet,' Max said to the soldiers. 'He'll keep my brother honest.'

He looked between Charlie and Vasco, distaste written across his features. 'You lovesick fool,' he muttered, shaking his head with a scornful look at Vasco. 'You could have had everything, but you turned your back on it – and all for what?' Max's lip curled as he threw a black look at Charlie. 'Some sewer rat with a pretty face and a pair of big brown eyes?'

Charlie felt his cheeks burn with shame, his gaze falling to the flagstones beneath his feet. The silence went on and on, and it hurt. He wished the ground would swallow him up.

'I hope he was worth it,' Max sneered, turning his back on them.

From beside him, Charlie heard Vasco's words, calm and clear. 'He was.'

Charlie's eyes shot to him, his heart suddenly racing in his chest. 'Vasco, you …'

Vasco smiled back, his dark eyes soft and sad. 'You were worth everything, Charlie.'

'I …' Charlie's ears were ringing, his chest tight. He blinked, confused. 'You …'

Max, who had frozen, addressed the soldiers without turning around. 'Lock them up.'

CHAPTER 24

With a strangled scream, Charlie's eyes shot open. His heart was racing. It took him some time to process that he was not drowning under a sea of blood and bodies, but was safe, lying with his head in Vasco's lap.

'It's all right, Charlie, it's all right,' Vasco said, his voice soft and calm as he stroked Charlie's hair. 'You're not there anymore. I'm here with you. You're safe with me.'

Hesitantly, Charlie raised himself into a sitting position. He became aware of the sound of a chain dragging across the flagstone floor as he moved. There was a heavy weight bearing down on his shoulders. He touched his fingers to the iron collar around his throat, his eyes finding its twin around Vasco's neck. He let his gaze follow the length of chain to an iron hook set into the stone wall, which restricted their movements to a few feet. He drew his fingernails along the skin of his forearm, his mind oddly blank.

Vasco was watching him. 'You had a nightmare? You were crying out in your sleep.'

'I was?' Charlie felt his heart sink, hazy details returning to him. 'What did I say?'

'Nothing, really,' Vasco said, after a long pause. 'You blacked out in the Vaults. I was worried you –' Lapsing into silence, he held out his hand, offering Charlie a piece of bread. 'The guards brought this earlier. I thought you might be hungry when you woke up.'

'You can have it.'

'When was the last time you ate something?' Vasco asked, frowning, the bread still in his outstretched hand. 'I don't think I've ever seen you eat. You need to get your strength back.'

'I'm fine,' Charlie said, with a shrug and a shake of his head. 'I don't think I can face the idea of eating right now.' He glanced around the gloomy cell. 'Where are we, anyway?'

'The Castle dungeons. We've already been here a few hours, I think. It must be close to sunrise by now.'

'Vasco,' Charlie began, running his finger along a crack in one of the flagstones between them. 'I wanted to say – before, in the Vaults – thank you, for not leaving me behind.'

Vasco gave him a small smile. 'You're my friend. I'll never leave you behind.'

'Your friend.' Charlie felt one of his eyebrows quirk. 'And is … is that all I am?'

'Charlie, I –' Vasco glanced away as Charlie looked up at him. 'I never want to do anything to hurt you.'

'Come over here for a second.'

'What is it?' Charlie watched Vasco's eyes dart across his face. 'Is something wrong?'

'I just want to check something.'

Charlie kept his tone casual. A smile lifted one corner of his mouth as, with some hesitation, Vasco leant in, bringing his face close to Charlie's, his brown eyes round and questioning.

'Yeah, you know, I was right.' Tilting his face, Charlie brushed his lips against Vasco's. 'Up close, you don't look like such a damn hothead.' Drawing away, he opened his eyes, an affectionate smile blooming across his face at the sight of Vasco's startled expression. 'Honestly, I'm starting to think you're actually pretty adorable. You hid it well there, for a while.'

'You have freckles,' Vasco said, his voice soft, the tip of his tongue skirting his teeth. He looked somewhat dazed. 'I never noticed them before.' His gaze travelled between Charlie's eyes before dropping to his lips. 'And … and your nose is kind of crooked. You … you're really –' Vasco broke off, reddening, and Charlie's smile grew even wider.

Shuffling closer, Charlie batted his eyelashes. 'I heard you like big brown eyes and a pretty face.'

'One of your sewer rat friends tell you that, did they?' Vasco snorted, shifting closer to Charlie in turn, and brushed his thumb against Charlie's cheek. 'Did you know I have a soft spot for smart-mouthed idiots with ridiculous hairstyles, too?' He raised a hand and caressed Charlie's hair, a tender smile coming to his face as he did so. 'I always wanted to do that, since the first time I ever ...'

'Always? You mean you –' Charlie released a breath of unexpected pleasure. It had never felt like this before. 'Now you've done it,' he warned, a broad grin spreading across his face as he wrapped his arms around Vasco's neck, pulling him closer. 'C-Can I –?'

'Yes.' Vasco was nodding his head, the tip of his nose touching Charlie's. 'I want –'

For a single moment, everything was perfect. Then a memory flashed behind Charlie's closed eyes. Suddenly, the hands on his back and in his hair were no longer Vasco's, the tongue in his mouth was that of a stranger, and the heat he felt building inside of him was no longer intoxicating, but suffocating.

He tore himself out of Vasco's grip, his breathing ragged. He had ruined everything. Shame burnt beneath his skin as he was struck with the understanding that it would never stop being this way for him. He dug his fingernails into his arms and relished the pain. Forcing the tears from his eyes, he realised he should have known better than to think that the world would allow him this kind of happiness. And now –

'I'm sorry,' was all he could say.

'No, I ...' Vasco was staring at him, pale-faced and anxious. 'I shouldn't have –'

'It's not your fault,' Charlie hastened to explain. 'It's just that ... I – I can't –' He braced a fist against his forehead, furious at himself. The rising panic spiralling inside him was choking off his words. He could not stop it. 'There's a lot you still don't know about me, and I can't –'

'Can you try to explain it to me?' Vasco asked, his voice even, as he fixed Charlie with his serious, steady gaze. 'I promise, I'll listen to you. Please try. For … for me?'

'I can't.'

'It doesn't have to be everything, but if I knew, maybe I could help you.'

Charlie gritted his teeth. 'If you knew the truth about me, you wouldn't want –'

'There's nothing you could say that would make me change my mind about you.'

Looking up into Vasco's sombre face, Charlie shook his head. 'I don't believe you.'

'Give me a chance to earn your trust, Charlie,' Vasco said, resting his hand gently on top of Charlie's. 'You know I'd never turn my back on you, don't you?'

'I was –'

Charlie stared at Vasco's hand for a few seconds, letting the silence that fell between them ease some of the tension in his shoulders. Gradually, his breathing began to deepen.

'When I was –'

Frowning, he attempted to find the right words.

'I used to be –'

His throat was too tight to speak.

'I'm sorry,' he said, the words shuddering out of him. 'I can't.'

'I know it's hard,' Vasco said, still in the same gentle tone that Charlie was not sure he had ever heard anyone use for him before. 'Thank you for trying, all right? I'm proud of you.'

Charlie felt something threatening to snap inside him. Glancing up at Vasco, his defences raised, Charlie was ready to lash out. But the sight of Vasco's sad-eyed expression made him pause.

'You're actually serious, aren't you?' he murmured, his anger deflating at once. 'Why are you like this? You're always so … *kind* to me.'

'I care about you,' Vasco said, smiling at the flagstones. 'I'll never forget watching you jump out of that helicopter. When I saw you leap into the air, it was like, just for a moment, you could fly.'

As he looked up, Charlie met his fierce gaze. 'You looked invincible.'

'You don't have to do this.'

'Let me say it once,' Vasco said, holding up a hand with a quick shake of his head, 'or I'll regret it.' He took a deep breath. 'All the time we were apart, I couldn't stop thinking about you. You're the bravest person I've ever known, and I've never met anyone else who makes me feel the way you do.' It was only now that his eyes left Charlie's face. 'That's all I wanted to say.'

'I …' Charlie's hand had found the nape of his own neck, a tentative smile creeping across his face, despite himself. 'You're a real dark horse, aren't you? Who knew you were such a smooth talker?'

'It's how I feel,' Vasco said, shrugging. 'I wanted to tell you, before …' He looked away, rubbing the back of his palm against his eyes. 'Before it was too late.'

'You're better off staying away from me and finding someone who's less damaged.'

'I don't want them.'

'You deserve better than me.' Charlie could hear the edge of urgency in his words as he tried to make Vasco understand. 'I'm not … I wouldn't even know how to begin –'

'We could work it out together, couldn't we? One step at a time. We could try.'

Charlie sighed. 'I can't promise you anything. I need you to understand that.'

'I want to be there to support you,' Vasco said. 'Whatever it takes, no matter what happens. That's all I want.'

Charlie felt a weak smile tug at the corners of his mouth. 'Even if there's no hope?'

'If one day I could help you see that you're not alone,' Vasco said, closing the space between them and laying his hand on Charlie's knee, 'that would be enough for me. I'm here for you, Charlie. I always will be.'

Charlie closed his eyes. He had to tell him the truth. 'Vasco, I'm–'

At the sound of a key scraping against metal, both of their heads turned towards the door to the dungeon. Their eyes were fixed on the person who stood on the threshold. A look of triumph on his face, Arron Dragomir led the way into the cell towards Charlie and Vasco, the two soldiers who had arrested them following in his wake.

'Well, now, you two are looking pretty cosy down here, aren't you?' Dragomir surveyed Charlie with his arms folded, a nasty smirk playing across his face. 'Back in the game, already, switch hitter? Consider me impressed. I didn't think you'd even be able to walk yet.'

'Leave him alone.'

Trembling on the flagstones, his mind empty, Charlie felt himself returning to reality at the sound of Vasco defending him. He curled his palms into fists, forcing himself to breathe.

Dragomir snorted. 'Are you serious, Kovalev?' His cold gaze travelled between the two of them, seemingly nonplussed. 'Take it from me, he's nothing special. Just another one of Faulkner's worn-out rent boys.' A cruel grin slipped across his face as his eyes pierced Charlie. 'Honestly, I'm surprised. I never thought you'd lower yourself to taking my sloppy seconds.'

Vasco's eyes flashed. 'I'm going to kill you for that.' He had gone very still and quiet.

'Whatever you say, Vasya,' Dragomir said with a wave of his hand. Looking entirely untroubled, he strode towards Charlie and dragged him up off his knees by the chain. 'As for *you*,' he growled, his face so close to Charlie's that Charlie could feel the heat of his breath, 'you behave yourself, and your new boyfriend might just get out of this alive. Make any trouble for me, and I'll put him down right in front of your eyes. You got that?'

'Don't listen to him, Charlie,' Vasco said, his voice a low snarl. 'Don't stop fighting!'

Dragomir gave Charlie a rough shake. 'You understand me, you little bitch?'

Doing his best to stop shaking, Charlie forced himself to nod, his chest tight.

'I can't hear you,' Dragomir said, his voice soft.

'Yes.'

'Yes *what?*'

'*Yes, sir, I understand you!*' Charlie yelped, as Dragomir wrenched his hair back.

'Good.' Dragomir let Charlie fall to his knees on the stone. 'Take them to the throne room.'

Their hands were tied behind their backs, then the two soldiers pulled Charlie and Vasco to their feet. With a tug on their chains, they were forced up a flight of stone steps, out of the dungeons and into the Elysian Castle.

As they were marched along dank passageways lit with flaming torches, and brought into the upper levels of the castle, Charlie glanced through a set of mullioned windows. He wanted to catch sight of the outside world one last time.

By now, it was approaching daybreak. In the far distance, across the mountains, the horizon was blood red. Bursts of pink and gold spilled over the cloudless expanse above the hills. Charlie's eyes lingered on the sight as the sky gradually lightened to periwinkle blue, the last stars still twinkling overhead. He knew that this would likely be the last sunrise he ever saw.

The huge doors to the throne room swung open, revealing an enormous chamber with a cavernous ceiling. It was empty but for a carved wooden throne that stood on top of a dais. Marble pillars supporting high arches lined the room, while stony-faced soldiers stood to attention, evenly spaced in the gaps between them.

Sprawled on the throne, his elbow propped up on one curved armrest, one long leg crossed lazily over the other, was Nikolai Ignatiev. He glanced up as Charlie and Vasco were led into the throne room, a cruel smile spreading across his face.

'Finally,' he said, striding forwards after gracefully rising to his feet. 'We can begin.'

'Why are you doing this to him?' Charlie demanded, as Vasco was chained to one of the marble pillars by the soldier who had been guarding him. 'I don't know what you want from me. Just let him go – this has nothing to do with him!'

Without taking his eyes from Charlie's face, Nikolai Ignatiev lifted his chain from the other soldier's grip and twined it around his palm, drawing Charlie closer. 'Allow me to make myself clear,' he said, gripping a fistful of Charlie's hair in his other hand. 'Your days in hiding are officially over. One way or another, I am getting what I want out of you.' He shoved Charlie to his knees on the flagstones. 'Today, my long years of waiting will at last come to an end.'

Teeth gritted, Charlie stared up at him. 'What the hell are you talking about?'

'I am not unreasonable,' Nikolai Ignatiev said, his voice mild, his head cocked slightly to one side. 'I will allow you to choose how you meet your fate. Will you yield your power to me with honour, or would you prefer for things between us to get more … complicated?'

'I'd rather die than give in to you!'

Nikolai Ignatiev blinked his long-lashed bright eyes, and flashed Charlie a bland smile. 'Be careful what you wish for, child,' he said, lowering himself to one knee, and pinching Charlie's chin between his long fingers. 'Do you suppose you have come to know a little about suffering thus far? I will gladly make you beg for something as sweet as what you had before.'

'Please. Don't hurt him.'

Both Charlie and Nikolai Ignatiev turned their heads towards Vasco, whose pained voice had cut the silence between them.

'Shut your mouth, traitor.' Charlie flinched as Dragomir punched Vasco in the face.

'No, let us hear what he has to say,' Nikolai Ignatiev said, getting to his feet with an amused chuckle. 'Go ahead, Vaska. Show us all where your loyalty truly lies.'

Catching sight of the hungry look on Nikolai Ignatiev's face, Charlie tried to plead with his eyes for Vasco to stay silent. Begging for mercy would only make it worse.

'Please …' Vasco hung limp in his chains, his dark eyes on Charlie. 'Don't do this.'

At this, Charlie made a strangled noise of frustration in his throat. He was still desperately trying to signal Vasco with his eyes, to make him understand that he needed to stop talking. Charlie knew his best hope for getting Vasco out of this situation alive was to draw their tormenters' attention and keep it on himself for as long as he could. But if Vasco kept –

'I am afraid you are going to have to be a little more specific than that …'

A sly smile spread across Nikolai Ignatiev's face as he gripped Charlie's injured shoulder and forced him down onto his back. The Great Protector was strong, but it was the unnervingly tender look in his eyes as he pushed Charlie onto the flagstones that kept Charlie frozen under his grip.

He did not resist as a cloth was forced between his teeth and tied behind his head. As Nikolai Ignatiev pushed his t-shirt up, Charlie turned his face away from Vasco and went still. He had to survive this. He knew how. He had done it before.

'Well, Vaska, what is it that you do not wish me to do?' A knife had appeared in the Great Protector's hand. 'This? *This?*' It came away red and dripping. '*Well?* Speak up, you worthless wretch!'

'I'm begging you to let him go! *Please* stop hurting him!'

Charlie caught the despair in Vasco's voice as he lay on the cold stones, his limbs trembling. A low moan escaped him as he caught sight of the dark gashes on his chest, oozing blood.

'He's a civilian,' Vasco was saying, barely-contained panic in his every word. 'He's done *nothing* wrong! You surely can't think he poses any threat to you? Please – I'll – if you ever cared for me – *please* show him mercy!'

Nikolai Ignatiev snorted. 'Pathetic. You *dare* ask me to show this creature mercy?'

Dimly, Charlie became aware of the Great Protector drawing away from him. Out of the corner of his eye, he watched as the older man approached Vasco, the bloody knife at his side. Something unthinkable flashed in front of his eyes, and Charlie fought to free his mouth.

'For how long has this weakness been festering inside you, Vaska? How did you ever think you could hope to win my respect when you are so pitifully inadequate?'

Charlie summoned all his courage. 'He's worth a *thousand* of you!' he spat furiously.

'I don't care what you think of me anymore,' Vasco said quickly, and Nikolai Ignatiev turned to face him again, ignoring Charlie. 'Your words can't do anything to hurt me.'

'Are you so sure of that?' The Great Protector's voice was cold. 'Did you think I was unaware of how desperately you longed for me to acknowledge you as my son? I always suspected you were a good-for-nothing dog under my table. But I confess, I still thought I would be able to put you to some use in the end.'

Charlie felt his blood boil. 'You shut your mouth!' he yelled. 'Vasco, don't listen to him!'

'But it matters not.' Nikolai Ignatiev had returned to Charlie's side. Charlie braced himself, feeling his own blood wet his face as the Great Protector drew the blade of his knife along the skin of his cheek. 'I have found my true son, and now I have his power in my grasp.'

As though from far away, Charlie heard Vasco. 'Leave him alone! Don't touch him!'

'Lieutenant Dragomir.' A frown crossing his face, Nikolai Ignatiev raised his voice. 'Please do something about that terrible racket. I am beginning to get a headache, and this work will require my full concentration.'

'Lights out, Vasya …'

Hearing the crack of something solid against bone, Charlie craned his neck to the side, straining to see. Vasco had gone limp and still, his eyes closed, a trickle of blood sliding down his forehead. Dragomir was standing beside him looking satisfied with himself, his eyes cold.

'Vasco! Can you hear me? *Vasco*! Va-'

Nikolai Ignatiev's fingers gripped his jaw, forcing Charlie's head back towards him, so that they were face to face. The Great Protector's bright eyes gleamed. 'Don't you think you have enough to worry about right now, without concerning yourself with the troubles of that failure?'

'I'm going to make you pay for hurting him,' Charlie whispered. 'I swear, I'll –'

Nikolai Ignatiev cut him off with a longsuffering sigh. 'I am growing tired of this. In my experience, pain and fear are usually enough to provoke your kind into bringing their corruption to the surface.' The knife sliced skin, and Charlie screamed. 'However, it may be different in your case. Perhaps after everything you have survived, you have become numb to that particular method … I suppose we can only try.' The brief moment of relief was followed by excruciating pain as Charlie thrashed and sobbed. 'We will find out, one way or another.'

His world shrank to the eye of a needle, his only thought that of surviving the pain.

'I know you're there. It's hiding somewhere inside you, buried underneath your skin.'

Between his screaming, begging, weeping, and cursing, Charlie lost track of himself.

'Don't you get tired of all these ridiculous histrionics? Must I carve it out of you?'

Nikolai Ignatiev brought the blade of his knife to Charlie's throat, and Charlie went still. Stars whirled in front of his eyes. His head was spinning.

'You are trying my patience.' A voice like ice. 'Could it be that I have been going about this all the wrong way? Perhaps I should turn my attention to the girl, and have you watch? Or would her younger sister be the better choice?'

'Don't even think about it, you sick fuck,' Charlie snarled, gasping for breath.

'I think – *yes*!' A broad grin spread across Nikolai Ignatiev's face, his features coming alive with excitement. 'Is that *fire* I see in your eyes?' His hands gripping Charlie's shoulders, he leant in closer. 'Let it out. Do it. Trust me, you will feel so much better afterwards.'

'I swear …' Charlie's eyes were rolling in his head. 'I'll kill every last one of you …'

'Everything you have been holding back …' Charlie shuddered at the brush of skin as Nikolai Ignatiev stroked a finger along his jaw. 'You have my permission to release it all.'

'I won't!' Something was burning just beneath his skin. 'I won't give in to you …'

'Why hide from what you are?' Nikolai Ignatiev cupped his cheek, and Charlie stared, horrified, into his dazzlingly green eyes.

'You are a coward.' He drew closer, his breath a gentle whisper in Charlie's ear. 'Why do you still refuse to accept it? Do you not see? If you had only been brave enough to face the truth of your own nature before now, you would have had the power to save them.'

'You …'

Charlie did not know what happened after that. Where there should have been memories, he found only a blank, quiet space in his mind. All he knew was that when he came back to himself, he was on his feet, the ropes that had bound his wrists smouldering around him on the flagstones.

The glass in the high windows had shattered. Sputtering flames licked the marble pillars. Dragomir was sprawled on the floor, his face ashen. Some of the soldiers had been knocked out, while others had fled. Those that remained were on their knees, staring at him with wide eyes and slack jaws.

Standing before him, Nikolai Ignatiev's pitiless laughter rang in Charlie's ears.

'So,' he said, a triumphant light blazing in his face, 'I see it is rage that has awoken you at last, Bloodwitch.'

CHAPTER 25

'Tell me again,' Charlie murmured, his shoulders shaking, 'how I wasn't brave enough to save them.'

His breathing fast and unsteady, Charlie rounded on Nikolai Ignatiev, grinding his teeth in his fury. But the Great Protector held up a hand in front of him, halting him in his tracks.

'I would prefer to tell you a story about your mother,' he said, light dancing in his eyes.

Charlie felt what little strength he had left draining away. 'I don't want to hear it.'

'You would be welcome to consider it a sort of reward, if you like – you deserve one.'

Charlie curled his hands into fists, flames licking his skin. 'Don't you *talk* about her!'

'I had set my heart on having a son by a witch,' Nikolai Ignatiev said, his eyes burning into Charlie's face, his expression ravenous. 'But when the traditional path brought only failure, I set my sights elsewhere.'

'What?' Charlie had gone cold.

'Seventeen years ago, I brought my full force down on the Darkwood coven. I crushed it, erased its existence entirely, and dragged the last daughter of that ruined clan back to Elysia with me to be my broodmare.' Nikolai Ignatiev smiled at the look of horror on Charlie's face. 'Then I kept her in chains under the ground for the next nine months. Coincidentally, it actually happens that I locked her up in the very same dungeon that you and Vaska spent the night in yourselves ...'

'You don't mean –' Numb, Charlie forced the words out, his throat like sandpaper. 'That was – that was where ...'

'There was little she could do to fight me, although she certainly tried her best. I was never under any illusions that she wanted me.' Nikolai Ignatiev gave a slight shrug, a lazy smile curving his lips. 'But that was not her choice to make ... I wonder, do you think she ever wanted *you*? Personally, I am having trouble imagining it.'

Faster than Charlie had expected, Nikolai Ignatiev was in front of him. His grip was tight on the iron collar around Charlie's neck, his mouth a twisted snarl. 'Look at you. Who could ever want a monster like you?'

'Why are you telling me this?' Charlie had sunk to his knees. 'Just *shut up* about it.'

'My hands were the first to claim you. I held you when you were pulled from her body.'

'Stop.' Charlie covered his ears with his hands, shaking his head, his eyes screwed up. He was certain he was about to be sick. 'Why are you doing this to me? Why won't you *stop*?'

'I gave you a name. You are Zuriel Ignatiev, the rock on which I will build my kingdom. You will lay siege to my enemies – a harbinger of doom to all those who stand in my way.'

'No ...'

'I had a vision that the sound of your name would strike fear into the hearts of all those who opposed me, all those who would dare challenge my power. I saw your future – how you would make them wail and scream before your storms of fire. You, the true Deathbringer.'

'No.'

'But Erin escaped my clutches.' Nikolai Ignatiev let out a long sigh, running his fingers through his hair as the tension sagged from his shoulders. 'That mercenary witch brought you into the world at my behest and stole you from me the very same day. Ever since then, I have been searching for you. I vowed that I would never cease until I had you under my command.'

'You never will.' Charlie glared up at the handsome, mask-like face of the man – the monster – who stood above him. 'I don't care what you do to me. I will *never* give in to you.'

'Oh, my favourite child …' Shaking his head, Nikolai Ignatiev stroked his fingers through Charlie's hair, cradling his head in his other hand with a fondness that made Charlie's skin crawl. 'Do you still not understand? Soon enough, you will become the greatest weapon in my arsenal.'

'I *won't.*'

'You will be my right hand in the fight against the covens,' Nikolai Ignatiev said, turning away from Charlie, his arms outstretched as he stared up into the vaulted ceiling. 'And then, when your purpose has been fulfilled, when the witches have been purged once and for all,' he added, with a smirk in Charlie's direction, 'I will leash you to my throne for the rest of your miserable life, and relish the sight of you kneeling at my feet like the abomination you are.'

'I will *never* kneel for you. I'll die first.' Charlie was trembling. 'You can *go to hell*.'

'Lieutenant Dragomir,' Nikolai Ignatiev said, not taking his eyes from Charlie's face.

'S-Sire?' Dragomir's voice was unsteady. He was leaning against the marble pillar.

'Fetch the Casimir witch.' Nikolai Ignatiev's smile broadened as he caught sight of the look of horrified understanding on Charlie's face. 'It is time for me to teach this wayward son of mine a lesson in obedience.'

Sliding down onto the cold flagstones, Charlie curled up on his side, breathing through the pain. His t-shirt was sticky with his own blood. The scent of himself was overpowering.

For a while, his father amused himself by throwing the knife at him like a dart, but he seemed to tire of this quickly. Charlie allowed his mind to drift, a high-pitched ringing in his ears. A familiar, numb sensation had already begun stealing its way through his bones.

'*Luckily for these three kids, though,*' Charlie heard himself saying, as, in his mind, he watched the children squealing happily on the floor, *'there was a brave knight who lived nearby called Charlie, and he saw how frightened they were by the monsters, and it made him sad.'*

'Charlie is my favourite.' He remembered Ruby's gap-toothed smile as she said that.

'He knew he wanted to help the three children somehow.' Charlie smiled as he told himself the story, staring into the middle distance with unseeing eyes. *'So, one day, he went out with his sword and he fought for them. He fought off all the witch covens and the gangs and the bad men. Then they were gone, forever, and the three kids were happy.'*

'What happened to Charlie?' he heard the echo of Dima's voice ask. *'You never tell us.'*

'He was happy too,' Charlie whispered, his eyes burning, 'because he knew he had saved the children.'

'What happens at the end?' Ruby's voice was asking. *'You never tell us that part either.'*

'Yeah, you never tell us!' Leo had always wanted to know how it ended. *'You never tell us how he kills everyone!'*

Charlie went to a quiet, empty place, where nothing could hurt him, and where he could forget. But when he saw a pair of jackbooted feet approaching him, he wrenched himself up onto his knees again. He was not about to go down without a fight.

With a flash of fury, Charlie saw that Seren lay at Dragomir's feet. Like him, she had a chain fastened to a collar around her neck. She was sprawled on the flagstones of the throne room floor, apparently unconscious. Charlie forced the image of his family – lying motionless in the dying light – out of his mind, as he was assaulted by memories.

But no, the red waves pooling around her were not her blood, only her hair. He yelled her name and saw her stir at the sound of his voice. He strained against the chain, and it was only Nikolai Ignatiev holding him back that prevented Charlie from racing over to Seren and killing Dragomir with his bare hands.

'What have you done to Seren?' he shouted, his words choked off. 'Let her go – now!'

Dragomir laughed nastily and shoved Seren's body forward with the toe of his boot. Charlie saw her cringe as the soldier's foot made impact with her spine in the gap between her shoulder blades. He heard her whimper in pain. Something snapped inside of him, and he managed to force himself an inch or two forwards. Nikolai Ignatiev reacted immediately, cuffing Charlie around the back of the head and sending him sprawling to the floor.

'Naughty boy,' he murmured. 'Don't you know how to behave yourself? Lieutenant.'

Charlie flinched as Dragomir pulled hard on the length of chain in his hands. Seren let out a strangled cry as she was wrenched back with him and dragged into an upright position. Then she was resting on her knees, her eyes lowered.

'Let's get this over with. He won't be able to resist. I imagine you are hungry by now?'

Ignoring the pressure against his throat as Nikolai Ignatiev shook his chain, Charlie fixed his eyes on Seren, willing her to look up at him. She was shivering, her thin arms bare. Someone had taken her green jumper from her, and she was barefoot again.

The chain in Dragomir's hands was connected to a shorter one that kept her hands manacled together. She was wearing the same kind of restraints on her wrists and ankles as when they had first met in the prison cells at the Volya Facility. He had helped free her from those once before.

No matter what it cost him, he had to try again.

'Seren, look at me,' Charlie said softly. 'Don't worry. You're not alone. I'm here.'

At the sound of his voice, Seren raised her eyes to his. A crust of dried blood had already set across her forehead. Dark red smudges were smeared across her face, now ghostly pale. Her eyes were shining, and her lips trembled as she stared into his face. She seemed to be trying to communicate something to him without using words. Growing desperate, Charlie glanced from Dragomir's openly mocking expression to Nikolai Ignatiev's look of mild amusement.

Rage blazed within him, smouldering away inside of his bones.

'Get on with it, monster,' Dragomir hissed. His eyes fixed on Charlie, he brought the blade of his hunting knife to Seren's neck and made a cut directly above her collarbone. Paying no attention to her distress, he kicked her forwards, onto her hands and knees. 'Feed.'

'What the hell?' Charlie whirled around to face Nikolai Ignatiev. 'I won't do this.'

'What a stubborn troublemaker my son has turned out to be.' Nikolai Ignatiev stared down at him, his head tilted to one side as he scratched the back of his head. 'I suppose I should have expected this. No doubt it is all thanks to the manner in which you were raised …'

'I won't hurt her,' Charlie whispered, an acrid taste in the back of his throat.

'You are determined to defy me, aren't you?' As something in his face changed, Nikolai Ignatiev released a sigh. 'Very well. Know that you brought this on her yourself. *Surrender.*'

Confused, Charlie stared up into his father's gleaming eyes. Then he caught sight of movement beside him. Turning his head, he saw Seren crawling towards him. Her eyes glazed, she shuffled across the flagstones, tugging the front of her dress down with one hand as she went. She had turned her face away from her open wound as the blood dripped down her chest.

'No.' Charlie backed off, horrified, but was dragged closer by his father.

'For you,' Seren said, leaning closer to him, her voice flat and empty, 'I give my life.'

'Feast on her.' A feverish whisper from above. 'Become what you were born to be.'

'Come on, Seren,' Charlie urged, hearing the fear in his own voice as he edged away from her. The smell of her blood was cloying in his nostrils. His stomach growled violently. 'I know you're scared, but – but we can fight this – together – you and me, right? I know you don't want to do this …'

'How long do you intend to keep up this delusional farce, you miserable wretch?' Nikolai Ignatiev hissed. 'Do you still not see? I have broken her mind. She belongs to *me*.'

'I don't,' Seren blinked, something flickering in her misty eyes, 'want …'

'You're my friend.' Charlie's voice cracked. 'I don't ever want to hurt you.'

'My friend …' With great effort, Seren turned her face to his, frowning. 'Charlie …'

Charlie heard his father whisper something that sounded like '*Impossible*,' but he refused to break eye contact with Seren. He watched as she blinked her long-lashed eyes, sending a single tear falling down her pale cheek. Something in his heart broke at the sight of it.

'Seren, come with me,' Charlie said, extending his hand slowly towards her. 'We need to find Saga, right? You remember Saga? Your little sister is waiting for us rescue her.'

'Saga.' Seren released her sister's name like a purifying breath. 'I need to … save her.'

'That's right,' Charlie whispered, as Seren touched his fingers. 'We're going to get her back – together. The two of us, we're going to save her, so don't you *dare* give in now!' He drew the back of his other hand roughly across his eyes, his arm shaking. 'Don't ever stop fighting!'

Seren looked at him for a long time, a frown creasing her forehead, before the fog seemed to clear from her eyes. Recognition dawned on her face. 'Charlie … you're here …' She gazed around her as though in shock, completely ignoring the two men beside them. 'Where did you go? I thought you were –'

'I'm here, Seren. I'll always be here.' Charlie was so close to her now that their foreheads were touching. Exhausted, he felt relief wash over him. She was safe. 'No matter what happens,' he told her, 'I'll always be right here with you.'

'So …' His heart sinking, Charlie's eyes snapped to Nikolai Ignatiev. He was looming above them, his face thunderous. 'You think you can make a fool out of me, do you, you worthless guttersnipe? I'll show you what happens to slaves who step out of line.'

'Seren …' Charlie breathed, reading the look on his father's face, 'help me.'

With vicious speed, Nikolai Ignatiev wrenched the chain backwards, dragging Charlie to his feet and pulling him forward by the collar around his throat. 'You have sealed your fate,' he hissed, spittle flecking his lips. 'I will crawl inside your mind,' he said, his fingernails digging into Charlie's ears, 'and once I am there, you will never be able to escape me again.'

'I –' Charlie's words died on his lips at the murderous smile on Nikolai Ignatiev's face.

'The Shadow Cells have been pining for you,' he whispered, 'and thanks to all those memories you so generously divulged during your last stay with us, I know exactly where I should begin with your punishment.'

Charlie flinched as his father brought his lips to his ear.

'Do you see the truth of your existence now? Anyone who might ever have loved you – they have abandoned you. You were born from hate, and will die in the darkness, alone.'

'No …'

Trembling, Seren had got to her feet, golden light rippling from her hands. Behind her, Dragomir was white-faced. Though he was tugging at the chain connected to her collar with all his might, it had no effect whatsoever.

'I will never let anyone …' Striding forward, Seren's voice rose to a deafening roar. '*Nobody treats my family like that!*'

His eyes fixed on Seren, his mouth hanging open, Nikolai Ignatiev released his grip on Charlie's collar. Collapsing to the flagstones, Charlie had just enough time to shield his eyes before a brilliant glare erupted from Seren's body. Bracing himself against a wave of heat, Charlie looked up to see her standing before him, engulfed in a white-hot light that pulsated like flames.

A furious wind was picking up around her. Dragomir was knocked backwards towards Vasco, his head hitting a marble pillar. Squinting through the fierce light, Charlie watched as Seren ripped through the manacles that bound her hands as easily as tearing through a sheet of paper. She ripped the collar from her throat, then threw her arm out towards him. His collar was broken into pieces, which were sent scattering to the stone floor beside the discarded knife.

Fighting not to be engulfed in the whirlwind of heat and light that Seren had created, Charlie crawled behind a pillar. He wrapped his arms around the smooth marble, watching as terrified soldiers raced out into the passageway while Seren wreaked havoc on the throne room.

When at last the wind and the heat had died down, Charlie braved a glance around the pillar. There was a huge crack in the wall behind the empty throne, running all the way up to the cavernous roof. Seren was standing by the throne, gazing up at the arched ceiling, her hair cascading down her back as the light uncoiled itself from her arms. His father was nowhere to be seen.

'You sure can fight,' Charlie said, grinning at Seren as the glow began to fade.

'Vasco is awake,' she said, staring calmly at the throne. 'Free him. You have the strength to do it now. We're going to find my sister – and this time, no one is getting left behind.'

'You got it.' Charlie raced over to the pillar where Vasco had been chained up.

'Charlie …' Vasco blinked slowly, his voice low and tired. 'Charlie … did … did he hurt you?'

'Hey,' Charlie said gently, pushing Vasco's hair out of his eyes and examining the deep wound on his head with some apprehension. 'I'm here. I'm going to get you out of these chains, all right? So stay with me and just take it easy.'

'I knew you wouldn't give up.' A weak smile passed across Vasco's pale face as Charlie ripped the collar from his neck, before tearing through the chains that bound him to the marble pillar with his bare hands. 'You never stop fighting.' Placing one hand on Charlie's left shoulder to steady himself, Vasco met his eyes, adding, in a clear voice, 'That's what I love about you.'

Charlie let out a soft laugh, scratching his face as he felt warmth bloom under his skin. 'You took a pretty bad knock to the head, huh? How many fingers am I holding up right now?'

'I'm serious. If we somehow manage to get out of here alive, I want to be with you.'

'I sure hope you haven't set your heart on a quiet life. I tend to attract a lot of trouble.'

Vasco smiled at him, a playful light in his dark eyes. 'I'm looking forward to it already.'

'You're such an idiot,' Charlie said, grinning despite himself as he covered his face with one hand. Looking at Vasco, he said, seriously, 'I'm really glad I have you on my side.'

Vasco nodded. 'You always will,' he said, before his eyes darted to Dragomir, who was beginning to stir on the floor behind them. 'You and Seren need to get out of here – fast.'

'Come with us,' Charlie urged him. The idea of leaving Vasco behind was intolerable.

'Help Seren rescue the other prisoners,' Vasco said. 'I'll hold him off until then.'

'All this sentimentality ...' Dragomir had forced himself to his feet, his mouth twisted as he looked from Charlie to Vasco. 'It makes me sick. You won't get away from me this time.'

Charlie stumbled backwards. 'But, Vasco ...' he said, his chest tight. 'What if –?'

'Take Seren and get out of here,' Vasco ordered, pushing him away. 'Now, Charlie!'

Turning on his heel, Charlie fled towards Seren, Dragomir's warning to Vasco pounding in his ears. 'You had better kill me while you have the chance, you traitorous coward. Because I swear to you now, if you don't, I'm going to make sure you live to regret being so weak.'

'Don't die,' Charlie chanted the words under his breath as he ran, hoping that if he said them enough, it might make a difference. 'Please, don't let him die. Don't take him away from me, too ...'

'Charlie, hurry up!' Seren stood at the threshold of the throne room, the doors wide open before her, beckoning to him. 'Our friends are all still waiting for us to rescue them.'

Pulling the cloth tie from around his neck, Charlie handed it to her to staunch the bleeding along her collarbone. He had to fight to clear his vision. There was a gnawing hunger deep inside his bones.

'I'm right behind you.'

Forcing himself not to look back, Charlie followed Seren out of the throne room. She led the way with such speed and confidence that he guessed she was retracing a familiar route back to the prison cells where she had been held. The Castle was not heavily guarded, and the sound of their footsteps as they ran thundered along the corridors. It seemed as though much of the force that had been stationed there had fled during Seren's attack. Whenever they did happen to come across a soldier, Seren simply blasted them out of the way as if it were nothing.

'Why did you never tell me,' she asked, as they raced towards the cells, 'that your mother was a Darkwood clan witch?'

'I never knew. She and my –' Charlie broke off. 'She died when I was still a kid. The war.'

'Did I ever tell you that my mother disappeared a couple of years ago?'

It took him a moment to respond. 'No, you didn't.'

'One day, she just vanished,' Seren said, her eyes fixed ahead as she ran. 'I searched everywhere for her, but she was gone. I went to my grandfather and begged him to let me keep looking for her beyond the borders of our land, but he refused. I never understood how he could just abandon her without a fight. It was only when the Witch Hunters returned for my sister and I that I finally understood what had happened to my mother.'

'I swear to you, Seren,' Charlie said, his jaw clenched, 'I'm going to make sure he pays with his life for everything he's done to us. I'll make him feel what we've felt, and much worse.'

Seren came to a halt, whirled around, and took Charlie's head in her hands. It was so unexpected that he did not attempt to resist.

'I know you're in pain, Charlie,' she said, pressing her forehead to his, as memories he thought he had sealed up forever came spilling back into his mind. 'I know how badly you've been hurt. But I need you to understand something.'

'I didn't say you could look there,' he whispered. 'Those things are – they're private.'

'You've inherited a treacherous, brutal legacy,' Seren said, as she stared into his eyes. 'The power of the Bloodwitch is a double-edged sword. It's not a bad thing to be afraid of it.'

'I'm not afraid of this power … I finally have a way to fight back. I can beat them now.'

Seren bit her lip, her forehead creased with concern. 'Pain like this needs to be held in gentle hands, Charlie,' she said. 'Think of saving an animal from a trap. If you treat it kindly, it has a chance to heal. But if you try to corner it or push it too hard, it'll turn on you, and you'll only end up hurting yourself more. Either way, you won't be the same. It will transform you.'

'If it means I have the chance to wield strength like yours, I'll do whatever it takes.'

'It's not going to be easy,' she said. 'But I promise, I'll be there to support you … through it all.'

They had reached the cells. Seren led them purposefully towards a heavy iron door that stood locked and bolted. With a curt nod to one another, they lashed out at the door, Charlie with a vicious kick, and Seren with a ferocious blast of air.

The door burst open and they entered the dark cell. A huge cage took up most of the room, looming out of the shadows.

'Charlie, Seren, is that you?' Alya's face, wan and frightened, appeared between the bars. 'What are you doing here?'

'Isn't it obvious?' Charlie said, grinning at her. 'We've come to rescue you.'

CHAPTER 26

'Stand back.'

The witches in the cell followed Charlie's warning. Seren waited until they had all edged a few steps closer towards the far end of the cage, then threw both her hands out, smashing a hole through the bars. It was so wide that they could all climb through without any difficulty. The witches emerged one by one through the clouds of dust, picking their way through the rubble and twisted metal around them. Pushing a frantic path through them, Seren rushed into the cage.

Alya flung herself towards Charlie with tears in her eyes. 'You're safe.' As she wrapped him in a tight embrace, he patted her gingerly on the head. 'I'm so glad. I was so worried about you.'

'Did they hurt you?' he asked, his eyes scanning the group of Lilith coven witches, some of whom shook their heads in response. 'Then why didn't you escape before now? If Seren could use her powers to break you out so easily –'

'She was strong enough to break the ward on her own,' Jasmine explained, stepping forward out of the gloom. 'We tried, but even with our combined strength, it wasn't enough.'

'How did she gain such strength?' Eva Brightheart asked, eyeing Seren closely.

'She was imprisoned here and experimented on,' Charlie answered, extricating himself from his sister's grip and drawing closer to Seren. 'How are you feeling? Do you need to rest?'

Seren wheeled around, her eyes wide. 'Where's my sister? Where is Saga?'

'She's not here,' Jasmine said, drawing her arm around Seren's shoulders, and leading her out of the cell. 'I'm sorry. We don't know where she is. We tried to find out anything we could from the guards, but –'

'But she must *be* here.' Seren gripped her head in her hands. 'Everyone *else* is here.'

'We'll find her, Seren,' Charlie said, meeting Jasmine's troubled gaze with a brief nod. 'Don't worry. I'll go straight to the Shadow Cells and search for her. Don't give up, all right?'

'Where is she, Charlie?' Seren was biting her nails. 'What have they done to her?'

'Try to focus on staying calm,' he said, chewing his lip. 'We won't leave without her.'

'Charlie …' At the sound of Alya's tentative voice, he glanced over his shoulder. 'Where's Vasco? Is he –?'

'He stayed behind to hold Dragomir off,' he answered, his own fears mirrored in Alya's horrified expression. 'We need to get to the throne room and back him up as soon as we can.'

At this, Eva Brightheart stiffened. 'No,' she said, waving his words away with a swipe of her hand. 'We need to leave this place as soon as we can. We *must* escape, and quickly.'

'*What?*' Charlie rounded on her, furious. 'You're not telling me you're planning to just leave him behind, are you? You'd abandon him, even after everything he's done to help you?'

Her blue eyes narrowed, Eva Brightheart regarded him coldly. 'He is not one of us.'

'Neither am I!'

'Are you not?'

Shaking off the sinking feeling in his stomach at the knowing arch of her brow, Charlie appealed to the others. 'Vasco risked his life to give me and Seren a chance to escape. We need to go back and help him before it's too late!'

'I am responsible for the safety of the daughters of my coven,' Eva Brightheart said, as the other witches turned towards her. 'I will not put their lives in danger for the sake of a Witch Hunter.'

As murmurs of assent rose from all around him, Charlie ground his teeth, his fists clenched. 'How about for Saga Casimir, then?'

he demanded, his rage burning a bright, clear path in his mind. 'How about for a little girl who's still trapped somewhere in this place, all alone and frightened? She's a witch, isn't she, just like all of you?' He rounded on the High Witch, who was watching him with a stony expression, her lip curled in disdain. 'Is she a good enough person in your eyes to be worth saving?'

'A single life can never outweigh the survival of an entire coven.'

Charlie snorted. 'Whatever. Alya, come on. Seren and I are going back.' Taking Seren's hand, Charlie led her towards the cell door. 'We're not leaving before we rescue her sister.'

'I … I'm going to lead the Lilith coven up to the roof of the Volya Facility.'

Standing on the threshold, Charlie looked back to see Alya staring him down. A determined furrow had settled across her brow as she met his gaze.

'There are military helicopters up there, large enough to carry everyone. We have a chance to get everyone out alive, and to get far enough away that they won't be able to follow us. But I'm the only one who knows the way. I can't go with you.'

'How are you going to fly without a pilot?' Charlie asked, his voice flat.

'We have no need for one.' One of Eva Brightheart's hands had come to rest on Alya's shoulder. 'That boy is of no use to us.'

'There's room enough on board for all of you, too,' Alya added, almost desperately.

'We'll wait for you as long as we can,' Jasmine said, giving him a gentle punch on the arm.

Charlie met their eyes, and knew he was beaten. 'Fine. Just take care of yourselves.'

Alya nodded, flashing him a weak smile. 'You too, Charlie.'

'Don't take too long.' Jasmine's face was set. 'Darkwoods don't leave family behind.'

Charlie was so taken aback by her words that his grip went slack on Seren's hand. She slipped away from him in an instant. By the time he had managed to shake himself back to reality, Seren had disappeared down the passageway, retracing their route towards the throne room. He pelted after her, raising his voice so that his words had a chance of reaching her.

'Seren, where are you going? I thought we were heading to the Shadow Cells?'

'I'm tired of running around in circles. I need answers, and *he* can give them to me.'

'You mean …' Charlie's heart was hammering. 'Wait for me – I'm coming with you!'

Seren ran as though she had the wind at her back, and Charlie soon lost sight of her. Bursting through the throne room doors, he saw Vasco leaning against a marble pillar, his shoulders rising and falling rapidly. When Charlie entered the room, Vasco glanced up, joy breaking over his pale face at the sight of him.

Seeing the exhaustion in Vasco's eyes, Charlie rushed towards him and dropped to his knees, checking to see if he had been hurt. Mercifully, it looked as though he had avoided anything worse than a few punches. Charlie let out a sigh of relief, his eyes scanning the flagstones for his knife, but it was nowhere to be seen.

'Did you find them?' Vasco asked, tension lining his face. 'Is Alexandra safe?'

'Yes. She's with her mother. They're planning to fly a military helicopter out of here with everyone on board. They're heading to the roof right now.'

'Really?' Vasco tilted his head back against the pillar, his hair falling into his eyes as a grim smile lifted the corners of his mouth. 'That plan might just be crazy enough to work.'

'Are you all right?' Charlie asked, brushing a fingertip against Vasco's cheek. It was somewhat swollen, and reddened under his touch. 'Did you see where Seren went?'

Vasco frowned, wincing as he pressed a hand to his ribs. 'She went after Dragomir.'

Charlie sighed. 'This time tomorrow, you're going to be waking up with a black eye.'

'It'll be worth it if I'm waking up beside you.'

Charlie rolled his eyes, smiling despite his better judgement. 'You do realise you could have been killed, right?' he said, as he pushed Vasco's hair out of his eyes and gave his hand a gentle squeeze. 'Why didn't you ask us to stay and help you?'

Vasco blinked, his eyes on Charlie's hand. Then he glanced up, looking as though the answer was obvious. 'You told me you didn't want Seren to use her powers unnecessarily, remember?'

At his words, Charlie went still, his mind racing. Vasco was right. *He* was the one who had been determined to rescue Seren from Nikolai Ignatiev's clutches without relying on her powers. Yet, in the end, he had been the one to beg Seren for help to save him from his father. He had witnessed how she had let her power loose, all for his sake.

If his own weakness led to her getting hurt …

'Charlie, what's wrong?'

Glancing towards the throne, Charlie registered that the crack in the wall behind it had already climbed all the way up to the roof. Seren had just broken a ward that all the witches of the Lilith coven could not overcome with their combined strength. Now she was attempting to face Dragomir alone. Charlie gritted his teeth and got to his feet, pulling Vasco with him.

'We're going after her.'

Vasco nodded at him wordlessly, his fingers curling around a handgun that lay discarded on the flagstone floor. Together, they plunged down a narrow stone passageway leading off from the throne room. When he felt a shiver across his spine, Charlie brought them both to a halt, flinging out one arm to stop Vasco from going any further.

'He's out there.' Steeling himself, Charlie took a step forward. 'Cover me from here.'

Vasco grabbed his wrist, holding him back. 'You can't!'

'Let go of me!' Charlie spat, whirling around as he attempted to free himself.

'Don't you remember what happened last time?' There was a desperate look in Vasco's eyes. 'You can't seriously expect me to sit back and let you do this?'

'I'm warning you, don't get in my way,' Charlie said, wrenching himself out of Vasco's grip and striding out into the open. 'I'm right here, Dragomir, you piece of shit!'

'Well,' came Dragomir's voice, 'I'm impressed at your tenacity if nothing else.'

'Get out here and face me, or are you not done playing hide and seek yet?'

'As you wish.' Smirking, Dragomir stepped out from behind a pillar into the light.

His heart plummeting, Charlie saw that the soldier was alone. There was no sign of Seren anywhere.

'Where is she?' he asked, forcing himself to keep his voice steady. 'Let her go right now, or you'll regret it.'

'You and I have been down this road before, haven't we?' Dragomir's cruel smile widened, and he folded his arms. 'Are you going to make the same mistake again, Charlie?'

'Charlie –! Get out of here –!'

He could hear her voice, and the sound of a struggle, but Seren was nowhere to be seen.

'I know you're using Seren to bait me, just like you did with my family,' Charlie said, his hands balled into fists as he glared at Dragomir. 'It's not going to work this time.'

'Feeling lucky today, are we? Don't you want to save your pretty little friend?'

'Run away, Charlie!' The sound of Seren's voice was growing fainter.

Grinding his teeth, Charlie fought the rage building inside him. 'Let – her – *go.*'

'You could always take her place,' Dragomir said, his voice light, a sneer curving his mouth. 'All you have to do is ask. I know how much you always looked forward to those visits I used to pay to your cell, no matter how coy you tried to be about it.'

Charlie froze. 'Wh-What the hell are you talking about?' he murmured, his voice shaking. 'I said no ... I told you to stop.' He felt sick. 'I said I didn't want you to do it ...'

'For a while, sure,' Dragomir said, shrugging, 'but that didn't last long, did it? In the end, you gave up your act of pretending to fight me off. You and I both know that's the truth. Besides, if you really didn't want it, you would never have put yourself in that position in the first place.'

'I –' Charlie's mouth had gone dry. 'It was – it was the only way I could – I never wanted –'

'Faulkner told me all about you.' As Dragomir prowled towards him, Charlie stumbled backwards, his hands trembling. 'You've been used like that ever since you were a kid, haven't you? You're used to it. I mean, really,' Dragomir added, with a soft laugh, 'what else are you good for, at this point? You think anyone would want you now, knowing where you've been?'

'I …'

'In all honesty, I think you should start taking a bit more responsibility for yourself.'

'*What?*' He wanted to shout, but it came out as a horrified whisper instead.

'You like to act tough and mouth off, but you're just playing hard to get, aren't you?'

'No, that's – that's not –'

'You always insisted on provoking me. It was like it was all a game to you. You can't expect me not to react.' Dragomir raised his hand to touch Charlie's face, but Charlie knocked it away. Dragomir let out a low chuckle of amusement. 'You're just too good to resist. We shared some good times together, didn't we?' His smile broadened. 'Lots of fond memories.'

'Don't …'

'I still think about you a lot, you know. Do you think about me sometimes, too, at night?'

Dragomir was so close to Charlie's face now that Charlie felt frozen under his cold stare. His mind had gone utterly blank. When he tried to force himself to think, a wave of sickening terror crashed over him.

The ghostly sensations of rough hands on his skin, and memories of a pain that seemed to never end, were all that he could find in his head. It was as if his whole body were covered with invisible bruises, and the man in front of him was busy pushing down on them, one by one.

'You're mine now, demon.'

A hand grabbed his throat, fingernails digging into his skin.

'Not on my watch, scum!'

A single gunshot split the air, and Dragomir staggered back.

'Vasco …' On his knees with his hands at his neck, Charlie felt his pulse racing beneath his fingers.

'Kovalev, have you lost your mind? I'll *kill* you for this!'

Dragomir was on his back on the flagstone floor, his arms trembling beneath him as he attempted to prop himself up. His teeth were gritted in pain, his face grey. Charlie's eyes travelled over his body and saw a dark stain at his pelvis, spreading steadily across his uniform.

With a shiver of mingled horror and awe, he stared up at his rescuer. Vasco's dark eyes were burning with rage, his face white. But his hand was steady, as he kept his gun trained on Dragomir.

'You won't have the chance,' Vasco answered. Then he shot both of Dragomir's kneecaps.

'Why are you *protecting* him?' Dragomir demanded, gasping with pain as his screams subsided. '*He's the Bloodwitch*! He's the one we've been hunting all this time. If you let him walk out of here alive, our nation will fall.'

'I won't let that happen.'

'You're going to turn your back on everything we've worked for our whole lives?'

'I don't care about any of that.' Vasco stared down at him, expressionless. 'Not anymore.'

Dragomir's eyes were wild, spit flying from his mouth. 'You're the Witchkiller! Your hands are stained in their blood! You can't wash it off now, so – so what's a little more? Kill him, right now, before he has the chance to destroy *everything*!'

'You're right.' Vasco's voice had grown dangerously soft. He bent down on one knee, his face level with Dragomir's. 'I've come this far. After all I've done, what's a little more blood on my hands?' Slowly, he pressed the muzzle of his gun directly between Dragomir's eyes. 'You sealed your own fate, the moment you first put your hands on him. You will never hurt anyone I love – ever again.'

Charlie, whose body seemed to no longer be listening to him, could not look away. He heard the final shot as it rang out, watched as though in slow motion as Dragomir's body fell backwards over the flagstones and lay still. It was a long time before he found himself able to tear his eyes away from the pool of blood gathering around Dragomir's body. He expected to feel something about it, but he only felt hollow.

'Are you all right, Charlie?' Vasco was standing beside him, stripping the gun in his hand with practised care and cleaning it intently. 'It's all over now.'

'He's …'

'I'm not sorry,' Vasco said, his voice even. 'No one treats you like that.'

'You …' Charlie was still on his knees, his entire body trembling.

'He got off easy. If it had been the other way around, he would have made you suffer much worse than that. He deserved it.' Finished with his work, Vasco holstered the gun and pulled Charlie to his feet with a scowl. 'When it comes to protecting you, I won't hesitate.'

'Seren … Saga …' His legs unsteady beneath him, Charlie stumbled forward. He had to shake his head to clear it of the images of dead bodies flashing before his eyes. 'We need to find them soon. If we don't make it to the helicopter in time …'

'You go after Seren,' Vasco said. 'I have a good idea where her sister might be.'

'Watch out for my brother.' Charlie did not know why he said it, but the same ominous feeling he had felt before, in the Vaults, was prickling the back of his neck. 'He's bound to be around here somewhere. And …' He swallowed hard. 'And make sure you –'

'Don't worry, we'll find them.' The shadow of a smile passed across Vasco's sombre face. 'Stay alive. I'm coming back for you, and I won't come back alone, either.'

Charlie watched as Vasco headed down the passageway, retracing their route towards the throne room. When he finally lost sight of him, Charlie continued his solitary journey. His mind was blank, his hands still shaking. Feeling oddly numb, he hugged his arms against his chest. Struggling to make sense of what he had just witnessed, he kept his eyes on his feet as he stumbled on.

'You see, Doctor? Didn't I tell you he wouldn't be able to resist playing the hero?'

At the sound of a horribly familiar voice, Charlie glanced up, only to find himself face to face with his brother. Standing beside Doctor Ivanov was Faulkner. He held Seren still by her long hair, which he had wrapped tightly around his hand. Her eyes were glazed, and only half-open. She looked pale and exhausted.

'It's you ...'

Although Charlie had known for some time that it was the truth, a part of him had never genuinely believed that his brother Max could be the Doctor Ivanov who had hurt so many people. He felt the pieces slotting into place inside him with a kind of cold finality.

'I'm afraid to say that this is the end of the road for you, little brother.'

'So it's really true?' Charlie murmured. 'You've been working with *him* – all along?'

'I need a steady supply of materials to make progress in my work,' Ivanov said, shrugging. 'I hope that puts it in terms simple enough so that even you can understand them. Now, don't move. I need to decide what to do with you.'

'You think you're the one who gets to choose how this ends, do you?'

Ivanov smiled coldly. 'You may be faced with your own choice, one day.'

Charlie stared him down without flinching. 'When that day comes, I will not hesitate.'

'Those are brave words, Charlie.' Sounding mildly impressed, Faulkner shoved Seren towards Ivanov, who caught her before she had a chance to escape. 'Leave your brother to me, Doctor. I know exactly how to deal with him.'

'I'll keep the witch secure,' Ivanov said to Faulkner, as he dragged Seren away. 'Do whatever you like to him, just make sure he suffers long enough before you put an end to him.'

Charlie surged forward, enraged. 'You're not going anywhere! Let her go!'

Faulkner stepped in front of his path, Charlie's knife in his hand. 'Not so fast, Charlie.'

'Get out of my way!'

Faulkner shook his head with a smirk. 'You owe me, and it's time for you to pay up.'

'I'm warning you. If you don't –'

Charlie broke off, his hand clutching his ribs as he fell to his knees. When it came away, he realised that his blood had soaked through his t-shirt. The wounds his father had inflicted on him in the throne room were still bleeding. His head was swimming. Black spots swam in front of his eyes.

'You're not looking so good, Charlie.' Faulkner loomed above him, a nasty laugh playing around his mouth as he spun the knife in his hand. 'What should I carve into you this time? Do you still have the scars? Will you let me see them once more, for old times' sake?'

'*Fuck* you!' Charlie snarled at him. 'You're never touching me again.'

'I never could resist a challenge.' Charlie cried out as Faulkner grabbed his scarred shoulder and twisted his fingers. '*Oh*, does it still hurt?' he cooed, his lips pressed to Charlie's ear. 'You've always been weak. When it counted, you could never do anything for anyone.'

Charlie caught a flash of light against the blade, then his left shoulder was on fire.

'It's been such a long time,' Faulkner murmured, as he buried the knife deeper into Charlie's skin, forcing him onto his back. 'I can't wait to find out how you've changed.'

Immobilised by the pain, Charlie could do nothing to resist as Faulkner lowered himself onto his body, his breathing fast and hot against Charlie's neck. All that existed were the flames.

'Don't look away from me ...' he whispered, tilting Charlie's head towards his. 'Don't let me miss that look in your eyes. Who's free now, Charlie? You're mine, always and forever.'

Something skipped in Charlie's mind. He had been in this position before, years ago. The fall of rain hammered in his ears.

A flash of lightning illuminated the crimson velvet drapes behind Faulkner's head. He saw himself as a child.

Back then, the same knife that was now buried deep in his shoulder had been in his hand instead, as he slashed wildly at Faulkner's face. There had been blood on his skin then, too. It had only taken one surprise attack to throw Faulkner off-balance, for Charlie to mount his escape. Faulkner's arrogance had been his undoing then, just as it would be now.

With a roar of effort, his jaw clenched against the pain, Charlie wrenched the knife from his shoulder. He caught sight of Faulkner's eyes, wide with shock. Adjusting his grip, Charlie took a deep breath, and let his mind be free.

When he returned to himself, he was standing above Faulkner, breathing heavily. One arm hung limp at his side, while blood dripped steadily from the blade in his other hand. Sweat fell from his hair as his own blood pounded in his veins. He felt elated.

He felt alive.

'What – the hell – did you just do to me?'

Faulkner was ashen-faced and gravely wounded. The sight of the fear in his eyes was better than anything Charlie could ever have imagined.

'Why did I wait so long to do this to you?' he wondered aloud, between soft laughter.

'Who do you think you are to stand up to me?' Faulkner demanded, hissing with pain.

'I thought you couldn't wait to find out how I've changed?' Sinking to his knees, Charlie pressed the blade of his knife into Faulkner's skin and let it enter his flesh slowly. 'No,' he said, his voice low, as Faulkner squeezed his eyes shut with an agonised scream. 'Don't you *dare* look away from me ... I don't want to miss that look in your eyes ... You're *mine* now.'

When Charlie was done, the man gasping for breath before him was unrecognisable.

'I ... never did manage ... to tame you ... did I?' Faulkner mumbled, his voice thick. The light was beginning to fade from his eyes as blood bubbled up from his mouth and flooded through his open chest. 'I wonder ... what will it take to ... truly break you?'

'Nothing in this world can break me,' Charlie said quietly, as he watched Faulkner die.

'One of these days, Charlie …' Faulkner's voice was becoming weaker with every passing moment, a long rattle sounding from his throat with each breath he took. 'One day soon, you'll find out that there's been someone waiting … with a knife in the dark for you as well … all this time.'

Towering above the bloody corpse at his feet, Charlie felt a smile spread slowly across his face. 'Well,' he murmured, dragging the back of his hand across his mouth and tasting blood on his lips, 'I guess I'll just have to kill them too, then, won't I?'

CHAPTER 27

Charlie stalked down the passageway, a furious hunger gnawing at his insides, his skin prickling with scorching heat. It did not take long before he found who he was looking for.

His brother had managed to reach the end of the passage and had dragged Seren back into the throne room. At the sight of Charlie appearing out of the darkness, he raised his gun, aiming it straight at Charlie's heart.

'Think carefully about this, Charlie,' he said. 'This is your last chance to walk away.'

Coming to a halt, Charlie's eyes travelled from the gun in his brother's hand to Seren, struggling under Ivanov's grip. He was holding her by the wrist, so tightly that his fingers had gone white with effort. She appeared to be fighting him with all the strength she had left. But, from the beads of sweat on her pale face, and her harsh breathing, it was clear that she was exhausted. When she caught sight of Charlie, she went completely still, her face falling as she covered her mouth with her free hand.

'Charlie ...' Seren whispered, looking as though she might start to cry. 'Your eyes ...'

Ivanov laughed coldly. 'So, you killed him, did you? I didn't think you had it in you.'

Charlie, who had raised a hand to his eyes at the sound of the fear in Seren's voice, ground his teeth at his brother's words. He clenched his fist, letting his arm fall to his side. 'I'm done playing games with you,' he said, pointing his knife at his brother. 'I'm warning you, you had better let Seren go, right now.'

Ivanov's eyes narrowed. 'And what are you going to do about it if I don't?'

Charlie took a step forward, tightening his grip on the knife, which was trembling in his fingers as he held it out towards his brother. A nauseous feeling swirled in his stomach. His heart racing, Charlie felt his legs buckle beneath him before his knees hit the flagstones. The knife was still in his hand, the tip of the blade aimed at his brother's heart. But his hand was now shaking so badly that he needed to grip his wrist with his other hand to keep it steady.

'You can't do it, can you?' Ivanov's voice was soft, holding notes of surprise and pity.

'Please, Max ...' From his knees, Charlie stared up at his brother. 'Don't make me –'

The sound of a single gunshot cut off the rest of Charlie's words, followed an instant later by Seren's terrible scream. For a second, he thought she was the one who had been shot.

Then he felt blistering fire somewhere near his chest. Confused, Charlie reached for the source of the pain at his side. He blinked slowly down at his hand, as it came away covered in blood.

His vision blurred as he sank onto his side, whatever strength he had left flowing out of him like a surging torrent. He knew, without a doubt, that he was dying. He had managed to outrun his fate until now, but a part of him had always known that he could never truly be free.

'H-How could you shoot your own brother?' he heard Seren whimper through her tears.

'Some brother he was. My brother abandoned me. He's been dead to me for years.'

His breathing ragged and laboured, Charlie's eyes came to rest on his brother's highly polished shoes as he crouched down beside him. 'You always were stubborn,' Ivanov said quietly, resting his chin against his palm as he gazed down at Charlie. 'Your problem is that you never learned to recognise when you can't win. Look at where it's brought you in the end.'

'He's your family!' Charlie heard Seren shriek. 'How could you *do* this to him?'

'He is nothing to me,' Ivanov said, straightening up and turning on his heel. 'Now —'

'You killed my friend.' Seren sounded frighteningly calm. 'I am going to *destroy* you.'

Charlie felt something tight seize his chest as he forced himself to edge further onto his side, searching for Seren. He clenched his fists, desperately trying to breathe through the fierce pain lancing through his upper body. By now, the slightest movement sent him into convulsions of agony. His brother was sprinting away across the throne room, towards the double doors.

Seren had stepped forward, her hands moving in arcs as she sent gusts of air and beams of light in all directions. At the sight of her waves of fire, Charlie shielded his head with his hands, bracing himself against the oncoming wash of intense heat.

An ominous crack sounded somewhere high above them, followed by the deep groans of wood and metal starting to give way. With a roar of broken glass and splintered beams, the roof began to collapse in on them.

Lying on the floor, Charlie had only a vague awareness of what was going on around him. He was starting to grow deeply, bone-achingly tired. He felt as though he was sinking into a deep sleep. The smell of charred flesh was on the air as particles of ash drifted past him.

Another menacing rumble, like that of oncoming thunder, sounded above his head, as debris began to fall all around him. Somewhere in the distance, Charlie could hear people shouting and screaming. As clouds of thick dust threatened to choke him, he fought to cover his mouth, nose and eyes. By the time they had cleared, his brother was gone.

'Charlie, can you still hear me? Stay with me, Charlie, all right?'

'Seren ...' His eyes were blurry, his cheeks wet. 'Why do you sound ... so sad?'

'Come on, tough guy.' Seren laughed, then sniffed. 'You're not leaving me like this.'

'I think I … wanted … to do something … worthwhile … just once … before …'

'It's not so bad,' she tried to reassure him. She touched her fingertips to his forehead, and he opened his eyes to see a concerned frown shadowing her face. 'Hold on. I'll help you.'

'No.' Charlie took a deep, shuddering breath, pulling away. 'I don't want you to.'

'Don't be an idiot.' Seren cradled his shoulders and touched him. 'Let me help you.'

'*No*, Seren.' Though he could feel himself growing weaker every moment, he put all his strength into his last words. 'I don't want you to get hurt … because of me.'

'You came back for me. I only found the power to stop being their puppet because of you.' She spoke slowly, softly, her eyes drinking him in. 'I can't leave you like this, Charlie. I won't do it.'

'There's not much time,' Charlie said, his voice becoming fainter. 'You – have to get out of here. You have to leave me behind.' He tried to smile, to mask his fear, but it was there.

'You would never leave *me* behind,' she murmured, a small smile crossing her face.

He laughed – then regretted it, because it hurt – and blinked back tears. Remorse for what he had left unsaid pierced him as badly as the pain in his chest. 'I've known this was coming … for a long time. I'm sorry for not telling you sooner, but –'

'Don't talk like that. I knew when I first came here looking for my sister that there was a good chance I would never make it home again.' Seren smiled at him as light began to blossom from her fingertips and run along the skin of her arms. 'I never thought I would make some friends along the way. I'm grateful for that.' Her face was illuminated in a halo of light. 'I'm only sad because I failed to rescue Saga. I'm not afraid to die. Not if I can save you.'

'Seren, you have to let me go.'

'No,' she said simply. 'No, I won't let you do that.' Shuffling closer to him on her knees, she placed her hands on his chest, directly over his heart, and closed her eyes. 'I won't give up on you. You're not going anywhere.'

'*Please* don't do this.' He was begging now. With the last of his breath, he was begging. He might once have felt ashamed. Now nothing mattered to him but keeping her alive and safe.

Seren's eyes snapped open at his words, and she gazed at him imploringly. 'This is *my* decision. Don't you understand, Charlie? I want to do this for you – because you're my friend.'

Tears were trickling steadily down his face. 'But I – I don't want you to forget me.'

'Charlie, I could never forget you.'

'But you *will*,' he insisted. 'If you do this, something bad will happen to you, and I couldn't live – I couldn't go on, knowing I survived because you sacrificed yourself for me.'

'And I couldn't live with myself if I let you die,' she whispered, tears spilling from her eyes. 'I can save you – I can do it. Please … please trust me.'

Her hair brushed his face as she leant in closer towards him. She took one of his hands in hers and squeezed gently, her thumb running along his, her touch warm and comforting.

'I promise,' she said, her breath tickling his ear, 'if we ever meet again, even if I seem different than I am now, even if it seems … Please, never doubt that I … that somewhere deep, deep down inside myself … that I remember you.'

'Why would you risk your life for me?' Charlie asked softly. 'I'm not … I'm not –'

'You're my family. I know you have the power to save everyone else. I trust that.'

'I don't understand why … why you would –'

'I need you to promise that you'll do something for me in return,' Seren murmured, as she closed her eyes. 'Promise me that you'll find a way to forgive yourself. If you don't, your Gift will be too unstable. I know I said I would help you … but I think I'll have to –'

'Seren, please don't do this …' She was shimmering in front of him through his tears.

'I'm going to save you,' she said quietly. She pushed her weight through her hands and onto his chest, her brow knitted in intense concentration. 'I promise. I *will* save you, Charlie.'

Something was happening beneath his skin. It felt like needles were working their way inside his body, pricking at him, tingling throughout his whole being. Their touch was light but insistent. The air around him was becoming warmer. When he opened his eyes, Seren was surrounded by light. Her hair fanned out in waves of red, orange and gold, like it was on fire.

'I'm going to tell you something important now, Charlie.' Her words held a vague echo, despite how calmly she spoke them. 'Don't ever forget … I have the power to heal the damage to your body, but only you have the power to heal the pain in your heart. Don't give up …'

Charlie thought she looked peaceful, deep in concentration. Her eyes were gently closed, with only the merest trace of a frown on her face. The light seemed to be coming from inside her, yet somehow shining down upon her at the same time. It was growing more and more intense with every passing moment.

Charlie attempted to shield his eyes, but he no longer had any strength left to lift his hand. He squinted against the bright light, seeking her face. He could feel himself fading, his eyes gradually closing, as Seren's slowly opened. Eventually, all he could see of Seren was her deep brown eyes, and the small smile that held so much unspoken sadness, as she looked down upon him.

'Will you promise me one more thing?' she asked, her voice soft. 'If you don't mind?'

'Anything.' He was too exhausted to open his eyes, but the pain was leaving him.

'Please don't leave me behind.' She sniffed, heaved a sigh, and squeezed his hand. 'When they capture me again … please try to rescue me. Don't leave me here all on my own.'

Charlie held her hand tightly, a single tear falling from his lashes. 'I won't leave you.'

'Don't blame yourself anymore. No matter what anyone says, it wasn't your fault.'

*

'Find Experimental Subject 1740904.'

'Sir, we should leave – the building is unstable. It's a miracle the roof hasn't caved in.'

'Find her, or all my research will have come to nothing.'

'She's over here, Doctor Ivanov. She's still alive – just.'

'Then we have everything we need.'

'What do you want us to do with the Bloodwitch? The Great Protector will want –'

'Leave him to bleed out. He's as good as dead already. Bring the girl. We still need to find Kovalev and the witches he escaped with.'

Charlie felt Seren's fingers slip from his own. He had no strength left to resist. He did not know how long he lay there, motionless, as his life gradually returned to him. When at last he found the strength to sit up, his head was clear. The lightness that came with the absence of pain in his heart and his chest was palpable.

He staggered to his feet, leaning against a marble pillar for support, hardly daring to believe that he was still alive. Seren, Doctor Ivanov, and his father's soldiers were gone. He was alone.

He was reborn.

'Charlie!' Vasco was racing towards him. 'You're safe? All saints, I thought you –'

'You came back for me.' Charlie rubbed his eyes frantically. 'You really came back.'

'I told you I would, didn't I?' With a gentle touch, Vasco rested his hand against the small of Charlie's back, frowning with concern as he peered into his face. 'Your eyes are red. Did you get smoke in them? Where's Seren, by the way? I've got a present for her.'

'Huh?' Glancing down, Charlie saw a small, red-headed figure nestled in the crook of Vasco's arm. Her face was buried against his chest, a fistful of his t-shirt balled in her hand. It was Saga. 'You rescued her … you really did it. You saved her, and you're … you're alive.'

'It must be a blue moon,' Vasco said, with a glint in his eye that made Charlie's heart skip a beat. 'That's the only explanation. But seriously, where's Seren?' His eyes downcast, Vasco rocked slowly from foot to foot, humming a soft tune that Charlie did not recognise. 'This little one needs her sister.'

'She sacrificed herself to protect me,' Charlie said at last, gripping his arms tightly.

Vasco went still. He resettled Saga in his arms before meeting Charlie's eyes. 'Then we need to get out of here, right now,' he said. 'This whole place could collapse at any moment.'

Lowering his gaze to the floor, Charlie nodded. 'Vasco ...' he began. 'I think I'm –'

'Whatever you want to say, I'll listen to you later.' Vasco was arming himself with the weapons the soldiers had left scattered around the throne room during Seren's attack. 'Let's take it one step at a time. For now, we'll head to the roof and just hope to all the saints that they haven't left yet.'

His mind empty of thought, Charlie followed Vasco through the Castle, into the Facility, and up to the rooftop. There were no dead bodies to greet him this time – no soldiers, or injections, or chains, or prison cells, or knives. He was safe.

He tried to see if he could find some kind of emotion connected with that realisation. But when he went looking for how he was supposed to feel, he found that there was only a deep, aching emptiness inside of himself. Something told him that it would be with him for a long time to come.

'Charlie! Vasco!' Alya was waving at them from the helicopter. 'Over here – hurry!'

They raced towards her, and had almost reached the helicopter, when Eva Brightheart stepped in front of them. She placed herself firmly between them and the witches of her coven.

'What are you doing?' Charlie asked coldly, his skin burning. 'Get out of our way.'

'Give me the Casimir girl,' she said, her hand outstretched, her face impassive.

'Saga is frightened.' Charlie could tell Vasco was trying hard to maintain a respectful tone as he glanced uncertainly between him and the High Witch. 'I don't think she wants to let go of me ...'

'Then *make* her let go.' Eva Brightheart's lip curled. 'The child is confused. She needs to be with her own people.' She stepped forward, reaching for Saga. 'Give her to me, Witchkiller.'

Charlie planted himself in front of Vasco, forcing the High Witch to pause. 'Why can't she stay with Vasco until she's ready to let go?' he demanded. '*He's* the one who rescued her.'

Eva Brightheart's cold eyes narrowed. 'He is not welcome here. He is not our kind.'

Charlie shrugged. 'Then we're done talking. If he's not going then neither are we.'

'You are risking all of our lives with this ridiculous behaviour!' she hissed furiously.

'If you want me or Saga on that helicopter with you, then Vasco comes too.'

Eva Brightheart turned on her heel, her cloak flying out behind her. 'Get us in the air.'

'But, Mother,' Alya said, looking stricken, 'we can't possibly leave them behind!'

'What about the little girl?' another witch asked, to troubled murmurs of assent from the other witches.

Jasmine had risen to her feet and come to stand at Alya's side. 'Commander,' she began, in a carefully level voice, 'what was the point of waiting here all this time if we're just going to fly off without them?'

Charlie watched with mild interest as Eva Brightheart stared into the eyes of his sister and his cousin, wondering what she would do next. Her eyes scanned the faces of the witches in her coven. When her shoulders sagged, he knew that she saw she was beaten. He felt a smile of triumphant satisfaction spread across his face as warmth flickered and curled under his skin.

'Very well,' she said, turning back to them. Fury burnt in her chalk-white face as she stared directly at Charlie. 'I want you all on board at once – before I change my mind.'

Smirking, Charlie saw Vasco and Saga onto the helicopter first. With a last look behind him at the Volya Facility and the Elysian Castle, Charlie followed Vasco's footsteps. No sooner had he pulled the door closed behind him than the helicopter started to rise off the concrete roof. As he and Vasco made their way to the end of a row of benches, Charlie sensed every pair of eyes in the helicopter on them. They sat together in the corner, side by side, in silence.

The helicopter was large enough to fit all the escaped prisoners, although they had to squash close together to ensure everyone had a space to sit down. Vasco had propped the rifle he had taken from the throne room up beside him. He was looking suitably uncomfortable at the venomous stares the witches closest to them were throwing his way. With a small smile, Charlie noticed Vasco shift his body slightly, as though attempting to hide the weapon from view. He decided to say nothing about it, as they began to fly higher into the air.

'You two have made quite the impression already,' Jasmine said, taking a seat opposite them. 'So, what's your game, Witchkiller?' she asked, her eyes snapping towards Vasco. 'You thought you'd rescue Seren's kid sister and lull us all into a false sense of security?'

'Take that back!' Charlie warned her, leaping to his feet, his anger blazing like fire.

'Try to keep your voices down,' Vasco said gently, squeezing Charlie's hand. 'I think Saga's fallen asleep. Oh, and also,' he added, meeting Jasmine's fierce gaze, 'please don't call me by that name anymore. Whatever it takes, I'm going to find a way to leave who I was behind me.'

Jasmine snorted and stood up. 'You think it's going to be as easy as that, do you?'

'Where are we going?' Charlie called after her, as she strode down to the front of the helicopter.

'We can't return to the hideout. We're flying north, to the Casimir coven.'

Charlie and Vasco watched Jasmine go. Beyond her, they could just make out Eva Brightheart and a small circle of older witches moving their hands above their heads in wide circles. They were using their powers to keep the helicopter airborne, steady, and moving at speed.

Charlie grinned at Vasco, intrigued to discover what he would make of all this. But his smile quickly faded when he noticed how wide Vasco's eyes had become. His pale face had taken on a distinctly greenish tinge.

'Why don't you look out of the window?' Charlie suggested, but Vasco shook his head.

Charlie said nothing, as Vasco closed his eyes and tilted his head back, breathing fast. He did, however, give Vasco's knee a brief pat, before looking around them. Jasmine was walking to and fro among the former prisoners, counting on her fingers. Charlie saw that she would smile occasionally when she noticed the children looking up at her with curious glances.

Alya was handing out blankets and food parcels. Charlie supposed he should have guessed that his sister would have thought to stop for supplies before they made their escape. She appeared to be trying to speak to as many people as she could.

When she caught sight of Charlie watching her, she inclined her head towards him in a little nod of acknowledgement. He turned away to stare out of the window as the Volya Facility, the Elysian Castle, and the city of Penumbra all grew smaller and smaller below them. Someone important was missing.

She was down there, somewhere.

'I'll come back for you, Seren.'

He spoke the words under his breath, his eyes lingering on the castle in the mountains with its caved-in roof. Drawing his knife from his pocket, he saw that it was still stained with blood – although whose blood it was, he could no longer be sure.

'I won't leave you behind.'

Without flinching, he sliced the blade along his palm, clenching his fist to his face.

'I promise, no matter what it takes, I'll find you again.'

Vasco shifted beside him, as Saga stirred in his arms and gave a wide yawn. 'I guess I'm going to have to learn how to be a big brother now,' he said, an expression of mingled apprehension and wonder on his face as she blinked up at them both. 'You've got two of us now, Saga,' he added, putting an arm around Charlie's shoulders and smiling at her. 'What d'you think of that? Two big brothers – me and Charlie. But you know Charlie already, don't you?'

Charlie watched as Saga turned her large eyes on him, her thumb in her mouth. She blinked silently up at him. He stared back at her, seeing the ghost of her sister in every aspect of her face. He clenched his fists tighter to stop his hands from shaking, his jaw set. Blood dripped from his open wound, and Charlie gritted his teeth.

He was starving.

Saga's eyes grew wary, and she clung tighter to Vasco, burying her face in his t-shirt again without making a sound. Rubbing his hand in soothing circles against her back, Vasco cast Charlie an anxious look.

'Charlie?'

'What d'you want?'

'Oh, um ...' Vasco said, running his hand through his hair and tapping his feet. 'I guess I was just wondering ... but it doesn't matter at the moment. Don't worry about it, all right?'

'What are you talking about?'

'Forget it, it's not important.' Vasco sighed. 'I wonder what's going to happen to us now?'

'I have to go back.' His hand was throbbing painfully. 'I have to rescue Seren.'

Vasco nodded, giving no indication that Charlie's words came as a surprise to him.

'You can't stop me.'

'I don't plan to. In fact, you can count me in.'

'Huh.' He frowned, watching Vasco closely as the blood spread under his fingers. 'I thought you'd call me crazy – or say it's too dangerous. I didn't expect you to be on my side.'

Vasco smiled. 'I'll always be on your side, no matter what happens. I promise, Charlie.'

'Don't *call* me that,' he snapped.

He heard the anger in his own voice but found himself unable and unwilling to restrain it. It was *his* fault. But that weak, cowardly part of himself was gone. He would burn any last remnants of it out, until those memories were nothing more than smouldering ash.

'I never want to hear that name again, you understand me?'

'But ...' A frown of concern had darkened Vasco's features. 'But, Charlie –'

'No. He died in the Shadow Cells. From now on, I will live with the name I should have been given from the start.'

The blood had reached his wrist. He was so desperately hungry.

'My name is Zuriel Ignatiev.'

THE SWALLOW'S FLIGHT

a prequel

Emily Rooke

CHAPTER 1

T he house with the black door had been on Charlie's mind for the last three days. It was the huge bay windows that had first attracted him to it, since they offered such a welcoming view onto the life of the family who lived inside. The house stood on a wide, tidy street, shielded from the road by wrought iron fences. To get their attention, you had to climb a flight of whitewashed stone steps and ring the bellpull hanging by the front door. After that, a maid would appear, and you would be shown inside. He had worked it all out in his head. Nothing could go wrong.

This was what he was trying to explain to Sally, but he was not certain that she was paying much attention to him. She had done a good job of following his instructions all morning, holding his hand as they crossed over the Witchtrap Wall and left the dingy alleyways of Penumbra behind for the suburban streets of Elysia. However, now that they stood there, hidden in a spinney across the road from the house with the black door, she seemed to be getting cold feet. Charlie – who was conscious that the longer they lingered between the trees, the greater the chance that someone would discover them – was trying not to let his frayed nerves show.

'That's about it for what you have to do,' he told her. 'Have you been listening to me?'

'I'm listening.' The little girl was staring at the twigs and leaves below their feet, her thumb in her mouth. She seemed to be determined to avoid meeting his eyes.

'All right, then it's time for you to get going,' Charlie said, having scanned both sides of the street to check that no one was watching their location. 'Are you ready?'

Sally's lip was trembling as she shifted from foot to foot. When she looked up at him again, Charlie saw that her eyes were shining. Frowning, he lowered himself to his knees, so that their faces were at the same level. The pull across the small of his back that came with the movement made him wince, and he gritted his teeth to weather the pain.

'Why are you crying?' he asked, his voice gentle as he tucked her hair behind her ear.

'Do I have to go, Charlie?' Her words were somewhat muffled by her thumb.

'What's wrong?' His eyes travelled over her troubled expression. 'Are you scared?'

At his words, Sally nodded. In a hesitant voice, she said, 'Charlie, what if they don't want me?'

'Come here.' With a sigh, Charlie opened his arms, and Sally folded herself into his embrace, her body warm against his. 'That's impossible,' he said, as he patted her head and smiled down at her. 'Who wouldn't want you? Trust me, they're going to love you.'

With a sniff, Sally drew back a little, so that she was looking directly into his face. 'Will I ever see you again, Charlie?' she asked, her eyes wide with concern.

Charlie hesitated for a moment, his face falling, as he tried to decide what to tell her. 'I'll come see you sometime, if you like,' he said at last, forcing himself to keep his tone light. 'You're going to be having too much fun to worry about me, anyway. But I'll stop by sometime, I guess ... if you really want me to. You can show me all the books you've been reading, and your new fancy clothes, and all your new toys. So –'

'Can we still play together when you come to see me, Charlie?'

'We'll play as much as you want,' he said, getting to his feet and taking her hand. 'But listen,' he added, staring up and down the street once again, his heart beginning to beat a little faster. 'It's time for us to say goodbye for a while now, all right? You're going to find a real family. Forget about me, and everything else. You remember what you're supposed to say?'

Sally nodded. 'I tell them I'm lost, and that I don't know where my parents are, and I tell them that I need their help.' She took a deep breath, and, gazing at him seriously, went on. 'I don't *ever* tell them where I came from, or about you, or anything about –'

'Good. That's right.' Charlie let go of her hand. 'Off you go, then, while it's still quiet.'

She took a step forward, then looked back, biting her lip. 'I'll miss you, Charlie.'

'I'll miss you too,' Charlie said, his voice strained, his eyes darting around the empty street. 'Go on, hurry up,' he added, as he attempted to give her a nod of encouragement. 'And don't look back at me, all right? I'll be watching you, but you have to make it look like you're alone.'

The little girl gave him one last, fierce hug. 'Bye, Charlie,' she said, before stepping out into the light. 'Thank you for rescuing me.'

Charlie was so taken aback by her words that, by the time he managed to murmur his goodbye, she had already left him far behind. He concealed himself in the shadows, watching from behind the trunk of a huge oak tree as Sally crossed the street. With some hesitation, she climbed up the stone steps to the black door. Once on the threshold, she stretched out her arm, reaching for the bellpull.

For one horrible moment, Charlie thought that she was not going to be able to reach it, because she was so small. He had almost stepped out onto the street himself, when he saw one of her tiny hands grasp it and pull down hard. Drawing back from the light, Charlie waited until the door was opened, and the young maid he recognised had appeared.

His mouth dry, he recited the words he had taught Sally to say under his breath. Then he watched as, right on cue, the maid put her arm around Sally's shoulders, and led her into the house. Once the door was shut behind them, Charlie felt his shoulders sag with relief. His plan had worked. She was safe.

So, with Sally included, that made eleven.

Without a second thought, he took the shortest route back to the Witchtrap Wall, keeping to the backstreets as much as he could. He kept his head down and his hands in the pockets of his black sweatpants as he went. His mind was racing furiously. This was far from his first visit to the little spinney in the western suburb of the city. Over the last fourteen days, he had brought three children to three different houses in close proximity to it. Sally would have to be the last.

He had chosen that location specifically because it allowed him a place to stay hidden from view. From there, he could wait to make sure the children were taken safely into the houses. But he could not use it again. If he were ever recognised, it would all be over – not only for the kids, but for him as well. If any of the residents became suspicious, if any of them called the military police, they would swarm on the spinney in an instant.

He would need to scout out a new set of streets for the next few kids on his mental list. It would mean more nights in the autumn chill, more days without sleep, but none of that mattered to him. There was only one thought driving him now. Perhaps he would try the southern part of the city next. He needed to avoid any sort of pattern, and he needed to stay three steps ahead of Faulkner.

Charlie retraced the familiar route back through the streets of Penumbra to the Spike, pulling his shoulder-length hair down from its messy bun and tying it back up into a loose ponytail as he did so. He hated the feel of it, but that was how Faulkner liked it, and that was what mattered.

By the time he had returned to the Spike, the position of the sun told him it was close to midday. His stomach growling, Charlie rounded his shoulders as he caught sight of the two sentries on duty at the front of the hideout. He kept his eyes on his scuffed sneakers as he approached them.

'You're back late, kid,' one of them said – Mikhail, Charlie thought his name was.

'I'm back, aren't I?' Charlie muttered, pushing past them and reaching for the door.

'Busy night, was it?' the other guard chuckled. 'Need your beauty sleep now, do you?'

'Shut the hell up.'

Charlie had said it under his breath, but the guard heard him. He realised his mistake at once. It was Rorik, one of the Pen boys Maya had warned him to stay away from. Charlie thought he remembered her telling him something about how much Rorik loved tormenting the younger kids. At the time, all he had been able to focus on was the burning rage her words had made him feel.

Grabbing Charlie by his ponytail, Rorik wrenched his head backwards. 'You had better watch your mouth when you speak to me, you little brat,' he warned, his voice harsh as he shoved Charlie to the ground. 'You're nobody's favourite anymore, got that? Know your place. You kids are no better than dirt.'

Pain lanced through Charlie's lower back as he forced himself onto his knees. Trying to control his shaking, he dug his fingernails into the skin of his palms and glared up at the guard. 'You wanna fight?'

One of Rorik's eyebrows rose. 'You want me to teach you another lesson, do you?'

'Just leave it,' Mikhail said, his voice sharp. 'You, get inside,' he added to Charlie, with a flick of his head. 'If you're back here later than the nine bells tomorrow, I'll report you to the boss.'

'You do that. See if I care.'

Charlie slunk past them, shoving the door open with his shoulder, and entered the Pen gang's hideout. His upper arm was throbbing. He hoped it would bruise. No sooner had he slammed the door shut behind him than he heard a girl's accusing voice from over his shoulder.

'Where have *you* been all morning?' Maya was frowning at him. One of her hands rested on the bannister of the staircase that led up to Faulkner's rooms, her fingers tapping out a pattern. *Someone's listening.*

Crossing his arms, Charlie leant against the door and stared back at her, a mirthless smile stretching his lips. 'Where d'you think?'

Maya tilted her head to the side, her eyes narrowed in suspicion. 'All this time?'

Charlie's smile grew a little wider. 'I'm clearly in higher demand than you are.'

'That's funny.' After pulling her old woollen cardigan around her thin dress and wrapping her arms around herself, Maya took a couple of steps towards him. She threw a cautious look behind her before lowering her voice. 'Should you even be out there right now, Charlie? After what … I mean –' She dropped her gaze, her pale face flushing furiously. 'I'm sorry … I didn't mean –'

'Go on. Say it.' Charlie ground out each word. 'What *do* you mean?'

Chewing on her lip, Maya raised her head. 'You're still recovering, aren't you?'

His shoulders stiffening, Charlie shrugged himself off the door. 'I'm fine,' he said, as he strode past her, his fists buried in his pockets. 'If you're done treating me like I'm some little kid you need to take care of, I'll see you around later.'

'Where are you going?'

'I'm going to sleep. I'm exhausted.' It was only half a lie.

'You can't,' Maya said, her voice stiff. 'He wants to see you.'

'He wants to …' Charlie turned on his heel, his voice faltering. 'He wants to see me?'

Maya still had her back to him. 'Did you know that children have been disappearing from the Spike, Charlie?' she asked quietly, her head bent.

Charlie was silent for a moment. 'How many?'

'I don't know, maybe ten,' Maya said, turning to face him again at last, an uncertain look on her face. 'He wants to talk to you about it.'

'Maybe later,' Charlie said, stifling a yawn, 'if I feel like it.'

'Charlie, don't make him angry …'

'I wish you'd stop looking at me like you think I'm about to die, or something,' he mumbled, glaring at her as he fixed his ponytail and tugged his fingers through the ends of his hair. He had to try to untangle some of the knots before seeing Faulkner again. 'You never used to look at me like that.'

Maya's face fell, and she began to twist her fingers. 'I just want to help you.'

Charlie felt his jaw clench involuntarily. 'I don't need your help, or your pity,' he said. 'I'm fine on my own. I always have been.' He took a few paces down the corridor towards the dormitory, before coming to a halt, grinding his teeth as he spoke to the floorboards. 'You think I haven't noticed how no one around here can even look me in the eye anymore? No one can stand to be around me for more than a few seconds.' He gripped his arms, his nails digging into his skin. 'You think I don't know why? I'm not stupid. I know what everyone thinks of me, now that I –'

'You're not serious, Charlie? All the little ones here *love* you.' Her voice gentle, Maya took a few steps closer towards him, and Charlie looked away. 'They're just wary of you right now, that's all. They don't know how to act around you, after …' She had gathered up her long, silver-blonde ponytail, and was running her fingers through it, her eyes on the staircase. 'After what happened.'

'Ever since I came back, everyone's been treating me so different.' He had not intended to say it, and hated himself for doing so.

'We all care about you, Charlie. We want to look after you.' Maya was close enough to touch him now. She raised a tentative hand to his face, and Charlie stilled, a ringing in his ears. 'But you have to let us in.'

His heart racing, Charlie ducked past Maya, forcing himself to round the bannister before he lost his nerve. He had not so much as raised his eyes beyond that point in two and a half months. He had not thought he would ever be invited back inside. There was a small part of him that still wished –

'I'm going to see Faulkner,' he muttered, refusing to look back at her. 'I don't want to keep him waiting.'

Charlie started to climb the stairs, his legs wobbly beneath him. With every moan of creaking wood beneath his feet, his stomach clenched tighter. When he reached the closed door at the top of the staircase, he rapped on the pane of frosted glass with his knuckles – and waited. He was still not used to following all these new rules. Not so long ago, he had been allowed to come and go as he pleased. He had never needed to ask permission for anything.

Almost anything, a stern voice in his head reminded him, and Charlie shook himself. He pulled the hem of his grey t-shirt further down over his lower back, his teeth running along his lips. *Remember*, he's *the one who did this to you.*

'Come in.'

At the sound of Faulkner's voice, Charlie flinched, his eyes squeezing tightly shut. For a single, wild moment, he seriously considered running straight back down the stairs. But there was nowhere for him to run to. Faulkner hated to be kept waiting. Focusing on his breathing, Charlie slowly peeled open his eyes. Steeling himself, he grasped the doorknob to steady his trembling hand, and entered Faulkner's study.

There was a roaring fire blazing in the grate. Charlie shrank away from it at once, his eyes darting to the pokers and branding irons that stood beside it. Illuminated by the flames, their shapes cast flickering shadows along the threadbare rug, which covered most of the wooden floor.

Fighting the urge to escape, Charlie closed the door behind him. Faulkner hated draughts. Other than the kitchens when their food was being prepared, this was the only room in the hideout that ever held any warmth. As always, Faulkner kept the lamps in the study burning low, and the heavy crimson drapes closed. This was a place where the outside world was sealed off.

Tentatively, Charlie raised his eyes, and gazed around the familiar sights of the study. It was exactly how he remembered it, right down to the leatherbound diaries on the bookshelves and the silver letter-opener on Faulkner's mahogany desk. He had always thought that it was as though time stopped whenever he entered this space. He was already starting to feel dreamy.

'I sent a message for you hours ago.' Faulkner was standing behind his desk, his finger running down the page of the notebook that lay open in front of him. 'You know I don't like to be kept waiting.' Looking up, Faulkner fixed Charlie with his steely eyes. 'Or should I perhaps blame my choice of messenger?'

'It's not Maya's fault,' Charlie said, his throat dry. 'She told me as soon as I got back.'

A smirk crossed Faulkner's face. 'You haven't lost all your loyalty, I see,' he said, moving in front of the desk and leaning against it. 'It's good to see you.' His long-fingered hands came to rest on the polished surface as he surveyed Charlie. 'Truthfully speaking, I wasn't sure you'd come.'

Charlie blinked, and swallowed before answering. 'You told me to come, so I came.'

'Yes.' His ringed fingers brushing the handle of the letter-opener, Faulkner stared at the fire. The light sent shadows dancing across the planes of his handsome face. 'You're saying all the right things, as usual …'

His heart doing somersaults in his chest, Charlie stayed silent.

'Sit down, Charlie.' Faulkner held out his arm, indicating the cracked leather sofa that stood directly across the room from the fireplace. With his other hand, he drew a wooden comb from his pocket, and began turning it over in his fingers.

Wordlessly, Charlie did as he was told. He sat perched on the edge of the sofa, his shoulders hunched, tension singing through his body as he sensed Faulkner approaching him. When he felt a hand on his shoulder, Charlie went utterly still. His eyes locked onto the blazing fire. Faulkner had not been this close to him in two and a half months. Not since that night.

'It's been a while since you last stepped foot in here, hasn't it?' Faulkner murmured, as he took Charlie's hair down from its ponytail. 'How long has it been, Charlie? Two months?'

'And fourteen days.' He was not entirely aware of what he was saying anymore.

'And how are you feeling, after your bedrest?'

'Fine.'

'I'm glad to hear it.' As Faulkner ran his fingers through Charlie's hair, freeing the locks from one another, loose brown waves fell over Charlie's shoulders, brushing his face. 'In that case, you can start getting to work repaying what you owe me for having that doctor treat you, can't you?'

His hand moving of its own volition, Charlie reached into the pocket of his sweatpants. Without a word, he handed Faulkner everything he had earnt since first going out onto the streets almost two weeks ago.

He did not know what he was doing. He did not know what he hoped for. Perhaps there was still a tiny part of him that hoped Faulkner would say it had all been a bad dream, and that it was over now.

His fingers trailing across Charlie's, Faulkner took the money from him with a soft laugh. 'How enterprising of you. I thought from the smell of you that you'd been busy ...'

Without warning, Faulkner began to tug the comb through Charlie's hair, wrenching his way mercilessly through the tangles and knots. Charlie screwed his eyes up against the pain and made himself weather it. There was something satisfying about being able to bear pain like this. Faulkner had always praised him for that.

He bit down on his lower lip, forcing himself not to cry out, as Faulkner dug the teeth of the comb into his scalp and tore them across his head. Tasting blood in his mouth, Charlie sniffed, blinking fast to clear his watering eyes.

'You haven't been taking very good care of yourself, have you?' Faulkner said softly.

'It hurts.' Charlie heard how small his voice sounded, and he hated it. 'It hurts.'

'Do you want me to stop?' Faulkner had paused, the teeth of the comb positioned at Charlie's hairline, beneath his overgrown bangs. 'We're just playing a game, Charlie, that's all. If you want me to stop, you know what you have to say.'

Charlie's mind was racing, trying to find the right answer before he ran out of time. He remembered when he used to sit in this same spot, and have his hair brushed gently – sometimes before, sometimes after. He knew the answer he was supposed to give. 'No,' he whispered.

'What *do* you want?' Faulkner asked silkily, drawing away from him. 'Tell me.'

Charlie's stomach lurched. His head whipping over his shoulder, he stared up at Faulkner, his eyes wide. He did not know what he was supposed to say anymore. All thought had left him. Not since before he was branded had he … and after that, Faulkner had said –

'You're lucky I care about you so much.' His voice mild, Faulkner reached up, placing the comb on a high shelf with a sigh. He lowered himself onto the armrest beside Charlie, twisting a lock of Charlie's hair around his finger, and smiled. 'It's because I have such a soft spot for you,' he added, as he scraped Charlie's hair back and tied it up into a tight ponytail again.

'If you care about me,' Charlie began, staring at the rug, 'then why did you –'

'I remember the night you got this.' Faulkner had gripped his arm and pulled the sleeve of his t-shirt down over his shoulder, revealing the huge spiderweb tattoo Charlie had had since he was a child. 'Do you remember how you used to *beg* me to let you get your first tattoo?' His breath was a fierce hiss in Charlie's ear. 'You were such an annoying brat, even then. Always so jealous of the others. I always ended up giving you exactly what you wanted, didn't I? Just to shut you up for a while.'

Frozen under his grip, Charlie did not move again until Faulkner returned to his desk.

314

'It's a shame you decided to turn your back on me,' he was saying, as he collected his ledgers and stacked them into a neat pile at the edge of the desk. 'But maybe you can earn your way back up the ladder, in time. I know you can be very persistent when you want to be.'

'Do you want something from me?' Charlie asked stiffly, righting his t-shirt again.

'There are children going missing, Charlie. Did you know that?'

'Yeah, I did.' Charlie gazed into the fire. 'Maya told me, just before I came up here.'

'Ten children, Charlie. Ten children in the last fourteen days.'

Charlie said nothing. There was a crack in the wall. He traced the line with his eyes.

'You don't have much to say for yourself today, do you?' Faulkner's calm voice pulled him from his reverie. 'Has all that hard work of yours finally made you lose your voice?'

Recognising the particular tone that always meant danger, Charlie got to his feet. 'No.'

Faulkner was watching him with narrowed eyes, his index finger trailing circles around the handle of his letter-opener. 'If I find out that you have anything to do with this, you will see me get angry,' he said. 'Do you understand me, Charlie?'

Charlie gave him a terse nod, before turning on his heel to leave the study. He had to get away, quickly, before –

'I asked you a question, you filthy little *whore*.'

It had happened too fast for him to do anything to stop it. Charlie was on the floor, the room spinning around him. His ears were ringing, and his back was screaming in pain. When he looked at the fire, the flames swam and danced like stars in front of his eyes. He guessed Faulkner must have smashed his head against the brick wall.

'I –' he gasped, his shoulders shaking, 'I understand you. I understand you. I –'

'What are you still doing here?' From the leather chair behind his desk, Faulkner spared Charlie a single glance, distaste written across his features. 'You want me to kick you down the stairs, too? Stop being so needy. Get out of my sight – if you know what's good for you.' With that, he picked up his pen and returned to work.

'I —' Charlie scrambled to his feet, his shoulders hunched. 'I'm sorry …'

'Just get out.'

Cradling his head, Charlie edged his way down the stairs, his legs unsteady. Everything seemed to be swaying around him. He had to grab hold of the bannister to stop himself losing his footing.

When he reached the bottom of the staircase, he sat down on the last step and rested his forehead on his knees. Closing his eyes, he folded his hands over his head, massaging his scalp. It was a relief to be away from the heat of the fire. It was over. Nothing bad had happened.

There was blood on his hands when he brought them away from his head.

Once his heart had stopped thumping so fast, he got to his feet, and headed towards the dormitory. As far as Faulkner was aware, ten children had gone missing from the hideout. Charlie knew very well that he was wrong about that. It was not ten children, but eleven.

And now, he was about to make it twelve.

CHAPTER 2

C harlie found Yuliya asleep in the dormitory with the other children. It was a long, draughty room that looked as though it could have once been an assembly hall, or some other kind of meeting space, before the war. Rows and rows of children lay on the floor, curled up alongside one another under thin blankets. Most of them were huddled together in small groups, their hands reaching out to one another along the floorboards.

Over the last two weeks, Charlie had found little time to sleep. When he did, he tried his best to keep to a corner, by himself. Being one of the oldest, the others left him alone when he wanted them to, which he was grateful for. Just the idea of lying amongst so many bodies was enough to make his stomach turn over.

'Hey.' Easing himself onto the floorboards, Charlie lay a gentle hand on Yuliya's shoulder. 'Hey, Yulenka, it's me. It's time to wake up.'

'Charlie?' She rolled over, gazing at him with huge blue eyes. 'What's going on?'

'Careful,' he whispered, holding a finger to his lips. 'We don't want to wake the others.'

The little girl sat up, suddenly alert. 'Are we –?'

'I'm getting you out of here,' Charlie said, nodding. 'Come on, come with me.'

'But Charlie,' she said, rubbing her eyes and staring down at the hand he was holding out for her. 'I'm still sleepy ... I don't want to go ...'

'I'll carry you,' he said, gathering her up into his arms as he got to his feet. 'You can sleep on the way. But we've got to go *now*, you understand? And we've got to be very, *very* quiet.'

'Are we playing a game?' Yuliya asked in a hushed voice, settling herself against his body and draping her arms around his neck.

'Yes, we're playing a game,' Charlie whispered back, as he edged his way out of the dormitory and down one of the narrow corridors that led towards the gang's lounge area. 'We're playing the escape game,' he added, glancing over his shoulder and quickening his pace. 'I'll be the leader, so you have to help me by being as quiet as you can. Understand?'

Clapping her hands in front of her mouth, Yuliya stared up at him and nodded vigorously.

'Good, that's good,' Charlie said, as they reached the alcove between two storage rooms. After carefully lowering Yuliya to her feet, he reached up. His fingers were seeking the window with the latch that had been warped by the rain, which never fully closed anymore. 'Just stand there for a bit, all right?' he added, glancing down at her. 'You get extra points for standing perfectly still.'

Yuliya nodded, a serious expression settling on her face, and held herself as still as a statue. Meanwhile, Charlie forced the window open, listening hard for any sound of movement along the corridor. Once it was loosened from the frame, he bent down, picked up the little girl, and eased her through the open window.

'Bend your knees when you jump down,' he told her. He was standing on his tip-toes to hold the window open until she was through, so that her head was protected. 'It's not far. I'll be right behind you.'

When they had both jumped down into the alleyway, Charlie picked Yuliya up again. She was staring around in all directions, wide-eyed, and seemed unsure how to react to being out of doors again, having been separated from the outside world for so long.

Feeling her grip tighten around his neck, Charlie drew them both into the shadows along the wall. He glanced around them, determined to make sure that no one had noticed their escape. From somewhere above their heads, there was the sound of birdsong.

Charlie took a deep breath, his heart pounding in his chest. He had not thought this through, he had not planned any of it out, and he was skating on thin ice now. Faulkner might have tried to sound him out, but if he had any real suspicions, Charlie knew he would not be breathing freely right now. He had to save as many of the kids as he could, before he ran out of time.

He had made a promise.

Heading straight out of the alleyway, Charlie ducked down one of the side streets behind the townhouses, avoiding the eyes of the guards. They were out. Now they just needed to reach Elysia – and find a house where he could leave Yuliya.

'Charlie …' the little girl said, as they reached the crossing point at the Witchtrap Wall.

'What is it?' he asked. He made sure to avoid the eyes of the sentries, who were standing guard along the barbed wire, as they passed through the gate. 'Are you hungry? We'll get you something to eat soon, don't worry.'

'I want to get down and walk by myself now.'

'That's not …' Charlie chewed his lip, risking a glance over his shoulder as they entered the outskirts of Elysia. 'Can you wait a bit longer? We'll go faster if I keep carrying you.'

'I don't want to be carried anymore, I want to walk by myself.'

'I …' Biting the corner of his mouth, Charlie set her down on her feet. 'Fine. That's fine. But you have to hold my hand, all right? You need to stay close to me and do as I say.'

'Yes, Charlie,' Yuliya said, smiling happily as she took his hand.

As the streets widened, and the early afternoon sunlight broke through the clouds, Yuliya gradually began to lower her shoulders. She started looking from side to side as they walked further into Elysia, pointing out the neat gardens and attractive shopfronts as they went.

With some hesitation, Charlie allowed her to stop and pick a handful of daisies, which were growing by the wooden fencing that enclosed a small park. While she crouched down to gather them up, Charlie crossed his arms and leant against the fence, scanning the smartly-dressed people who were walking to and fro through the cobbled streets. There were too many eyes on them.

'We have to go now, Yuliya,' he said, his tone clipped, as he glared at a man in a suit and tie, who gave them both a wide berth as he passed them by.

'But I want to make a daisy chain,' Yuliya said, holding the flowers up to show him.

'I'll make one for you later,' Charlie told her, taking her other hand and pulling her along with him. 'First we have to find somewhere quiet. Come with me, we need to get going.'

'You're going too fast for me, Charlie …'

The first fluttering of panic was beginning to twist in Charlie's stomach. They were too exposed out here on the street, especially in their worn clothes. Not to mention the collars that marked them as Penumbran. There were no other children anywhere else in sight.

He tried to remember what day of the week it was, realising as he did so that the Elysian children were likely to all be in school at this time of day. He glanced down at Yuliya, understanding the danger he had put them both in for the first time. Then he halted in his tracks at the sight of two military policemen on horseback, heading directly towards them.

'Fucking *soldiers* …' Charlie gritted his teeth, his legs like lead. 'Why are they –'

'Charlie, what's happening?' Yuliya had gripped his hand tightly, her eyes fixed on the huge horses as she began to tremble violently.

'Shit, they're coming,' Charlie murmured, as he watched the two policemen dismount. He caught sight of them withdrawing what looked like batons from their belts. 'Yuliya, listen to me,' he said, his voice urgent, as he dropped to his knees, his back searing with pain at the sudden movement. 'You need to run.'

She shook her head, her lower lip wobbling, and grabbed his shoulders. 'But I don't want –'

'No, don't argue with me!' he said, pushing her off him. 'Run away, right now. Go find a mother with kids, all right? Tell her you're lost, and you need her help. You'll be all right.'

'But –'

'If you can't find a woman with kids, just find a lady, all right? Any lady is fine.' Trying to soften his tone, Charlie turned Yuliya around and gave her a slight shove in the back. He wanted to encourage her to head down a narrow alley behind the park, which he could see opened onto a wider street. 'Just – just stay away from any men. Don't talk to anyone else.'

'But Charlie –'

'Run, *now*, while I distract them!'

When he saw that she had done what he had told her to, Charlie clenched his fists and sprinted towards the two military policemen. He could not care less if they caught him, or if they tried to follow him. Let them chase him all the way through Elysia, if it meant he would be giving Yuliya a chance to get away without being hunted down. As long as they lost her, she would at least stand a chance of finding a better place than the one that was waiting for her back in Penumbra.

'Where d'you think *you're* going?'

Fierce pain tore through Charlie's scalp, and he realised one of the military policemen had grabbed him by the ponytail, just before he was thrown to the ground. Furious at himself for forgetting to fix it back into a bun as soon as he had left the Spike, Charlie struggled to get free.

He lashed out with one arm, only to have it wrenched behind him and held firmly in place – directly against the small of his back, where he had been branded. The sudden contact with the still-healing wound made him whine, but he refused to betray any other reaction.

'We've got you now, kid,' a voice above him said. 'You're not going anywhere.'

'Get the fuck off me,' Charlie snarled, fighting to force himself up.

'Stop fighting us,' the man snapped. He pulled Charlie's other arm behind his back and secured his wrists with a pair of steel handcuffs. 'Now, I want you to answer some questions,' he said, one of his hands pressing down on Charlie's shoulder, while the other remained on his hands. 'Who are you? Where did you come from? What are you doing roaming the streets?'

Charlie stayed silent, his eyes on the ground, biting down hard on the corner of his mouth. The touch of someone else's skin on his was almost more than he could bear, and he could not stand to be this close to an adult man without thinking of –

'He's Penumbran, he's got the collar.' Out of the corner of his eye, Charlie saw the other military policeman standing over him, his upper lip curling. 'I don't know what they're thinking, letting scum like this through the Wall …'

'What are you doing in Elysia, Penny?' the soldier who was holding him demanded, giving Charlie a fierce shake when he did not answer at once. 'Who are you? Who's the girl you were with back there?'

'She's my sister.'

The soldier let out a harsh laugh. 'Don't give me that. You two didn't exactly look alike. Come on,' he said, taking Charlie by the scruff of the neck, so that he was lifted off the pavement and forced to meet the man's eyes. 'Tell us the truth, and we'll let you go.'

They will only lie to you,' Faulkner had said, and from the glint in the soldier's eyes, Charlie knew that it was true. *'Don't trust anything they say. I am the only one who can protect you, after what you've done.'*

'He's not saying anything,' the other soldier said. Turning his back on both Charlie and his partner, he shook his head with an irritable exhale of breath, before striding away.

'Don't feel like talking?' The soldier who had arrested Charlie hauled him to his feet. Taking his upper arm in a vicelike grip, he dragged Charlie towards the horses. 'Let's see if you feel any different down at the station.'

While the first military policeman held Charlie still, the one who had walked off returned with a length of rope. He looped one end of it through the metal collar Charlie wore around his neck.

A strange cold stealing over him, Charlie watched as the soldier tied the other end of the rope to the pommel of his horse's saddle. The rough texture of the rope against his throat was forcing him to remember that night, two and a half months ago. But he closed his eyes, refusing to think about it.

As long as he kept himself numb, he would not have to feel anything at all.

He stayed still while the military policemen mounted their horses, staring down any passers-by in the street who dared to meet his eye. He did not resist as he was pulled forward with the horse's movement. They could do whatever they wanted to him.

By now, Yuliya would easily have had time to find a woman and ask for help. She was so small and sweet-natured, no one would be able to turn her away. As he was led down the street towards the police station, Charlie set his shoulders.

He had done what he had set out to do. He didn't care what happened to him next.

*

'And who's this?' a woman behind a tall desk asked, as they entered the police station. She lowered her glasses to gaze down at Charlie, a frown creasing her forehead as her eyes travelled to the two soldiers flanking him on either side. 'Tougher than he looks, is he, Yegorov?'

'Won't tell us his name,' the soldier who had arrested Charlie said, gripping his forearm again and pulling Charlie behind him. 'He's refusing to answer any questions, Katya. I'm taking him to the cells.'

'He's too young for that,' Katya said, with a firm shake of her head. She returned her glasses to the bridge of her nose and jerked her chin over Charlie's shoulder. 'Keep him here until the Captain is ready to make a decision.'

Charlie thought the woman seemed to be making a note of something, although he could not be sure, since he was not tall enough to see over the desk. Then he felt a pair of hands on his shoulders, and stiffened.

After being wheeled around, he was led over to the far side of the room, towards a square table surrounded by four metal chairs. The soldier unlocked Charlie's handcuffs before moving his wrists in front of his body and cuffing him again. Then he was unceremoniously shoved down into one of the chairs.

'You just sit down and stay there,' Yegorov said, jabbing a finger in Charlie's face, while Charlie glowered silently back at him. 'Don't make any trouble for me, got it?'

Once the soldier had stalked off, Charlie shifted slightly in his seat, and placed his hands in his lap. Most of his hair had come loose from his ponytail during the struggle, and he had to keep tossing his head to the side to clear his bangs out of his eyes. Keeping his shoulders hunched, he lifted his head a fraction, and began to scan the police station.

His eyes roved across the posters on the walls, taking in the men and women in khaki uniforms who rushed past him. Most of them ignored him, although some cast looks of concern his way as they passed by. Every single one of them was armed. He was too far away from the door to think about escaping. He did not have the slightest idea how he was supposed to get himself out of this situation.

Frowning, Charlie let out a deep sigh. His gaze travelling over towards the stairwell, Charlie's eyes settled on a teenage boy with wild, dark hair. He was wearing a black uniform, and was watching Charlie from the other side of the room, a puzzled look on his face.

Straightening up, Charlie glared back at him, and raised his voice. 'What are *you* looking at?'

'*Don't talk to police.*' That was what Faulkner had always said. '*Don't talk to soldiers. Where they'll take you is much worse, I can promise you that.*'

The teenage boy blinked, his eyebrows quirking. Charlie thought he looked as though he was about to say something. But then someone called his name, and he disappeared with a final glance in Charlie's direction.

Leaning back in his chair, Charlie let out a deep breath and stared at the ceiling, rocking backwards and forwards to occupy himself. His thoughts turned vaguely towards what he should do next. He guessed that Yegorov must have given orders that he should be kept isolated, because everyone left him alone.

Time dragged on, painfully slow, as he sat there in silence. In the end, he put his hands on the table and rested his head on them, deciding he might as well try to get some sleep. It seemed unlikely that anyone would try to do anything to him here, with so many people around.

'Can I join you?'

At the sound of an unfamiliar voice, Charlie's eyes shot open, his entire body tense and alert. He glanced up, and, seeing the same teenage boy who had been looking at him before, narrowed his eyes. 'I don't need you to babysit me, all right? I'm not a kid.'

The boy tilted his head to one side, his brow furrowed. 'Yes you are,' he said, in a voice that was serious, but not unkind. 'How old are you, anyway? Ten? Eleven?'

'I'm *thirteen*,' Charlie snarled back, incensed.

'Well, I'm fifteen, so I'm still older than you.'

'So what?' Charlie snapped. 'You think that means I have to do what you say? I don't care how old you are, you're not the boss of me. You can't tell me what to do.'

The boy's face broke into a grin, although he seemed to fight to suppress it at once. 'I wouldn't dream of it,' he said. 'I only came by to see you because I thought you might like some company. I thought maybe you would be hungry by now.'

Frowning, Charlie looked at him properly for the first time, and realised that the boy was carrying a plastic tray. A variety of different food was arranged neatly on top of it.

'Is that …' Charlie swallowed, his throat dry. Warily, he lifted his eyes to meet the boy's for the first time, finding himself taken aback by how deep and dark they were. 'For me?'

The boy nodded, smiling, and slid into the seat opposite Charlie's. 'I get cafeteria privileges while I'm stationed here, so,' he explained, shrugging, as he carefully set the tray of food down on the table between them. 'Help yourself.'

While the boy took a flick knife from his pocket and began peeling an apple with it, Charlie poked at what looked like some kind of spongey brown thing in a plastic wrapper.

'You're a dessert-before-the-main-course kind of guy, are you?'

'Huh?' Charlie looked up to find the boy smiling back at him, the entirety of the apple peel hanging off in one piece. 'What are you talking about?' With some misgivings, Charlie tore open the plastic and pulled off a piece of the brown food, which was oddly sticky. It was so over-sweetened that he gagged the second he put it in his mouth. 'That's *disgusting*.'

'Have this instead,' the boy said, handing him the apple. 'It's better for you, anyway.'

'Thanks,' Charlie mumbled, accepting the apple and biting off a tiny piece.

He was almost grateful for the handcuffs pulling his other hand with him as he brought the piece of fruit to his lips. They meant he would not have to explain his habit of keeping his mouth hidden whenever he ate anything. He had always hated eating in front of other people. No, not always. Only since –

'Can I tell you something?' the boy said, unscrewing the cap from a bottle of water as he gazed at Charlie with his sombre eyes. 'I thought you were a girl, the first time I saw you. Because of your hair. It's so long.'

Charlie gritted his teeth and glared back. 'It's not *my* choice to have it this long!'

The boy frowned, setting the bottle of water back on the table. 'It's your hair, isn't it?'

Charlie made a derisive snort. 'You don't know anything.'

'So explain it to me,' the boy said, watching calmly as Charlie placed the apple back on the tray and returned his hands to his lap.

Charlie rolled his eyes and shrugged, before staring at the ceiling. 'Don't feel like it.'

'I'm training to become a soldier,' the boy said, breaking the silence that had fallen between them. 'I'm in the Elysian Military Academy right now. This is my first year.'

Charlie felt his lip curl. *Fucking soldiers.* 'Is that supposed to impress me?' he asked, his voice like acid. 'You know how to kill people – big deal. You think I'm scared of you?'

'No,' the boy said quickly, his face falling. 'No, it's just – that's the only reason I'm here. It's part of my training, you see.'

'So what?' Charlie muttered, looking away. '*I* don't care.'

'I just thought … you obviously don't trust anyone here, so I wanted you to know that.'

Charlie's eyes shot back to the boy's, a fierce anger that he did not understand raging inside him. 'You want me to *trust* you? Good luck with that. You're wasting your time.'

'I don't feel like I am,' the boy said, his voice gentle. 'What's your name?'

'Nikolai Ignatiev,' Charlie said, shrugging, as a half-smile tugged a corner of his mouth.

The boy's eyes grew wide. 'Saints, *what* did you just say?' He let out a nervous laugh, glancing hastily around them. 'You're crazy ... you're *crazy* to say something like that here.'

'Don't *laugh* at me.' Charlie heard the edge in his voice as he clenched his fists.

'I'm sorry,' the boy said at once, holding his hands up in front of him in a gesture of surrender. 'I'm not laughing at you, I promise. It's only because ... but never mind. My name is –'

'I don't *care* what your name is,' Charlie spat back. 'Stop acting like you're my friend! Just get lost, already.' His shoulders sagging as his anger drained away, he slumped back against his chair and folded his arms on the table, his chin coming to rest on his hands. 'Leave me alone,' he mumbled, a hollow sensation in the pit of his stomach. 'Just leave me alone.'

'All right, I'll leave you alone.' His voice level, the boy got to his feet, leaving the tray of food behind him. 'I need to get back to work, anyway. Just ...' There was a pause, and, although he did not move his head, Charlie's eyes flicked up towards the boy's face. 'Are you all right? Are you sure you don't need any help?'

'What?' Charlie whispered, a strange tightness growing in his chest.

'I mean ... where do you live?' the boy asked, his pale face colouring slightly as he raked a hand through his messy hair. 'Who looks after you?'

'Why do you –' Charlie had sat bolt upright at once, and only just managed to hold himself back from saying too much. 'I don't need *anyone*,' he muttered, glaring down at his hands. 'I can look after myself.'

'You're not alone, you know,' the boy was saying, his voice soft. 'There are people out there who would take you in, take care of you. Foster parents, that sort of thing. They do exist.'

Charlie felt something burning behind his eyes. 'They would never want *me*.'

The boy shook his head firmly. 'You're wrong. That's not –'

Charlie looked up to see the teenage boy gazing down at him, his face full of concern. Just then, he heard a rough voice in his ear, and felt a strong hand gripping his upper arm.

'Come on, kid, get on your feet,' Yegorov said. 'I've had orders from the Captain. You don't want to tell us who you are, you'll be spending the night in the cells. See if you feel like talking after that.'

'Oh, I'm so *scared*,' Charlie sneered, before being promptly smacked around the head.

'Hey, don't hurt him!' the teenage boy said, his voice sharp. 'He's just a little kid.'

'You shut up and get back to work,' the soldier ordered, jabbing a finger at the teenage boy's chest and causing him to scowl. 'Don't think you can slack off just because of your connections.'

He did not know why he did it, but Charlie glanced over his shoulder as he was led towards the cells. He caught sight of the sad look in the teenage boy's dark eyes, but he did not understand it at all.

Yegorov dumped him in the cells without another word. Once the bars slid closed behind him, Charlie was left with nothing but his own thoughts, and the lonely silence.

CHAPTER 3

'You've got a visitor.'

At the sound of a gruff, male voice, Charlie's eyes shot open. He shifted on the bench, which was fixed into one of the walls of the cell. There was no sound of a key scraping in a lock, or of the door to the cell being wrenched open, but he was still immediately on edge.

He had stayed upright all night, knowing that his back would not be able to cope with the hard wood beneath him. Beyond that, he had found himself unable to tolerate the idea of sleeping in any other position in such an unfamiliar place.

Although he had closed his eyes, he had not slept. The sounds of movement in the darkness, whether real or imaginary, had sent him into such a state of panic that he had not been able to even make a sound. Only sunrise through the barred windows beyond the cell had brought a semblance of peace.

With a groan, Charlie stretched, massaging his neck and rolling his shoulders as he got to his feet. He could hear the shuffling footsteps of someone approaching from further along the corridor. Reaching the bars at the front of the cell, Charlie tilted his head, trying to discover the identity of his unexpected visitor. The only person he could think that might come to see him was Faulkner.

But there was no way the military police could have connected the two of them, with what little information Charlie had given them the previous day. He had barely said anything to anyone, and he knew what Faulkner said about not trusting cops, not trusting soldiers, not trusting adults of any kind. Faulkner had always made it perfectly clear what would happen to Charlie if he risked revealing the truth about himself to anyone else. The only person Charlie could trust was –

'Good morning, young man.'

An elderly woman with tightly curled grey hair was standing before him. She was only slightly taller than he was, although she seemed to command the space around her despite her small frame. From the collar around her neck, he saw that she was Penumbran, like him. She was dressed in a long skirt that almost brushed the floor, as well as a lumpy knitted jumper with enormous flowers embroidered across it. Her face was lined with deep wrinkles, but her grey eyes were sharp, and Charlie felt himself stiffen warily as she took him in.

'Who're *you*?' he asked, frowning as he crossed his arms in front of his chest. 'What d'you want?'

'My name is June. You can call me Granny if you like. I came here to visit you.'

'Why?' Charlie's eyes narrowed in suspicion. 'Who told you about me? What do you *want*?'

A small smile lifted the corners of the old woman's thin mouth. 'May I ask you your name, young man, since you asked me mine?'

'Charlie.'

'It's very nice to meet you, Charlie.'

'Why are you *here*?' he demanded, his tone sharpening as he remembered what Faulkner had said would be waiting for him if he ever told anyone what had happened to him. 'What are you, some – some sort of special doctor or something?'

'No, I'm certainly not anything like that,' June said, a hint of laughter in her voice. 'The reason I came here this morning is because I was told there was someone who might need my help.'

Charlie set his jaw. 'I don't need you. I never asked for your help. Just get lost.'

'I've taken in a lot of children over these last few years,' June said gently, her voice steady as she looked him up and down. She spoke slowly, as though choosing her words carefully, and a sad light had come to her eyes. 'I find I can always tell when someone needs me.'

'I'm not a *child*,' Charlie snapped. 'I don't need anyone's pity. And you –' He swallowed, unable to stop the words from escaping him. 'You wouldn't want me, anyway …'

Something seemed to change in the elderly woman's face at this. 'But I do,' she said, an urgent note creeping into her voice, as Charlie caught the sound of heavy footsteps echoing along the corridor. 'I do want you, for as long as you want to stay with me. I mean that sincerely, Charlie.'

Struggling to know what he was supposed to say, Charlie opened his mouth. But at the sight of Yegorov appearing in front of the bars, he closed it again at once. Shrinking back against the far wall as the soldier entered the cell, Charlie averted his eyes from both adults and tried to force himself further into the corner. He wished he could just disappear.

'Visiting time's over, Granny,' Yegorov said, grabbing Charlie and hauling him out of the cell. 'Time for your interview, kid. I hope you're feeling more talkative today.'

'Think about what I said,' June told him, as the soldier led him away. 'Please. My home will always be open to you, I promise.'

'You're wasting your time with this one, lady,' Yegorov said, with a dismissive snort. 'Punk kids like you always end up the same way,' he added, giving Charlie a rough shake and causing him to stumble. 'It's not even worth the effort of trying to help you.'

'Whatever,' Charlie muttered, as he was led unwillingly back into the familiar space of the holding area. 'As if I care what *you* think about me. I don't give a –'

'*Charlie!*'

At the sound of a child's terrified voice, Charlie froze. He glanced around the room, desperately seeking the person who had called his name. Then he caught sight of a blonde little girl with a tear-stained face. She was standing between two military policemen and a tall, well-dressed woman who he had never seen before. At the sight of her, his stomach dropped.

'Yuliya …'

'Charlie, I'm so sorry!' Before anyone had a chance to catch her, Yuliya had ducked out of the grasp of the adults and sprinted towards him. She grabbed him around the hips, her face pressed against his stomach, and began to cry into his t-shirt. 'I didn't mean to! I didn't mean to do it! I'm so sorry, Charlie. *Please* don't be angry with me.'

'I'm not angry,' Charlie murmured, forcing himself to ease some of the tension in his body as he tried to reassure her. Her hands were resting against the brand at the small of his back. The soldier's hands bearing down on his wrists and shoulder were reminding him of the night he had fought so hard to forget. 'I'm not angry.'

The Elysian woman strode towards them. Her expression was fierce, and she held a long umbrella gripped in her hand. 'Are *you* the reason this poor child is so frightened?'

Charlie shrank away from her, his eyes on the umbrella, as Yegorov let go of him and stepped in between them. Yuliya was sobbing loudly now, the noise making Charlie feel dizzy.

'Ma'am,' Yegorov said, his voice firm, 'please calm down and explain. What's happened?'

As the Elysian woman launched into a furious tirade, Charlie raised his cuffed wrists over Yuliya's head and held her close to him. 'Are you all right?' he asked softly, but she could only shake her head, her small hands balled up into fists against her eyes.

'This little Penumbran girl ran up to me on the street and told me she was in danger,' the woman was saying. 'She said there was a man trying to hurt her. When I brought her here she became hysterical, and now look at her reaction to seeing *him*! What on Earth have you done to her, you nasty creature?' she demanded, as she glared at Charlie. 'Look at the state of you. They should lock you up and throw away the key.'

'*Charlie.*' Yuliya whined his name through her tears. 'I'm frightened ...'

'It's all right, Yulenka, you're safe.' Charlie rested his chin on her head, ignoring the woman and the soldiers and the ringing in his ears. 'No one's going to hurt you, I promise.'

The adults seemed to have come to a stalemate. Charlie's eyes tracked around the room. He knew that any thought of an escape attempt with Yuliya in tow was pointless, especially with so many soldiers around.

Out of the corner of his eye, he caught sight of the teenage boy with the wild black hair who had sat and talked to him the day before. He was standing alone, his gaze fixed on Charlie, his expression darkening by the moment.

Just then, a broad-shouldered man with stars on his lapels appeared from behind the door of a small office. Charlie steeled himself, as a strange shiver of recognition passed through him.

'Get this kid into the interview room,' the man told Yegorov, as Charlie looked away, concentrating on the scent of Yuliya's hair. 'I think I know what's going on here.'

'Yes, Captain,' Yegorov said at once.

'Sir, is this the best time to interview him?'

At the sound of a concerned voice, Charlie glanced up to see the teenage boy standing beside him. He was facing the Captain with clenched fists.

The Captain stared back at him, his jaw set. 'Are you questioning me, boy?'

'No, sir,' he said quickly, meeting the older man's gaze without flinching. 'But there's something else going on here, something we don't know about – I'm sure of it.'

'Oh, you're so *sure* of it, are you, Cadet?' the Captain sneered, and Charlie gritted his teeth.

'He looks unwell to me, sir,' the boy insisted. A stubborn look that made Charlie think he was settling in for a fight had appeared on his face. 'Has anyone even checked to make sure he's all right?' He turned to Charlie, a scowl darkening his features, his eyes blazing. 'Are you all right?'

'Why are you ...' Charlie gazed back at him, his throat tight, not knowing what he was supposed to say. He could not remember ever feeling so lost. 'I don't ... I'm not ...' He shook his head, his eyes on the floor, before he forced himself to raise them again. 'I – I'm sorry.'

The boy's face fell as he stared at Charlie. Charlie thought he looked as though he wanted to say something else. But then the Captain barged past him and grasped Charlie's upper arm, wrenching Yuliya away from him at the same time. Yuliya was screaming his name, the sound of her terror putting Charlie in mind of his own.

Craning his head desperately over his shoulder, Charlie caught sight of the teenage boy holding her back. His face was full of unease as he looked from Yuliya to Charlie, his unspoken questions clear on his face.

The Captain of the military police led Charlie into the interview room. They were followed by Yegorov, who had apparently managed to extricate himself from the situation with the Elysian woman. The interview room was a small, cramped space, with a low ceiling, and no windows. There was enough space for a table with two chairs on either side, but not for much else.

While the younger soldier took a seat in one of the chairs facing away from the door, the Captain pushed Charlie into a seat on the opposite side of the table. He half-leaned against it, a triumphant look on his face as he stared down at Charlie.

'I know who this brat is, and I know how to get him to cooperate.'

'Don't you fucking *touch* me!' Charlie hissed, recoiling from the older man as he grabbed Charlie's t-shirt and pulled at the neckline.

'You see?' the Captain said, a vindictive note in his voice as he took in the spiderweb tattoo across Charlie's shoulder. 'What did I tell you? This piece of trash is one of the Pen boys.'

'He's a bit young for that, isn't he, sir?' Yegorov said, sounding dubious.

'Not for the work they'll be having him do,' the Captain said, his tone dark. He raised his baton and lifted Charlie's hair away from his ear, revealing the collection of metal piercings around his helix. 'Go and prepare the statement,' he said to Yegorov, dismissing him with a wave of his hand.

Once the younger soldier had left, Charlie glared at the floor, his hands shoved between his thighs. The room was silent for a while, until the Captain spoke, in a voice like silk.

'There were so many of us that night, you probably don't remember me, do you?'

Charlie's gaze shot up, his eyes wide as he stared, horrified, at the man in front of him. He tried to speak, but his throat had closed up. Only a strangled, pitiful noise escaped him as the older man nodded back at him, confirming his worst fear. His mind was screaming at him to run, but his body had locked into place, just as it had that night, when –

'You almost caused me a world of trouble,' the Captain growled, leaning closer to Charlie as he lowered his voice. 'I'd like to hear what Faulkner has to say when he finds out that *you're* the one behind this mess, you little slut.'

The door opened with a click, and the Captain slowly drew away from Charlie as Yegorov returned to the interview room.

'The statement is ready, sir.'

'You can leave, Constable,' the Captain said, his eyes on Charlie, who was still sitting frozen in his seat. 'I'll deal with the rest.'

'Sir,' Yegorov said. After placing a sheet of paper on the table, he inclined his head respectfully towards the Captain, before leaving the room again.

Once the door was closed, the Captain took a pen from his breast pocket, and placed it on the table in front of Charlie. 'Sign it,' he said, sliding the piece of paper towards him.

'Wh-What does it say?' Charlie asked, his voice trembling, as he looked up from the wavy lines of black handwriting into the older man's face. 'I – I don't know how to –'

'You just worry about signing it,' the Captain said, a sneer playing around his mouth. 'Leave the rest to me and your old man. We'll handle this mess for you, don't worry.'

Tentatively, Charlie picked up the pen in front of him and passed it between his right and left hands. He remembered that both of his names began with the same letter, sort of like a half-circle. He pressed the pen to the paper hesitantly, and awkwardly traced the two shapes. His hand shook, making the lines he drew unsteady. Then he lay the pen down again, his face burning. He kept his head bent, refusing to meet the older man's eyes.

'You'll be returned to the custody of your guardian,' the Captain said smartly, folding the piece of paper and returning the pen to his breast pocket as he got to his feet. 'And that'll be the end of this little adventure.' He stared down at Charlie, a derisive look on his face. 'And of you, too, I shouldn't wonder,' he added. Gripping Charlie by the arm, he forced him to his feet and marched him out of the room.

Charlie did nothing to resist, as he was deposited in a chair near to the desk at the entrance to the station. He said nothing, as he was told to wait there until his guardian came to collect him. The thought of what Faulkner would do to him when he arrived made him feel sick.

At some point, someone had removed his handcuffs. He wrapped his arms around himself, wishing he knew what to do. He had seen no sign of Yuliya or the teenage boy since leaving the interview room. Everyone left him alone. No one wanted to talk to him anymore.

Faulkner arrived at the police station a few hours later. He sloped into the building with his hands deep in his pockets, a muscle working in his jaw as his eyes travelled around the holding area. He stood on the threshold, his gaze lingering on Charlie as a look of cold fury settled on his face.

Charlie quailed under his stare, pinned to the spot as though by knives. He watched Faulkner's eyes narrow, his upper lip curling as he turned his back on Charlie and addressed the Captain of the military police, who was waiting for him by the front desk.

'I see that one of my possessions is ready to be collected,' Faulkner said, his icy voice travelling over to Charlie. 'So where's the girl?'

The Captain shook his head at once, folding his meaty arms. 'No way, Blue Jay. There's too much heat on this case. She stays with us.'

'*What* did you say?'

Recognising the quiet warning in Faulkner's voice, Charlie's back curved instinctively, his shoulders rising as he braced himself for the oncoming storm.

'We can't let you walk off with both of them,' the Captain explained. 'Raises too many questions.' He cleared his throat, and Charlie glanced over to see that both men were staring straight at him. 'You're welcome to this one, though,' he added, with a sly smile.

'I see.' Though his voice remained calm, Faulkner was slowly clenching and unclenching his fists, his shoulders rising and falling. Charlie knew from the signs that he was close to losing control. 'Well, you have my thanks, *Captain*, as ever.'

Charlie's eyes came to rest on Faulkner's hands. They were balled into fists at his sides as he turned on his heel and strode away from the desk. He headed straight towards the line of chairs by the front entrance, to where Charlie was sitting alone. He planted himself in front of Charlie, towering above him, while Charlie's gaze drifted to the scuffmarks on the floor. The silence stretched on between them, and Charlie felt himself begin to tremble with fear.

'*You*,' Faulkner murmured, and Charlie glanced up, frozen under his steely glare. Faulkner was beckoning Charlie towards him with his index finger. 'Come with me, *now*.'

His mind blank, Charlie got to his feet. He followed in Faulkner's footsteps as they left the police station. When they reached a fountain in the square outside, Faulkner's fingers found Charlie's upper arm and ensnared him in their fierce grip. Faulkner lowered his face to Charlie's ear, and hissed three words.

'You are *dead*.'

'I – I –' Charlie stammered, but Faulkner cut him off.

'Tell me this, Charlie,' he said, as he began to drag him past the fountain. 'Is there ever going to be *one* single day in your miserable life when you don't do *something* to make me want to fucking smash your head against a brick wall?'

'I –'

'You think you're *so* clever, don't you? I bet you're feeling pretty pleased with yourself right now, aren't you?' When Charlie tried to deny it, Faulkner backhanded him straight across the face. 'We're done playing games now, you understand me?' he snarled, returning his grip to Charlie's upper arm and wrenching him forwards. 'I'm going to make sure you regret this decision for the rest of your life.'

'Wait!'

Faulkner halted in his tracks and glanced over his shoulder. Charlie followed his gaze, his eyes widening in horror as he recognised the teenage boy with the messy black hair. He was standing a few paces away from them both, so that the fountain was between them. The rush of water pounded furiously in Charlie's ears, matching the race of his heartbeat.

'What the fuck do *you* want, baby grunt?' Faulkner asked, his lip curling derisively.

The boy was silent for a few moments. His eyes were travelling between Charlie and Faulkner as though he were weighing something up. They came to rest on Charlie's face, just as Charlie felt something wet sliding down his temple, and noticed that his vision had gone blurry on one side. With Faulkner beside him, he did not dare do anything about it.

'*Well?*' Faulkner demanded, his fingers digging into Charlie's skin. 'Do you have something you'd like to say?'

'The Captain respectfully requests that you not leave just yet,' the boy said at last, drawing himself up to his full height as he stared straight back at Faulkner. 'There's still some paperwork left for you to sign. He sent me to tell you.'

Charlie heard Faulkner make a noise of irritation in his throat. He loosened his grip and shoved Charlie away from him. 'You stay right *here*,' he said, pointing downwards, his barely-contained rage blazing in his cold eyes. 'If I think you've moved even one inch from this exact spot by the time I get back, I'll split your head open on these cobblestones. Got it?'

Charlie nodded quickly, twisting his hands against his stomach. 'Yes.'

The teenage boy waited until Faulkner had disappeared into the police station again, before he strode straight towards Charlie. 'Run,' was all he said, his voice low and urgent.

'What?' Wiping the blood out of his eyes, Charlie's head shot towards the doors of the station. He half-expected Faulkner to come flying right out of them at this hint of treachery.

'You need to run away, *now*, before he comes back. Just go!' the boy urged, trying to push Charlie away. 'Find the old lady. She'll help you, I know she will.'

'I'm not running away from *anyone*,' Charlie snapped, shoving him right back. 'I'm *not* a coward. What the hell has this got to do with you, anyway? Why do you even *care*?'

'Why do I …' The boy's face fell, and he shook his head, frowning at Charlie as though he did not understand anything Charlie had just said. 'Isn't this what anyone would do?'

Charlie frowned back, his anger fading, an unfamiliar emotion replacing it. 'You …'

'If you're not going to run, then …' The boy took a small square of paper from his pocket and held it out to Charlie. 'Here, take this. It's her address. Keep it somewhere safe.'

Charlie stared at the piece of paper, his heart fluttering. This was the moment, and he knew it. It was time for him to make his decision. He swallowed hard, knowing that he would need to ask if he wanted to find out, knowing that he would need to rely on someone else's help.

'Would –' He bit his lip, drawing blood, and forced the words out. 'Would you … read it out to me … please?'

'Sure,' the boy said, and, without any hesitation, he read out the old woman's address. 'Do you know the Kharber Quarter?' he asked, folding up the piece of paper and tucking it into Charlie's pocket. 'It's somewhere in Penumbra, isn't it?'

Charlie nodded. 'I know where it is.'

'Will you remember the address?'

Charlie nodded again.

'Take this as well,' the boy said. He withdrew the flick knife from his pocket and placed it in Charlie's hand. 'If …' He took a deep breath, and stared directly at Charlie, meeting his eyes with a look of absolute sincerity on his face. 'When the time comes, don't hesitate. Use it. Save yourself.'

Charlie looked from the boy's grave expression to the knife he now held in his hand, and back again, before nodding his head the tiniest fraction. Without a word, he slipped the knife into his pocket. Just as he removed his hand, Faulkner re-appeared, and Charlie dropped his gaze to his sneakers.

'We're leaving,' Faulkner said, striding towards them and grabbing Charlie's forearm. 'Say goodbye to your *friend*,' he hissed, his fingers tightening around Charlie's wrist as he dragged him away. 'You won't be seeing him again for a long, long time.'

CHAPTER 4

'You had big plans, didn't you, Charlie?'

He had been brought straight to the room where the children ate their meals. It was the only place in the hideout that they were allowed to go without any escorts, other than the dormitory. A fire was already burning in the grate.

Charlie was held firmly in place between Mikhail and Rorik. They had searched him as soon as they returned to the hideout – and had handed the knife and piece of paper straight to Faulkner. Faulkner had merely taken a cursory glance at the address before ripping it up into tiny pieces. He had kept his eyes fixed on Charlie as he tossed them into the blazing fire.

'Get them in here,' he said, flicking the knife open and closed in his hand, while the other members of the Pen gang hastened to follow his orders. 'They're all going to watch this.'

'Leave them *alone*,' Charlie managed to say, his voice quavering with fear.

'Oh, I intend to.' Faulkner gave a curt nod to the two men holding Charlie, who both let go of him at once. 'You've got my full attention now, Charlie, don't worry about that.'

Without warning, Faulkner drew back his hand and slapped Charlie across the face, then brought his hand back and struck him again. Dazed, Charlie shook his head. He found himself on the floorboards, but did not remember falling. Looking up, he saw the children shuffling into the room, flanked by the older members of the gang.

'Charlie …'

Maya was watching him in horror, her face pale as she covered her mouth with her hands. Charlie saw her eyes dart around the room, taking in the adults blocking the doors, and Faulkner standing above him, before they shuttered.

As some of the younger children started to cry, Maya slowly lowered her hands. She gathered the children closer towards her, her arms snaking across their shoulders as she drew them in. Charlie heard one of the kids whimper his name, and set his shoulders, his face stinging as he stared at the floor. He was not about to let them see him cry.

'So *this* is your guardian angel, is it?' His words dripping scorn, Faulkner's gaze travelled from Charlie to the children and back again. His face hardened as he pointed the knife towards them. 'I want you all to watch this. This is what happens to you when you step out of line around here.'

Faulkner bent down on one knee, and Charlie fought to stop his arms from giving way. Try as he might, he could not bring himself to meet Faulkner's cool eyes. He wished he could do something – anything – but he was just a –

'You fucking moronic piece of trash,' Faulkner murmured, and Charlie winced as Faulkner twisted his loose hair around his hand and yanked mercilessly on it. 'What the hell made you think you were good for anything besides taking whatever I give you? Did you forget? Those two holes of yours are the only things about you worth anything at all.'

'Fucking *shut up* and leave me alone,' Charlie whimpered, tears springing to his eyes.

'You're not telling me that this is all because I got too carried away last time?' For a moment, there was a hint of curiosity in Faulkner's voice, before it suddenly hardened. 'It's my *right* to punish you, you little brat – I *own* you.'

'No you don't,' Charlie whispered, his eyes meeting Faulkner's at last. 'No. You *don't*.'

Faulkner unclenched his fist, letting Charlie's hair tumble around his shoulders. 'So, this was your plan, was it?' he asked, his voice soft. 'You spent the last two months confined to your bed coming up with *some way* to get back at me, and this pathetic little scheme is the best you could come up with?' Inhaling sharply, he straightened up, and slowly drew his foot back. 'You thought you'd fucking hurt me? I'll show you how you *really* hurt your enemies.'

Charlie braced himself, unable to move, and screwed his eyes tightly shut, as Faulkner lashed out at him. Kicked in the chest and stomach, again and again, the pain left Charlie gasping and crawling on the floor. As though from far away, he could hear the sound of a mass of children's voices, screaming and crying out his name.

'Is this all you've got, you worthless hustler?' Faulkner's boot connected with Charlie's face, before he stamped on Charlie's legs. 'Are you proud of yourself? You're *nothing*.'

Charlie was nodding. 'I know,' he said, his words thick with blood as it poured out of his mouth. 'I know, I know. I'm *sorry*, all right? I'm sorry. I shouldn't have –'

'You're not even worth my time,' Faulkner said, breathing hard as he shook his head and smoothed the front of his shirt. 'I can't believe I ever looked twice at you. You're a fucking disgrace, you know that? Don't you feel ashamed of yourself, after everything you've done?'

'Yes,' Charlie mumbled. 'Yes, I do feel ashamed.' His head on the floor, his eyes drifted over towards the children, who were still sobbing around Maya. 'I do feel ashamed.'

'You think they care about you?' Faulkner's gaze had followed his. He was staring down at Charlie, a cruel, knowing smile on his face. 'They can't *stand* you. You disgust them.'

Charlie nodded, tears welling up in his eyes. 'I already know that.'

'No one will ever want you, you hear me? Don't *ever* forget that. You're just a dirty whore. You have been all your life. The only difference is that, now, everyone can see it.'

'I …'

Charlie caught himself, suddenly remembering the old lady who had come to see him at the police station, and what she had said to him there. He could think of no reason why she would have lied to him. She had absolutely nothing to gain by doing so.

He remembered the teenage boy who had sat with him and made him feel less alone, when no one else had even bothered to ask him whether he was all right. Charlie had spent the whole time backtalking him, and he had never once raised his voice or retaliated, even when Charlie had tried to provoke him.

He did not understand why either of them had bothered with him, but …

'You're wrong,' Charlie said, pushing himself up on trembling arms, so that he was sitting upright on the floor. He raised his head to Faulkner, as blood dripped steadily from his nose and mouth. 'You're a liar. You've been lying to me my whole life. I'm … I'm not what you say I am.'

For a moment, something like surprise flashed across Faulkner's face. Then his eyes narrowed. 'It seems I've been wasting my time with you all these years,' he said, his voice cold and flat. 'Do you still not understand what I've been trying to teach you? You can keep trying to run away from me, but there's no point. Run as much as you want. You'll never be able to escape what you are.'

'That's … that's not –' Charlie faltered, and Faulkner seized the opportunity, kicking his arms out from under him.

'What am I going to do with you now?' he asked softly. Stooping down, he gathered Charlie into his arms, ignoring Charlie's weak protests. 'I'll have to think about it, won't I? Because my previous methods obviously fell on deaf ears …'

Faulkner was carrying him down a flight of stairs. Charlie could feel the chill creeping in. He stirred in Faulkner's arms, but Faulkner's grip on him tightened, and at his command to behave, Charlie stilled. Dread stole into his bones as he realised where he was being taken.

'Please …' he whispered, as a door creaked open. 'Please – don't do it.'

'I have to do it, Charlie,' Faulkner said, his voice mild, all the fury gone, as though it had never been there. 'You *made* me do it.' Settling Charlie on the cold stone floor of the cellar, Faulkner reached into the darkness for something, and Charlie choked back a sob as he heard the echo of a chain being dragged closer. 'When you behave like a bad dog, you get treated this way, don't you?' Faulkner attached the end of the chain to the collar around

Charlie's neck, ignoring his desperate entreaties. 'You never could learn how to make me happy, could you? You always leave me with no other choice.'

'No, *please*,' Charlie moaned, clawing at Faulkner as he got to his feet. '*Please*, not this!'

'You can stay down here in the dark and think about what you've done,' Faulkner told him. A smile curved across his mouth as he turned on his heel at the door, a shaft of light illuminating his face. 'Maybe I'll tell someone to let you out again in a few days or so … if I haven't forgotten all about you by then, that is.'

'No – please!' Charlie's mouth had gone dry at Faulkner's words. 'Please, *please*,' he begged, growing frantic as Faulkner slipped through the gap and closed the door, plunging Charlie into complete darkness. '*Please* …' he whispered, as he heard a padlock being secured on the other side of the door. 'Don't leave me …'

All the things he had tried so hard to forget came rushing back into his mind. He saw the branding iron in the fire, glowing in front of his eyes even when he closed them. He felt the ropes around his wrists and ankles, the hands holding him down. He smelt his own flesh burning, felt a dark shadow of the pain that burnt inside of him and consumed him whole. He heard the words Faulkner had said, knew that this was his punishment for trying to escape, knew that there was nothing he could do to stop it.

Yet, some small part of him had refused to believe that he deserved it. He had fought, until there were too many of them to fight, and then he had drifted into empty space. It had been days before he had woken up, immobilised on his stomach, lying in the same bed for months.

One single thought had kept him sane, as his body clung to life and his being pieced itself slowly back together. No matter what it took, he would save the others. Somehow, he would save the children. He would find a way to save them all.

But he had failed.

Charlie had been six years old the first time Faulkner had throttled him, telling him he hated the sound of his pathetic sobbing. After that, he had learnt how to cry silently. He allowed himself that, just for a while.

When a tiny sliver of light appeared between the cracks in the doorframe, he stopped, hastily wiping his eyes with the back of his hand. Then he heard Maya's voice, low and tentative, from the other side of the door.

'Charlie, it's me. Are you there? Can you hear me?'

'Mm.' He could not manage any words.

'The door's locked.' She sounded apologetic. 'I can't get you out.'

'That's all right,' Charlie mumbled into his knees.

'He's going to hurt you this time. It's going to be bad.'

Charlie nodded, and the chain dragged along the stone floor. 'I know.'

'I got you something,' Maya said, a hopeful note in her voice. 'For when it happens ... so that you at least have a chance ...'

At the sound of something being forced through the gap between the door and the floor, Charlie turned his head, his eyes widening as he realised what Maya had managed to bring him.

'You stole this from him?' he asked, marvelling as he examined the knife the teenage boy had given him, back at the fountain outside of the police station. 'How did you –'

'I'm sorry he burnt that piece of paper you had. Was it something important to you?'

'It doesn't matter,' Charlie said quickly, still stunned. 'Thank you for ... for this.'

'You've spent so many years looking out for the rest of us, Charlie,' Maya said, and Charlie thought he heard a strange sadness seeping into her words. 'I want you to take care of yourself from now on. You should try to forget about us – and about all of this. Goodbye.'

'Maya, no – I couldn't ...' Charlie paused, thinking he had caught the sound of light footsteps on the stairs. 'Maya?' he continued, in a hushed whisper. 'Are you still there? Maya?'

She did not answer, and Charlie sat there in the silence and the darkness, concentrating on taking slow, deep breaths. For some reason, now that he had the knife in his hand, he felt braver, somehow. He did not know how much time had passed before the door opened, and Faulkner re-appeared. In an instant, Charlie shoved the knife deep into his pocket.

'I've been doing some thinking while you've been down here,' Faulkner said, as Charlie shrank away from the door, 'and I think now that I finally understand.' He drew closer, untying the chain from Charlie's collar and patting his head. 'You just wanted some attention, didn't you, Charlie?' he crooned, drawing his finger along Charlie's jaw before gathering him up into his arms again. 'Don't worry, I can give you that. I can give you *exactly* what you want.'

Charlie was frozen still in his arms. He was no longer fully aware of what was in front of him. He had the sensation of being carried up some steps, then along the creaking floorboards of a corridor, and up another flight of stairs. He recognised the frosted glass of the door in front of him, and realised they were entering Faulkner's study.

From out of nowhere, a memory came to him of being dumped from someone's arms onto a bed. This time, Faulkner dropped him directly onto the floor. With a groan of pain, Charlie raised himself onto his knees. His eyes shot to the fire, burning fiercely in the grate, and to the metal pokers and branding irons stuck in the flames.

'You're still afraid of the dark, aren't you?' Faulkner was saying. Charlie caught the last words over the ringing in his ears, just as a flash of lightning illuminated the room. 'You've always been such a baby.'

Faulkner was standing beside the fire, his hand reaching out for one of the metal rods being heated in it. 'Have you ever thought about what it would be like to live in permanent darkness?' he asked, his voice light, as he lifted the thin poker out of the flames and rounded on Charlie with it.

There was a rumble of thunder in the distance.

'How about I help you find out? Then you can tell me everything about it. I'll listen to you for as long as you want.'

Charlie had gone numb. His mind was blank. He knew he had to run if he wanted to survive, but it was as though he was no longer in control of his body. It felt like he had somehow already fled, but also left himself behind. All he could hear was the crackling of wood under the heat of the flames, and the hammering of rain on the windowpanes from the violent storm outside. He thought he caught the scent of burning flesh, and his stomach turned over.

'I need to make sure you can never pretend to be a hero ever again,' Faulkner said, his voice low, his eyes on the fire. 'But first,' he added, sliding the poker back into the flames, 'I'll make sure my face is the last thing you remember seeing.'

Charlie saw it all happening in front of his eyes, and knew there was nothing he could do to stop it. He was on his back, Faulkner's body on top of his – his hands, his breath, his scent, everywhere.

'You really do have such beautiful eyes. It's a shame you have to lose them.'

'I *hate* you.' Charlie managed to choke the words out. 'I hate you, I *hate* you!'

'Without me, you would be alone. Forever. You have *no one* else. You are *nothing.*'

Unbidden, the image of the teenage boy's solemn face came swimming into Charlie's mind. Charlie recalled the words he had said to him in the police station.

'You're not alone.'

His fingers reached for the knife in his pocket. Thunder boomed overhead.

'When the time comes, don't hesitate. Use it.'

Charlie gritted his teeth and clenched his fingers around the hilt of the knife.

'Save yourself.'

With the next flash of lightning, Charlie lashed out and sliced at Faulkner's face. Warm blood spattered his skin, the sharpness of it cloying in his nostrils.

With a guttural cry, Faulkner reeled backwards, his hands clutching his face. Charlie remained motionless on the floor, staring at the blood spilling past Faulkner's fingers. He had crashed into the desk, his face still covered by his hands.

His chest rising and falling rapidly, Charlie backed away, the feeling gradually returning to his legs as he scrambled to his feet.

'Get *back* here, you little bastard,' Faulkner spat. 'Where d'you think you're going?'

Charlie froze at the venom in Faulkner's voice. He turned, one hand on the doorhandle, to see Faulkner staring at him through a gap in his fingers, rage blazing in his eyes.

'You just dug your own grave,' Faulkner whispered. 'You won't even live to regret this.'

'I'm leaving now,' Charlie heard himself say, 'and I'm never coming back. Not ever.'

'You're not going *anywhere*!' Faulkner snarled, lunging towards him.

But Charlie was out of the door in an instant, slamming it behind him and racing down the staircase. He took the bottom half of the stairs at a flying leap, and crashed through the doors to the hideout without so much as a backwards glance. If there were any guards posted on duty, he had sprinted away from them into the darkness before they had a chance to know what had hit them.

It was the dead of night. The rain was beating down on the cobblestones relentlessly, muffling the sound of his racing footsteps and his gasping breath as he fled the Spike. His breath rose in a mist before him as he shook his head to clear the pouring rain from out of his eyes.

His throat was tight and burning. He did not know how he could still stand after the beating he had taken, let alone how he could manage to race through the city as though he were soaring on wings. But he was not about to waste any time thinking about it. He just had to run.

His feet led him towards the narrow streets and rundown houses of the Kharber Quarter. It had been razed almost to the ground during the war, and the buildings that still remained standing were blown-out shells, desolate in the shadows of the night. He crossed a bridge over a fast-flowing river, crawled through a hole in the barbed wire, and fought to steady his breathing.

He had to think. He could picture the note the teenage boy had written for him, with the old lady's address on it. He had not paid any attention to the scribbled writing. It had meant nothing to him.

But Charlie was good at remembering things. He knew her address. Now he just had to find it.

He closed the flick knife at last, and returned it to his sock, the weight of it comforting against his ankle. From out of his pocket, he withdrew his spare hair tie, and tied his hair back up into a loose bun, his fingers clumsy in the icy rain. There was still a chance that he might be able to make a good impression – if he really tried. He had to find her, and hope that she had not changed her mind about him.

No one was out on the streets in the downpour. Whenever he caught sight of candlelight in any of the houses he passed, Charlie hammered on the doors for a while. Mostly, people just ignored him. But, from time to time, someone would answer, looking frightened at the sight of a blood-spattered, rain-soaked teenage boy standing on their threshold.

Charlie asked the same question of everyone who opened their door to him: where could he find the old lady's address? Little by little, he got closer to her house. He followed the instructions of the people who answered their doors to him, knocking on another set of doors whenever he lost his way.

Eventually, he ended up in front of what looked like an abandoned tenement block. Under the light of the moon, he could make out a patch of scrub that had been cleared to plant flowers. He frowned, unsure whether he had seen anything like that before. Then he raised his fist and banged on the door.

'J-June?' he called out, his teeth chattering. 'It's – it's Ch- Charlie. P-Please …' He gritted his teeth, forcing himself to shout the words out above the pouring rain. *'Please will you let me in?'*

A moment later, the door opened. The old woman was standing there, wrapped in a shawl and bearing a candleholder.

'Charlie …' Her eyes widened behind her round glasses as she took in his bedraggled appearance. 'Are you all right? Why are you out here alone so late?' Her voice sharpened as she glanced up and down the street. 'You're in trouble, aren't you? Tell me what's happened.'

'Please can I …' Charlie said, hugging his arms around his body to stop himself from shaking, and gazing directly into her eyes. 'Please can I stay with you? I'll really try my –'

'Of course you can,' June said at once, stepping aside to let him through. 'Come in, Charlie, come in. Dear me, you'll catch your death if you stay out in this weather much longer.'

Feeling as though he was in a daze, Charlie followed her along a dark corridor and down a flight of wooden steps. June led him into a basement that had been made into a makeshift home.

It was small, but much cosier than anything he was used to. On one side of the room there was a tiny kitchen. A round wooden table had been placed by the bottom of the stairs. Across the room from the kitchen, a bed stood beside a foggy window.

'You sit down here, Charlie,' June told him, pulling one of the wooden chairs out from under the table.

While Charlie sat down and began looking tentatively around, June bustled about in the kitchen.

'You'll start feeling better as soon as you've had something warm to drink,' she told him, lighting the gas stove. 'You've been in the wars, haven't you, you poor thing?'

Charlie's eyes lingered on the blue flames as he removed his earrings and lay the pieces of metal down on the table. An idea had drifted into his mind. His hand came to rest on his tattooed shoulder, and he made a mental note to watch for where June kept the cutlery. He would need a spoon.

'You must be hungry, too,' June said, returning with a chipped mug and pressing it into his hands. 'I'll make you something to eat.'

His empty stomach churning, Charlie shook his head. 'I don't want anything.' After a pause, he remembered to add a mumbled, 'Thank you.' Now that he held the hot mug in his hands, some of the feeling was starting to come back into his fingers.

'You need to eat, you know,' she said, moving out of sight into another room, though her voice carried over to him. 'Growing boys like you need lots of healthy food if they want to become strong.' She returned, bearing a stack of towels. 'Have you ever thought about what you want to do with your life, when you're a bit older?' she asked, shaking out one of the smaller towels. After carefully taking down his bun and handing the elastic to him, she began to pat Charlie's hair dry. 'What would be your dream – if you could do anything at all?'

Charlie sat there, lost for words, as she towel-dried his hair for him. No one had ever asked him questions like these before. At first, his shoulders were hunched, tensed for the smack or cuff that he knew would be coming. But it never did. Her hands were firm but gentle, and he eased into the feeling of being cared for, wondering how long it had been since anyone had done this for him without expecting something else in return.

'If you take off your wet clothes, I'll make sure they're dried for you,' June said, after she had used another towel to dry his arms. 'The bathroom is over there,' she added, seeing the change in his expression. 'Put these on afterwards. You'll soon get warm.' She handed him a pair of tartan-patterned pyjama pants, and a black hooded sweatshirt, both of which looked far too large for him. 'This belonged to one of my sons,' she explained, patting the folded sweater affectionately. 'It's still a little too big for you, but I'm sure you'll grow into it, soon enough.'

In the bathroom, Charlie tied his hair back up, then got dressed, pulling the sweater over his head. Immediately, he felt better for having his arms covered. 'It's really soft,' he said, pulling it down as far as it would go, and hiding his hands inside the long sleeves. As he returned to the main room, he lowered his eyes, suddenly nervous. 'Th-Thank you … for –'

'It's very late,' June said gently, as Charlie stifled a huge yawn with one sleeve. 'Time for you to go to bed, I think. Let's see if we can do something about those shadows under your eyes, shall we?'

June pulled back the duvet, and Charlie climbed into the bed, his limbs aching and heavy. A bone-deep sense of exhaustion was crashing down upon him. As June pulled the blanket back over him and smoothed out the edges, Charlie realised that, for the first time in as long as he could remember, he was about to fall asleep without fear. Somehow, he already felt safe here.

His thoughts turned to Maya, and to the other children that he had left behind in the hideout. A hot, sick sensation of guilt swept through him. He had – he had just run away and left them there. He could never make up for that. Out of his own selfishness, his own self-preservation, he had found a safe place, and he had abandoned them all.

The only way he could think to atone for it was to never act in the same way again. That would be his new promise. From now on, whenever someone needed his help, he would save them, no matter what. He would never be able to forgive himself. But perhaps, someday, he could learn to live with what he had done.

'What are you thinking about?' June asked, her voice soft. 'Let me help you, Charlie.'

'Nothing,' he mumbled, closing his eyes and heaving a deep sigh. 'It's nothing. I'm fine.'

'You should get some sleep,' she said, laying a blanket over the top of the duvet. 'I won't wake you up tomorrow morning. You can sleep for as long as you want. When you're ready, we can talk about what happens next.'

'There's something I still can't figure out,' Charlie murmured, opening his eyes. 'Why did you come to visit me at the police station? Why were you even in Elysia that morning?'

'The night before I came to visit you, a young man came to see me,' June said, as she perched on the edge of the bed and adjusted the blanket. 'He was the one who told me about you.'

'*What?*' Charlie yelped, bolting upright at once. 'He … he what?'

'He was a few years older than you, I think,' June said, tapping her chin with one of her fingers. 'Black hair. Earnest … yes, that's how I would describe him.' She smiled at Charlie's puzzled look. 'I do remember he seemed very serious for someone his age, I must say, especially considering he was Elysian. You don't see many of their sort around here, I can promise you that. I'm not sure how he found this address, either. Perhaps he looked through some of the older records and realised I would be willing to help you.'

'He …' Charlie's heart was beating fast. 'Did you … did he tell you his name?'

June shook her head, a kind smile on her face. 'He was entirely focused on you, I think.'

Charlie frowned, not understanding what she meant, and sank back against the pillow.

'You need to rest now, Charlie,' she said, getting to her feet. A fond expression on her face, she tucked a strand of his hair behind his ear. 'Is there anything else I can do for you?'

Charlie took a deep breath. 'Granny, please would you ...' Pulling the hair tie from the back of his head, Charlie shook his hair over his shoulders, letting the damp waves spill out from the bun. He gazed up at her, his throat growing tight, as hot tears began to shimmer in front of his eyes. 'Please would you cut my hair for me?'

THE END

Author's Note

I hope you enjoyed reading *The Dying Light*. I would be incredibly grateful if you could leave an honest review on Amazon and Goodreads. Ratings and reviews are extremely important to authors because they help new readers find our books, and give them an idea of what they can expect from the story. Besides purchasing a copy of this book, leaving a review is the best thing you can do to help support me! Thank you so much for reading *The Dying Light*.

This story, and these characters, have now been living inside my head for close to three years. One night in Berlin, I started daydreaming about a teenage boy sitting on a window ledge in a rundown basement, surrounded by small children. I did not know how any of them got there, or what the connection between them was, but I knew that he was telling them a story. I also knew, without a doubt, that he would do anything for them. That was Charlie. Little by little, I started – for want of a better word – gaining his trust. Together, we went to some genuinely dark places, and I wrote about things that I had thought I would never be able to share.

Writing Charlie has been an experience unlike anything I have ever attempted to do before. Through him, I have explored topics and themes that have been on my heart for many years. Now that the novel is complete, my shoulders feel lighter. I hope that Charlie will carve out a little space for himself in the hearts of readers of *The Dying Light*. He is definitely tenacious enough to do so, although he would probably claim not to care what anyone else thinks. If you are interested in listening to the music that inspired *The Dying Light*, search for 'The Dying Light – Writing Soundtrack' on YouTube. For *The Swallow's Flight*, search for 'The Swallow's Flight – Writing Soundtrack' on YouTube.

If you would like to stay up to date with my writing progress, and be among the first to find out about what comes next for Charlie, make sure you are subscribed to my newsletter through my website at www.emily-rooke.com. You can follow me on Tumblr (www.emilyrooke.tumblr.com), Instagram (@rooke_emily), and Twitter (@rooke_emily), as well as on Goodreads.

Thank you so much for purchasing this book and for meeting Charlie. If you enjoyed it, please consider leaving a review and recommending it to a friend. I would be so grateful!

Emily Rooke

About the Author

Emily Rooke is the author of *The Dying Light*, *A Silent Night*, and *The Swallow's Flight*. She has lived in a number of different cities, including Osaka and Berlin. She was born in the south-east of England and is a graduate of the University of York and King's College London. She currently lives and writes in Tbilisi, Georgia. You can find out more about the *Bloodwitch* series by visiting her website: www.emily-rooke.com. You can also follow her on Tumblr (www.emilyrooke.tumblr.com), Instagram (@rooke_emily), and Twitter (@rooke_emily), as well as on Goodreads.

Also by this Author

A Silent Night: A Christmas story from Penumbra

Content Warnings

Emily Rooke's novels often deal with serious topics. You may be concerned that *The Dying Light* may contain a topic that is distressing or triggering for you.

This page contains a comprehensive list of the content in *The Dying Light* that may be distressing or triggering for some individuals. Please read safely and contact the author if you feel that something is missing from this list.

- Abduction
- Abuse (emotional; mental; physical; sexual)
- Amnesia
- Anxiety
- Child abuse
- Death
- Depersonalisation
- Derealisation
- Disordered eating
- Gaslighting
- Human trafficking
- Incarceration
- Loss of loved ones
- Mental illness

- Mind control
- Needles
- Paedophilia
- Panic attacks
- Post-Traumatic Stress Disorder
- Pregnancy (not depicted on-page)
- Prostitution (referenced, not depicted on-page)
- Rape
- Self-harm
- Sexual assault
- Suicidal ideation
- Suicidal thoughts
- Terminal illness
- Terrorism (referenced)
- Torture
- Trauma
- Violence

Acknowledgements

Although I have been writing since I was a small child, until *The Dying Light* (and its companion Christmas novella *A Silent Night* and prequel *The Swallow's Flight*) I had never written anything that I felt was worth sharing, let alone worthy of being published. It was only when I started tentatively reaching out to the writing community online, and was encouraged to join The Writer Community on Instagram by Megan, that my confidence started growing. I am so grateful for all the support I have received from this wonderful community. I would not have had the confidence to publish this book without your kindness and support. By joining this community of writers, I have made some true friends from across the globe. You all mean the world to me.

There are a few people I have to think in particular. Gee, thank you for believing in this story, these characters, and me, from the very beginning. Esme, thank you for being the very first person to share your feedback on the story with me – I still treasure your email. Kat, thank you for clearing my head and for going back and forth with me as I worked on the blurb. Ellie and Alex, thank you for your live reactions, fan casts and memes. I am so grateful to everyone on my ARC team for their support, encouragement and enthusiasm; as well as to Cathrel (@lordzuuko), whose beautiful pieces of official art for *The Dying Light* and *A Silent Night* brought Charlie and Vasco to life; and to Dane and the team at ebooklaunch.com for creating such a stunning book cover.

Finally, I would like to thank my husband, Dillon, for his endless love and support. He was the first person I trusted to read my early drafts, and I still remember when we sat up for hours talking about these characters and their stories and the world I had created. I felt like my heart was so full it could have burst. Thank you for bringing me 'Charlie songs' and 'Vasco songs'; for asking me who would voice each character in the Japanese anime version; and for being my first fan. I am so thankful to have such a wonderful person to call my own. I don't know what I did to deserve you, but thank you for always being there for me, my love. You will never know how much it means to me that you saw me and believed in me.

Made in the USA
Monee, IL
23 November 2021

82833174R00203